The Innsmouth Cycle

The Taint of the Deep Ones
in Thirteen Tales and Three Poems

More Titles from Chaosium

Call of Cthulhu® Fiction

Robert Bloch's Mysteries of the Worm
Cthulhu's Heirs
The Book of Iod
Made in Goatswood
The Dunwich Cycle
The Disciples of Cthulhu Second Edition
The Cthulhu Cycle
The Necronomicon
The Xothic Legend Cycle
The Nyarlathotep Cycle
The Hastur Cycle Second Edition
Singers of Strange Songs

Call of Cthulhu® Fiction

The Innsmouth Cycle
The Taint of the Deep Ones

H. P. Lovecraft

Virginia Anderson

R. Flavie Carson

Robert W. Chambers

Irvin S. Cobb

Lord Dunsany

John Glasby

Roger Johnson

Stephen Mark Rainey

Stanley C. Sargent

Ann K. Schwader

Franklyn Searight

Lewis Theobald III

Henry J. Vester III

James Wade

Selected and Edited by Robert M. Price
Cover art by H. E. Fassl
Interior art by Dave Carson

A Chaosium Book
2006

FIRST EDITION

2 3 4 5 6 7 8 9 10

Chaosium Publication 6017. Published in February 1998.

ISBN 1-56882-199-9

Printed in USA.

Contents

INTRODUCTION *Robert M. Price*......................................vii

OF YOHARNETH-LAHAI *Lord Dunsany*.......................1

THE HARBOR-MASTER *Robert W. Chambers*.................3

FISHHEAD *Irvin S. Cobb*...24

THE SHADOW OVER INNSMOUTH *H. P. Lovecraft*.......34

THE DEEP ONES *James Wade*......................................88

A DARKER SHADOW OVER INNSMOUTH
James Wade...120

THE INNSMOUTH HEAD *Franklyn Searight*..............125

INNSMOUTH GOLD *Henry J. Vester III*.....................142

CUSTOS SANCTORUM *Roger Johnson*.........................165

RAPTURE IN BLACK *Stephen Mark Rainey*................178

LIVE BAIT *Stanley C. Sargent*....................................189

DEVIL REEF *John Glasby*...206

THE TRANSITION OF ZADOK ALLEN
Lewis Theobald III..224

THREE POEMS *Virginia Anderson, R. Flavie Carson,
and Ann K. Schwader*...229

Respectfully dedicated to
Ben Chapman,
the Creature from the Black Lagoon

Introduction

Ontogeny Recapitulates Phylogeny

Coming of Age in Y'ha-nthlei

Innsmouth is perhaps the best example of Lovecraft's full-blown alien civilizations. As with the empires of the Old Ones in Antarctica and the Great Race in Australia, Lovecraft mapped out the culture of a wholly imaginary race. This in itself was nothing new. Lovecraft's great inspiration, Edgar Rice Burroughs, had done the same many times over, as had just about every writer of Lost Race novels. Lovecraft himself did a more comprehensive job with his Antarctican and Australian races. But in Innsmouth we see HPL's most effective, most evocative performance. Less detail is filled in; the culture of the deep ones is but sketched in with broad strokes. The story is all the more effective for that: More is left to the imagination. Even so, there is easily enough depicted for us to play the role of participant observer in this alien culture. Let us put on our pith helmets and play anthropologists in Innsmouth. Remember, no fraternizing with the natives!

Anthropologists study various cultural phenomena and isolate common elements and trends and then, by induction, formulate "ideal types" (Max Weber). These are not quite descriptive categories, as if all the phenomena would fit neatly into them. Rather, ideal types are yardsticks, textbook definitions, to which no one example conforms exactly, but which may be used profitably in analyzing the specific phenomena. We may measure them against the generalization, the ideal type, and where this particular case happens not to conform to it, we have the distinctive feature of it. Revitalization Movements (Anthony F. C. Wallace) are a good example. This rubric covers movements as diverse as the Ghost Dance of the Paiute, Sioux, Kiowa, and other tribes (James Mooney, *The Ghost Dance Religion and Wounded Knee*; Weston La Barre, *Ghost Dance: The Origins of Religion*), Melanesian Cargo Cults (Peter Worsley, *The Trumpet Shall Sound*), and the Boxer Rebellion. These movements gestate in the womb of cultural crisis when a native culture is suddenly overwhelmed by the invasion of a more powerful and aggressive culture, usually that of imperialist colonizers. Their technology, weapons, dress, manners, and religion threaten to swallow up the native culture. Foreign armies take over and humiliate the native elders, making their "wisdom" seem superfluous and obsolete. The foreigners' technology seems magical and beguiling. Modernization destroys the sacred cosmos, loosing the hold of traditional beliefs and practices.

Alternatively, if the imperialists themselves are religious, their missionaries will succeed in converting many of the natives, since, as with conquerors of old, their gods will seem to have proven themselves greater than those of the conquered people. This is what was happening when Judea became part of the Seleucid Empire. Antiochus Epiphanes wanted, in the spirit of Alexander the Great, to Hellenize his new subjects. It was their "White Man's Burden." Many Jews liked the idea, and Judaism was forever Hellenized. Even the institution of the Rabbinate is a borrowing from the Greek philosophical schools, while the great hermeneutical rules of

Hillel and others were borrowed from Greek hermeneutics. But many Jews were assimilating to the point of embracing the Greek gods (which, I think, explains a lot of the manifest influence of Dionysus on the Christ concept) and repudiating the Torah. What happened? Lucky for Judaism, a band of stubborn priests decided not to take all this lying down. Mattathias and his sons, foremost of whom was Judah the Hammer, mounted a guerrilla war that ended by forcing the Seleucids out of the land, much like the Afghan Mujahedeen sending the Soviets home with their tails between their legs. This was a Revitalization Movement.

Revitalization Movements, then, try to arrest the decay of the traditional culture/religion (two names for the same thing through most of the history in most of the world). In order to do this, the prophets of the movements will, ironically, make significant innovations in order to preserve the "old time religion." They figure that there must be something to the religion (and the technology) of the outsiders, or they wouldn't be so successful. But maybe their weapons can be turned against them. (Thus the Ayatollah Khomeini, a devotee of medieval Islam, used Western technology—first audiocassettes, then jet fighters—to oust the modernizing, Westernizing, secularizing Shah.) So the prophets have a revelation directing them to combine elements of the conquerors' religion with their own in order to save their own. Thus the Melanesian Cargo Cults added Jesus to their pantheon and piously expected his imminent return aboard a Western ship or airplane laden with refrigerators, stereos, and washing machines for the faithful, and wrath for the Western oppressors. Of course, the risk is that the "new and improved" version of the "old-time religion" will seem to the tribal elders merely another new-fangled heresy to be rejected. Or a new religion may begin.

Something similar may result even if there is no significant resistance from the side of the colonized natives. The dominating culture may find certain aspects of the native religion irresistibly attractive. The result will be a syncretic mixture, just like the neo-religion of the Revitalization Movement. Buddhism is often understood as such a mix of indigenous Indian mysticism with the Vedic religion of the Aryan invaders. European Christianity took over various elements of the paganism it sought to replace. Or the old religion may continue covertly under the names and forms of the new, as in Voudun ("Voodoo"), a religion of spirit-possession in which the native *loa* merely adopt the religiously-correct aliases of Roman Catholic saints. In any case, what we have is a survival of the old, indigenous religion by the expedient of hybridization with the new.

Consider the case of the Kanaka islanders whose culture was vitiated by the incursion of the deep ones, who may be understood as colonizers, since their goals included intermarriage with the islanders, as well as tribute paid in the form of human sacrifices. In return for these favors, they offered the blessings of plentiful fishing as well as trinkets made of Atlantean electrum. This amounted to the establishment of a traditional patron-client relationship. We must assume that the Kanakas had adopted the worship of Cthulhu as their own, though whether Lovecraft would have envisioned a mixture with their traditional religion (as August Derleth seems to have contemplated), we do not know. But once Obed Marsh contacts the Kanaka culture, the influence is strictly all the other way. Obed imports the religion of the Kanakas into Innsmouth, lock, stock, and barrel. It is a Cargo Cult in the full sense, since the whole point is to secure the economic blessings of the Kanaka culture by adopting their religion.

Obed Marsh functions as the Cargo Cult prophet, summoning the endangered native culture to adopt new ways, those of the foreigners'. Innsmouth's traditional culture is threatened in two ways. Their economy was already slipping, something the Christian religion did nothing to arrest, as Obed liked to point out. And, once he had crossed the Rubicon by summoning the deep ones up from the sea off Innsmouth, their possible invasion threatened the town, so that his alliance with them was somewhat in the nature of a protection racket. The sacrifices and interbreeding were later accommodations, tribute paid to the deep ones. "Remember, I ain't sayin' Obed was set on hevin' things jest like they was on that Kanaky isle."

Obed manages to run all the clergy of the traditional faith (Christianity) out of town, and yet the new Cargo Cult, the Esoteric Order of Dagon, has to some extent clothed itself in the trappings of the old. Hence the use of the name Dagon, the Philistine fish-god mentioned in the Bible. When Lovecraft wanted to convey something like the indigenous name of one of the Old Ones, he coined some unpronounceable jumble. By contrast, the name "Dagon" is a direct borrowing from familiar sources and implies that Marsh and his confederates had chosen the closest biblical analogy to the real object of worship of the deep ones, namely Great Cthulhu. Similarly, Mother Hydra comes straight from familiar classical mythology. To be consistent, HPL might have named her Rahab, the name of a female dragon-titan mentioned frequently in biblical mythology.

I have always had the impression that the Order of Dagon was but a transitional Sunday School version of the Deep Things taught in Y'ha-nthlei. When one had fully matured and dived off Devil's Reef, one would have "put away childish things." Having seen hitherto through a glass darkly, one would see henceforth face to face. That is, we can measure an implicit gap between the full faith of the deep ones themselves and that of the vestigially human Innsmouthers. This means that the Order of Dagon is a syncretic Revitalization Movement, though admittedly the surviving elements of the traditional Innsmouth religion (Protestant Christianity and Masonry) are pretty minimal. The Protestant clergy fled the town, rejecting the prophet Obed's new faith as itself being too innovative and no less dangerous to the old-time religion than the encroachment of the deep ones themselves. In this they were like tribal elders who rejected the Ghost Dance or the John Prum cult, even though these sought to preserve the threatened culture. This makes it hard to see that, according to the ideal type of the Revitalization Movement, Obed's new religion must be recognized, surprisingly, as an attempt to preserve some vestige of the traditional Innsmouth religion and culture!

Black Magical Rites Tonight

"The Shadow over Innsmouth" is all about transition, passage, metamorphosis. Here, too, the imaginary Innsmouth culture rings true, for all cultures have a set of "rites of passage." Arnold van Gennep (*Rites of Passage*) is the pioneer here. Unlike our modern Western (bacterial) culture, overwhelmed and vitiated almost completely by capitalism, traditional cultures understood that the course of biological life and maturity is a series of discrete stages, each characterized by a different set of roles and responsibilities. Passage to and from each stage is marked by prescribed public rituals which not only celebrate/commemorate the passage, but actually facilitate it. The rituals serve to usher the neophyte from one stage to the next in the sight of the whole community and with their affirmation.

For lack of effective rituals of this kind, people in our culture fail to recognize where they are in their life's course. No one told the aging, pot-bellied, toupéed playboys who dump their first wives for their sexy secretaries that they have left youth behind, that they must move on to the next stage, not pathetically try to re-enter the previous one. Think of all the mess of divorces, palimony suits, single-parent families. The 1960's witnessed a sophomoric disdain for marriage ceremonies: "Why do we need a piece of paper from City Hall?" This question could never have arisen if marriage, like the other rites of passage in America, had not already been largely reduced to a mere formality, icing on the wedding cake. Marriage has nothing to do with morality, as if premarital sex were somehow "immoral." No, the reason for it is to mark the passage from one life-stage to another. Once my brother-in-law's wife found his wedding ring in his jeans pocket while doing the laundry. What happened? He would take it off while visiting the bar with his buddies. He wasn't cruising for chicks; he just wanted to be one of the boys again. He hadn't been made to understand that the bachelor had died the day he got married, the same day the husband was born. His transition into marriage was incomplete and therefore unsuccessful. No wonder he and his (former) wife now live in different states.

The basic rites of passage in all cultures share the same syntagmic axis, since all are built on the maturation process of the common human organism. Where they differ is in the nonessentials, the paradigmatic axis, i.e., the different choices made by different cultures to fill in the same blanks. First, there are birth rituals in which the baby, having been born biologically, must also be born culturally, into the symbolic community of meaning. These rituals include naming, baptism, circumcision, touching to the ground, breathing into the face, etc.

Second, there are puberty rites in which the youngster becomes an adult. Parents and/or tribal elders catechize the youngster in three areas: sex, death, and the sacred, telling them the privileged secrets of adults. What is implicit in all rites of passage is explicit in puberty rites, namely that each transition is a death to the old and a rebirth into the new. This may be symbolized in puberty rites of immersion in water, burial in leaves or sand, isolation in a sweat lodge or smoke hut, etc. One enters the tomb and then exits the womb, reborn and resurrected, like the caterpillar that goes into the cocoon and comes out a butterfly. Henceforth the youngster is regarded as a young adult, with emphasis on the "adult."

Soon the ritual of marriage follows, and finally the funeral rites of transition to the next world. Other cultures add or subtract some. Hinduism, for example, has one that we sorely need but lack, a retirement ritual ushering the older person not out to pasture but into a new state of freedom and spiritual self-enrichment.

One of the most important contributions to the study of rites of passage is Victor Turner's essay "Betwixt and Between: The Liminal Period in Rites of Passage" (available in his book *The Forest of Symbols*). Turner shows that the lines one crosses in rites of passage are just as important as the fact of their crossing. The lines between life-stage categories are high and thick. We do not ordinarily allow them to be crossed. It is the grossest kind of transgression when, for instance, the adult-child boundary is crossed in incest or child molestation. Or think of "The Loved Dead." You get the picture. It cannot be a transgression to cross the line by growing up, since this is inevitable. But the culture cannot make it a light thing to cross the line even in that case, lest people begin to think the line may be easily crossed by anyone at any time. So we make the passage something of a gauntlet to run.

In the plays and dances attending rites of passage, and in the myths recited on those occasions, Turner points out, there will be depictions and descriptions of curious hybrid beings, neither fish nor foul, or rather both. Angels, centaurs, minotaurs, virgin mothers, and such creatures straddle the fence; they are positioned "on the boundary", as Tillich used to say. Of course, they are embodiments of the liminality, the border-line or "interstitial" character of the initiate who is undergoing the passage.

It is not only attendant symbols which partake of liminality. The initiate himself is marginalized for the duration of the ritual period, driven forth from the village into the hills, the forest, the desert, the smoke-hut, etc. He is allowed or instructed to behave in liminal ways, engaging in acts of sex or violence that would ordinarily be strictly off limits. Homosexuality between uncles and nephews, not recognized as a lifestyle otherwise, may be required at the time of transition. One is temporarily beyond good and evil since one is for the time being outside the realm in which such rules are designed to apply. By the same token, one must be isolated from the society during this time lest the aberrant behavior infect the community at large. In the same way, there may be yearly rites in which the whole community engages in allowed anomalous behavior: Mischief Night, the Feast of Fools, Sadie Hawkins Day, etc. These allow the society to let off steam, as with the Red Hour in the *Star Trek* episode "Return of the Archons." Such occasions are necessary to "manage chaos", but by the same token they must be carefully circumscribed.

There are also rituals in which the initiate is personally "liminalized." This may entail wearing the clothes of the opposite sex, or adopting the costume or behavior of animals, or actual physical transformation, such as subincision, the ritual in which the underside of the penis is slit open to form a symbolic male vagina (see Bruno Bettelheim, *Symbolic Wounds: Puberty Rites and the Envious Male*) so as to restore the initiate to the primordial condition of androgyny before the gods split the Primal Human into two sexes. Get it? The boy becomes an androgyne on the way to becoming a man. He becomes the line, then crosses the line.

"The Shadow over Innsmouth" is loaded with the imagery of rites of passage and liminality, dripping with it. Rites of passage provide the punctuation for a life that would otherwise be a meaningless run-on sentence (see Mircea Eliade's discussion of rites of passage as a case of sacred time intersecting profane time and charging it with meaning in *The Sacred and the Profane* and *Rites and Symbols of Initiation*). Even so, they provide the structure of Lovecraft's tale, as well as much of the meat that clothes this skeleton. It is no exaggeration to say that the whole of the story is that of Robert Olmstead's rite of passage. We are virtually told as much right up front: "I was celebrating my coming of age by a tour of New England." He doesn't realize he has embarked on a Vision Quest, but that is exactly what he has done. He has left home, Ohio, and is thus beyond the bounds of the community. In

Arkham he learns of Innsmouth and, heeding some inner instinct, goes there. Innsmouth is, of course, itself an interstitial space of liminality. For one thing, it is a sea port, straddling land and sea like the angel of Revelation 10:1-2. Second, it is the dwelling of the hybrid Innsmouthers, themselves merfolk such as the mythic beings described by Turner as the accouterments of passage rituals. Third, it is a timeless zone where the steeple clocks are stilled and missing hands, thus outside the normal temporal sequence.

Puberty rites often immerse the initiate in the reality of death, the daunting knowledge of which shadows adult life. Death is unknown to children who see Elmer Fudd obliterated by dynamite in one scene and back intact in the next, but they learn of it in the form of a psychodrama, such as the symbolic burials already described, or actually in a situation of risk, as the youth is brought on a hunt or into a war. In the rituals he undergoes symbolic death; in the hunt or the battle, he inflicts real death. Narrator Olmstead finds himself running for his life, calling on resources untapped by most Lovecraftian protagonists: making a sheet ladder, shinnying down a drainpipe, dodging into darkened doorways, etc. It is an ordeal; he is playing "the most dangerous game." And a game is what it is, since he later discovers they meant him no harm. It was a welcoming committee he fled from, not a lynch mob. They did not mean to lead him a merry chase; he gave them no time to explain. But the result is tantamount to a danger ritual. The effect is to push him to the extreme and boundary of his preliminary human existence, to drive him to the threshold of his next stage.

Before coming to accept his own identity, Olmstead first learns of the transition of the Innsmouth folk, the same process he himself will undergo. He hears the tale of Obed Marsh and of the horrific hybridizing and dismisses it as a myth. The situation is in effect that of a youth of the tribe (which is in fact what he is, a descendant of Obed Marsh himself) being catechized by a tribal elder, Zadok Allen. As he hears the myth, Olmstead judges that it has nothing to do with him, no more than the child who hears the hero myths of Robin Hood, King Arthur, Gilgamesh, or Jesus thinks they have anything to do with his own life. What he does not know, but which Jung, Joseph Campbell, and Vladimir Propp knew, was that the myth of the heroic quest has everything to do with him, and with everyone: The hero myth is the script of Everyman's life, including the hurdles he must jump, the reverses he must overcome, finally to win the Princess, the Grail, etc., and to live happily ever after. You are to follow the path thus marked out for you, though only you can tell what your Grail will be.

In precisely the same way, old Zadok's tale, which he himself lived through at the period of his own adolescence, forms the basis for Olmstead's eventual course of action. The tale which once seemed so outlandish later provides the only framework within which Olmstead is able to make sense of his dreams, the facts of his family's genealogy, etc. They guide him to final fulfillment amid the eternal wonder and glory of Y'ha-nthlei. For want of such knowledge, such a script-myth, Olmstead's Uncle Douglas shot himself in confusion, just as Robert Bly observes that urban youth become gang thugs because they do not know what to do with their dawning male energy, lacking the myth of Iron John and anyone to initiate them according to that script.

Olmstead sees in Innsmouth numerous signs of liminality on the part of others who are slowly undergoing the change. Joe Sargent and all those possessing the Innsmouth look bear marks, Olmstead first thinks, of inbreeding, i.e., incest. He is wrong, and significantly wrong. Inbreeding among siblings or cousins would constitute a failure to pass over the lines separating families, a line that must be passed over for healthy reproduction. Inbreeding keeps things "all in the family" to an excessive degree. In fact, the appearance of the Innsmouthers denoted *inter*breeding, a crossing of lines for reproductive purposes. Once Olmstead does discover this, he finds it even more repellent, thinking that no ritual can rightly navigate one's passage across such an inviolable line. It would constitute unspeakable bestiality. (Of course, such sexual traffic was symbolic of interethnic miscegenation, detested by the white supremacist HPL.)

We are even informed that the Order of Dagon provided an explicit set of degrees of initiation, three successive "oaths of Dagon." The Latin for "oath" is *sacramentum*. The idea of ritual sacraments came from the induction oaths of Roman soldiers who swore allegiance to Caesar as to a god. An oath of Dagon is a sacramental rite of initiation, and there are successive degrees. Of these, young Zadok took two but balked at the third, a marriage sacrament. Nonetheless, the two he had taken were apparently sufficient to give him immortality in the flesh, even if not to accomplish his transition into an amphibian. If these oaths are not rites of passage in a life-cycle, what is? (Interestingly, the implication is that the life-cycle in view is literally circular, since we end where we began, with the no-longer-vestigial gills we sported for a while in our mother's womb.)

The monstrously deformed Innsmouthers behind boarded-up windows along the streets Olmstead walks are themselves liminal myth-figures present, like ritual man-animal masks, on the scene at a puberty rite. They are, of course, half human/half Deep One, as well as being "fish-frogs", doubly double. For Olmstead to walk through their midst is itself a dramatized rite of passage, an initiatory gauntlet. The hidden Innsmouthers are themselves in an extended period of transition and are thus shut away in liminal space, hidden alike from the human sojourners tolerated in Innsmouth, from the immature Innsmouthers not yet manifesting "the look", and from the fully mature deep ones. If they had simply become fishy-looking, why weren't they swimming free off Devil Reef? So the boarded-up windows in the decaying houses are analogous to the sweat lodges and smoke huts of the American Indians. Similarly, Olmstead's cousin Lawrence, confined in an insane asylum, is biding his time in a liminal, interstitial space, from which he is soon to emerge and head for Y'ha-nthlei.

At the end of the story, having himself attained maturity by the very device of writing down his memoir and sorting out his experiences, Olmstead has crossed the boundary and now looks with favor on the intermating that has at length begotten him. The notion of boundary-crossing miscegenation is the fundamental myth-image facilitating his own personal passage over the threshold into maturity. This tells us an important thing about the scene of narration: Writing the tale has itself been the effective ritual of passage for Olmstead. Why does the story end as it does? That is, why does it not end, as it might have, after Olmstead makes his pilgrimage to Y'ha-nthlei? Because we, the readers, are not initiates, not deep ones. We remain in the human stage, while Olmstead has gone beyond. We can envision what lies beyond no more than the tadpole can be given to understand the surface-dwelling of the adult toad.

***

This collection is planned as the first of a pair. *The Innsmouth Cycle* should be followed by *Tales of Innsmouth*, which will contain all new works of fishy fiction. This time around, however, I must thank Ken Silvestri and Paul Berglund, who brought one or another of these items to my attention.

Robert M. Price
Sunken Ruins of Y'ha-nthlei
Hour of the Unspeakable Snorkeling
December 7, 1996

"The Innsmouth Look" *from H.P. Lovecraft's "Shadow over Innsmouth."*

About "Of Yoharneth-Lahai"

Toward the end of "The Shadow over Innsmouth" the narrator, suddenly taking a second, "Innsmouth", look at recent events, repents. The conversion he has undergone is less like the philosophical enlightenment of Plato's troglodyte than it is like that of Saul into Paul on the road to Damascus. Thus the borrowed cadences of Psalm 23 at the close of the story, when the narrator blissfully envisions the blessings awaiting him off Devil Reef.

Only he doesn't call it "Devil Reef" anymore, does he? No, for he doesn't view the deep ones as "them devils" anymore, having become one of them. Now he uses the deep ones' own name for their salt-water Shangri-La, Y'ha-nthlei. Have you ever wondered how he knew this name? Presumably he learned it, as Lovecraft himself learned the names "Nyarlathotep" and "Necronomicon", in his dreams. Presumably, also, the name is a specimen of the language of R'lyeh (see Philip Marsh, *R'lyehian as a Toy Language*).

As with many other names, Lovecraft seems to have borrowed this one, either consciously or unconsciously, from Lord Dunsany. We know he had read the following tale, and it is evident that Y'ha-nthlei is Lovecraft's contraction of "Yoharneth-Lahai." No doubt Dunsany came to mind once Lovecraft decided to have his narrator enter into a state of conversion-bliss. If Psalm 23 came to mind, inevitably so did Lord Dunsany, a far better pasticheur of the King James Bible than Joseph Smith. Specifically, the name Yoharneth-Lahai is probably based specifically on a place name in Judges 15:17, Ramath-Lehi, a spring of water that Yahve obligingly supplies the thirsty Samson after a hard day spent butchering Philistines. The name means "Well of the Jawbone", ostensibly because Samson used a jawbone to kill his foes, but actually because of the topography of the place: It was located at a sloping ridge with a pile of boulders, which gave the general impression of a big jawbone. Wells were given names like this so travelers could find them readily. A similar one occurs in Genesis 16:14, Beerlahairoi, "Well of the Antelope's Jawbone."

"Of Yoharneth-Lahai" originally appeared in *The Gods of Pegāna* in 1905.

Of Yoharneth-Lahai

(The God of Little Dreams and Fancies)

by Lord Dunsany

Yoharneth-Lahai is the god of little dreams and fancies.

All night he sendeth little dreams out of PEGĀNA to please the people of Earth.

He sendeth little dreams to the poor man and to The King.

He is so busy to send his dreams to all before the night be ended that oft he forgetteth which be the poor man and which be The King.

To whom Yoharneth-Lahai cometh not with little dreams and sleep he must endure all night the laughter of the gods, with highest mockery, in PEGĀNA.

All night long Yoharneth-Lahai giveth peace to cities until the dawn hour and the departing of Yoharneth-Lahai, when it is time for the gods to play with men again.

Whether the dreams and the fancies of Yoharneth-Lahai be false and the Things that are done in the Day be real, or the Things that are done in the Day be false and the dreams and the fancies of Yoharneth-Lahai be true, none knoweth saving only MĀNA-YOOD-SUSHAI, *who hath not spoken.*

About "The Harbor-Master"

In an October 17, 1930 letter to his apprentice Frank Belknap Long, Lovecraft lists a number of volumes he has just acquired, among them Robert W. "Chambers's *In Search of the Unknown* (God! The Harbour-Master!!!)." 'Nuff said, I guess. But he says just a bit more in a letter to J. Vernon Shea (January 28, 1933): "I think The Yellow Sign is the most fascinating product of Chambers's pen, & altogether one of the greatest weird tales ever written. The brooding, gathering atmosphere is actually tremendous. I must read it again & see how it strikes me after many years. The Harbour-Master gave me quite a wallop in 1926 when I read it - although I did not care for the rest of the volume." The story is indeed quite effective, one may say, until the ending, which seems to descend into silliness. The collection in which it appeared (*In Search of the Unknown*) was published in 1904.

If Lovecraft borrowed the "Innsmouth look" from the hapless Fishhead in Irvin S. Cobb's story of that title, he would appear to have derived the appearance of the full-fledged deep ones from Chambers' harbor-master. Remember, the deep ones provide one half of the chromosomes of your average Innsmouther, the other half being human.

Beyond this, the major debt owed to "The Harbor-Master" by "The Shadow over Innsmouth" is the device of Devil's Reef, a crevasse in the sea floor descending to problematical depths but located surprisingly close to an inhabited coast.

The Harbor-Master

by Robert W. Chambers

Where the slanting forest eaves,
Shingled tight with greenest leaves,
Sweep the scented meadow-sedge,
Let us snoop along the edge;
Let us pry in hidden nooks,
Laden with our nature books,
Scaring birds with happy cries,
Chloroforming butterflies,
Rooting up each woodland plant,
Pinning beetle, fly, and ant,
So we may identify
What we've ruined, by-and-by.

I

Because it all seems so improbable—so horribly impossible to me now, sitting here safe and sane in my own library—I hesitate to record an episode which already appears to me less horrible than grotesque. Yet, unless this story is written now, I know I shall never have the courage to tell the truth about the matter—not from fear of ridicule, but because I myself shall soon cease to credit what I now know to be true. Not scarcely a month has elapsed since I heard the stealthy purring of what I believed to be the shoaling undertow—scarcely a month ago, with my own eyes, I saw that which, even now, I am beginning to believe never existed. As for the harbor-master—and the blow I am now striking at the old order of things—. But of that I shall not speak now, or later; I shall try to tell the story simply and truthfully, and let my friends testify as to my probity and the publishers of this book corroborate them.

On the 29th of February I resigned my position under the government and left Washington to accept an offer from Professor Farrago—whose name he kindly permits me to use—and on the first day of April I entered upon my new and congenial duties as general superintendent of the water-fowl department connected with the Zoological Gardens then in course of erection at Bronx Park, New York.

For a week I followed the routine, examining the new foundations, studying the architect's plans, following the surveyors through the Bronx thickets, suggesting arrangements for water-courses and pools destined to be included in the enclosures for swans, geese, pelicans, herons, and such of the waders and swimmers as we might expect to acclimate in Bronx Park.

It was at that time the policy of the trustees and officers of the Zoological Gardens neither to employ collectors nor to send out expeditions in search of specimens. The society decided to depend upon voluntary contributions, and I was always busy, part of the day, in dictating answers to correspondents who wrote offering their services as hunters of big game, collectors of all sorts of fauna, trappers, snarers, and also to those who offered specimens for sale, usually at exorbitant prices.

To the proprietors of the five-legged kittens, mangy lynxes, moth-eaten coyotes, and dancing bears I returned courteous but uncompromising refusals—of course, first submitting all such letters, together with my replies, to Professor Farrago.

One day toward the end of May, however, just as I was leaving Bronx Park to return to town, Professor Lesard, of the reptilian department, called out to me that Professor Farrago wanted to see me a moment; so I put my pipe into my pocket again and retraced my steps to the temporary wooden building occupied by Professor Farrago, general superintendent of the Zoological Gardens. The professor, who was sitting at his desk before a pile of letters and replies submitted for approval by me, pushed his glasses down and looked over them at me with a whimsical smile that suggested amusement, impatience, annoyance, and perhaps a faint trace of apology.

"Now, here's a letter," he said, with a deliberate gesture toward a sheet of paper impaled on a file, "a letter that I suppose you remember." He disengaged the sheet of paper and handed it to me.

"Oh, yes," I replied, with a shrug. "Of course the man is mistaken—or—"

"Or what?" demanded Professor Farrago, tranquilly, wiping his glasses.

"—or a liar," I replied.

After a silence he leaned back in his chair and bade me read the letter to him again, and I did so with a contemptuous tolerance for the writer, who must have been either a very innocent victim or a very stupid swindler. I said as much to Professor Farrago, but, to my surprise, he appeared to waver.

"I suppose," he said, with his near-sighted, embarrassed smile, "that nine hundred and ninety-nine men in a thousand would throw that letter aside and condemn the writer as a liar or a fool?"

"In my opinion," said I, "he's one or the other."

"He isn't—in mine," said the professor, placidly.

"What!" I exclaimed. "Here is a man living all alone on a strip of rock and sand between the wilderness and the sea, who wants you to send somebody to take charge of a bird that doesn't exist!"

"How do you know," asked Professor Farrago, "that the bird in question does not exist?"

"It is generally accepted," I replied sarcastically, "that the great auk has been extinct for years. Therefore I may be pardoned for doubting that our correspondent possesses a pair of them alive."

"Oh, you young fellows," said the professor, smiling wearily, "you embark on a theory for destinations that don't exist."

He leaned back in his chair, his amused eyes searching space for the imagery that made him smile.

"Like swimming squirrels, you navigate with the help of Heaven and a stiff breeze, but you never land where you hope to—do you?"

Rather red in the face, I said, "Don't you believe the great auk to be extinct?"

"Audubon saw the great auk."

"Who has seen a single specimen since?"

"Nobody—except our correspondent here," he replied, laughing.

I laughed, too, considering the interview at an end, but the professor went on, coolly: "Whatever it is that our correspondent has—and I am daring to believe that it *is* the great auk itself—I want you to secure it for the society."

When my astonishment subsided my first conscious sentiment was one of pity. Clearly, Professor Farrago was on the verge of dotage—ah, what a loss to the world!

I believe now that Professor Farrago perfectly interpreted my thoughts, but he betrayed neither resentment nor impatience. I drew a chair up beside his desk—there was nothing to do but to obey, and this fool's errand was none of my conceiving.

Together we made out a list of articles necessary for me and itemized the expenses I might incur, and I set a date for my return, allowing no margin for a successful termination to the expedition.

"Never mind that," said the professor. "What I want you to do is to get those birds here safely. Now, how many men will you take?"

"None," I replied, bluntly. "It's a useless expense, unless there is something to bring back. If there is I'll wire you, you may be sure."

"Very well," said Professor Farrago, good-humoredly, "you shall have all the assistance you may require. Can you leave tonight?"

The old gentleman was certainly prompt. I nodded, half-sulkily, aware of his amusement.

"So," I said, picking up my hat, "I am to start north to find a place called Black Harbor, where there is a man named Halyard who possesses, among other household utensils, two extinct great auks—"

We were both laughing by this time. I asked him why on earth he credited the assertion of a man he had never before heard of.

"I suppose," he replied, with the same half-apologetic, half-humorous smile, "it is instinct. I feel, somehow, that this man Halyard *has* got an auk—or perhaps two. I can't get away from the idea that we are on the eve of acquiring the rarest of living creatures. It's odd for a scientist to talk as I do; doubtless you're shocked—admit it, now!"

But I was not shocked; on the contrary, I was conscious that the same strange hope that Professor Farrago cherished was beginning, in spite of me, to stir my pulses, too.

"If he has—" I began, then stopped.

The professor and I looked hard at each other in silence.

"Go on," he said, encouragingly.

But I had nothing more to say, for the prospect of beholding with my own eyes a living specimen of the great auk produced a series of conflicting emotions within me which rendered speech profanely superfluous.

As I took my leave Professor Farrago came to the door of the temporary wooden office and handed me the letter written by the man Halyard. I folded it and put it into my pocket, as Halyard might require it for my own identification.

"How much does he want for the pair?" I asked.

"Ten thousand dollars. Don't demur—if the birds are really—"

"I know," I said, hastily, not daring to hope too much.

"One more thing," said Professor Farrago, gravely. "You know, in that last paragraph of his letter, Halyard speaks of something else in the way of specimens—an undiscovered species of amphibious biped—just read that paragraph again, will you?"

I drew the letter from my pocket and read as he directed:

When you have seen the two living specimens of the great auk, and have satisfied yourself that I tell the truth, you may be wise enough to listen without prejudice to a statement I shall make concerning the existence of the strangest creature ever fashioned. I will merely say, at this time, that the creature referred to is an amphibious biped and inhabits the ocean near this coast. More I cannot say, for I personally have not seen the animal, but I have

a witness who has, and there are many who affirm that they have
seen the creature. You will naturally say that my statement
amounts to nothing; but when your representative arrives, if he
be free from prejudice, I expect his reports to you concerning this
sea-biped will confirm the solemn statements of a witness I *know*
to be unimpeachable.

> Yours truly,
> BURTON HALYARD.
> BLACK HARBOR.

"Well," I said, after a moment's thought, "here goes for the wild-
goose chase."

"Wild auk, you mean," said Professor Farrago, shaking hands with me.
"You will start tonight, won't you?"

"Yes, but Heaven knows how I'm ever going to land in this man
Halyard's door-yard. Good-bye!"

"About that sea-biped——" began Professor Farrago, shyly.

"Oh, don't!" I said. "I can swallow the auks, feathers and claws, but if
this fellow Halyard is hinting he's seen an amphibious creature resembling
a man——"

"——or a woman," said the professor, cautiously.

I retired, disgusted, my faith shaken in the mental vigor of Professor
Farrago.

II

The three days' voyage by boat and rail was irksome. I bought my kit at
Sainte Croix, on the Central Pacific Railroad, and on June 1st I began the
last stage of my journey via the Sainte Isole broad-gauge, arriving in the
wilderness by daylight. A tedious forced march by blazed trail, freshly spotted on the wrong side, of course, brought me to the northern terminus of
the rusty, narrow-gauge lumber railway which runs from the heart of the
hushed pine wilderness to the sea.

Already a long train of battered flat-cars, piled with sluice props and
roughly hewn sleepers, was moving slowly off into the brooding forest
gloom when I came in sight of the track; but I developed a gratifying and
unexpected burst of speed, shouting all the while. The train stopped; I
swung myself aboard the last car, where a pleasant young fellow was sitting
on the rear brake, chewing spruce and reading a letter.

"Come aboard, sir," he said, looking up with a smile. "I guess you're the
man in a hurry."

"I'm looking for a man named Halyard," I said, dropping rifle and knapsack on the fresh-cut, fragrant pile of pine. "Are you Halyard?"

"No, I'm Francis Lee, bossing the mica pit at Port-of-Waves," he replied, "but this letter is from Halyard, asking me to look out for a man in a hurry from Bronx Park, New York."

"I'm that man," said I, filling my pipe and offering him a share of the weed of peace, and we sat side by side smoking very amiably, until a signal from the locomotive sent him forward and I was left alone, lounging at ease, head pillowed on both arms, watching the blue sky flying through the branches overhead.

Long before we came in sight of the ocean I smelled it; the fresh, salt aroma stole into my senses, drowsy with the heated odor of pine and hemlock, and I sat up, peering ahead into the dusky sea of pines.

Fresher and fresher came the wind from the sea, in puffs, in mild, sweet breezes, in steady, freshening currents, blowing the feathery crowns of the pines, setting the balsam's blue tufts rocking.

Lee wandered back over the long line of flats, balancing himself nonchalantly as the cars swung around a sharp curve, where water dripped from a newly propped sluice that suddenly emerged from the depths of the forest to run parallel to the railroad track.

"Built it this spring," he said, surveying his handiwork, which seemed to undulate as the cars swept past. "It runs to the cove—or ought to——." He stopped abruptly with a thoughtful glance at me.

"So you're going over to Halyard's?" he continued, as though answering a question asked by himself.

I nodded.

"You've never been there—of course?"

"No," I said, "and I'm not likely to go again."

I would have told him why I was going if I had not already begun to feel ashamed of my idiotic errand.

"I guess you're going to look at those birds of his," continued Lee, placidly.

"I guess I am," I said, sulkily, glancing askance to see whether he was smiling.

But he only asked me, quite seriously, whether a great auk was really a very rare bird; and I told him that the last one ever seen had been found dead off Labrador in January, 1870. Then I asked him whether these birds of Halyard's were really great auks, and he replied, somewhat indifferently, that he supposed they were—at least, nobody had ever before seen such birds near Port-of-Waves.

"There's something else," he said, running a pine sliver through his pipe-stem—"something that interests us all here more than auks, big or little. I suppose I might as well speak of it, as you are bound to hear about it sooner or later."

He hesitated, and I could see that he was embarrassed, searching for the exact words to convey his meaning.

"If," said I, "you have anything in this region more important to science than the great auk, I should be very glad to know about it."

Perhaps there was the faintest tinge of sarcasm in my voice, for he shot a sharp glance at me and then turned slightly. After a moment, however, he put his pipe into his pocket, laid hold of the brake with both hands, vaulted to his perch aloft, and glanced down at me.

"Did you ever hear of the harbor-master?" he asked, maliciously.

"Which harbor-master?" I inquired.

"You'll know before long," he observed, with a satisfied glance into perspective.

This rather extraordinary observation puzzled me. I waited for him to resume, and, as he did not, I asked him what he meant.

"If I knew," he said, "I'd tell you. But, come to think of it, I'd be a fool to go into details with a scientific man. You'll hear about the harbor-master—perhaps you will see the harbor-master. In that event I should be glad to converse with you on the subject."

I could not help laughing at his prim and precise manner, and after a moment he also laughed, saying: "It hurts a man's vanity to know he knows a thing that somebody else knows he doesn't know. I'm damned if I say another word about the harbor-master until you've been to Halyard's!"

"A harbor-master," I persisted, "is an official who superintends the mooring of ships—isn't he?"

But he refused to be tempted into conversation, and we lounged silently on the lumber until a long, thin whistle from the locomotive and a rush of stinging salt wind brought us to our feet. Through the trees I could see the bluish-black ocean, stretching out beyond black headlands to meet the clouds; a great wind was roaring among the trees as the train slowly came to a standstill on the edge of the primeval forest.

Lee jumped to the ground and aided me with my rifle and pack, and then the train began to back away along a curved side-track which, Lee said, led to the mica pit and company stores.

"Now what will you do?" he asked, pleasantly. "I can give you a good dinner and a decent bed tonight if you like—and I'm sure Mrs. Lee would be very glad to have you stop with us as long as you choose."

I thanked him, but said that I was anxious to reach Halyard's before dark, and he very kindly led me along the cliffs and pointed out the path.

"This man Halyard," he said, "is an invalid. He lives at a cove called Black Harbor, and all his truck goes through to him over the company's road. We receive it here, and send a pack-mule through once a month. I've met him; he's a bad-tempered hypochondriac, a cynic at heart, and a man whose word is never doubted. If he says he has a great auk, you may be satisfied he has."

My heart was beating with excitement at the prospect; I looked out across the wooded headlands and tangled stretches of dune and hollow, trying to realize what it might mean to me, to Professor Farrago, to the world, if I should lead back to New York a live auk.

"He's a crank," said Lee; "frankly, I don't like him. If you find it unpleasant there, come back to us."

"Does Halyard live alone?" I asked.

"Yes—except for a professional trained nurse—poor thing!"

"A man?"

"No," said Lee, disgustedly.

Presently he gave me a peculiar glance, hesitated, and finally said: "Ask Halyard to tell you about his nurse and—the harbor-master. Good-bye— I'm due at the quarry. Come and stay with us whenever you care to; you will find a welcome at Port-of-Waves."

We shook hands and parted on the cliff, he turning back into the forest along the railway, I starting northward, pack slung, rifle over my shoulder. Once I met a group of quarrymen, faces burned brick-red, scarred hands swinging as they walked. As I passed them with a nod, turning, I saw that they also had turned to look after me, and I caught a word or two of their conversation, whirled back to me on the sea wind.

They were speaking of the harbor-master.

III

Toward sunset I came out on a sheer granite cliff where the sea birds were whirling and clamoring, and the great breakers dashed rolling in double-thundered reverberations on the sun-dyed, crimson sands below the rock.

Across the half-moon of beach towered another cliff, and, behind this, I saw a column of smoke rising in the still air. It certainly came from Halyard's chimney, although the opposite cliff prevented me from seeing the house itself.

I rested a moment to refill my pipe, then resumed rifle and pack, and cautiously started to skirt the cliffs. I had descended halfway toward the beach, and was examining the cliff opposite, when something on the very top of the rock arrested my attention—a man darkly outlined against the sky. The next moment, however, I knew it could not be a man, for the object suddenly glided over the face of the cliff and slid down the sheer, smooth face like a lizard. Before I could get a square look at it, the thing crawled into the surf—or, at least, it seemed to—but the whole episode occurred so suddenly, so unexpectedly, that I was not sure I had seen anything at all.

However, I was curious enough to climb the cliff on the land side and make my way toward the spot where I imagined I had seen the man. Of course, there was nothing there—not a trace of a human being, I mean. Something *had* been there—a sea otter, possibly—for the remains of a freshly killed fish lay on the rock, eaten to the backbone and tail.

The next moment, below me, I saw the house, a freshly painted, trim, flimsy structure, modern, and very much out of harmony with the splendid savagery surrounding it. It struck a nasty, cheap note in the noble, gray monotony of headland and sea.

The descent was easy enough. I crossed the crescent beach, hard as pink marble, and found a little trodden path among the rocks that led to the front porch of the house.

There were two people on the porch—I heard their voices before I saw them—and when I set my foot upon the wooden steps, I saw one of them, a woman, rise from her chair and step hastily toward me.

"Come back!" cried the other, a man with a smooth-shaven, deeply lined face, and a pair of angry, blue eyes; and the woman stepped back quietly, acknowledging my lifted hat with a silent inclination.

The man, who was reclining in an invalid's rolling chair, clapped both large, pale hands to the wheels and pushed himself out along the porch. He had shawls pinned about him, an untidy, drab-colored hat on his head, and, when he looked at me, he scowled.

"I know who you are," he said, in an acid voice; "you're one of the Zoological men from Bronx Park. You look like it, anyway."

"It is easy to recognize you from your reputation," I replied, irritated at his discourtesy.

"Really," he replied, with something between a sneer and a laugh, "I'm obliged for your frankness. You're after my great auks, are you not?"

"Nothing else would have tempted me into this place," I replied, sincerely.

"Thank Heaven for that," he said. "Sit down a moment; you've interrupted us." Then, turning to the young woman, who wore the neat gown and tiny cap of a professional nurse, he bade her resume what she had been saying. She did so, with a deprecating glance at me, which made the old man sneer again.

"It happened so suddenly," she said, in her low voice, "that I had no chance to get back. The boat was drifting in the cove; I sat in the stern, reading, both oars shipped, and the tiller swinging. Then I heard a scratching under the boat, but thought it might be seaweed—and, next moment, came those soft thumpings, like the sound of a big fish rubbing its nose against a float."

Halyard clutched the wheels of his chair and stared at the girl in grim displeasure.

"Didn't you know enough to be frightened?" he demanded.

"No—not then," she said, coloring faintly, "but when, after a few moments, I looked up and saw the harbor-master running up and down the beach, I was horribly frightened."

"Really?" said Halyard, sarcastically. "It was about time." Then, turning to me, he rasped out: "And that young lady was obliged to row all the way to Port-of-Waves and call to Lee's quarrymen to take her boat in."

Completely mystified, I looked from Halyard to the girl, not in the least comprehending what all this meant.

"That will do," said Halyard, ungraciously, which curt phrase was apparently the usual dismissal for the nurse.

She rose, and I rose, and she passed me with an inclination, stepping noiselessly into the house.

"I want beef-tea!" bawled Halyard after her; then he gave me an unamiable glance.

"I was a well bred man," he sneered. "I'm a Harvard graduate, too, but I live as I like, and I do what I like, and I say what I like."

"You certainly are not reticent," I said, disgusted.

"Why should I be?" he rasped. "I pay that young woman for my irritability; it's a bargain between us."

"In your domestic affairs," I said, "there is nothing that interests me. I came to see those auks."

"You probably believe them to be razor-billed auks," he said, contemptuously. "But they're not; they're great auks."

I suggested that he permit me to examine them, and he replied, indifferently, that they were in a pen in his backyard, and that I was free to step around the house when I cared to.

I laid my rifle and pack on the verandah, and hastened off with mixed emotions, among which hope no longer predominated. No man in his senses would keep two such precious prizes in a pen in his backyard, I argued, and I was perfectly prepared to find anything from a puffin to a penguin in that pen.

I shall never forget, as long as I live, my stupor of amazement when I came to the wire-covered enclosure. Not only were there two great auks in the pen, alive, breathing, squatting in bulk majesty on their seaweed bed, but one of them was gravely contemplating two newly hatched chicks, all bill and feet, which nestled sedately at the edge of a puddle of salt water, where some small fish were swimming.

For a while excitement blinded, nay, deafened me. I tried to realize that I was gazing upon the last individuals of an all but extinct race—the sole survivors of the gigantic auk, which, for thirty years, has been accounted an extinct creature.

I believe that I did not move muscle nor limb until the sun had gone down and the crowding darkness blurred my straining eyes and blotted the great, silent, bright-eyed birds from sight.

Even then I could not tear myself away from the enclosure; I listened to the strange, drowsy note of the male bird, the fainter responses of the female, the thin plaints of the chicks, huddling under her breast; I heard their flipper-like, embryotic wings beating sleepily as the birds stretched and yawned their beaks and clacked them, preparing for slumber.

"If you please," came a soft voice from the door, "Mr. Halyard awaits your company to dinner."

IV

I dined well—or rather, I might have enjoyed my dinner if Mr. Halyard had been eliminated and the feast consisted exclusively of a joint of beef, the pretty nurse, and myself. She was exceedingly attractive—with a disturbing fashion of lowering her head and raising her dark eyes when spoken to.

As for Halyard, he was unspeakable, bundled up in his snuffy shawls, and making uncouth noises over his gruel. It is only just to say that his table was worth sitting down to and his wine was sound as a bell.

"Yah!" he snapped. "I'm sick of this cursed soup—and I'll trouble you to fill my glass—"

"It is dangerous for you to touch claret," said the pretty nurse.

"I might as well die at dinner as anywhere," he observed.

"Certainly," said I, cheerfully passing the decanter, but he did not appear overpleased with the attention.

"I can't smoke, either," he snarled, hitching the shawls around until he looked like Richard the Third.

However, he was good enough to shove a box of cigars at me, and I took one and stood up, as the pretty nurse slipped past and vanished into the little parlor beyond.

We sat there for a while without speaking. He picked irritably at the bread-crumbs on the cloth, never glancing in my direction. I, tired from my long foot-tour, lay back in my chair, silently appreciating one of the best cigars I had ever smoked.

"Well," he rasped out at length, "what do you think of my auks—and my veracity?"

I told him that both were unimpeachable.

"Didn't they call me a swindler down there at your museum?" he demanded.

I admitted that I had heard the term applied. Then I made a clean breast of the matter, telling him that it was I who had doubted; that my chief, Professor Farrago, had sent me against my will; and that I was ready and glad to admit that he, Mr. Halyard, was a benefactor of the human race.

"Bosh!" he said. "What good does a confounded wobbly, bandy-toed bird do to the human race?"

He was pleased, nevertheless; and presently he asked me, not unamiably, to punish his claret again.

"I'm done for," he said; "good things to eat and drink are no good to me. Some day I'll get mad enough to have a fit, and then—"

He paused to yawn.

"Then," he continued, "that little nurse of mine will drink up my claret and go back to civilization, where people are polite."

Somehow or other, in spite of the fact that Halyard was an old pig, what he had said touched me. There was certainly not much left in life for him—as he regarded life.

"I'm going to leave her this house," he said, arranging his shawls. "She doesn't know it. I'm going to leave her my money, too. She doesn't know that. Good Lord! What kind of a woman can she be to stand my bad temper for a few dollars a month!"

"I think," said I, "that it's partly because she's poor, partly because she's sorry for you."

He looked up with a ghastly smile.

"You think she really is sorry?"

Before I could answer he went on: "I'm no mawkish sentimentalist, and I won't allow anybody to be sorry for me—do you hear?"

"Oh, I'm not sorry for you!" I said, hastily, and, for the first time since I had seen him, he laughed heartily, without a sneer.

We both seemed to feel better after that; I drank his wine and smoked his cigars, and he appeared to take a certain grim pleasure in watching me.

"There's no fool like a young fool," he observed, presently.

As I had no doubt he referred to me, I paid him no attention.

After fidgeting with his shawls, he gave me an oblique scowl and asked me my age.

"Twenty-four," I replied.

"Sort of a tadpole, aren't you?" he said.

As I took no offense, he repeated the remark.

"Oh, come," said I, "there's no use in trying to irritate me. I see through you; a row acts like a cocktail on you—but you'll have to stick to gruel in my company."

"I call that impudence!" he rasped out, wrathfully.

"I don't care what you call it," I replied, undisturbed, "I am not going to be worried by you. Anyway," I ended, "it is my opinion that you could be very good company if you chose."

The proposition appeared to take his breath away—at least, he said nothing more; and I finished my cigar in peace and tossed the stump into a saucer.

"Now," said I, "what price do you set upon your birds, Mr. Halyard?"

"Ten thousand dollars," he snapped, with an evil smile.

"You will receive a certified check when the birds are delivered," I said, quietly.

"You don't mean to say that you agree to that outrageous bargain—and I won't take a cent less, either—good Lord!—haven't you any spirit left?" he cried, half rising from his pile of shawls.

His piteous eagerness for a dispute sent me into laughter impossible to control, and he eyed me, mouth open, animosity rising visibly.

Then he seized the wheels of his invalid chair and trundled away, too mad to speak; and I strolled out into the parlor, still laughing.

The pretty nurse was there, sewing under a hanging lamp.

"If I am not indiscreet—" I began.

"Indiscretion is the better part of valor," said she, dropping her head but raising her eyes.

So I sat down with a frivolous smile peculiar to the appreciated.

"Doubtless," said I, "you are hemming a 'kerchief.'"

"Doubtless I am not," she said; "this is a night-cap for Mr. Halyard."

A mental vision of Halyard in a night-cap, very mad, nearly set me laughing again.

"Like the King of Yvetot, he wears his crown in bed," I said, flippantly.

"The King of Yvetot might have made that remark," she observed, rethreading her needle.

It is unpleasant to be reproved. How large and red and hot a man's ears feel.

To cool them, I strolled out to the porch. After a while, the pretty nurse came out, too, and sat down in a chair not far away. She probably regretted her lost opportunity to be flirted with.

"I have so little company—it is a great relief to see somebody from the world," she said. "If you can be agreeable, I wish you would."

The idea that she had come out to see me was so agreeable that I remained speechless until she said, "Do tell me what people are doing in New York."

So I seated myself on the steps and talked about the portion of the world inhabited by me, while she sat sewing in the dull light that straggled out from the parlor windows.

She had a certain coquetry of her own, using the usual methods with an individuality that was certainly fetching. For instance, when she lost her needle—and, another time, when we both, on hands and knees, hunted for her thimble.

However, directions for these pastimes may be found in contemporary classics.

I was as entertaining as I could be—perhaps not quite as entertaining as a young man usually thinks he is. However, we got on very well together until I asked her tenderly who the harbor-master might be, whom they all discussed so mysteriously.

"I do not care to speak about it," she said, with a primness of which I had not suspected her capable.

Of course I could scarcely pursue the subject after that—and, indeed, I did not intend to—so I began to tell her how I fancied I had seen a man on the cliff this afternoon, and how the creature slid over the sheer rock like a snake.

To my amazement, she asked me kindly to discontinue the account of my adventures, in an icy tone, which left no room for protest.

"It was only a sea otter," I tried to explain, thinking perhaps she did not care for snake stories.

But the explanation did not appear to interest her, and I was mortified to observe that my impression upon her was anything but pleasant.

She doesn't seem to like me and my stories, thought I, *but she is too young, perhaps, to appreciate them.*

So I forgave her—for she was even prettier than I had thought her at first—and I took my leave, saying that Mr. Halyard would doubtless direct me to my room.

Halyard was in his library, cleaning a revolver, when I entered.

"Your room is next to mine," he said. "Pleasant dreams, and kindly refrain from snoring."

"May I venture an absurd hope that you will do the same!" I replied, politely.

That maddened him, so I hastily withdrew.

I had been asleep for at least two hours when a movement by my bedside and a light in my eyes awakened me. I sat bolt upright in bed, blinking at Halyard, who, clad in a dressing-gown and wearing a night-cap, had wheeled himself into my room with one hand, while with the other he solemnly waved a candle over my head.

"I'm so cursed lonely," he said. "Come, there's a good fellow—talk to me in your own original, impudent way."

I objected strenuously, but he looked so worn and thin, so lonely and bad-tempered, so lovelessly grotesque, that I got out of bed and passed a spongeful of cold water over my head.

Then I returned to bed and propped the pillows up for a back-rest, ready to quarrel with him if it might bring some little pleasure into his morbid existence.

"No," he said, amiably, "I'm too worried to quarrel, but I'm much obliged for your kindly offer. I want to tell you something."

"What?" I asked, suspiciously.

"I want to ask you if you ever saw a man with gills like a fish?"

"Gills?" I repeated.

"Yes, gills! Did you?"

"No," I replied, angrily, "and neither did you."

"No, I never did," he said, in a curiously placid voice, "but there's a man with gills like a fish who lives in the ocean out there. Oh, you needn't look that way—nobody ever thinks of doubting my word, and I tell you that there's a man—or a thing that looks like a man—as big as you are, too—all slate-colored—with nasty red gills like a fish!—and I've a witness to prove what I say!"

"Who?" I asked, sarcastically.

"The witness? My nurse."

"Oh! She saw a slate-colored man with gills?"

"Yes, she did. So did Francis Lee, superintendent of the Mica Quarry Company at Port-of-Waves. So have a dozen men who work in the quarry. Oh, you needn't laugh. It's an old story here, and anybody can tell you about the harbor-master."

"The harbor-master!" I exclaimed.

"Yes, that slate-colored thing with gills, that looks like a man—and—by Heaven! *is* a man—that's the harbor-master. Ask any quarryman at Port-of-Waves what it is that comes purring around their boats at the wharf and unties painters and changes the mooring of every cat-boat in the cove at night! Ask Francis Lee what it was he saw running and leaping up and down the shoal at sunset last Friday! Ask anybody along the coast what sort of a thing moves about the cliffs like a man and slides over them into the sea like an otter—"

"I saw it do that!" I burst out.

"Oh, did you? Well, *what was it?*"

Something kept me silent, although a dozen explanations flew to my lips.

After a pause, Halyard said: "You saw the harbor-master, that's what you saw!"

I looked at him without a word.

"Don't mistake me," he said, pettishly; "I don't think that the harbor-master is a spirit or a sprite or a hobgoblin, or any sort of damned rot. Neither do I believe it to be an optical illusion."

"What do you think it is?" I asked.

"I think it's a man—I think it's a branch of the human race—that's what I think. Let me tell you something; the deepest spot in the Atlantic Ocean is a trifle over five miles deep—and I suppose you know that this place lies only about a quarter of a mile off this headland. The British exploring vessel, *Gull*, Captain Marotte, discovered and sounded it, I believe. Anyway, it's there, and it's my belief that the profound depths are inhabited by the remnants of the last race of amphibious human beings!"

This was childish; I did not bother to reply.

"Believe it or not, as you will," he said, angrily. "One thing I know, and that is this: The harbor-master has taken to hanging around my cove, and he is attracted to my nurse! I won't have it! I'll blow his fishy gills out of his head if I ever get a shot at him! I don't care whether it's homicide or not—anyway, it's a new kind of murder and it attracts me!"

I gazed at him incredulously, but he was working himself into a passion, and I did not choose to say what I thought.

"Yes, this slate-colored thing with gills goes purring and grinning and spitting about after my nurse—when she walks, when she rows, when she sits on the beach! Gad! It drives me nearly frantic. I won't tolerate it, I tell you!"

"No," said I, "I wouldn't either." And I rolled over in bed and convulsed with laughter.

The next moment I heard my door slam. I smothered my mirth and rose to close the window, for the land-wind blew cold from the forest, and a drizzle was sweeping the carpet as far as my bed.

That luminous glare which sometimes lingers after the stars go out threw a trembling, nebulous radiance over sand and cove. I heard the seething currents under the breakers' softened thunder—louder than I ever heard it. Then, as I closed my window, lingering for a last look at the crawling tide, I saw a man standing, ankle-deep, in the surf, all alone there in the night. But—was it a man? For the figure suddenly began running over the beach on all fours like a beetle, waving its limbs like feelers. Before I could throw open the window again it darted into the surf, and, when I leaned out into the chilling drizzle, I saw nothing save the flat ebb crawling on the coast—I heard nothing save the purring of bubbles on seething sands.

V

It took me a week to perfect my arrangements for transporting the great auks, by water, to Port-of-Waves, where a lumber schooner was to be sent from Petite Sainte Isole, chartered by me for a voyage to New York.

I had constructed a cage made of osiers, in which my auks were to squat until they arrived at Bronx Park. My telegrams to Professor Farrago were brief. One merely said "Victory!" Another explained that I wanted no assistance, and a third read: "Schooner chartered. Arrive New York July 1st. Send furniture van to foot of Bluff Street."

My week as a guest of Mr. Halyard proved interesting. I wrangled with that invalid to his heart's content, I worked all day on my osier cage, I hunted the thimble in the moonlight with the pretty nurse. We sometimes found it.

As for the thing they called the harbor-master, I saw it a dozen times, but always either at night or so far away and so close to the sea that of course no trace of it remained when I reached the spot, rifle in hand.

I had quite made up my mind that the so-called harbor-master was a demented darky—wandered from Heaven knows where—perhaps ship-wrecked and gone mad from his sufferings. Still, it was far from pleasant to know that the creature was strongly attracted by the pretty nurse.

She, however, persisted in regarding the harbor-master as a sea crea-ture; she earnestly affirmed that it had gills, like a fish's gills, that it had a soft, fleshy hole for a mouth, and that its eyes were luminous and lidless and fixed.

"Besides," she said with a shudder, "it's all slate color, like a porpoise, and it looks as wet as a sheet of India rubber in a dissecting room."

The day before I was to set sail with my auks in a cat-boat bound for Port-of-Waves, Halyard trundled up to me in his chair and announced his intention of going with me.

"Going where?" I asked.

"To Port-of-Waves and then to New York," he replied, tranquilly.

I was doubtful, and my lack of cordiality hurt his feelings.

"Oh, of course, if you need the sea-voyage—" I began.

"I don't; I need you," he said, savagely. "I need the stimulus of our daily quarrel. I never disagreed so pleasantly with anybody in my life; it agrees with me; I am a hundred percent better than I was last week."

I was inclined to resent this, but something in the deep-lined face of the invalid softened me. Besides, I had taken a hearty liking to the old pig.

"I don't want any mawkish sentiment about it," he said, observing me closely. "I won't permit anybody to feel sorry for me—do you understand?"

"I'll trouble you to use a different tone in addressing me," I replied, hotly; "I'll feel sorry for you if I choose to!" And our usual quarrel proceeded, to his deep satisfaction.

By six o'clock next evening I had Halyard's luggage stowed away in the cat-boat, and the pretty nurse's effects corded down, with the newly hatched auk chicks in a hat-box on top. She and I placed the osier cage aboard, securing it firmly, and then, throwing tablecloths over the auks' heads, we led those simple and dignified birds down the path and across the plank at the little wooden pier. Together we locked up the house, while Halyard stormed at us both and wheeled himself furiously up and down the beach below. At the last moment she forgot her thimble, but we found it, I forget where.

"Come on!" shouted Halyard, waving his shawls furiously. "What the devil are you about up there?"

He received our explanation with a sniff, and we trundled him aboard without further ceremony.

"Don't run me across the plank like a steamer trunk!" he shouted, as I shot him dexterously into the cockpit. But the wind was dying away, and I had no time to dispute with him then.

The sun was setting above the pine-clad ridge as our sail flapped and partly filled, and I cast off and began a long track, east by south, to avoid the spouting rocks on our starboard bow.

The sea birds rose in clouds as we swung across the shoal, the black surf-ducks scuttered out to sea, the gulls tossed their sun-tipped wings in the ocean, riding the rollers like bits of froth.

Already we were sailing slowly out across that great hole in the ocean, five miles deep, the most profound sounding ever taken in the Atlantic. The presence of great heights or great depths, seen or unseen, always impresses the human mind—perhaps oppresses it. We were very silent; the sunlight stain on the cliff and beach deepened to crimson, then faded into somber purple gloom that lingered long after the rose tint died out in the zenith.

Our progress was slow; at times, although the sail filled with the rising land breeze, we scarcely seemed to move at all.

"Of course," said the pretty nurse, "we couldn't be aground in the deepest hole in the Atlantic."

"Scarcely," said Halyard, sarcastically, "unless we've grounded on a whale."

"What's that soft thumping?" I asked. "Have we run afoul of a barrel or log?"

It was almost too dark to see, but I leaned over the rail and swept the water with my hand.

Instantly something smooth glided under it, like the back of a great fish, and I jerked my hand back to the tiller. At the same moment the whole

surface of the water seemed to begin to purr, with a sound like the breaking of froth in a champagne glass.

"What's the matter with you?" asked Halyard, sharply.

"A fish came up under my hand," I said, "a porpoise or something—"

With a low cry, the pretty nurse clasped my arm in both her hands.

"Listen!" she whispered. "It's purring around the boat."

"What the devil's purring?" shouted Halyard. "I won't have anything
purring around me!"

At that moment, to my amazement, I saw that the boat had stopped
entirely, although the sail was full and the small pennant fluttered from the
mast-head. Something, too, was tugging at the rudder, twisting and jerking
it until the tiller strained and creaked in my hand. All at once it snapped;
the tiller swung useless and the boat whirled around, heeling in the stiffen-
ing wind, and drove shoreward.

It was then that I, ducking to escape the boom, caught a glimpse of
something ahead—something that a sudden wave seemed to toss on deck
and leave there, wet and flapping—a man with round, fixed, fishy eyes, and
soft, slaty skin.

But the horror of the thing were the two gills that swelled and relaxed
spasmodically, emitting a rasping, purring sound—two gasping, blood-red
gills, all fluted and scalloped and distended.

Frozen with amazement and repugnance, I stared at the creature; I felt
the hair stirring on my head and the icy sweat on my forehead.

"It's the harbor-master!" screamed Halyard.

The harbor-master had gathered himself into a wet lump, squatting
motionless in the bows under the mast; his lidless eyes were phosphorescent,
like the eyes of living codfish. After a while I felt that either fright or disgust was going to strangle me where I sat, but it was only the arms of the
pretty nurse clasped around me in a frenzy of terror.

There was not a firearm aboard that we could get at. Halyard's hand
crept backward where a steel-shod boat-hook lay, and I also made a clutch
at it. The next moment I had it in my hand, and staggered forward, but the
boat was already tumbling shoreward among the breakers, and the next I
knew the harbor-master ran at me like a colossal rat, just as the boat rolled
over and over through the surf, spilling freight and passengers among the
seaweed-covered rocks.

When I came to myself I was thrashing about knee-deep in a rocky
pool, blinded by the water and half suffocated, while under my feet, like a
stranded porpoise, the harbor-master made the water boil in his efforts to
upset me. But his limbs seemed soft and boneless; he had no nails, no teeth,
and he bounced and thumped and flapped and splashed like a fish, while I
rained blows on him with the boat-hook that sounded like blows on a foot-

ball. All the while his gills were blowing out and frothing, and purring, and his lidless eyes looked into mine, until, nauseated and trembling, I dragged myself back to the beach, where already the pretty nurse alternately wrung her hands and her petticoats in ornamental despair.

Beyond the cove, Halyard was bobbing up and down, afloat in his invalid's chair, trying to steer shoreward. He was the maddest man I ever saw.

"Have you killed that rubber-headed thing yet?" he roared.

"I can't kill it!" I shouted, breathlessly. "I might as well try to kill a football!"

"Can't you punch a hole in it?" he bawled. "If I can only get at him—"

His words were drowned in a thunderous splashing, a roar of great, broad flippers beating the sea, and I saw the gigantic forms of my two great auks, followed by their chicks, blundering past in a shower of spray, driving headlong out into the ocean.

"Oh, Lord!" I said. "I can't stand that," and, for the first time in my life, I fainted peacefully—and appropriately—at the feet of the pretty nurse.

It is within the range of possibility that this story may be doubted. It doesn't matter; nothing can add to the despair of a man who has lost two great auks.

As for Halyard, nothing affects him—except his involuntary sea-bath, and that did him so much good that he writes me from the south that he's going on a walking tour through Switzerland—if I'll join him. I might have joined him if he had not married the pretty nurse. I wonder whether—but, of course, this is no place for speculation.

In regard to the harbor-master, you may believe it or not, as you choose. But if you hear of any great auks being found, kindly throw a table-cloth over their heads and notify the authorities at the new Zoological Gardens in Bronx Park, New York. The reward is ten thousand dollars.

About "Fishhead"

Of this story by Irvin S. Cobb (1876-1944) H. P. Lovecraft had this to say:

Still further carrying on our spectral tradition is the gifted and versatile humorist Irvin S. Cobb, whose work both early and recent contains some finely weird specimens. "Fishhead", an early achievement, is banefully effective in its portrayal of unnatural affinities between a hybrid idiot and the strange fish of an isolated lake, which at the last avenge their biped kinsman's murder (*Supernatural Horror in Literature*).

Lovecraft would have read the story in *The Cavalier* for January 1913.

The influence of this story upon Lovecraft's "The Shadow over Innsmouth" cannot be doubted. In terms of specifics, notice the facial appearance of Fishhead himself and the fact that fish tended to throng more thickly about his domicile than anywhere else on the lake. If any one character in "The Shadow over Innsmouth" may be taken as corresponding to Fishhead, it is surely the Ralph Kramden of Innsmouth, bus driver Joe Sargent, the first Innsmouther we get to see, and thus the stereotype standard bearer for the whole class he belongs to.

Perhaps more importantly, Fishhead embodies unambiguously the basic premise of "The Shadow over Innsmouth" in that, while the product of "loathsome miscegenation", he is the son of a Negro and an American Indian, not of a human and a deep one. This, of course, is really what Lovecraft found revolting in the idea of interacial marriage: not the ludicrous notion of human and inhuman producing offspring, but the subtextual hook of different ethnic races mating and "polluting" the gene pool (as though the result would not rather be genetically enhancing!).

But how did Cobb envision the interbreeding as resulting in Fishhead's ichthyic traits? The narration doesn't seem to side with the popular superstition that Fishhead's mother was scared by a catfish while pregnant. We may wonder if he intended that the product of two "inferior" races would result in an atavistic freak, combining the near-animal recessive genes of both "degenerate" parents. At least it would not be surprising if Lovecraft had read Cobb this way.

Fishhead

by Irvin S. Cobb

It goes past the powers of my pen to try to describe Reelfoot Lake for you so that you, reading this, will get the picture of it in your mind as I have it in mine.

For Reelfoot Lake is like no other lake that I know anything about. It is an afterthought of Creation.

The rest of this continent was made and had dried in the sun for thousands of years—millions of years, for all I know—before Reelfoot came to be. It's the newest big thing in nature on this hemisphere, probably, for it was formed by the great earthquake of 1811.

That earthquake of 1811 surely altered the face of the Earth on the then far frontier of this country.

It changed the course of rivers, it converted hills into what are now the sunken lands of three states, and it turned the solid ground to jelly and made it roll in waves like the sea.

And in the midst of the retching of the land and the vomiting of the waters it depressed to varying depths a section of the Earth's crust sixty miles long, taking it down—trees, hills, hollows, and all; and a crack broke through to the Mississippi River so that for three days the river ran upstream, filling the hole.

The result was the largest lake south of the Ohio, lying mostly in Tennessee, but extending up across what is now the Kentucky line, and taking its name from a fancied resemblance in its outline to the splay, reeled foot of a cornfield Negro. Niggerwool Swamp, not so far away, may have got its name from the same man who christened Reelfoot; at least so it sounds.

Reelfoot is, and has always been, a lake of mystery.

In places it is bottomless. Other places the skeletons of the cypress trees that went down when the earth sank still stand upright so that if the sun shines from the right quarter, and the water is less muddy than common, a man, peering face downward into its depths, sees, or thinks he sees, down below him the bare top limbs upstretching like drowned men's fingers, all coated with the mud of years and bandaged with pennons of the green lake slime.

In still other places the lake is shallow for long stretches, no deeper than breast high to a man, but dangerous because of the weed growths and the sunken drifts which entangle a swimmer's limbs. Its banks are mainly mud; its waters are muddied, too, being a rich coffee color in the spring and a copperish yellow in the summer, and after the spring floods, when the dried sediment covers the tree trunks with a thick, scrofulous-looking coat.

There are stretches of unbroken woodland around it, and slashes where the cypress knees rise countlessly like headstones and footstones for the dead snags that rot in the soft ooze.

There are deadenings with the lowland corn growing high and rank below and the bleached, fire-blackened girdled trees rising above, barren of leaf and limb.

There are long, dismal flats where in the spring the clotted frogspawn cling like patches of white mucus among the weed-stalks, and at night the turtles crawl out to lay clutches of perfectly round, white eggs with tough, rubbery shells in the sand.

There are bayous leading off to nowhere, and sloughs that wind aimlessly, like great, blind worms, finally to join the big river that rolls its semi-liquid torrents a few miles to the westward.

So Reelfoot lies there, flat in the bottoms, freezing lightly in the winter, streaming torridly in the summer, swollen in the spring when the woods have turned a vivid green and the buffalo-gnats by the million and the billion fill the flooded hollows with their pestilential buzzing, and in the fall ringed about gloriously with all the colors which the first frost brings—gold of hickory, yellow-russet of sycamore, red of dogwood and ash, and purple-black of sweet-gum.

But the Reelfoot country has its uses. It is the best game and fish country, natural or artificial, that is left in the South today.

In their appointed seasons the duck and the geese flock in, and even semi-tropical birds, like the brown pelican and the Florida snake-bird, have been known to come there to nest.

Pigs, gone back to wildness, range the ridges, each razor-backed drove captained by a gaunt, savage, slab-sided old boar. By night the bullfrogs, inconceivably big and tremendously vocal, bellow under the banks.

It is a wonderful place for fish—bass and crappie, and perch, and the snouted buffalo fish.

How these edible sorts live to spawn, and how their spawn in turn live to spawn again is a marvel, seeing how many of the big fish-eating canni-bal-fish there are in Reelfoot.

Here, bigger than anywhere else, you find the garfish, all bones and appetite, and horny plates, with a snout like an alligator, the nearest link, naturalists say, between the animal life of today and the animal life of the Reptilian Period.

The shovel-nose cat, really a deformed kind of fresh-water sturgeon, with a great fan-shaped membranous plate jutting out from his nose like a bowsprit, jumps all day in the quiet places with mighty splashing sounds, as though a horse had fallen into the water.

On every stranded log the huge snapping turtles lie on sunny days in groups of four and six, baking their shells black in the sun, with their little snaky heads raised watchfully, ready to slip noiselessly off at the first sound of oars grating in the row-locks. But the biggest of them all are the catfish!

These are monstrous creatures, these catfish of Reelfoot—scaleless, slick things, with corpsy, dead eyes and poisonous fins, like javelins, and huge whiskers dangling from the sides of their cavernous heads.

Six and seven feet long they grow to be, and weigh 200 pounds or more, and they have mouths wide enough to take in a man's foot or a man's fist, and strong enough to break any hook save the strongest, and greedy enough to eat anything, living or dead or putrid, that the horny jaws can master.

Oh, but they are wicked things, and they tell wicked tales of them down there. They call them man-eaters, and compare them, in certain of their habits, to sharks.

Fishhead was of a piece with this setting.

He fitted into it as an acorn fits its cup. All his life he had lived on Reelfoot, always in the one place, at the mouth of a certain slough.

He had been born there, of a Negro father and a half-breed Indian mother, both of them now dead, and the story was that before his birth his mother was frightened by one of the big fish, so that the child came into the world hideously marked.

Anyhow, Fishhead was a human monstrosity, the veritable embodiment of nightmare!

He had the body of a man—a short, stocky, sinewy body—but his face was as near to being the face of a great fish as any face could be and yet retain some trace of human aspect.

His skull sloped back so abruptly that he could hardly be said to have a forehead at all; his chin slanted off right into nothing. His eyes were small and round with shallow, glazed, pale-yellow pupils, and they were set wide apart in his head, and they were unwinking and staring, like a fish's eyes.

His nose was no more than a pair of tiny slits in the middle of the yellow mask. His mouth was the worst of all. It was the awful mouth of a catfish, lipless and almost inconceivably wide, stretching from side to side.

When Fishhead became a man grown his likeness to a fish increased, for the hair upon his face grew out into two tightly kinked slender pendants that drooped down either side of the mouth like the beards of a fish!

If he had any other name than Fishhead, none excepting he knew it. As Fishhead he was known, and as Fishhead he answered. Because he knew the waters and the woods of Reelfoot better than any other man there, he was valued as a guide by the city men who came every year to hunt or fish; but there were few such jobs that Fishhead would take.

Mainly he kept to himself, tending his corn patch, netting the lake, trapping a little, and in season pot hunting for the city markets. His neighbors, ague-bitten and malaria-proof Negroes alike, left him to himself.

Indeed, for the most part they had a superstitious fear of him. So he lived alone, with no kith or kin, nor even a friend, shunning his kind and shunned by them.

His cabin stood just below the state line, where Mud Slough runs into the lake. It was a shack of logs, the only human habitation for four miles up or down.

Behind it the thick timber came shouldering right up to the edge of Fishhead's small truck patch, enclosing it in thick shade except when the sun stood just overhead.

He cooked his food in a primitive fashion, outdoors, over a hole in the soggy earth or upon the rusted red ruin of an old cookstove, and he drank the saffron water of the lake out of a dipper made of a gourd, faring and fending for himself, a master hand at skiff and net, competent with duck gun and fish spear, yet a creature of affliction and loneliness, part savage, almost amphibious, set apart from his fellows, silent and suspicious.

In front of his cabin jutted out a long fallen cottonwood trunk, lying half in and half out of the water, its top side burnt by the sun and worn by the friction of Fishhead's bare feet until it showed countless patterns of tiny scrolled lines, its underside black and rotted, and lapped at unceasingly by little waves like tiny licking tongues.

Its farther end reached deep water. And it was a part of Fishhead, for no matter how far his fishing and trapping might take him in the daytime, sunset would find him back there, his boat drawn up on the bank, and he on the other end of this log.

From a distance men had seen him there many times, sometimes squatted motionless as the big turtles that would crawl upon its dipping tip in his absence, sometimes erect and motionless like a creek crane, his misshapen yellow form outlined against the yellow sun, the yellow water, the yellow banks—all of them yellow together.

If the Reelfooters shunned Fishhead by day they feared him by night and avoided him as a plague, dreading even the chance of a casual meeting. For there were ugly stories about Fishhead—stories which all the Negroes and some of the whites believed.

They said that a cry which had been heard just before dusk and just after, skittering across the darkened waters, was his calling cry to the big cats, and at his bidding they came trooping in, and that in their company he swam in the lake on moonlight nights, sporting with them, diving with them, even feeding with them on what manner of unclean things they fed.

The cry had been heard many times, that much was certain, and it was certain also that the big fish were noticeably thick at the mouth of Fishhead's slough. No native Reelfooter, white or black, would willingly wet a leg or arm there.

Here Fishhead had lived, and here he was going to die. The Baxters were going to kill him, and this day in late summer was to be the time of the killing.

The two Baxters—Jake and Joel—were coming in their dugout to do it!

This murder had been a long time in the making. The Baxters had to brew their hate over a slow fire for months before it reached the pitch of action.

They were poor whites, poor in everything, repute, and worldly goods, and standing—a pair of fever-ridden squatters who lived on whiskey and tobacco when they could get it, and on fish and cornbread when they couldn't.

The feud itself was of months' standing.

Meeting Fishhead one day in the spring on the spindly scaffolding of the skiff landing at Walnut Log, and being themselves far overtaken in liquor and vainglorious with a bogus alcoholic substitute for courage, the brothers had accused him, wantonly and without proof, of running their trout-line and stripping it of the hooked catch—an unforgivable sin among the water dwellers and the shanty boaters of the South.

Seeing that he bore this accusation in silence, only eyeing them steadfastly, they had been emboldened then to slap his face, whereupon he turned and gave them both the beating of their lives—bloodying their noses and bruising their lips with hard blows against their front teeth, and finally leaving them, mauled and prone, in the dirt.

Moreover, in the onlookers a sense of the everlasting fitness of things had triumphed over race prejudice and allowed them—two freeborn, sovereign whites—to be licked by a nigger! Therefore they were going to get the nigger!

The whole thing had been planned out amply. They were going to kill him on his log at sundown. There would be no witnesses to see it, no retribution to follow after it. The very ease of the undertaking made them forget even their inborn fear of the place of Fishhead's habitation.

For more than an hour they had been coming from their shack across a deeply indented arm of the lake.

Their dugout, fashioned by fire and adz and draw-knife from the hide of a gum-tree, moved through the water as noiselessly as a swimming mallard, leaving behind it a long, wavy trail on the stilled waters.

Jake, the better oarsman, sat flat in the stern of the round-bottomed craft, paddling with quick, splashless strokes. Joel, the better shot, was squatted forward. There was a heavy, rusted duck gun between his knees.

Though their spying upon the victim had made them certain sure he would not be about the shore for hours, a doubled sense of caution led them to hug closely the weedy banks. They slid along the shore like shadows, moving so swiftly and in such silence that the watchful mud turtles barely turned their snaky heads as they passed.

So, a full hour before the time, they came slipping around the mouth of the slough and made for a natural ambuscade which the mixed-breed had left within a stone's jerk of his cabin to his own undoing.

Where the slough's flow joined deeper water a partly uprooted tree was stretched, prone from shore, at the top still thick and green with leaves that drew nourishment from the earth in which the half-uncovered roots yet held, and twined about with an exuberance of trumpet vines and wild fox-grapes. All about was a huddle of drift—last year's cornstalks, shreddy strips of bark, chunks of rotted weed, all the riffle and dunnage of a quiet eddy.

Straight into this green clump glided the dugout and swung, broadside on, against the protecting trunk of the tree, hidden from the inner side by the intervening curtains of rank growth, just as the Baxters had intended it should be hidden, when days before in their scouting they marked this masked place of waiting and included it, then and there, in the scope of their plans.

There had been no hitch or mishap. No one had been abroad in the late afternoon to mark their movements—and in a little while Fishhead ought to be due. Jake's woodsman's eye followed the downward swing of the sun speculatively.

The shadows, thrown shoreward, lengthened and slithered on the small ripples. The small noises of the day died out; the small noises of the coming night began to multiply.

The green-bodied flies went away and big mosquitoes, with speckled gray legs, came to take the places of the flies.

The sleepy lake sucked at the mud banks with small mouthing sounds, as though it found the taste of the raw mud agreeable. A monster crawfish, big as a chicken lobster, crawled out of the top of his dried mud chimney and perched himself there, an armored sentinel on the watchtower.

Bull bats began to flitter back and forth, above the tops of the trees. A pudgy muskrat, swimming with head up, was moved to sidle off briskly as he met a cottonmouth moccasin snake, so fat and swollen with summer poison that it looked almost like a legless lizard as it moved along the surface of the water in a series of slow torpid *s*'s. Directly above the head of either of the waiting assassins a compact little swarm of midges hung, holding to a sort of kite-shaped formation.

A little more time passed and Fishhead came out of the woods at the back, walking swiftly, with a sack over his shoulder.

For a few seconds his deformities showed in the clearing; then the black inside of the cabin swallowed him up.

By now the sun was almost down. Only the red nub of it showed above the timber line across the lake, and the shadows lay inland a long way. Out beyond, the big cats were stirring, and the great smacking sounds as their twisting bodies leaped clear and fell back in the water came shoreward in a chorus.

But the two brothers, in their green covert, gave heed to nothing except the one thing upon which their hearts were set and their nerves tensed. Joel gently shoved his gun barrels across the log, cuddling the stock to his shoulder and slipping two fingers caressingly back and forth upon the triggers. Jake held the narrow dugout steady by a grip upon a fox-grape tendril.

A little wait and then the finish came!

Fishhead emerged from the cabin door and came down the narrow footpath to the water and out upon the water on his log.

He was barefooted and bareheaded, his cotton shirt open down the front to show his yellow neck and breast, his dungaree trousers held about his waist by a twisted tow string.

His broad splay feet, with the prehensile toes outspread, gripped the polished curve of the log as he moved along its swaying, dipping surface until he came to its outer end and stood there erect, his chest filling, his chinless face lifted up, and something of mastership and dominion in his poise.

And then—his eye caught what another's eyes might have missed— the round, twin ends of the gun barrels, the fixed gleam of Joel's eyes, aimed at him through the green tracery!

In that swift passage of time, too swift almost to be measured by seconds, realization flashed all through him, and he threw his head still higher and opened wide his shapeless trap of a mouth, and out across the lake he sent skittering and rolling his cry.

And in his cry was the laugh of a loon, and the croaking bellow of a frog, and the bay of a hound, all the compounded night noises of the lake. And in it, too, was a farewell, and a defiance, and an appeal!

The heavy roar of the duck gun came!

At twenty yards the double charge tore the throat out of him. He came down, face forward, upon the log and clung there, his trunk twisting distortedly, his legs twitching and kicking like the legs of a speared frog; his shoulders hunching and lifting spasmodically as the life ran out of him all in one swift coursing flow.

His head canted up between the heaving shoulders, his eyes looked full on the staring face of his murderer, and then the blood came out of his mouth, and Fishhead, in death still as much fish as man, slid flopping, head first, off the end of the log, and sank, face downward slowly, his limbs all extended out.

One after another a string of big bubbles came up to burst in the middle of a widening reddish stain on the coffee-colored water.

The brothers watched this, held by the horror of the thing they had done, and the cranky dugout, having been tipped far over by the recoil of the gun, took water steadily across its gunwale; and now there was a sudden stroke from below upon its careening bottom and it went over and they were in the lake.

But shore was only twenty feet away, the trunk of the uprooted tree only five. Joel, still holding fast to his shotgun, made for the log, gaining it with one stroke. He threw his free arm over it and clung there, treading water, as he shook his eyes free.

Something gripped him—some great, sinewy, unseen thing gripped him fast by the thigh, crushing down on his flesh!

He uttered no cry, but his eyes popped out, and his mouth set in a square shape of agony, and his fingers gripped into the bark of the tree like grapples. He was pulled down and down, by steady jerks, not rapidly but steadily, so steadily, and as he went his fingernails tore four little white strips in the tree-bark. His mouth went under, next his popping eyes, then his erect hair, and finally his clawing, clutching hand, and that was the end of him.

Jake's fate was harder still, for he lived longer—long enough to see Joel's finish. He saw it through the water that ran down his face, and with a great surge of his whole body, he literally flung himself across the log and jerked his legs up high into the air to save them. He flung himself too far, though, for his face and chest hit the water on the far side.

And out of this water rose the head of a great fish, with the lake slime of years on its flat, black head, its whiskers bristling, its corpsy eyes alight. Its horny jaws closed and clamped on the front of Jake's flannel shirt. His hand struck out wildly and was speared with a great yell, and a whirling and churning of the water that made the cornstalks circle on the edges of a small whirlpool.

But the whirlpool soon thinned away into widening rings of ripples, and the cornstalks quit circling and became still again, and only the multiplying night noises sounded about the mouth of the slough.

The bodies of all three came ashore on the same day near the same place. Except for the gaping gunshot wound where the neck met the chest, Fishhead's body was unmarked.

But the bodies of the two Baxters were so marred and mauled that the Reelfooters buried them together on the bank without ever knowing which might be Jake's and which might be Joel's.

About "The Shadow over Innsmouth"

Lovecraft made no attempt to harmonize the details between his various stories and their depictions of his myth cycle. Or, better, he attempted not to harmonize them. He realized that actual ancient myth cycles abound in contradictions and variants. To lend his own artificial mythology the semblance of reality, he allowed contradictions to stand. Was Cthulhu the leader of the Old Ones in "The Call of Cthulhu" but only their cousin in "The Dunwich Horror?" So be it. Cthulhu in R'lyeh wasn't losing any sleep over it, and neither was HPL. One of the most important contradictions concerns the relative chronology of the extraterrestrial races. According to "The Whisperer in Darkness" (1930), where the crustacean Outer Ones make their first appearance, the Yuggoth spawn were on Earth before R'lyeh sank beneath the waves, while in the next year's epic, *At the Mountains of Madness*, we are told that the war of the Cthulhu spawn with the crinoid Old Ones of Antarctica was cut short by the sinking of R'lyeh, and that only subsequently did the Outer Ones appear on earth.

Ironically, this pair of stories marks the beginning of a belated attempt by Lovecraft to knit his stories into a more coherent whole. The links become stronger with each new tale. The space devils from Yuggoth, as we have just seen, make an encore cameo appearance in *At the Mountains of Madness*. Then the starfish-headed Old Ones are glimpsed by Walter Gilman in one of his bad trips in "The Dreams in the Witch-House" (1932). They are also mentioned as the enemies of the Great Race of Yith in "The Shadow Out of Time" (1934-35). It must be the crinoids again to whom Zadok Allen alludes as "the lost Old Ones" in "The Shadow over Innsmouth", as we also hear of shoggoths as allies of the deep ones who worship Cthulhu. Finally, the bulge-eyed Innsmouth folk appear again in "The Thing on the Doorstep" (1933), though as bit players.

Putting these fragments together, we would have to guess that the deep ones somehow correspond to the "Cthulhu spawn" of *At the Mountains of Madness*, even though there they were called "cosmic octopi." They had been enemies of the Old Ones of Antarctica, as were the shoggoths later on, who turned on the Old Ones and destroyed them. Thus it makes some sense that the shoggoths should now be allied with the deep ones of Cthulhu, even though their common enemy has vanished. But there are missing pieces here.

Where do "the Old Ones' signs" fit in, those swastika talismans Zadok describes to the incredulous narrator of "The Shadow over Innsmouth?" Why even mention them in the story if they refer neither backward nor forward to anything else? Can this detail be a loose end left over from an earlier draft of the story? And what exactly is the implied relation between the cosmic octopi and the fish-frog deep ones? One almost wonders if there might have been another tale in the sequence, now lost, that would have plugged these gaps. Perhaps it floats somewhere, on the Serenarian Sea, in a bottle of strange workmanship, waiting to be caught in some fisherman's net.

"The Shadow over Innsmouth" first appeared in *Weird Tales* of January 1942, but that version was an unauthorized abridged version. The version we include here is the complete story.

The Shadow over Innsmouth

by H. P. Lovecraft

I

During the winter of 1927-28 officials of the federal government made a strange and secret investigation of certain conditions in the ancient Massachusetts seaport of Innsmouth. The public first learned of it in February, when a vast series of raids and arrests occurred, followed by the deliberate burning and dynamiting—under suitable precautions—of an enormous number of crumbling, worm-eaten, and supposedly empty houses along the abandoned waterfront. Uninquiring souls let this occurrence pass as one of the major clashes in a spasmodic war on liquor.

Keener news-followers, however, wondered at the prodigious number of arrests, the abnormally large force of men used in making them, and the secrecy surrounding the disposal of the prisoners. No trials, or even definite charges, were reported; nor were any of the captives seen thereafter in the regular gaols of the nation. There were vague statements about disease and concentration camps, and later about dispersal in various naval and military prisons, but nothing positive ever developed. Innsmouth itself was left almost depopulated, and it is even now only beginning to show signs of a sluggishly revived existence.

Complaints from many liberal organisations were met with long confidential discussions, and representatives were taken on trips to certain camps and prisons. As a result, these societies became surprisingly passive and reticent. Newspaper men were harder to manage, but seemed largely to cooperate with the government in the end. Only one paper—a tabloid always discounted because of its wild policy—mentioned the deep-diving submarine that discharged torpedoes downward in the marine abyss just beyond Devil Reef. That item, gathered by chance in a haunt of sailors, seemed indeed rather farfetched, since the low, black reef lies a full mile and a half out from Innsmouth Harbour.

People around the country and in the nearby towns muttered a great deal among themselves, but said very little to the outer world. They had talked about dying and half-deserted Innsmouth for nearly a century, and nothing new could be wilder or more hideous than what they had whispered and hinted years before. Many things had taught them secretiveness, and there was no need to exert pressure on them. Besides, they really knew little; for wide salt marshes, desolate and unpeopled, kept neighbours off from Innsmouth on the landward side.

But at last I am going to defy the ban on speech about this thing. Results, I am certain, are so thorough that no public harm save a shock of repulsion could ever accrue from a hinting of what was found by those horrified raiders at Innsmouth. Besides, what was found might possibly have more than one explanation. I do not know just how much of the whole tale has been told even to me, and I have many reasons for not wishing to probe more deeply. For my contact with this affair has been closer than that of any other layman, and I have carried away impressions which are yet to drive me to drastic measures.

It was I who fled frantically out of Innsmouth in the early morning hours of July 16, 1927, and whose frightened appeals for government inquiry and action brought on the whole reported episode. I was willing enough to stay mute while the affair was fresh and uncertain, but now that it is an old story, with public interest and curiosity gone, I have an odd craving to whisper about those few frightful hours in that ill-rumoured and evilly shadowed seaport of death and blasphemous abnormality. The mere telling helps me to restore confidence in my own faculties, to reassure myself that I was not simply the first to succumb to a contagious nightmare hallucination. It helps me, too, in making up my mind regarding a certain terrible step which lies ahead of me.

I never heard of Innsmouth till the day before I saw it for the first and—so far—last time. I was celebrating my coming of age by a tour of New England—sightseeing, antiquarian, and genealogical—and had planned to go directly from ancient Newburyport to Arkham, whence my mother's family was derived. I had no car, but was travelling by train, trolley, and motor-coach, always seeking the cheapest possible route. In Newburyport they told me that the steam train was the thing to take to Arkham; it was only at the station ticket-office, when I demurred at the high fare, that I learned about Innsmouth. The stout, shrewd-faced agent, whose speech shewed him to be no local man, seemed sympathetic toward my efforts at economy, and made a suggestion that none of my other informants had offered.

"You could take that old bus, I suppose," he said with a certain hesitation, "but it ain't thought much of hereabouts. It goes through Innsmouth—you may have heard about that—and so the people don't like it. Run by an Innsmouth fellow—Joe Sargent—but never gets any customers from here, or Arkham either, I guess. Wonder it keeps running at all. I s'pose it's cheap enough, but I never see mor'n two or three people in it—nobody but those Innsmouth folks. Leaves the Square—front of Hammond's Drug Store—at 10 a.m. and 7 p.m. unless they've changed lately. Looks like a terrible rattletrap—I've never been on it."

That was the first I ever heard of shadowed Innsmouth. Any reference to a town not shown on common maps or listed in recent guidebooks would have interested me, and the agent's odd manner of allusion roused something like real curiosity. A town able to inspire such dislike in its neighbours, I thought, must be at least rather unusual, and worthy of a tourist's attention. If it came before Arkham I would stop off there—and so I asked the agent to tell me something about it. He was very deliberate, and spoke with an air of feeling slightly superior to what he said.

"Innsmouth? Well, it's a queer kind of a town down at the mouth of the Manuxet. Used to be almost a city—quite a port before the War of 1812—but all gone to pieces in the last hundred years or so. No railroad now—B. and M. never went through, and the branch line from Rowley was given up years ago.

"More empty houses than there are people, I guess, and no business to speak of except fishing and lobstering. Everybody trades mostly either here or in Arkham or Ipswich. Once they had quite a few mills, but nothing's left now except one gold refinery running on the leanest kind of part time.

"That refinery, though, used to a big thing, and old man Marsh, who owns it, must be richer'n Croesus. Queer old duck, though, and sticks mighty close in his home. He's supposed to have developed some skin disease or deformity late in life that makes him keep out of sight. Grandson of Captain Obed Marsh, who founded the business. His mother seems to've been some kind of foreigner—they say a South Sea islander—so everybody raised Cain when he married an Ipswich girl fifty years ago. They always do that about Innsmouth people, and folks here and hereabouts always try to cover up any Innsmouth blood they have in 'em. But Marsh's children and grandchildren look just like anyone else so far's I can see. I've had 'em pointed out to me here—though, come to think of it, the elder children don't seem to be around lately. Never saw the old man.

"And why is everybody so down on Innsmouth? Well, young fellow, you mustn't take too much stock in what people around here say. They're hard to get started, but once they do get started they never let up. They've been telling things about Innsmouth—whispering 'em, mostly—for the last hundred years, I guess, and I gather they're more scared than anything else. Some of the stories would make you laugh—about old Captain Marsh driving bargains with the devil and bringing imps out of hell to live in Innsmouth, or about some kind of devil-worship and awful sacrifices in some place near the wharves that people stumbled on around 1845 or thereabouts—but I come from Panton, Vermont, and that kind of story don't go down with me.

"You ought to hear, though, what some of the old-timers tell about the black reef off the coast—Devil Reef, they call it. It's well above water a good part of the time, and never much below it, but at that you could hardly call it an island. The story is that there's a whole legion of devils seen sometimes on that reef—sprawled about, or darting in and out of some kind of caves near the top. It's a rugged, uneven thing, a good bit over a mile out, and toward the end of shipping days the sailors used to make big detours just to avoid it.

"That is, sailors that didn't hail from Innsmouth. One of the things they had against old Captain Marsh was that he was supposed to land on it sometimes at night when the tide was right. Maybe he did, for I dare say the rock formation was interesting, and it's just barely possible he was looking for pirate loot and maybe finding it; but there was talk of his dealing with demons there. Fact is, I guess on the whole it was really the Captain that gave the bad reputation to the reef.

"That was before the big epidemic of 1846, when over half the folks in Innsmouth was carried off. They never did quite figure out what the trouble was, but it was probably some foreign kind of disease brought from China or somewhere by the shipping. It surely was bad enough—there was riots over it, and all sorts of ghastly doings that I don't believe ever got outside of town—and it left the place in awful shape. Never came back—there can't be more'n 300 or 400 people living there now.

"But the real thing behind the way folks feel is simply race prejudice—and I don't say I'm blaming those that hold it. I hate those Innsmouth folks myself, and I wouldn't care to go to their town. I s'pose you know—though I can see you're a Westerner by your talk—what a lot our New England ships used to have to do with queer ports in Africa, Asia, the South Seas, and everywhere else, and what queer kinds of people they sometimes brought back with 'em. You've probably heard about the Salem man that came home with a Chinese wife, and maybe you know there's still a bunch of Fiji Islanders somewhere around Cape Cod.

"Well, there must be something like that back of the Innsmouth people. The place always was badly cut off from the rest of the country by marshes and creeks, and we can't be sure about the ins and outs of the matter; but it's pretty clear that old Captain Marsh must have brought home some odd specimens when he had all three of his ships in commission back in the twenties and thirties. There certainly is a strange kind of streak in the Innsmouth folks today—I don't know how to explain it, but it sort of makes you crawl. You'll notice a little in Sargent if you take his bus. Some of 'em have queer narrow heads with flat noses and bulgy, stary eyes that never seem to shut, and their skin ain't quite right. Rough and scabby, and the sides of their necks are all shrivelled or creased up. Get bald, too, very young. The older fellows look the worst—fact is, I don't believe I've ever seen a very old chap of that kind. Guess they must die of looking in the glass! Animals hate 'em—they used to have lots of horse trouble before autos came in.

"Nobody around here or in Arkham or Ipswich will have anything to do with 'em, and they act kind of offish themselves when they come to town or when anyone tries to fish on their grounds. Queer how fish are always thick off Innsmouth Harbour when there ain't any anywhere else around— but just try to fish there yourself and see how the folks chase you off! Those people used to come here on the railroad—walking and taking the train at Rowley after the branch was dropped—but now they use that bus.

"Yes, there's a hotel in Innsmouth—called the Gilman House—but I don't believe it can amount to much. I wouldn't advise you to try it. Better stay over here and take the ten o'clock bus tomorrow morning; then you can get an evening bus there for Arkham at eight o'clock. There was a factory inspector who stopped at the Gilman a couple of years ago and he had a lot of unpleasant hints about the place. Seems they get a queer crowd there, for this fellow heard voices in other rooms—though most of 'em was empty— that gave him the shivers. It was a foreign talk, he thought, but he said the bad thing about it was the kind of voice that sometimes spoke. It sounded so unnatural—slopping-like, he said—that he didn't dare undress and go to sleep. Just waited up and lit out the first thing in the morning. The talk went on most all night.

"This fellow—Casey, his name was—had a lot to say about how the Innsmouth folks watched him and seemed kind of on guard. He found the Marsh refinery a queer place—it's an old mill on the lower falls of the Manuxet. What he said tallied up with what I'd heard. Books in bad shape, and no clear account of any kind of dealings. You know it's always been a kind of mystery where the Marshes get the gold they refine. They've never seemed to do much buying in that line, but years ago they shipped out an enormous lot of ingots.

"Used to be talk of a queer foreign kind of jewellery that the sailors and refinery men sometimes sold on the sly, or that was seen once or twice on some of the Marsh women-folks. People allowed maybe old Captain Obed traded for it in some heathen port, especially since he always ordered stacks of glass beads and trinkets such as seafaring men used to get for native trade. Others thought and still think he'd found an old pirate cache out on Devil Reef. But here's a funny thing. The old Captain's been dead these sixty years, and there ain't been a good-sized ship out of the place since the Civil War; but just the same the Marshes still keep on buying a few of those native trade things—mostly glass and rubber gewgaws, they tell me. Maybe the Innsmouth folks like 'em to look at themselves—Gawd knows they've gotten to be about as bad as South Sea cannibals and Guinea savages.

"That plague of '46 must have taken off the best blood in the place. Anyway, they're a doubtful lot now, and the Marshes and other rich folks are as bad as any. As I told you, there probably ain't more'n 400 people in the whole town in spite of all the streets they say there are. I guess they're what they call 'white trash' down South—lawless and sly, and full of secret doings. They got a lot of fish and lobsters and do exporting by truck. Queer how the fish swarm right there and nowhere else.

"Nobody can ever keep track of these people, and state school officials and census men have a devil of a time. You can bet that prying strangers ain't welcome around Innsmouth. I've heard personally of more'n one business or government man that's disappeared there, and there's loose talk of one who went crazy and is out at Danvers now. They must have fixed up some awful scare for that fellow.

"That's why I wouldn't go at night if I was you. I've never been there and have no wish to go, but I guess a daytime trip couldn't hurt you—even though the people hereabouts will advise you not to make it. If you're just sightseeing, and looking for old-time stuff, Innsmouth ought to be quite a place for you."

And so I spent a part of that evening at the Newburyport Public Library looking up data about Innsmouth. When I had tried to question the natives in the shops, the lunchroom, the garages, and the fire station, I had found them even harder to get started than the ticket agent had predicted; and realised that I could not spare the time to overcome their first instinctive reticences. They had a kind of obscure suspiciousness, as if there were something amiss with anyone too much interested in Innsmouth. At the Y.M.C.A., where I was stopping, the clerk merely discouraged my going to such a dismal, decadent place; and the people at the library shewed much the same attitude. Clearly, in the eyes of the educated, Innsmouth was merely an exaggerated case of civic degeneration.

The Essex County histories on the library shelves had very little to say, except that the town was founded in 1643, noted for shipbuilding before the Revolution, a seat of great marine prosperity in the early 19th century, and later a minor factory centre using the Manuxet as power. The epidemic and riots of 1846 were very sparsely treated, as if they formed a discredit to the county.

References to decline were few, though the significance of the later record was unmistakable. After the Civil War all industrial life was confined to the Marsh Refining Company, and the marketing of gold ingots formed the only remaining bit of major commerce aside from the eternal fishing. That fishing paid less and less as the price of the commodity fell and large-scale corporations offered competition, but there was never a dearth of fish around Innsmouth Harbour. Foreigners seldom settled there, and there was some discreetly veiled evidence that a number of Poles and Portuguese who had tried it had been scattered in a peculiarly drastic fashion.

Most interesting of all was a glancing reference to the strange jewellery vaguely associated with Innsmouth. It had evidently impressed the whole countryside more than a little, for mention was made of specimens in the museum of Miskatonic University at Arkham, and in the display room of the Newburyport Historical Society. The fragmentary descriptions of these things were bald and prosaic, but they hinted to me an undercurrent of persistent strangeness. Something about them seemed so odd and provocative that I could not put them out of my mind, and despite the relative lateness of the hour I resolved to see the local sample—said to be a large, queerly proportioned thing evidently meant for a tiara—if it could possibly be arranged.

The librarian gave me a note of introduction to the curator of the Society, a Miss Anna Tilton, who lived nearby, and after a brief explanation that ancient gentlewoman was kind enough to pilot me into the closed building, since the hour was not outrageously late. The collection was a notable one indeed, but in my present mood I had eyes for nothing but the bizarre object which glistened in a corner cupboard under the electric lights.

It took no excessive sensitiveness to beauty to make me literally gasp at the strange, unearthly splendour of the alien, opulent phantasy that rested there on a purple velvet cushion. Even now I can hardly describe what I saw, though it was clearly enough a sort of tiara, as the description had said. It was tall in front, and with a very large and curiously irregular periphery, as if designed for a head of almost freakishly elliptical outline. The material seemed to be predominantly gold, though a weird lighter lustrousness hinted at some strange alloy with an equally beautiful and scarcely identifiable metal. Its condition was almost perfect, and one could have spent hours in studying the striking and puzzlingly untraditional designs—some simply geometrical, and some plainly marine—chased or moulded in high relief on its surface with a craftsmanship of incredible skill and grace.

The longer I looked, the more the thing fascinated me; and in this fascination there was a curiously disturbing element hardly to be classified or accounted for. At first I decided that it was the queer otherworldly quality of the art which made me uneasy. All other art objects I had ever seen either belonged to some known racial or national stream, or else were consciously modernistic defiances of every recognised stream. This tiara was neither. It clearly belonged to some settled technique of infinite maturity and perfection, yet that technique was utterly remote from any—Eastern or Western, ancient or modern—which I had ever heard of or seen exemplified. It was as if the workmanship were that of another planet.

However, I soon saw that my uneasiness had a second and perhaps equally potent source residing in the pictorial and mathematical suggestions of the strange designs. The patterns all hinted of remote secrets and unimaginable abysses in time and space, and the monotonously aquatic nature of the reliefs became almost sinister. Among these reliefs were fabulous monsters of abhorrent grotesqueness and malignity—half ichthyic and half batrachian in suggestion—which one could not dissociate from a certain haunting and uncomfortable sense of pseudomemory, as if they called up some image from deep cells and tissues whose retentive functions are wholly primal and awesomely ancestral. At times I fancied that every contour of these blasphemous fish-frogs was overflowing with the ultimate quintessence of unknown and inhuman evil.

In odd contrast to the tiara's aspect was its brief and prosy history as related by Miss Tilton. It had been pawned for a ridiculous sum at a shop in State Street in 1873, by a drunken Innsmouth man shortly afterward killed in a brawl. The Society had acquired it directly from the pawnbroker, at once giving it a display worthy of its quality. It was labelled as of probable East Indian or Indo-Chinese provenance, though the attribution was frankly tentative.

Miss Tilton, comparing all possible hypotheses regarding its origin and its presence in New England, was inclined to believe that it formed part of some exotic pirate hoard discovered by old Captain Obed Marsh. This view was surely not weakened by the insistent offers of purchase at a high price which the Marshes began to make as soon as they knew of its presence, and which they repeated to this day despite the Society's unvarying determination not to sell.

As the good lady shewed me out of the building she made it clear that the pirate theory of the Marsh fortune was a popular one among the intelligent people of the region. Her own attitude toward shadowed Innsmouth—which she had never seen—was one of disgust at a community slipping far down the cultural scale, and she assured me that the rumours of devil-worship were partly justified by a peculiar secret cult which had gained force there and engulfed all the orthodox churches.

It was called, she said, "The Esoteric Order of Dagon", and was undoubtedly a debased, quasipagan thing imported from the East a century before, at a time when the Innsmouth fisheries seemed to be going barren. Its persistence among a simple people was quite natural in view of the sudden and permanent return of abundantly fine fishing, and it soon came to be the greatest influence in the town, replacing Freemasonry altogether and taking up headquarters in the old Masonic Hall on New Church Green.

All this, to the pious Miss Tilton, formed an excellent reason for shunning the ancient town of decay and desolation; but to me it was merely a fresh incentive. To my architectural and historical anticipations was now added an acute anthropological zeal, and I could scarcely sleep in my small room at the "Y" as the night wore away.

II

Shortly before ten the next morning I stood with one small valise in front of Hammond's Drug Store in old Market Square waiting for the Innsmouth bus. As the hour for its arrival drew near I noticed a general drift of the loungers to other places up the street, or to the Ideal Lunch across the square. Evidently the ticket-agent had not exaggerated the dislike which local people bore toward Innsmouth and its denizens. In a few moments a small motor-coach of extreme decrepitude and dirty grey colour rattled down State Street, made a turn, and drew up at the curb beside me. I felt immediately that it was the right one, a guess which the half-legible sign on the windshield—*Arkham-Innsmouth-Newb'port*—soon verified.

There were only three passengers—dark, unkempt men of sullen visage and somewhat youthful cast—and when the vehicle stopped they clumsily shambled out and began walking up State Street in a silent, almost furtive fashion. The driver also alighted, and I watched him as he went into the drug store to make some purchase. This, I reflected, must be the Joe Sargent mentioned by the ticket-agent; and even before I noticed any details there spread over me a wave of spontaneous aversion which could be neither checked nor explained. It suddenly struck me as very natural that the local people should not wish to ride on a bus owned and driven by this man, or to visit any oftener than possible the habitat of such a man and his kinsfolk.

When the driver came out of the store I looked at him more carefully and tried to determine the source of my evil impression. He was a thin, stoop-shouldered man not much under six feet tall, dressed in shabby blue civilian clothes and wearing a frayed golf cap. His age was perhaps thirty-five, but the odd, deep creases in the sides of his neck made him seem older when one did not study his dull, expressionless face. He had a narrow head, bulging, watery-blue eyes that seemed never to wink, a flat nose, a receding forehead and chin, and singularly undeveloped ears. His long thick lips and coarse-pored, greyish cheeks seemed almost beardless except for some sparse yellow hairs that straggled and curled in irregular patches; and in places the surface seemed queerly irregular, as if peeling from some cutaneous disease. His hands were large and heavily veined, and had a very unusual greyish-blue tinge. The fingers were strikingly short in proportion to the rest of the structure, and seemed to have a tendency to curl closely into the huge palm. As he walked toward the bus I observed his peculiarly shambling gait and saw that his feet were inordinately immense. The more I studied them the more I wondered how he could buy any shoes to fit them.

A certain greasiness about the fellow increased my dislike. He was evidently given to working or lounging around the fish docks, and carried with him much of their characteristic smell. Just what foreign blood was in him I could not even guess. His oddities certainly did not look Asiatic, Polynesian, Levantine, or Negroid, yet I could see why the people found him alien. I myself would have thought of biological degeneration rather than alienage.

I was sorry when I saw there would be no other passengers on the bus. Somehow I did not like the idea of riding alone with this driver. But as leaving time obviously approached I conquered my qualms and followed the man aboard, extending him a dollar bill and murmuring the single word "Innsmouth." He looked curiously at me for a second as he returned forty cents change without speaking. I took a seat far behind him, but on the same side of the bus, since I wished to watch the shore during the journey.

At length the decrepit vehicle started with a jerk, and rattled noisily past the old brick buildings of State Street amidst a cloud of vapour from the exhaust. Glancing at the people on the sidewalks, I thought I detected in them a curious wish to avoid looking at the bus—or at least a wish to avoid seeming to look at it. Then we turned to the left into High Street, where the going was smoother—flying by stately old mansions of the early republic and still older colonial farmhouses, passing the Lower Green and Parker River, and finally emerging into a long, monotonous stretch of open shore country.

The day was warm and sunny, but the landscape of sand, sedge-grass, and stunted shrubbery became more and more desolate as we proceeded. Out the window I could see the blue water and the sandy line of Plum Island, and we presently drew very near the beach as our narrow road veered off from the main highway to Rowley and Ipswich. There were no visible houses, and I could tell by the state of the road that traffic was very light hereabouts. The small, weather-worn telephone poles carried only two wires. Now and then we crossed crude wooden bridges over tidal creeks that wound far inland and promoted the general isolation of the region.

Once in a while I noticed dead stumps and crumbling foundation-walls above the drifting sand, and recalled the old tradition quoted in one of the histories I had read, that this was once a fertile and thickly settled country-side. The change, it was said, came simultaneously with the Innsmouth epidemic of 1846, and was thought by simple folk to have a dark connexion with hidden forces of evil. Actually, it was caused by the unwise cutting of woodlands near the shore, which robbed the soil of its best protection and opened the way for waves of wind-blown sand.

At last we lost sight of Plum Island and saw the vast expanse of the open Atlantic on our left. Our narrow course began to climb steeply, and I felt a singular sense of disquiet in looking at the lonely crest ahead where the rutted roadway met the sky. It was as if the bus were about to keep on its ascent, leaving the sane earth altogether and merging with the unknown arcana of upper air and cryptical sky. The smell of the sea took on ominous implications, and the silent driver's bent, rigid back and narrow head became more and more hateful. As I looked at him I saw that the back of his head was almost as hairless as his face, having only a few straggling yellow strands upon a grey scabrous surface.

Then we reached the crest and beheld the outspread valley beyond, where the Manuxet joins the sea just north of the long line of cliffs that culminate in Kingsport Head and veer off toward Cape Ann. On the far misty horizon I could just make out the dizzy profile of the Head, topped by the queer ancient house of which so many legends are told; but for the moment all my attention was captured by the nearer panorama just below me. I had, I realised, come face to face with rumour-shadowed Innsmouth.

It was a town of wide extent and dense construction, yet one with a portentous dearth of visible life. From the tangle of chimney-pots scarcely a wisp of smoke came, and the three tall steeples loomed stark and unpainted against the seaward horizon. One of them was crumbling down at the top, and in that and another there were only black gaping holes where clock-dials should have been. The vast huddle of sagging gambrel roofs and peaked gables conveyed with offensive clearness the idea of wormy decay, and as we approached along the now descending road I could see that many roofs had wholly caved in. There were some large square Georgian houses, too, with hipped roofs, cupolas, and railed "widow's walks." These were mostly well back from the water, and one or two seemed to be in moderately sound condition. Stretching inland from among them I saw the rusted, grass-grown line of the abandoned railway, with leaning telegraph poles now devoid of wires, and the half-obscured lines of the old carriage roads to Rowley and Ipswich.

The decay was worst close to the waterfront, though in its very midst I could spy the white belfry of a fairly well preserved brick structure which looked like a small factory. The harbour, long clogged with sand, was enclosed by an ancient stone breakwater, on which I could begin to discern the minute forms of a few seated fishermen, and at whose end were what looked like the foundations of a bygone lighthouse. A sandy tongue had formed inside this barrier, and upon it I saw a few decrepit cabins, moored dories, and scattered lobster-pots. The only deep water seemed to be where the river poured out past the belfried structure and turned southward to join the ocean at the breakwater's end.

Here and there the ruins of wharves jutted out from the shore to end in indeterminate rottenness, those farthest south seeming the most decayed. Far out at sea, despite a high tide, I glimpsed a long, black line scarcely rising above the water yet carrying a suggestion of odd latent malignancy. This, I knew, must be Devil Reef. As I looked, a subtle, curious sense of beckoning seemed superadded to the grim repulsion; and oddly enough, I found this overtone more disturbing than the primary impression.

We met no one on the road, but presently began to pass deserted farms in varying stages of ruin. Then I noticed a few inhabited houses with rags stuffed in the broken windows and shells and dead fish lying about the littered yards. Once or twice I saw listless-looking people working in barren gardens or digging clams on the fishy-smelling beach below, and groups of dirty, simian-visaged children playing around weed-grown doorsteps. Somehow these people seemed more disquieting than the dismal buildings, for almost everyone had certain peculiarities of face and motions which I instinctively disliked without being able to define or comprehend them. For a second I thought this typical physique suggested some picture I had seen, perhaps in a book, under circumstances of particular horror or melancholy; but this pseudorecollection passed very quickly.

As the bus reached a lower level I began to catch the steady note of a waterfall through the unnatural stillness. The leaning, unpainted houses grew thicker, lined both sides of the road, and displayed more urban tendencies than did those we were leaving behind. The panorama ahead had contracted to a street scene, and in spots I could see where a cobblestone pavement and stretches of brick sidewalk had formerly existed. All the houses were apparently deserted, and there were occasional gaps where tumble-down chimneys and cellar walls told of buildings that had collapsed. Pervading everything was the most nauseous fishy odour imaginable.

Soon cross streets and junctions began to appear—those on the left leading to shoreward realms of unpaved squalor and decay, while those on the right shewed vistas of departed grandeur. So far I had seen no people in the town, but there now came signs of a sparse habitation—curtained windows here and there, and an occasional battered motorcar at the curb. Pavement and sidewalks were increasingly well defined, and though most of the houses were quite old—wood and brick structures of the early 19th century—they were obviously kept fit for habitation. As an amateur antiquarian I almost lost my olfactory disgust and my feeling of menace and repulsion amidst this rich, unaltered survival from the past.

But I was not to reach my destination without one very strong impression of poignantly disagreeable quality. The bus had come to a sort of open
concourse or radial point with churches on two sides and the bedraggled
remains of a circular green in the centre, and I was looking at a large pillared hall on the right-hand junction ahead. The structure's once white
paint was now grey and peeling, and the black and gold sign on the pediment was so faded that I could only with difficulty make out the words
"Esoteric Order of Dagon." This, then, was the former Masonic Hall now
given over to a degraded cult. As I strained to decipher this inscription my
notice was distracted by the raucous tones of a cracked bell across the street,
and I quickly turned to look out the window on my side of the coach.

The sound came from a squat-towered stone church of manifestly later
date than most of the houses, built in a clumsy Gothic fashion and having
a disproportionately high basement with shuttered windows. Though the
hands of its clock were missing on the side I glimpsed, I knew that those
hoarse strokes were tolling the hour of eleven. Then suddenly all thoughts
of time were blotted out by an onrushing image of sharp intensity and unaccountable horror which had seized me before I knew what it really was. The
door of the church basement was open, revealing a rectangle of blackness
inside. As I looked, a certain object crossed or seemed to cross that dark rectangle, burning into my brain a momentary conception of nightmare which
was all the more maddening because analysis could not shew a single nightmarish quality in it.

It was a living object—the first except the driver that I had seen since
entering the compact part of the town—and had I been in a steadier mood
I would have found nothing whatever of terror in it. Clearly, as I realised a
moment later, it was the pastor, clad in some peculiar vestments doubtless
introduced since the Order of Dagon had modified the ritual of the local
churches. The thing which had probably caught my first subconscious
glance and supplied the touch of bizarre horror was the tall tiara he wore,
an almost exact duplicate of the one Miss Tilton had shown me the previous evening. This, acting on my imagination, had supplied nameless sinister qualities to the indeterminate face and robed, shambling form beneath
it. There was not, I soon decided, any reason why I should have felt that
shuddering touch of evil pseudomemory. Was it not natural that a local
mystery cult should adopt among its regimentals an unique type of headdress made familiar to the community in some strange way—perhaps as a
treasure-trove?

A very thin sprinkling of repellent-looking youngish people now became visible on the sidewalks—lone individuals, and silent knots of two or three. The lower floors of the crumbling houses sometimes harboured small shops with dingy signs, and I noticed a parked truck or two as we rattled along. The sound of waterfalls became more and more distinct, and presently I saw a fairly deep river-gorge ahead, spanned by a wide, iron-railed highway bridge beyond which a large square opened out. As we clanked over the bridge, I looked out on both sides and observed some factory buildings on the edge of the grassy bluff or part way down. The water far below was very abundant, and I could see two vigorous sets of falls upstream on my right and at least one downstream on my left. From this point the noise was quite deafening. Then we rolled into the large semicircular square across the river and drew up on the right-hand side in front of a tall, cupola-crowned building with remnants of yellow paint and with a half-effaced sign proclaiming it to be the Gilman House.

I was glad to get out of that bus, and at once proceeded to check my valise in the shabby hotel lobby. There was only one person in sight—an elderly man without what I had come to call the "Innsmouth look"—and I decided not to ask him any of the questions which bothered me, remembering that odd things had been noticed in this hotel. Instead, I strolled out on the square, from which the bus had already gone, and studied the scene minutely and appraisingly.

One side of the cobblestoned open space was the straight line of the river; the other was a semicircle of slant-roofed brick buildings of about the 1800 period, from which several streets radiated away to the southeast, south, and southwest. Lamps were depressingly few and small—all low-powered incandescents—and I was glad that my plans called for departure before dark, even though I knew the moon would be bright. The buildings were all in fair condition, and included perhaps a dozen shops in current operation, of which one was a grocery of the First National chain, others a dismal restaurant, a drug store, and a wholesale fish-dealer's office, and still another, at the eastward extremity of the square near the river, an office of the town's only industry—the Marsh Refining Company. There were perhaps ten people visible, and four or five automobiles and motor trucks stood scattered about. I did not need to be told that this was the civic centre of Innsmouth. Eastward I could catch blue glimpses of the harbour, against which rose the decaying remains of three once-beautiful Georgian steeples. And toward the shore on the opposite bank of the river I saw the white belfry surmounting what I took to be the Marsh refinery.

For some reason or other I chose to make my first inquiries at the chain grocery, whose personnel was not likely to be native to Innsmouth. I found a solitary boy of about seventeen in charge, and was pleased to note the brightness and affability which promised cheerful information. He seemed exceptionally eager to talk, and I soon gathered that he did not like the place, its fishy smell, or its furtive people. A word with any outsider was a relief to him. He hailed from Arkham, boarded with a family who came from Ipswich, and went back whenever he got a moment off. His family did not like him to work in Innsmouth, but the chain had transferred him there and he did not wish to give up his job.

There was, he said, no public library or chamber of commerce in Innsmouth, but I could probably find my way about. The street I had come down was Federal. West of that were the fine old residence streets—Broad, Washington, Lafayette, and Adams—and east of it were the shoreward slums. It was in these slums—along Main Street—that I would find the old Georgian churches, but they were all long abandoned. It would be well not to make oneself too conspicuous in such neighbourhoods—especially north of the river—since the people were sullen and hostile. Some strangers had even disappeared.

Certain spots were almost forbidden territory, as he had learned at considerable cost. One must not, for example, linger much around the Marsh refinery, or around any of the still used churches, or around the pillared Order of Dagon Hall at New Church Green. Those churches were very odd—all violently disavowed by their respective denominations elsewhere, and apparently using the queerest kind of ceremonials and clerical vestments. Their creeds were heterodox and mysterious, involving hints of certain marvellous transformations leading to bodily immortality—of a sort—on this earth. The youth's own pastor—Dr. Wallace of Asbury M.E. Church in Arkham—had gravely urged him not to join any church in Innsmouth.

As for the Innsmouth people—the youth hardly knew what to make of them. They were as furtive and seldom seen as animals that live in burrows, and one could hardly imagine how they passed the time apart from their desultory fishing. Perhaps—judging from the quantities of bootleg liquor they consumed—they lay for most of the daylight hours in an alcoholic stupor. They seemed sullenly banded together in some sort of fellowship and understanding—despising the world as if they had access to other and preferable spheres of entity. Their appearance—especially those staring, unwinking eyes which one never saw shut—was certainly shocking enough; and their voices were disgusting. It was awful to hear them chanting in their churches at night, especially during their main festivals or revivals, which fell twice a year, on April 30th and October 31st.

They were fond of the water, and swam a great deal in both river and harbour. Swimming races out to Devil Reef were very common, and everyone in sight seemed well able to share in this arduous sport. When one came to think of it, it was generally only rather young people who were seen about in public, and of these the oldest were apt to be the most tainted-looking. When exceptions did occur, they were mostly persons with no trace of aberrancy, like the old clerk at the hotel. One wondered what became of the bulk of the older folk, and whether the "Innsmouth look" were not a strange and insidious disease-phenomenon which increased its hold as years advanced.

Only a very rare affliction, of course, could bring about such vast and radical anatomical changes in a single individual after maturity—changes involving osseous factors as basic as the shape of the skull—but then, even this aspect was no more baffling and unheard-of than the visible features of the malady as a whole. It would be hard, the youth implied, to form any real conclusions regarding such a matter, since one never came to know the natives personally no matter how long one might live in Innsmouth.

The youth was certain that many specimens even worse than the worst visible ones were kept locked indoors in some places. People sometimes heard the queerest kind of sounds. The tottering waterfront hovels north of the river were reputedly connected by hidden tunnels, being thus a veritable warren of unseen abnormalities. What kind of foreign blood—if any—these beings had, it was impossible to tell. They sometimes kept certain especially repulsive characters out of sight when government agents and others from the outside world came to town.

It would be of no use, my informant said, to ask the natives anything about the place. The only one who would talk was a very aged but normal-looking man who lived at the poorhouse on the north rim of the town and spent his time walking about or lounging around the fire station. This hoary character, Zadok Allen, was 96 years old and somewhat touched in the head, besides being the town drunkard. He was a strange, furtive creature who constantly looked over his shoulder as if afraid of something, and when sober could not be persuaded to talk at all with strangers. He was, however, unable to resist any offer of his favourite poison, and once drunk would furnish the most astonishing fragments of whispered reminiscence.

After all, though, little useful data could be gained from him, since his stories were all insane, incomplete hints of impossible marvels and horrors which could have no source save in his own disordered fancy. Nobody ever believed him, but the natives did not like him to drink and talk with strangers; and it was not always safe to be seen questioning him. It was probably from him that some of the wildest popular whispers and delusions were derived.

Several non-native residents had reported monstrous glimpses from time to time, but between old Zadok's tales and the malformed inhabitants it was no wonder such illusions were current. None of the non-natives ever stayed out late at night, there being a widespread impression that it was not wise to do so. Besides, the streets were loathsomely dark.

As for business—the abundance of the fish was certainly almost uncanny, but the natives were taking less and less advantage of it. Moreover, prices were falling and competition was growing. Of course, the town's real business was the refinery, whose commercial office was on the square only a few doors east of where we stood. Old Man Marsh was never seen, but sometimes went to the works in a closed, curtained car.

There were all sorts of rumours about how Marsh had come to look. He had once been a great dandy, and people said he still wore the frock-coated finery of the Edwardian age, curiously adapted to certain deformities. His sons had formerly conducted the office in the square, but latterly they had been keeping out of sight a good deal and leaving the brunt of affairs to the younger generation. The sons and their sisters had come to look very queer, especially the elder ones; and it was said that their health was failing.

One of the Marsh daughters was a repellent, reptilian-looking woman who wore an excess of weird jewellery clearly of the same exotic tradition as that to which the strange tiara belonged. My informant had noticed it many times, and had heard it spoken of as coming from some secret hoard, either of pirates or of demons. The clergymen—or priests, or whatever they were called nowadays—also wore this kind of ornament as a headdress, but one seldom caught glimpses of them. Other specimens the youth had not seen, though many were rumoured to exist around Innsmouth.

The Marshes, together with the other three gently bred families of the town—the Waites, the Gilmans, and the Eliots—were all very retiring. They lived in immense houses along Washington Street, and several were reputed to harbour in concealment certain living kinsfolk whose personal aspect forbade public view, and whose deaths had been reported and recorded.

Warning me that many of the street signs were down, the youth drew for my benefit a rough but ample and painstaking sketch map of the town's salient features. After a moment's study I felt sure that it would be of great help, and pocketed it with profuse thanks. Disliking the dinginess of the single restaurant I had seen, I bought a fair supply of cheese crackers and ginger wafers to serve as a lunch later on. My programme, I decided, would be to thread the principal streets, talk with any non-natives I might encounter, and catch the eight o'clock coach for Arkham. The town, I could see, formed a significant and exaggerated example of communal decay; but being no sociologist I would limit my serious observations to the field of architecture. Thus I began my systematic though half-bewildered tour of Innsmouth's narrow, shadow-blighted ways. Crossing the bridge and turning toward the roar of the lower falls, I passed close to the Marsh refinery, which seemed to be oddly free from the noise of industry. This building stood on the steep river bluff near a bridge and an open confluence of streets which I took to be the earliest civic centre, displaced after the revolution by the present Town Square.

Recrossing the gorge on the Main Street bridge, I struck a region of utter desertion which somehow made me shudder. Collapsing huddles of gambrel roofs formed a jagged and fantastic skyline, above which rose the ghoulish, decapitated steeple of an ancient church. Some houses along Main Street were tenanted, but most were tightly boarded up. Down unpaved side streets I saw the black, gaping windows of deserted hovels, many of which leaned at perilous and incredible angles through the sinking of part of the foundation. Those windows stared so spectrally that it took courage to turn eastward toward the waterfront. Certainly, the terror of a deserted house swells in geometrical rather than arithmetical progression as houses multiply to form a city of stark desolation. The sight of such endless avenues of fishy-eyed vacancy and death, and the thought of such linked infinities of black, brooding compartments given over to cobwebs and memories and the conqueror worm, start up vestigial fears and aversions that not even the stoutest philosophy can disperse.

Fish Street was as deserted as Main, though it differed in having many brick and stone warehouses still in excellent shape. Water Street was almost its duplicate, save that there were great seaward gaps where wharves had been. Not a living thing did I see except for the scattered fishermen on the distant break-water, and not a sound did I hear save the lapping of the har-bour tides and the roar of the falls in the Manuxet. The town was getting more and more on my nerves, and I looked behind me furtively as I picked my way back over the tottering Water Street bridge. The Fish Street bridge, according to the sketch, was in ruins.

North of the river there were traces of squalid life—active fish-packing houses in Water Street, smoking chimneys and patched roofs here and there, occasional sounds from indeterminate sources, and infrequent shambling forms in the dismal streets and unpaved lanes—but I seemed to find this even more oppressive than the southerly desertion. For one thing, the peo-ple were more hideous and abnormal than those near the centre of town, so that I was several times evilly reminded of something utterly fantastic which I could not quite place. Undoubtedly the alien strain in the Innsmouth folk was stronger here than farther inland—unless, indeed, the "Innsmouth look" were a disease rather than a blood strain, in which case this district might be held to harbour the more advanced cases.

One detail that annoyed me was the distribution of the few faint sounds I heard. They ought naturally to have come wholly from the visibly inhabited houses, yet in reality were often strongest inside the most rigidly boarded-up facades. There were creakings, scurryings, and hoarse doubtful noises; and I thought uncomfortably about the hidden tunnels suggested by the grocery boy. Suddenly I found myself wondering what the voices of those denizens would be like. I had heard no speech so far in this quarter, and was unaccountably anxious not to do so.

Pausing only long enough to look at two fine but ruinous old churches at Main and Church Streets, I hastened out of that vile waterfront slum. My next logical goal was New Church Green, but somehow or other I could not bear to repass the church in whose basement I had glimpsed the inexplicably frightening form of that strangely diademed priest or pastor. Besides, the grocery youth had told me that churches, as well as the Order of Dagon Hall, were not advisable neighbourhoods for strangers.

Accordingly I kept north along Main to Martin, then turning inland, crossing Federal Street safely north of the Green, and entering the decayed patrician neighbourhood of northern Broad, Washington, Lafayette, and Adams Streets. Though these stately old avenues were ill-surfaced and unkempt, their elm-shaded dignity had not entirely departed. Mansion after mansion claimed my gaze, most of them decrepit and boarded up amidst neglected grounds, but one or two in each street shewing signs of occupancy. In Washington Street there was a row of four or five in excellent repair and with finely tended lawns and gardens. The most sumptuous of these—with wide terraced parterres extending back the whole way to Lafayette Street—I took to be the home of Old Man Marsh, the afflicted refinery owner.

In all these streets no living thing was visible, and I wondered at the complete absence of cats and dogs from Innsmouth. Another thing which puzzled and disturbed me, even in some of the best preserved mansions, was the tightly shuttered condition of many third-storey and attic windows. Furtiveness and secretiveness seemed universal in this hushed city of alien-age and death, and I could not escape the sensation of being watched from ambush on every hand by sly, staring eyes that never shut.

I shivered as the cracked stroke of three sounded from a belfry on my left. Too well did I recall the squat church from which those notes came. Following Washington Street toward the river, I now faced a new zone of former industry and commerce, noting the ruins of a factory ahead, and see-ing others, with the traces of an old railway station and covered railway bridge beyond, up the gorge on my right.

The uncertain bridge now before me was posted with a warning sign, but I took the risk and crossed again to the south bank where traces of life reappeared. Furtive, shambling creatures stared cryptically in my direction, and more normal faces eyed me coldly and curiously. Innsmouth was rapid-ly becoming intolerable, and I turned down Paine Street toward the Square in the hope of getting some vehicle to take me to Arkham before the still-distant starting-time of that sinister bus.

It was then that I saw the tumble-down fire station on my left, and noticed the red-faced, bushy-bearded, watery-eyed old man in nondescript rags who sat on a bench in front of it talking with a pair of unkempt but not abnormal-looking firemen. This, of course, must be Zadok Allen, the half-crazed, liquorish nonagenarian whose tales of old Innsmouth and its shadow were so hideous and incredible.

III

It must have been some imp of the perverse—or some sardonic pull from dark, hidden sources—which made me change my plans as I did. I had long before resolved to limit my observations to architecture alone, and I was even then hurrying toward the Square in an effort to get quick transportation out of this festering city of death and decay; but the sight of old Zadok Allen set up new currents in my mind and made me slacken my pace uncertainly.

I had been assured that the old man could do nothing but hint at wild, disjointed, and incredible legends, and I had been warned that the natives made it unsafe to be seen talking with him; yet the thought of this aged witness to the town's decay, with memories going back to the early days of ships and factories, was a lure that no amount of reason could make me resist. After all, the strangest and maddest of myths are often merely symbols or allegories based upon truth—and old Zadok must have seen everything which went on around Innsmouth for the last ninety years. Curiosity flared up beyond sense and caution, and in my youthful egotism I fancied I might be able to sift a nucleus of real history from the confused, extravagant outpouring I would probably extract with the aid of raw whiskey.

I knew that I could not accost him then and there, for the firemen would surely notice and object. Instead, I reflected, I would prepare by getting some bootleg liquor at a place where the grocery boy had told me it was plentiful. Then I would loaf near the fire station in apparent casualness, and fall in with old Zadok after he had started on one of his frequent rambles. The youth had said that he was very restless, seldom sitting around the station for more than an hour or two at a time.

A quart bottle of whiskey was easily, though not cheaply, obtained in the rear of a dingy variety store just off the Square in Eliot Street. The dirty-looking fellow who waited on me had a touch of the staring "Innsmouth look", but was quite civil in his way, being perhaps used to the custom of such convivial strangers—truckmen, gold-buyers, and the like—as were occasionally in town.

Reentering the Square I saw that luck was with me, for—shuffling out of Paine Street around the corner of the Gilman House—I glimpsed nothing less than the tall, lean, tattered form of old Zadok Allen himself. In accordance with my plan, I attracted his attention by brandishing my newly purchased bottle, and soon realised that he had begun to shuffle wistfully after me as I turned into Waite Street on my way to the most deserted region I could think of.

I was steering my course by the map the grocery boy had prepared, and was aiming for the wholly abandoned stretch of southern waterfront which I had previously visited. The only people in sight there had been the fishermen on the distant breakwater; by going a few squares south I could get beyond the range of these, finding a pair of seats on some abandoned wharf and being free to question old Zadok unobserved for an indefinite time. Before I reached Main Street I could hear a faint and wheezy "Hey Mister!" behind me, and I presently allowed the old man to catch up and take copious pulls from the quart bottle.

I began putting out feelers as we walked amidst the omnipresent desolation and crazily tilted ruins, but found that the aged tongue did not loosen as quickly as I had expected. At length I saw a grass-grown opening toward the sea between crumbling brick walls, with the weedy length of an earth and masonry wharf projecting beyond. Piles of moss-covered stones near the water promised tolerable seats, and the scene was sheltered from all possible view by a ruined warehouse on the north. Here, I thought, was the ideal place for a long secret colloquy; so I guided my companion down the lane and picked out spots to sit in among the mossy stones. The air of death and desertion was ghoulish, and the smell of fish almost insufferable; but I was resolved to let nothing deter me.

About four hours remained for conversation if I were to catch the eight o'clock coach for Arkham, and I began to dole out more liquor to the ancient tippler, meanwhile eating my own frugal lunch. In my donations I was careful not to overshoot the mark, for I did not wish Zadok's vinous garrulousness to pass into a stupor. After an hour his furtive taciturnity shewed signs of disappearing, but much to my disappointment he still sidetracked my questions about Innsmouth and its shadow-haunted past. He would babble of current topics, revealing a wide acquaintance with newspapers and a great tendency to philosophise in a sententious village fashion.

Toward the end of the second hour I feared my quart of whiskey would not be enough to produce results, and was wondering whether I had better leave old Zadok and go back for more. Just then, however, chance made the opening which my questions had been unable to make, and the wheezing ancient's rambling took a turn that caused me to lean forward and listen alertly. My back was toward the fishy-smelly sea, but he was facing it, and

something or other had caused his wandering gaze to light on the low, distant line of Devil Reef, then shewing plainly and almost fascinatingly above
the waves. The sight seemed to displease him, for he began a series of weak
curses which ended in a confidential whisper and a knowing leer. He bent
toward me, took hold of my coat lapel, and hissed out some hints that could
not be mistaken.

"Thar's whar it all begun—that cursed place of all wickedness whar the
deep water starts. Gate o' hell—sheer drop daown to a bottom no soundin'-
line kin tech. Ol' Cap'n Obed done it—him that faound aout more'n was
good fer him in the Saouth Sea islands.

"Everybody was in a bad way them days. Trade fallin' off, mills losin'
business—even the new ones—an' the best of our menfolks kilt a-priva-
terin' in the War of 1812 or lost with the *Elizy* brig an' the *Ranger* scow—
both on 'em Gilman venters. Obed Marsh he had three ships afloat—brig-
antine *Columby*, brig *Hetty*, an' barque *Sumatry Queen.* He was the only one
as kep' on with the East-Injy an' Pacific trade, though Esdras Martin's
barkentine *Malay Bride* made a venter as late as twenty-eight.

"Never was nobody like Cap'n Obed—old limb o' Satan! Heh, heh! I
kin mind him a-tellin' abaout furren parts, an' callin' all the folks stupid fer
goin' to Christian meetin' an' bearin' their burdens meek an' lowly. Says
they'd orter git better gods like some o' the folks in the Injies—gods as ud
bring 'em good fishin' in return for their sacrifices, an' ud reely answer
folks's prayers.

"Matt Eliot, his fust mate, talked a lot too, only he was agin' folks's
doin' any heathen things. Told abaout an island east of Otaheite whar they
was a lot o' stone ruins older'n anybody knew anything abaout, kind o' like
them on Ponape, in the Carolines, but with carvin's of faces that looked like
the big statues on Easter Island. Thar was a little volcanic island near thar,
too, whar they was other ruins with diff'rent carvin's—ruins all wore away
like they'd ben under the sea onct, an' with picters of awful monsters all
over 'em.

"Wal, Sir, Matt he says the natives araound thar had all the fish they
cud ketch, an' sported bracelets an' armlets an' head rigs made aout o' a
queer kind o' gold an' covered with picters o' monsters jest like the ones
carved over the ruins on the little island—sorter fish-like frogs or frog-like
fishes that was drawed in all kinds o' positions like they was human bein's.
Nobody cud git aout o' them whar they got all the stuff, an' all the other
natives wondered haow they managed to find fish in plenty even when the
very next islands had lean pickin's. Matt he got to wonderin' too an' so did
Cap'n Obed. Obed he notices, besides, that lots of the han'some young folks
ud drop aout o' sight fer good from year to year, an' that they wan't many

old folks araound. Also, he thinks some of the folks looked durned queer even for Kanakys.

"It took Obed to git the truth aout o' them heathen. I dun't know haow he done it, but he begun by tradin' fer the gold-like things they wore. Ast 'em whar they come from, an' ef they cud git more, an' finally wormed the story aout o' the old chief—Walakea, they called him. Nobody but Obed ud ever a believed the old yeller devil, but the Cap'n cud read folks like they was books. Heh, heh! Nobody ever believes me naow when I tell 'em, an' I dun't s'pose you will, young feller—though come to look at ye, ye hev kind o' got them sharp-readin' eyes like Obed had."

The old man's whisper grew fainter, and I found myself shuddering at the terrible and sincere portentousness of his intonation, even though I knew his tale could be nothing but drunken phantasy.

"Wal, Sir, Obed he larnt that they's things on this arth as most folks never heerd about—an' wouldn't believe ef they did hear. It seems these Kanakys was sacrificin' heaps o' their young men an' maidens to some kind o' god-things that lived under the sea, an' gittin' all kinds o' favour in return. They met the things on the little islet with the queer ruins, an' it seems them awful picters o' frog-fish monsters was supposed to be picters o' these things. Mebbe they was the kind o' critters as got all the mermaid stories an' sech started. They had all kinds o' cities on the sea-bottom, an' this island was heaved up from thar. Seems they was some of the things alive in the stone buildin's when the island come up sudden to the surface. That's haow the Kanakys got wind they was daown thar. Made sign-talk as soon as they got over bein' skeert, an' pieced up a bargain afore long.

"Them things liked human sacrifices. Had had 'em ages afore, but lost track o' the upper world arter a time. What they done to the victims it ain't fer me to say, an' I guess Obed wa'n't none too sharp abaout askin'. But it was all right with the heathens, because they'd ben havin' a hard time an' was desp'rate abaout everything. They give a sarten number o' young folks to the sea-things twice every year—May-Eve an' Hallowe'en—reg'lar as cud be. Also give some o' the carved knick-knacks they made. What the things agreed to give in return was plenty o' fish—they druv 'em in from all over the sea—an' a few gold-like things naow an' then.

"Wal, as I says, the natives met the things on the little volcanic islet—goin' thar in canoes with the sacrifices et cet'ry, and bringin' back any of the gold-like jools as was comin' to 'em. At fust the things didn't never go onto the main island, but arter a time they come to want to. Seems they hankered arter mixin' with the folks, an' havin' j'int ceremonies on the big days—May-Eve an' Hallowe'en. Ye see, they was able to live both in an' aout o' water—what they call amphibians, I guess. The Kanakys told 'em as haow folks from the other islands might wanta wipe 'em aout ef they got wind o' their bein' thar, but they says they dun't keer much, because they cud wipe aout the hull brood o' humans ef they was willin' to bother—that is, any as didn't hev sarten signs sech as was used onct by the lost Old Ones, whoever they was. But not wantin' to bother, they'd lay low when anybody visited the island.

"When it come to matin' with them toad-lookin' fishes, the Kanakys kind o' balked, but finally they larnt something as put a new face on the matter. Seems that human folks has got a kind o' relation to sech water-beasts—that everything alive come aout o' the water onct, an' only needs a little change to go back agin. Them things told the Kanakys that ef they mixed bloods there'd be children as ud look human at fust, but later more'n more like the things, till finally they'd take to the water an' jine the main lot o' things daown thar. An' this is the important part, young feller—them as turned into fish things an' went into the water wouldn't never die. Them things never died excep' they was kilt violent.

"Wal, Sir, it seems by the time Obed knowed them islanders they was all full o' fish blood from them deep water things. When they got old an' began to shew it, they was kep' hid until they felt like takin' to the water an' quittin' the place. Some was more teched than others, an' some never did change quite enough to take to the water; but mostly they turned out jest the way them things said. Them as was born more like the things changed arly, but them as was nearly human sometimes stayed on the island till they was past seventy, though they'd usually go daown under for trial trips afore that. Folks as had took to the water gen'rally come back a good deal to visit, so's a man ud often be a-talkin' to his own five-times-great-grandfather who'd left the dry land a couple o' hundred years or so afore.

"Everybody got aout o' the idee o' dyin'—except in canoe wars with the other islanders, or as sacrifices to the sea gods daown below, or from snake-bites or plague or sharp gallopin' ailments or somethin' afore they cud take to the water—but simply looked forrad to a kind o' change that wa'n't a bit horrible arter a while. They thought what they'd got was well wuth all they'd had to give up—an' I guess Obed kind o' come to think the same hisself when he'd chewed over old Walakea's story a bit. Walakea, though, was one of the few as hadn't got none of the fish blood—bein' of a royal line that intermarried with royal lines on other islands.

"Walakea he shewed Obed a lot o' rites an' incantations as had to do with the sea things, an' let him see some o' the folks in the village as had changed a lot from human shape. Somehaow or other, though, he never would let him see one of the reg'lar things from right aout o' the water. In the end he give him a funny kind o' thingumajig made aout o' lead or something, that he said ud bring up the fish things from any place in the water whar they might be a nest o' 'em. The idee was to drop it daown with the right kind o' prayers an' sech. Walakea allaowed as the things was scattered all over the world, so's anybody that looked abaout cud find a nest an' bring 'em up ef they was wanted.

"Matt he didn't like this business at all, an' wanted Obed shud keep away from the island; but the Cap'n was sharp fer gain, an' faound he cud git them gold-like things so cheap it ud pay him to make a specialty of 'em. Things went on that way for years, an' Obed got enough o' that gold-like stuff to make him start the refinery in Waite's old run-daown fullin' mill. He didn't dass sell the pieces like they was, for folks ud be all the time askin' questions. All the same his crews ud git a piece an' dispose of it naow and then, even though they was swore to keep quiet; an' he let his womenfolks wear some o' the pieces as was more human-like than most.

"Wal, come abaout 'thutty-eight—when I was seven year' old—Obed he faound the island people all wiped aout between v'yages. Seems the other islanders had got wind o' what was goin' on, and had took matters into their own hands. S'pose they must a had, after all, them old magic signs as the sea things says was the only things they was afeard of. No tellin' what any o' them Kanakys will chance to git a holt of when the sea-bottom throws up some island with ruins older'n the deluge. Pious cusses, these was—they didn't leave nothin' standin' on either the main island or the little volcanic islet excep' what parts of the ruins was too big to knock daown. In some places they was little stones strewed abaout—like charms—with somethin' on 'em like what ye call a swastika naowadays. Prob'ly them was the Old Ones' signs. Folks all wiped aout, no trace o' no gold-like things, an' none o' the nearby Kanakys ud breathe a word abaout the matter. Wouldn't even admit they'd ever been any people on that island.

"That naturally hit Obed pretty hard, seein' as his normal trade was doin' very poor. It hit the whole of Innsmouth, too, because in seafarin' days what profited the master of a ship gen'lly profited the crew proportionate. Most of the folks araound the taown took the hard times kind o' sheeplike an' resigned, but they was in bad shape because the fishin' was peterin' aout an' the mills wan't doin' none too well.

"Then's the time Obed he begun a-cursin' at the folks fer bein' dull sheep an' prayin' to a Christian heaven as didn't help 'em none. He told 'em he'd knowed o' folks as prayed to gods that give somethin' ye reely need, an' says ef a good bunch o' men ud stand by him, he cud mebbe git a holt o' sarten paowers as ud bring plenty o' fish an' quite a bit o' gold. O' course them as sarved on the *Sumatry Queen,* an' seed the island knowed what he meant, an' wa'n't none too anxious to git clost to sea-things like they'd heerd tell on, but them as didn't know what 'twas all abaout got kind o' swayed by what Obed had to say, and begun to ast him what he cud do to set 'em on the way to the faith as ud bring 'em results."

Here the old man faltered, mumbled, and lapsed into a moody and apprehensive silence, glancing nervously over his shoulder and then turning back to stare fascinatedly at the distant black reef. When I spoke to him he did not answer, so I knew I would have to let him finish the bottle. The insane yarn I was hearing interested me profoundly, for I fancied there was contained within it a sort of crude allegory based upon the strangeness of Innsmouth and elaborated by an imagination at once creative and full of scraps of exotic legend. Not for a moment did I believe that the tale had any really substantial foundation; none the less the account held a hint of genuine terror if only because it brought in references to strange jewels clearly akin to the malign tiara I had seen in Newburyport. Perhaps the ornaments had, after all, come from some strange island; and possibly the wild stories were lies of the bygone Obed himself rather than of this antique toper.

I handed Zadok the bottle, and he drained it to the last drop. It was curious how he could stand so much whiskey, for not even a trace of thickness had come into his high, wheezy voice. He licked the nose of the bottle and slipped it into his pocket, then beginning to nod and whisper softly to himself. I bent close to catch any articulate words he might utter, and thought I saw a sardonic smile behind the stained bushy whiskers. Yes—he was really forming words, and I could grasp a fair proportion of them.

"Poor Matt—Matt he allus was agin' it—tried to line up the folks on his side, an' had long talks with the preachers—no use—they run the Congregational parson aout o' taown, an' the Methodist feller quit—never did see Resolved Babcock, the Baptist parson, agin—Wrath o' Jehovy—I was a mightly little critter, but I heerd what I heerd an' seen what I seen— Dagon an' Ashtoreth—Belial an' Beelzebub—Golden Calf an' the idols o' Canaan an' the Philistines—Babylonish abominations—*Mene, mene, tekel, upharsin*—."

He stopped again, and from the look in his watery blue eyes I feared he was close to a stupor after all. But when I gently shook his shoulder he turned on me with astonishing alertness and snapped out some more obscure phrases.

"Dun't believe me, hey? Heh, heh, heh—then jest tell me, young feller, why Cap'n Obed an' twenty odd other folks used to row aout to Devil Reef in the dead o' night an' chant things so laoud ye cud hear 'em all over taown when the wind was right? Tell me that, hey? An' tell me why Obed was allus droppin' heavy things daown into the deep water t'other side o' the reef whar the bottom shoots daown like a cliff lower'n ye kin saound? Tell me what he done with that funny-shaped lead thingumajig as Walakea give him? Hey, boy? An' what did they all haowl on May-Eve, an' agin the next Hallowe'en? An' why'd the new church parsons—fellers as used to be sailors—wear them queer robes an' cover theirselves with them gold-like things Obed brung? Hey?"

The watery blue eyes were almost savage and maniacal now, and the dirty white beard bristled electrically. Old Zadok probably saw me shrink back, for he began to cackle evilly.

"Heh, heh, heh, heh! Beginnin' to see, hey? Mebbe ye'd like to a ben me in them days, when I seed things at night aout to sea from the cupalo top o' my haouse. Oh, I kin tell ye' little pitchers hev big ears, an' I wa'n't missin' nothin' o' what was gossiped abaout Cap'n Obed an' the folks aout to the reef! Heh, heh, heh! Haow abaout the night I took my pa's ship's glass up to the cupalo an' seed the reef a-bristlin' thick with shapes that dove off quick soon's the moon riz? Obed an' the folks was in a dory, but them shapes dove off the far side into the deep water an' never come up. ... Haow'd ye like to be a little shaver alone up in a cupalo a-watchin' *shapes as wa'n't human shapes?* ... Hey? Heh, heh, heh ...."

The old man was getting hysterical, and I began to shiver with a name-less alarm. He laid a gnarled claw on my shoulder, and it seemed to me that its shaking was not altogether that of mirth.

"S'pose one night ye seed somethin' heavy heaved offen Obed's dory beyond the reef, and then learned nex' day a young feller was missin' from home. Hey! Did anybody ever see hide or hair o' Hiram Gilman agin? Did they? An' Nick Pierce, an' Luelly Waite, an' Adoniram Saouthwick, an' Henry Garrison. Hey? Heh, heh, heh, heh. ... Shapes talkin' sign language with their hands ... them as had reel hands. ...

"Wal, Sir, that was the time Obed begun to git on his feet agin. Folks see his three darters a-wearin' gold-like things as nobody'd never see on 'em afore, an' smoke started comin' aout o' the refin'ry chimbly. Other folks was prosp'rin', too—the fish begun to swarm into the harbour fit to kill, an' heaven knows what sized cargoes we begun to ship aout to Newb'ryport, Arkham, an' Boston. 'Twas then Obed got the ol' branch railrud put through. Some Kingsport fishermen heerd abaout the ketch an' come up in sloops, but they was all lost. Nobody never see 'em agin. An' jest then our folks organised the Esoteric Order o' Dagon' an' bought Masonic Hall offen Calvary Commandery for it. ... Heh, heh, heh! Matt Eliot was a Mason an' agin' the sellin', but he dropped aout o' sight jest then.

"Remember, I ain't sayin' Obed was set on hevin' things jest like they was on that Kanaky isle. I dun't think he aimed at fust to do no mixin', nor raise no younguns to take to the water an' turn into fishes with eternal life. He wanted them gold things, an' was willin' to pay heavy, an' I guess the others was satisfied fer a while. ...

"Come in 'forty-six the taown done some lookin' an thinkin' fer itself. Too many folks missin'—too much wild preachin' at meetin' of a Sunday—

too much talk abaout that reef. I guess I done a bit by tellin' Selecman Mowry what I see from the cupalo. They was a party one night as follered Obed's craowd aout to the reef, an' I heerd shots betwixt the dories. Nex' day Obed and thutty-two others was in gaol, with everybody a-wonderin' jest what was afoot and jest what charge agin' 'em cud be got to holt. God, ef anybody'd look'd ahead ... couple o' weeks later, when nothin' had ben throwed into the sea fer thet long ...."

Zadok was shewing signs of fright and exhaustion, and I let him keep silence for a while, though glancing apprehensively at my watch. The tide had turned and was coming in now, and the sound of the waves seemed to arouse him. I was glad of that tide, for at high water the fishy smell might not be so bad. Again I strained to catch his whispers.

"That awful night ... I seed 'em. I was up in the cupalo ... hordes of 'em ... swarms of 'em ... all over the reef an' swimmin' up the harbour into the Manuxet. ... God, what happened in the streets of Innsmouth that night ... they rattled our door, but Pa wouldn't open ... then he clumb aout the winder with his musket to find Selecman Mowry an' see what he cud do. ... Maounds o' the dead an' the dyin' ... shots and screams ... shaoutin' in Ol' Squar an' Taown Squar an' New Church Green—gaol throwed open ... proclamation ... treason ... called it the plague when folks come in an' faound half our people missin' ... nobody left but them as ud jine in with Obed an' them things or else keep quiet ... never heerd o' my pa no more. ...."

The old man was panting, and perspiring profusely. His grip on my shoulder tightened.

"Everything cleaned up in the mornin'—but they was *traces*. ... Obed he kinder takes charge an' says things is going' to be changed ... *others'll* worship with us at meetin' time, an' sarten haouses hez got to entertain *guests* ... they wanted to mix like they done with the Kanakys, an' he fer one didn't feel baound to stop 'em. Far gone, was Obed ... jest like a crazy man on the subjeck. He says they brung us fish an' treasure, an' shud hev what they hankered after. ...

"Nothin' was to be diff'runt on the aoutside, only we was to keep shy o' strangers ef we knowed what was good fer us. We all hed to take the Oath o' Dagon, an' later on they was secon' an' third Oaths that some on us took. Them as ud help special, ud git special rewards—gold an' sech—no use balkin', fer they was millions of 'em down thar. They'd ruther not start risin' an' wipin' aout human-kind, but ef they was gave away an' forced to, they cud do a lot toward jest that. We didn't hev them old charms to cut 'em off like folks in the Saouth Sea did, an' them Kanakys wudn't never give away their secrets.

"Yield up enough sacrifices an' savage knick-knacks an' harbourage in the taown when they wanted it, an' they'd let well enough alone. Wudn't bother no strangers as might bear tales aoutside—that is, withaout they got pryin'. All in the band of the faithful—Order o' Dagon—an' the children shud never die, but go back to the Mother Hydra an' Father Dagon what we all come from onct. ... *Iä! Iä! Cthulhu fhtagn! Ph'nglui mglw'nafh Cthulhu R'lyeh wgah-nagl fhtagn*—"

Old Zadok was fast lapsing into stark raving, and I held my breath. Poor old soul—to what pitiful depths of hallucination had his liquors plus his hatred of the decay, alienage, and disease around him, brought that fertile, imaginative brain! He began to moan now, and tears were coursing down his channelled cheeks into the depths of his beard.

"God, what I seen senct I was fifteen year' old—*Mene, mene, tekel, upharsin!*—the folks as was missin', an' them as kilt theirselves—them as told things in Arkham or Ipswich or sech places was all called crazy, like you're a callin' me right naow—but God, what I seen—they'd a kilt me long ago for what I know, only I'd took the fust an' secon' Oaths o' Dagon offen Obed, so was pertected unlessen a jury of 'em proved I told things knowin' an' delib'rit ... but I wudn't take the third Oath—I'd a died ruther'n take that—

"It got wuss araound Civil War time, *when children born senct 'forty-six begun to grow up*—some of 'em, that is. I was afeared—never did no pryin' arter that awful night, an' never seen one o'—*them*—clost to in all my life. That is, never no full-blooded one. I went to the war, an' ef I'd a had any guts or sense I'd a never come back, but settled away from here. But folks wrote me things wa'n't so bad. That, I s'pose, was because gov'munt draft men was in taown arter 'sixty-three. Arter the war it was jest as bad agin. People begun to fall off—mills an' shops shet daown—shippin' stopped an' the harbour choked up—railrud give up—but *they* ... they never stopped swimmin' in an' aout o' the river from that cursed reef o' Satan—an' more an' more attic winders got a-boarded up, an' more an' more noises was heerd in haouses as wa'n't s'posed to hev nobody in 'em. ...

"Folks aoutside hev their stories abaout us—s'pose you've heerd a plenty on 'em, seein' what questions ye ast—stories abaout things they've seed naow an' then, an' abaout that queer joolry as still comes in from somewhars an' ain't quite all melted up—but nothin' never gits def'nite. Nobody'll believe nothin'. They call them gold-like things pirate loot, an' allaow the Innsmouth folks hez furren blood or is distempered or somethin'. Besides, them that lives here shoo off as many strangers as they kin, an' encourage the rest not to git very cur'ous, specially raound night time. Beasts balk at the critters—hosses wuss'n mules—but when they got autos that was all right.

"In 'forty-six Cap'n Obed took a second wife that *nobody in the taown never seed*—some says he didn't want to, but was made to by them as he'd called in—had three children by her—two as disappeared young, but one gal as looked like anybody else an' was eddicated in Europe. Obed finally got her married off by a trick to an Arkham feller as didn't suspect nothin'. But nobody aoutside'll hev nothin' to do with Innsmouth folks naow. Barnabas Marsh that runs the refin'ry naow is Obed's grandson by his fust wife—son of Onesiphorus, his eldest son, *but his mother was another o' them as wa'n't never seed aoutdoors.*

"Right naow Barnabas is abaout changed. Can't shet his eyes no more, an' is all aout o' shape. They say he still wears clothes, but he'll take to the water soon. Mebbe he's tried it already—they do sometimes go daown fer little spells afore they go daown for good. Ain't ben seed abaout in public fer nigh on ten year'. Dun't know haow his poor wife kin feel—she come from Ipswich, an' they nigh lynched Barnabas when he courted her fifty odd year' ago. Obed he died in 'seventy-eight, an' all the next gen'ration is gone naow—the *fust* wife's children dead, an' the rest ... God knows. ...."

The sound of the incoming tide was now very insistent, and little by little it seemed to change the old man's mood from maudlin tearfulness to watchful fear. He would pause now and then to renew those nervous glances over his shoulder or out toward the reef, and despite the wild absurdity of his tale, I could not help beginning to share his vague apprehensiveness. Zadok now grew shriller, and seemed to be trying to whip up his courage with louder speech.

"Hey, yew, why dun't ye say somethin'? Haow'd ye like to be livin' in a taown like this, with everything a-rottin' an' a-dyin', an' boarded-up monsters crawlin' an' bleatin' an barkin' an' hoppin' araoun' black cellars an' attics every way ye turn? Hey? Haow'd ye like to hear the haowlin' night arter night from the churches an' Order o' Dagon Hall, *an' know what's doin' part o' the haowlin'?* Haow'd ye like to hear what comes from that awful reef every May-Eve an' Hallowmass? Hey? Think the old man's crazy, eh? Wal, Sir, *let me tell ye that ain't the wust!*"

Zadok was really screaming now, and the mad frenzy of his voice disturbed me more than I care to own.

"Curse ye, dun't set thar a-starin' at me with them eyes—I tell Obed Marsh he's in hell, an' hez got to stay thar! Heh, heh ... in hell, I says! Can't git me—I hain't done nothin' nor told nobody nothin'—

"Oh, yew, young feller? Wal, even ef I hain't told nobody nothin' yet, I'm a-goin' to naow! Yew jest set still an' listen to me, boy—this is what I ain't never told nobody. ... I says I didn't get to do no pryin' arter that night—*but I faound things aout jest the same!*

"Yew want to know what the reel horror is, hey? Wal, it's this—it ain't what them fish devils *hez done,* but what *they're a-goin' to do!* They're a-bringin' things up aout o' whar they come from into the taown—ben doin' it fer years, an' slackenin' up lately. Them haouses north o' the river betwixt Water an' Main Streets is full of 'em—them devils *an' what they brung*—an' when they git ready ... I say, *when they git ready* ... ever hear tell of a *shoggoth?*

"Hey, d'ye hear me? I tell ye *I know what them things be—I seen 'em one night when* ... eh-ahhh-ah! e'yahhh ...."

The hideous suddenness and inhuman frightfulness of the old man's shriek almost made me faint. His eyes, looking past me toward the malodorous sea, were positively starting from his head, while his face was a mask of fear worthy of Greek tragedy. His bony claw dug monstrously into my shoulder, and he made no motion as I turned my head to look at whatever he had glimpsed.

There was nothing that I could see. Only the incoming tide, with perhaps one set of ripples more local than the long-flung line of breakers. But now Zadok was shaking me, and I turned back to watch the melting of that fear-frozen face into a chaos of twitching eyelids and mumbling gums. Presently his voice came back—albeit as a trembling whisper.

"*Git aout o' here!* Git aout o' here! *They seen us*—git aout fer your life! Dun't wait fer nothin'—*they know naow*—run fer it—quick—*aout o' this taown*—"

Another heavy wave dashed against the loosening masonry of the bygone wharf, and changed the mad ancient's whisper to another inhuman and blood-curdling scream. "*E-yaahhhh! ... Yhaaaaaaa! ...*"

Before I could recover my scattered wits he had relaxed his clutch on my shoulder and dashed wildly inland toward the street, reeling northward around the ruined warehouse wall.

I glanced back at the sea, but there was nothing there. And when I reached Water Street and looked along it toward the north there was no remaining trace of Zadok Allen.

IV

I can hardly describe the mood in which I was left by this harrowing episode—an episode at once mad and pitiful, grotesque and terrifying. The grocery boy had prepared me for it, yet the reality left me none the less bewildered and disturbed. Puerile though the story was, old Zadok's insane earnestness and horror had communicated to me a mounting unrest which joined with my earlier sense of loathing for the town and its blight of intangible shadow.

Later I might sift the tale and extract some nucleus of historic allegory; just now I wished to put it out of my head. The hour had grown perilously late—my watch said 7:15, and the Arkham bus left Town Square at eight—so I tried to give my thoughts as neutral and practical a cast as possible, meanwhile walking rapidly through the deserted streets of gaping roofs and leaning houses toward the hotel where I had checked my valise and would find my bus.

Though the golden light of late afternoon gave the ancient roofs and decrepit chimneys an air of mystic loveliness and peace, I could not help glancing over my shoulder now and then. I would surely be very glad to get out of malodorous and fear-shadowed Innsmouth, and wished there were some vehicle other than the bus driven by that sinister-looking fellow Sargent. Yet I did not hurry too precipitately, for there were architectural details worth viewing at every silent corner; and I could easily, I calculated, cover the necessary distance in a half-hour.

Studying the grocery youth's map and seeking a route I had not traversed before, I chose Marsh Street instead of State for my approach to Town Square. Near the corner of Fall Street I began to see scattered groups of furtive whisperers, and when I finally reached the Square I saw that almost all the loiterers were congregated around the door of the Gilman House. It seemed as if many bulging, watery, unwinking eyes looked oddly at me as I claimed my valise in the lobby, and I hoped that none of these unpleasant creatures would be my fellow passengers on the coach.

The bus, rather early, rattled in with three passengers somewhat before eight, and an evil-looking fellow on the sidewalk muttered a few indistinguishable words to the driver. Sargent threw out a mail-bag and a roll of newspapers, and entered the hotel; while the passengers—the same men whom I had seen arriving in Newburyport that morning—shambled to the sidewalk and exchanged some faint guttural words with a loafer in a language I could have sworn was not English. I boarded the empty coach and took the same seat I had taken before, but was hardly settled before Sargent reappeared and began mumbling in a throaty voice of peculiar repulsiveness.

I was, it appeared, in very bad luck. There had been something wrong with the engine, despite the excellent time made from Newburyport, and the bus could not complete the journey to Arkham. No, it could not possibly be repaired that night, nor was there any other way of getting transportation out of Innsmouth either to Arkham or elsewhere. Sargent was sorry, but I would have to stop over at the Gilman. Probably the clerk would make the price easy for me, but there was nothing else to do. Almost dazed by this sudden obstacle, and violently dreading the fall of night in this decaying and half-unlighted town, I left the bus and reentered the hotel lobby, where the sullen queer-looking night clerk told me I could have Room 428 on next the top floor—large, but without running water—for a dollar.

Despite what I had heard of this hotel in Newburyport, I signed the register, paid my dollar, let the clerk take my valise, and followed that sour, solitary attendant up three creaking flights of stairs past dusty corridors which seemed wholly devoid of life. My room, a dismal rear one with two windows and bare, cheap furnishings, overlooked a dingy court-yard otherwise hemmed in by low, deserted brick blocks, with a marshy countryside beyond. At the end of the corridor was a bathroom—a discouraging relique with ancient marble bowl, tin tub, faint electric light, and musty wooden panelling around all the plumbing fixtures.

It being still daylight, I descended to the Square and looked around for a dinner of some sort, noticing as I did so the strange glances I received from the unwholesome loafers. Since the grocery was closed, I was forced to patronise the restaurant I had shunned before, a stooped, narrow-headed man with staring, unwinking eyes, and a flat-nosed wench with unbelievably thick, clumsy hands being in attendance. The service was all of the counter type, and it relieved me to find that much was evidently served from cans and packages. A bowl of vegetable soup with crackers was enough for me, and I soon headed back for my cheerless room at the Gilman, getting an evening paper and a fly-specked magazine from the evil-visaged clerk at the rickety stand beside his desk.

As twilight deepened I turned on the one feeble electric bulb over the cheap, iron-framed bed, and tried as best I could to continue the reading I had begun. I felt it advisable to keep my mind wholesomely occupied, for it would not do to brood over the abnormalities of this ancient, blight-shadowed town while I was still within its borders. The insane yarn I had heard from the aged drunkard did not promise very pleasant dreams, and I felt I must keep the image of his wild, watery eyes as far as possible from my imagination.

Also, I must not dwell on what the factory inspector had told the Newburyport ticket-agent about the Gilman House and the voices of its nocturnal tenants—not on that, nor on the face beneath the tiara in the black church doorway, the face for whose horror my conscious mind could not account. It would perhaps have been easier to keep my thoughts from disturbing topics had the room not been so gruesomely musty. As it was, the lethal mustiness blended hideously with the town's general fishy odour and persistently focussed one's fancy on death and decay.

Another thing that disturbed me was the absence of a bolt on the door of my room. One had been there, as marks clearly shewed, but there were signs of recent removal. No doubt it had become out of order, like so many other things in this decrepit edifice. In my nervousness I looked around and discovered a bolt on the clothespress which seemed to be of the same size, judging from the marks, as the one formerly on the door. To gain a partial relief from the general tension I busied myself by transferring this hardware to the vacant place with the aid of a handy three-in-one device including a screwdriver which I kept on my keyring. The bolt fitted perfectly, and I was somewhat relieved when I knew that I could shoot it firmly upon retiring. Not that I had any real apprehension of its need, but that any symbol of security was welcome in an environment of this kind. There were adequate bolts on the two lateral doors to connecting rooms, and these I proceeded to fasten.

I did not undress, but decided to read till I was sleepy and then lie down with only my coat, collar, and shoes off. Taking a pocket flashlight from my valise, I placed it in my trousers, so that I could read my watch if I woke up later in the dark. Drowsiness, however, did not come; and when I stopped to analyse my thoughts I found to my disquiet that I was really unconsciously listening for something—listening for something which I dreaded but could not name. That inspector's story must have worked on my imagination more deeply than I had suspected. Again I tried to read, but found that I made no progress.

After a time I seemed to hear the stairs and corridors creak at intervals as if with footsteps, and wondered if the other rooms were beginning to fill up. There were no voices, however, and it struck me that there was something subtly furtive about the creaking. I did not like it, and debated whether I had better try to sleep at all. This town had some queer people, and there had undoubtedly been several disappearances. Was this one of those inns where travelers were slain for their money? Surely I had no look of excessive prosperity. Or were the townsfolk really so resentful about curious visitors? Had my obvious sightseeing, with its frequent map-consultations, aroused unfavourable notice? It occurred to me that I must be in a highly nervous state to let a few random creakings set me off speculating in this fashion—but I regretted none the less that I was unarmed.

At length, feeling a fatigue which had nothing of drowsiness in it, I bolted the newly outfitted hall door, turned off the light, and threw myself down on the hard, uneven bed—coat, collar, shoes, and all. In the darkness every faint noise of the night seemed magnified, and a flood of doubly unpleasant thoughts swept over me. I was sorry I had put out the light, yet was too tired to rise and turn it on again. Then, after a long, dreary interval, and prefaced by a fresh creaking of stairs and corridor, there came that soft, damnably unmistakable sound which seemed like a malign fulfillment of all my apprehensions. Without the least shadow of a doubt, the lock of my door was being tried—cautiously, furtively, tentatively—with a key.

My sensations upon recognising this sign of actual peril were perhaps less rather than more tumultuous because of my previous vague fears. I had been, albeit without definite reason, instinctively on my guard—and that was to my advantage in the new and real crisis, whatever it might turn out to be. Nevertheless the change in the menace from vague premonition to immediate reality was a profound shock, and fell upon me with the force of a genuine blow. It never once occurred to me that the fumbling might be a mere mistake. Malign purpose was all I could think of, and I kept deathly quiet, awaiting the would-be intruder's next move.

After a time the cautious rattling ceased, and I heard the room to the north entered with a pass key. Then the lock of the connecting door to my room was softly tried. The bolt held, of course, and I heard the floor creak as the prowler left the room. After a moment there came another soft rattling, and I knew that the room to the south of me was being entered. Again a furtive trying of a bolted connecting door, and again a receding creaking. This time the creaking went along the hall and down the stairs, so I knew that the prowler had realised the bolted condition of my doors and was giving up his attempt for a greater or lesser time, as the future would shew.

The readiness with which I fell into a plan of action proves that I must have been subconsciously fearing some menace and considering possible avenues of escape for hours. From the first I felt that the unseen fumbler meant a danger not to be dealt with, but only to be fled from as precipitately as possible. The one thing to do was to get out of that hotel alive as quickly as I could, and through some channel other than the front stairs and lobby.

Rising softly and throwing my flashlight on the switch, I sought to light the bulb over my bed in order to choose and pocket some belongings for a swift, valiseless flight. Nothing, however, happened; and I saw that the power had been cut off. Clearly, some cryptic, evil movement was afoot on a large scale—just what, I could not say. As I stood pondering with my hand on the now useless switch I heard a muffled creaking on the floor below, and thought I could barely distinguish voices in conversation. A moment later I felt less sure that the deeper sounds were voices, since the apparent hoarse barkings and loose-syllabled croakings bore so little resemblance to recognised human speech. Then I thought with renewed force of what the factory inspector had heard in the night in this mouldering and pestilential building.

Having filled my pockets with the flashlight's aid, I put on my hat and tiptoed to the windows to consider chances of descent. Despite the state's safety regulations there was no fire escape on this side of the hotel, and I saw that my windows commanded only a sheer three-storey drop to the cobbled courtyard. On the right and left, however, some ancient brick business blocks abutted on the hotel, their slant roofs coming up to a reasonable jumping distance from my fourth-storey level. To reach either of these lines of buildings I would have to be in a room two doors from my own—in one case on the north and in the other case the south—and my mind instantly set to work calculating what chances I had of making the transfer.

I could not, I decided, risk an emergence into the corridor, where my footsteps would surely be heard, and where the difficulties of entering the desired room would be insuperable. My progress, if it was to be made at all, would have to be through the less solidly built connecting doors of the rooms, the locks and blots of which I would have to force violently, using my shoulder as a battering ram whenever they were set against me. This, I thought, would be possible owing to the rickety nature of the house and its fixtures; but I realised I could not do it noiselessly. I would have to count on sheer speed, and the chance of getting to a window before any hostile forces became coordinated enough to open the right door toward me with a pass key. My own outer door I reinforced by pushing the bureau against it—little by little, in order to make a minimum of sound.

I perceived that my chances were very slender, and was fully prepared for any calamity. Even getting to another roof would not solve the problem, for there would then remain the task of reaching the ground and escaping from the town. One thing in my favour was the deserted and ruinous state of the abutting buildings, and the number of skylights gaping blackly open in each row.

Gathering from the grocery boy's map that the best route out of town was southward, I glanced first at the connecting door on the south side of the room. It was designed to open in my direction, hence I saw—after drawing the bolt and finding other fastenings in place—it was not a favorable one for forcing. Accordingly abandoning it as a route, I cautiously moved the bedstead against it to hamper any attack which might be made on it later from the next room. The door on the north was hung to open away from me, and this—though a test proved it to be locked or bolted from the other side—I knew must be my route. If I could gain the roofs of the buildings in Paine Street and descend successfully to the ground level, I might perhaps dart through the courtyard and the adjacent or opposite buildings to Washington or Bates—or else emerge in Paine and edge around southward into Washington. In any case, I would aim to strike Washington somehow and get quickly out of the Town Square region. My preference would be to avoid Paine, since the fire station there might be open all night.

As I thought of these things I looked out over the squalid sea of decaying roofs below me, now brightened by the beams of a moon not much past full. On the right the black gash of the river gorge clove the panorama, abandoned factories and railway station clinging barnacle-like to its sides. Beyond it the rusted railway and the Rowley road led off through a flat, marshy terrain dotted with islets of higher and dryer scrub-grown land. On the left the creek-threaded countryside was nearer, the narrow road to

Ipswich gleaming white in the moonlight. I could not see from my side of the hotel the southward route toward Arkham which I had determined to take.

I was irresolutely speculating on when I had better attack the northward door, and on how I could least audibly manage it, when I noticed that the vague noises underfoot had given place to a fresh and heavier creaking of the stairs. A wavering flicker of light shewed through my transom, and the boards of the corridor began to groan with a ponderous load. Muffled sounds of possible vocal origin approached, and at length a firm knock came at my outer door.

For a moment I simply held my breath and waited. Eternities seemed to elapse, and the nauseous fishy odour of my environment seemed to mount suddenly and spectacularly. Then the knocking was repeated—continuously, and with growing insistence. I knew that the time for action had come, and forthwith drew the bolt of the northward connecting door, bracing myself for the task of battering it open. The knocking waxed louder, and I hoped that its volume would cover the sound of my efforts. At last beginning my attempt, I lunged again and again at the thin panelling with my left shoulder, heedless of shock or pain. The door resisted even more than I had expected, but I did not give in. And all the while the clamour at the outer door increased.

Finally the connecting door gave, but with such a crash that I knew those outside must have heard. Instantly the outside knocking became a violent battering, while keys sounded ominously in the hall doors of the rooms on both sides of me. Rushing through the newly opened connexion, I succeeded in bolting the northerly hall door before the lock could be turned; but even as I did so I heard the hall door of the third room—the one from whose window I had hoped to reach the roof below—being tried with a pass key.

For an instant I felt absolute despair, since my trapping in a chamber with no window egress seemed complete. A wave of almost abnormal horror swept over me, and invested with a terrible but unexplainable singularity the flashlight-glimpsed dust prints made by the intruder who had lately tried my door from this room. Then, with a dazed automatism which persisted despite hopelessness, I made for the next connecting door and performed the blind motion of pushing at it in an effort to get through and—granting that fastenings might be as providentially intact as in this second room—bolt the hall door beyond before the lock could be turned from outside.

Sheer fortunate chance gave me my reprieve—for the connecting door before me was not only unlocked but actually ajar. In a second I was through, and had my right knee and shoulder against a hall door which was visibly opening inward. My pressure took the opener off guard, for the thing shut as I pushed, so that I could slip the well conditioned bolt as I had done with the other door. As I gained this respite I heard the battering at the two other doors abate, while a confused clatter came from the connecting door I had shielded with the bedstead. Evidently the bulk of my assailants had entered the southerly room and were massing in a lateral attack. But at the same moment a pass key sounded in the next door to the north, and I knew that a nearer peril was at hand.

The northward connecting door was wide open, but there was no time to think about checking the already turning lock in the hall. All I could do was to shut and bolt the open connecting door, as well as its mate on the opposite side—pushing a bedstead against the one and a bureau against the other, and moving a washstand in front of the hall door. I must, I saw, trust to such makeshift barriers to shield me till I could get out the window and on the roof of the Paine Street block. But even in this acute moment my chief horror was something apart from the immediate weakness of my defences. I was shuddering because not one of my pursuers, despite some hideous pantings, gruntings, and subdued barkings at odd intervals, was uttering an unmuffled or intelligible vocal sound.

As I moved the furniture and rushed toward the windows I heard a frightful scurrying along the corridor toward the room north of me, and perceived that the southward battering had ceased. Plainly, most of my opponents were about to concentrate against the feeble connecting door which they knew must open directly on me. Outside, the moon played on the ridgepole of the block below, and I saw that the jump would be desperately hazardous because of the steep surface on which I must land.

Surveying the conditions, I chose the more southerly of the two windows as my avenue of escape, planning to land on the inner slope of the roof and make for the nearest skylight. Once inside one of the decrepit brick structures I would have to reckon with pursuit; but I hoped to descend and dodge in and out of yawning doorways along the shadowed courtyard, eventually getting to Washington Street and slipping out of town toward the south.

The clatter at the northerly connecting door was now terrific, and I saw that the weak panelling was beginning to splinter. Obviously, the besiegers had brought some ponderous object into play as a battering ram. The bedstead, however, still held firm, so that I had at least a faint chance of making good my escape. As I opened the window I noticed that it was flanked by heavy velour draperies suspended from a pole by brass rings, and also that there was a large projecting catch for the shutters on the exterior. Seeing a possible means of avoiding the dangerous jump, I yanked at the hangings and brought them down, pole and all; then quickly hooked two of the rings in the shutter catch and flung the drapery outside. The heavy folds reached fully to the abutting roof, and I saw that the rings and catch would be likely to bear my weight. So, climbing out of the window and down the improvised rope ladder, I left behind me for ever the morbid and horror-infested fabric of the Gilman House.

I landed safely on the loose slates of the steep roof, and succeeded in gaining the gaping black skylight without a slip. Glancing up at the window I had left, I observed it was still dark, though far across the crumbling chimneys to the north I could see lights ominously blazing in the Order of Dagon Hall, the Baptist church, and the Congregational church which I recalled so shiveringly. There had seemed to be no one in the courtyard below, and I hoped there would be a chance to get away before the spreading of a general alarm. Flashing my pocket lamp into the skylight, I saw that there were no steps down. The distance was slight, however, so I clambered over the brink and dropped, striking a dusty floor littered with crumbling boxes and barrels.

The place was ghoulish-looking, but I was past minding such impressions and made at once for the staircase revealed by my flashlight— after a hasty glance at my watch, which shewed the hour to be 2 a.m. The steps creaked, but seemed tolerably sound; and I raced down past a barn-like second storey to the ground floor. The desolation was complete, and only echoes answered my footfalls. At length I reached the lower hall at one end of which I saw a faint luminous rectangle marking the ruined Paine Street doorway. Heading the other way, I found the back door also open, and darted out and down five stone steps to the grass-grown cobblestones of the courtyard.

The moonbeams did not reach down here, but I could just see my way about without using the flashlight. Some of the windows on the Gilman House side were faintly glowing, and I thought I heard confused sounds within. Walking softly over to the Washington Street side I perceived several open doorways, and chose the nearest as my route out. The hallway inside was black, and when I reached the opposite end I saw that the street door was wedged immovably shut. Resolved to try another building, I groped my way back toward the courtyard, but stopped short when close to the doorway.

For out of an opened door in the Gilman House a large crowd of doubtful shapes was pouring—lanterns bobbing in the darkness, and horrible croaking voices exchanging low cries in what was certainly not English. The figures moved uncertainly, and I realised to my relief that they did not know where I had gone; but for all that they sent a shiver of horror through my frame. Their features were indistinguishable, but their crouching, shambling gait was abominably repellent. Worst of all, I perceived that one figure was strangely robed, and unmistakably surmounted by a tall tiara of a design altogether too familiar. As the figures spread throughout the courtyard, I felt my fears increase. Suppose I could find no egress from this building on the street side? The fishy odour was detestable, and I wondered I could stand it without fainting. Again groping toward the street, I opened a door off the hall and came upon an empty room with closely shuttered but sashless windows. Fumbling in the rays of my flashlight, I found I could open the shutters; and in another moment had climbed outside and was carefully closing the aperture in its original manner.

I was now in Washington Street, and for the moment saw no living thing nor any light save that of the moon. From several directions in the distance, however, I could hear the sound of hoarse voices, of footsteps, and of a curious kind of pattering which did not sound quite like footsteps. Plainly I had no time to lose. The points of the compass were clear to me, and I was glad that all the street lights were turned off, as is often the custom on strongly moonlit nights in unprosperous rural regions. Some of the sounds came from the south, yet I retained my design of escaping in that direction. There would, I knew, be plenty of deserted doorways to shelter me in case I met any person or group who looked like pursuers.

I walked rapidly, softly, and close to the ruined houses. While hatless and dishevelled after my arduous climb, I did not look especially noticeable; and I stood a good chance of passing unheeded if forced to encounter any casual wayfarer. At Bates Street I drew into a yawning vestibule while two shambling figures crossed in front of me, but was soon on my way again and approaching the open space where Eliot Street obliquely crosses Washington at the intersection of South. Though I had never seen this space, it had looked dangerous to me on the grocery youth's map, since the moonlight would have free play there. There was no use trying to evade it, for any alternative course would involve detours of possibly disastrous visibility and delaying effect. The only thing to do was to cross it boldly and openly, imitating the typical shamble of Innsmouth folk as best I could, and trusting that no one—or at least no pursuer of mine—would be there.

Just how fully the pursuit was organised—and indeed, just what its purpose might be—I could form no idea. There seemed to be unusual activity in the town, but I judged that the news of my escape from the Gilman had not yet spread. I would, of course, soon have to shift from Washington to some other southward street, for that party from the hotel would doubtless be after me. I must have left dust prints in that last old building, revealing how I had gained the street.

The open space was, as I had expected, strongly moonlit; and I saw the remains of a park-like, iron-railed green in its centre. Fortunately no one was about, though a curious sort of buzz or roar seemed to be increasing in the direction of Town Square. South Street was very wide, leading directly down a slight declivity to the waterfront and commanding a long view out at sea; and I hoped that no one would be glancing up it from afar as I crossed in the bright moonlight.

My progress was unimpeded, and no fresh sound arose to hint that I had been spied. Glancing about me, I involuntarily let my pace slacken for a second to take in the sight of the sea, gorgeous in the burning moonlight at the street's end. Far out beyond the breakwater was the dim, dark line of Devil Reef, and as I glimpsed it I could not help thinking of all the hideous legends I had heard in the last thirty-four hours—legends which portrayed this ragged rock as a veritable gateway to realms of unfathomed horror and inconceivable abnormality.

Then, without warning, I saw the intermittent flashes of light on the distant reef. They were definite and unmistakable, and awaked in my mind a blind horror beyond all rational proportion. My muscles tightened for panic flight, held in only by a certain unconscious caution and half-hypnotic fascination. To make matters worse, there now flashed forth from the lofty cupola of the Gilman House, which loomed up to the northeast behind me, a series of analogous though differently spaced gleams which could be nothing less than an answering signal.

Controlling my muscles, and realising afresh how plainly visible I was, I resumed my brisker and feignedly shambling pace, though keeping my eyes on that hellish and ominous view of the reef as long as the opening of South Street gave me a seaward view. What the whole proceeding meant, I could not imagine, unless it involved some strange rite connected with Devil Reef, or unless some party had landed from a ship on that sinister rock. I now bent to the left around the ruinous green, still gazing toward the ocean as it blazed in the spectral summer moonlight, and watching the cryptical flashing of those nameless, unexplainable beacons.

It was then that the most horrible impression of all was borne in upon me—the impression which destroyed my last vestige of self-control and sent me running frantically southward past the yawning black doorways and fishily staring windows of that deserted nightmare street. For at a closer glance I saw that the moonlit waters between the reef and the shore were far from empty. They were alive with a teeming horde of shapes swimming inward toward the town; and even at my vast distance and in my single moment of perception I could tell that the bobbing heads and flailing arms were alien and aberrant in a way scarcely to be expressed or consciously formulated.

My frantic running ceased before I had covered a block, for at my left I began to hear something like the hue and cry of organised pursuit. There were footsteps and guttural sounds, and a rattling motor wheezed south along Federal Street. In a second all my plans were utterly changed—for if the southward highway were blocked ahead of me, I must clearly find another egress from Innsmouth. I paused and drew into a gaping doorway, reflecting how lucky I was to have left the moonlit open space before these pursuers came down the parallel street.

A second reflection was less comforting. Since the pursuit was down another street, it was plain that the party was not following me directly. It had not seen me, but was simply obeying a general plan of cutting off my escape. This, however, implied that all roads leading out of Innsmouth were similarly patrolled, for the people could not have known what route I intended to take. If this were so, I would have to make my retreat across country away from any road; but how could I do that in view of the marshy and creek-riddled nature of all the surrounding region? For a moment my brain reeled—both from sheer hopelessness and from a rapid increase in the omnipresent fishy odour.

Then I thought of the abandoned railway to Rowley, whose solid line of ballasted, weed-grown earth still stretched off to the northwest from the crumbling station on the edge of the river gorge. There was just a chance that the townsfolk would not think of that, since its briar-choked desertion made it half-impassable, and the unlikeliest of all avenues for a fugitive to choose. I had seen it clearly from my hotel window, and knew about how it lay. Most of its earlier length was uncomfortably visible from the Rowley road, and from high places in the town itself; but one could perhaps crawl inconspicuously through the undergrowth. At any rate, it would form my only chance of deliverance, and there was nothing to do but try it.

Drawing inside the hall of my deserted shelter, I once more consulted the grocery boy's map with the aid of the flashlight. The immediate problem was how to reach the ancient railway, and I now saw that the safest course was ahead to Babson Street, then west to Lafayette—there edging around but not crossing an open space homologous to the one I had traversed—and subsequently back northward and westward in a zigzagging line through Lafayette, Bates, Adams, and Bank Streets—the latter skirting the river gorge—to the abandoned and dilapidated station I had seen from my window. My reason for going ahead to Babson was that I wished neither to recross the earlier open space nor to begin my westward course along a cross street as broad as South.

Starting once more, I crossed the street to the right-hand side in order to edge around into Babson as inconspicuously as possible. Noises still continued in Federal Street, and as I glanced behind me I thought I saw a gleam of light near the building through which I had escaped. Anxious to leave Washington Street, I broke into a quiet dog-trot, trusting to luck not to encounter any observing eye. Next the corner of Babson Street I saw to my alarm that one of the houses was still inhabited, as attested by curtains at the window; but there were no lights within, and I passed it without disaster.

In Babson Street, which crossed Federal and might thus reveal me to the searchers, I clung as closely as possible to the sagging, uneven buildings; twice pausing in a doorway as the noises behind me momentarily increased. The open space ahead shone wide and desolate under the moon, but my route would not force me to cross it. During my second pause I began to detect a fresh distribution of vague sounds, and upon looking cautiously out from cover beheld a motor car darting across the open space, bound outward along Eliot Street, which there intersects both Babson and Lafayette.

As I watched—choked by a sudden rise in the fishy odour after a short abatement—I saw a band of uncouth, crouching shapes loping and shambling in the same direction, and knew that this must be the party guarding the Ipswich road, since that highway forms an extension of Eliot Street. Two of the figures I glimpsed were in voluminous robes, and one wore a peaked diadem which glistened whitely in the moonlight. The gait of this figure was so odd that it sent a chill through me—for it seemed to me the creature was almost hopping.

When the last of the band was out of sight I resumed my progress, darting around the corner into Lafayette Street and crossing Eliot very hurriedly, lest stragglers of the party be still advancing along that thoroughfare. I did hear some croaking and clattering sounds far off toward Town Square, but accomplished the passage without disaster. My greatest dread was in recrossing broad and moonlit South Street—with its seaward view—and I had to nerve myself for the ordeal. Someone might easily be looking, and possible Eliot Street stragglers could not fail to glimpse me from either of two points. At the last moment I decided I had better slacken my trot and make the crossing as before in the shambling gait of an average Innsmouth native.

When the view of the water again opened out—this time on my right—I was half-determined not to look at it at all. I could not, however, resist; but I cast a sidelong glance as I carefully and imitatively shambled toward the protecting shadows ahead. There was no ship visible, as I had half-expected there would be. Instead, the first thing which caught my eye was a small rowboat pulling in toward the abandoned wharves and laden with some bulky, tarpaulin-covered object. Its rowers, though distantly and indistinctly seen, were of an especially repellent aspect. Several swimmers were still discernible, while on the far black reef I could see a faint, steady glow unlike the winking beacon visible before, and of a curious colour which I could not precisely identify. Above the slant roofs ahead and to the right there loomed the tall cupola of the Gilman House, but it was completely dark. The fishy odour, dispelled for a moment by some merciful breeze, now closed in again with maddening intensity.

I had not quite crossed the street when I heard a muttering band advancing along Washington from the north. As they reached the broad open space where I had had my first disquieting glimpse of the moonlit water I could see them plainly only a block away—and was horrified by the bestial abnormality of their faces and the dog-like subhumanness of their crouching gait. One man moved in a positively simian way, with long arms frequently touching the ground, while another figure—robed and tiaraed— seemed to progress in an almost hopping fashion. I judged this party to be the one I had seen in the Gilman's courtyard—the one, therefore, most closely on my trail. As some of the figures turned to look in my direction I was transfixed with fright, yet managed to preserve the casual, shambling gait I had assumed. To this day I do not know whether they saw me or not. If they did, my stratagem must have deceived them, for they passed on across the moonlit space without varying their course—meanwhile croaking and jabbering in some hateful guttural patois I could not identify.

Once more in shadow, I resumed my former dog-trot past the leaning and decrepit houses that stared blankly into the night. Having crossed to the western sidewalk I rounded the nearest corner into Bates Street, where I kept close to the buildings on the southern side. I passed two houses shew- ing signs of habitation, one of which had faint lights in upper rooms, yet met with no obstacle. As I turned into Adams Street I felt measurably safer, but received a shock when a man reeled out of a black doorway directly in front of me. He proved, however, too hopelessly drunk to be a menace, so that I reached the dismal ruins of the Bank Street warehouses in safety.

No one was stirring in that dead street beside the river gorge, and the roar of the waterfalls quite drowned my footsteps. It was a long dog-trot to the ruined station, and the great brick warehouse walls around me seemed somehow more terrifying than the fronts of private houses. At last I saw the ancient arcaded station—or what was left of it—and made directly for the tracks that started from its farther end.

The rails were rusty but mainly intact, and not more than half the ties had rotted away. Walking or running on such a surface was very difficult, but I did my best, and on the whole made very fair time. For some distance the line kept on along the gorge's brink, but at length I reached the long covered bridge where it crossed the chasm at a dizzy height. The condition of this bridge would determine my next step. If humanly possible, I would use it; if not, I would have to risk more street wandering and take the near- est intact highway bridge.

The vast, barn-like length of the old bridge gleamed spectrally in the moonlight, and I saw that the ties were safe for at least a few feet within.

Entering, I began to use my flashlight, and was almost knocked down by the cloud of bats that flapped past me. About halfway across there was a perilous gap in the ties which I feared for a moment would halt me; but in the end I risked a desperate jump which fortunately succeeded.

I was glad to see the moonlight again when I emerged from that macabre tunnel. The old tracks crossed River Street at grade, and at once veered off into a region increasingly rural and with less and less of Innsmouth's abhorrent fishy odour. Here the dense growth of weeds and briars hindered me and cruelly tore my clothes, but I was none the less glad that they were there to give me concealment in case of peril. I knew that much of my route must be visible from the Rowley road.

The marshy region began very shortly, with the single track on a low, grassy embankment where the weedy growth was somewhat thinner. Then came a sort of island of higher ground, where the line passed through a shallow open cut choked with bushes and brambles. I was very glad of this partial shelter, since at this point the Rowley road was uncomfortably near according to my window view. At the end of the cut it would cross the track and swerve off to a safer distance, but meanwhile I must be exceedingly careful. I was by this time thankfully certain that the railway itself was not patrolled.

Just before entering the cut I glanced behind me, but saw no pursuer. The ancient spires and roofs of decaying Innsmouth gleamed lovely and ethereal in the magic yellow moonlight, and I thought of how they must have looked in the old days before the shadow fell. Then, as my gaze circled inland from the town, something less tranquil arrested my notice and held me immobile for a second.

What I saw—or fancied I saw—was a disturbing suggestion of undulant motion far to the south, a suggestion which made me conclude that a very large horde must be pouring out of the city along the level Ipswich road. The distance was great, and I could distinguish nothing in detail; but I did not at all like the look of that moving column. It undulated too much, and glistened too brightly in the rays of the now westering moon. There was a suggestion of sound, too, though the wind was blowing the other way— a suggestion of bestial scraping and bellowing even worse than the muttering of the parties I had lately overheard.

All sorts of unpleasant conjectures crossed my mind. I thought of those very extreme Innsmouth types said to be hidden in crumbling, centuried warrens near the waterfront. I thought, too, of those nameless swimmers I had seen. Counting the parties so far glimpsed, as well as those presumably covering other roads, the number of my pursuers must be strangely large for a town as depopulated as Innsmouth.

Whence could come the dense personnel of such a column as I now beheld? Did those ancient, unplumbed warrens teem with a twisted, uncatalogued, and unsuspected life? Or had some unseen ship indeed landed a legion of unknown outsiders on that hellish reef? Who were they? Why were they here? And if such a column of them was scouring the Ipswich road, would the patrols on the other roads be likewise augmented?

I had entered the brush-grown cut and was struggling along at a very slow pace when that damnable fishy odour again waxed dominant. Had the wind suddenly changed eastward, so that it blew in from the sea and over the town? It must have, I concluded, since I now began to hear shocking guttural murmurs from that hitherto silent direction. There was another sound, too—a kind of wholesale, colossal flopping or pattering which somehow called up images of the most detestable sort. It made me think illogically of that unpleasantly undulating column on the far-off Ipswich road.

Then both stench and sounds grew stronger, so that I paused shivering and grateful for the cut's protection. It was here, I recalled, that the Rowley road drew so close to the old railway before crossing westward and diverging. Something was coming along that road, and I must lie low till its passage and vanishment in the distance. Thank heaven these creatures employed no dogs for tracking—though perhaps that would have been impossible amidst the omnipresent regional odour. Crouched in the bushes of that sandy cleft I felt reasonably safe, even though I knew the searchers would have to cross the track in front of me not much more than a hundred yards away. I would be able to see them, but they could not, except by a malign miracle, see me.

All at once I began dreading to look at them as they passed. I saw the close moonlit space where they would surge by, and had curious thoughts about the irredeemable pollution of that space. They would perhaps be the worst of all Innsmouth types—something one would not care to remember.

The stench waxed overpowering, and the noises swelled to a bestial babel of croaking, baying, and barking without the least suggestion of human speech. Were these indeed the voices of my pursuers? Did they have dogs after all? So far I had seen none of the lower animals in Innsmouth. That flopping or pattering was monstrous—I could not look upon the degenerate creatures responsible for it. I would keep my eyes shut till the sound receded toward the west. The horde was very close now—the air foul with their hoarse snarlings, and the ground almost shaking with their alien-rhythmed footfalls. My breath nearly ceased to come, and I put every ounce of willpower into the task of holding my eyelids down.

I am not even willing to say whether what followed was a hideous actuality or only a nightmare hallucination. The later action of the government, after my frantic appeals, would tend to confirm it as a monstrous truth; but could not an hallucination have been repeated under the quasihypnotic spell of that ancient, haunted, and shadowed town? Such places have strange properties, and the legacy of insane legend might well have acted on more than one human imagination amidst those dead, stench-cursed streets and huddles of rotting roofs and crumbling steeples. Is it not possible that the germ of an actual contagious madness lurks in the depths of that shadow over Innsmouth? Who can be sure of reality after hearing things like the tale of old Zadok Allen? The government men never found poor Zadok, and have no conjectures to make as to what became of him. Where does madness leave off and reality begin? Is it possible that even my latest fear is sheer delusion?

But I must try to tell what I thought I saw that night under the mocking yellow moon—saw surging and hopping down the Rowley road in plain sight in front of me as I crouched among the wild brambles of that desolate railway cut. Of course my resolution to keep my eyes shut had failed. It was foredoomed to failure—for who could crouch blindly while a legion of croaking, baying entities of unknown source flopped noisomely past, scarcely more than a hundred yards away?

I thought I was prepared for the worst, and I really ought to have been prepared considering what I had seen before. My other pursuers had been accursedly abnormal—so should I not have been ready to face a strengthening of the abnormal element; to look upon forms in which there was no mixture of the normal at all? I did not open my eyes until the raucous clamour came loudly from a point obviously straight ahead. Then I knew that a long section of them must be plainly in sight where the sides of the cut flattened out and the road crossed the track—and I could no longer keep myself from sampling whatever horror that leering yellow moon might have to show.

It was the end, for whatever remains to me of life on the surface of this earth, of every vestige of mental peace and confidence in the integrity of nature and of the human mind. Nothing that I could have imagined—nothing, even, that I could have gathered had I credited old Zadok's crazy tale in the most literal way—would be in any way comparable to the demoniac, blasphemous reality that I saw—or believe I saw. I have tried to hint what it was in order to postpone the horror of writing it down baldly. Can it be possible that this planet has actually spawned such things; that human eyes have truly seen, as objective flesh, what man has hitherto known only in febrile phantasy and tenuous legend?

And yet I saw them in a limitless stream—flopping, hopping, croaking, bleating—surging inhumanly through the spectral moonlight in a grotesque, malignant saraband of fantastic nightmare. Some of them had tall tiaras of that nameless whitish-gold metal ... and some were strangely robed ... and one, who led the way, was clad in a ghoulishly humped black coat and striped trousers, and had a man's felt hat perched on the shapeless thing that answered for a head.

I think their predominant colour was a greyish-green, though they had white bellies. They were mostly shiny and slippery, but the ridges of their backs were scaly. Their forms vaguely suggested the anthropoid, while their heads were the heads of fish, with prodigious bulging eyes that never closed. At the sides of their necks were palpitating gills, and their long paws were webbed. They hopped irregularly, sometimes on two legs and sometimes on four. I was somehow glad that they had no more than four limbs. Their croaking, baying voices, clearly used for articulate speech, held all the dark shades of expression which their staring faces lacked.

But for all their monstrousness they were not unfamiliar to me. I knew too well what they must be—for was not the memory of the evil tiara at Newburyport still fresh? They were the blasphemous fish-frogs of the nameless design—living and horrible—and as I saw them I knew also of what that humped, tiaraed priest in the black church basement had fearsomely reminded me. Their number was past guessing. It seemed to me that there were limitless swarms of them—and certainly my momentary glimpse could have shewn only the least fraction. In another instant everything was blotted out by a merciful fit of fainting, the first I had ever had.

V

It was gentle daylight rain that awaked me from my stupor in the brush-grown railway cut, and when I staggered out to the roadway ahead I saw no trace of any prints in the fresh mud. The fishy odour, too, was gone. Innsmouth's ruined roofs and toppling steeples loomed up greyly toward the southeast, but not a living creature did I spy in all the desolate salt marshes around. My watch was still going, and told me that the hour was past noon.

The reality of what I had been through was highly uncertain in my mind, but I felt that something hideous lay in the background. I must get away from evil-shadowed Innsmouth—and accordingly I began to test my cramped, wearied powers of locomotion. Despite weakness, hunger, horror, and bewilderment I found myself after a time able to walk, so started slow-ly along the muddy road to Rowley. Before evening I was in the village, get-ting a meal and providing myself with presentable clothes. I caught the night train to Arkham, and the next day talked long and earnestly with government officials there, a process I later repeated in Boston. With the main result of these colloquies the public is now familiar—and I wish, for normality's sake, there were nothing more to tell. Perhaps it is madness that is overtaking me—yet perhaps a greater horror—or a greater marvel—is reaching out.

As may well be imagined, I gave up most of the foreplanned features of the rest of my tour—the scenic, architectural, and antiquarian diversions on which I had counted so heavily. Nor did I dare look for that piece of strange jewellery said to be in the Miskatonic University Museum. I did, however, improve my stay in Arkham by collecting some genealogical notes I had long wished to possess; very rough and hasty data, it is true, but capable of good use later on when I might have time to collate and codify them. The curator of the historical society there—Mr. E. Lapham Peabody—was very courteous about assisting me, and expressed unusual interest when I told him I was a grandson of Eliza Orne of Arkham, who was born in 1867 and had married James Williamson of Ohio at the age of seventeen.

It seemed that a maternal uncle of mine had been there many years before on a quest much like my own, and that my grandmother's family was a topic of some local curiosity. There had, Mr. Peabody said, been considerable discussion about the marriage of her father, Benjamin Orne, just after the Civil War, since the ancestry of the bride was peculiarly puzzling. That bride was understood to have been an orphaned Marsh of New Hampshire—a cousin of the Essex County Marshes—but her education had been in France and she knew very little of her family. A guardian had deposited funds in a Boston bank to maintain her and her French governess; but that guardian's name was unfamiliar to Arkham people, and in time he dropped out of sight, so that the governess assumed his role by court appointment. The Frenchwoman—now long dead—was very taciturn, and there were those who said she could have told more than she did.

But the most baffling thing was the inability of anyone to place the recorded parents of the young woman—Enoch and Lydia (Meserve) Marsh—among the known families of New Hampshire. Possibly, many suggested, she was the natural daughter of some Marsh of prominence—she certainly had the true Marsh eyes. Most of the puzzling was done after her early death, which took place at the birth of my grandmother—her only child. Having formed some disagreeable impressions connected with the name of Marsh, I did not welcome the news that it belonged on my own ancestral tree; nor was I pleased by Mr. Peabody's suggestion that I had the true Marsh eyes myself. However, I was grateful for data which I knew would prove valuable, and took copious notes and lists of book references regarding the well documented Orne family.

I went directly home to Toledo from Boston, and later spent a month at Maumee recuperating from my ordeal. In September I entered Oberlin for my final year, and from then till the next June was busy with studies and other wholesome activities—reminded of the bygone terror only by occasional official visits from government men in connexion with the campaign which my pleas and evidence had started. Around the middle of July—just a year after the Innsmouth experience—I spent a week with my late mother's family in Cleveland, checking some of my new genealogical data with the various notes, traditions, and bits of heirloom material in existence there, and seeing what kind of connected chart I could construct.

I did not exactly relish this task, for the atmosphere of the Williamson home had always depressed me. There was a strain of morbidity there, and my mother had never encouraged my visiting her parents as a child, although she always welcomed her father when he came to Toledo. My Arkham-born grandmother had seemed strange and almost terrifying to me, and I do not think I grieved when she disappeared. I was eight years old then, and it was said that she had wandered off in grief after the suicide of my Uncle Douglas, her eldest son. He had shot himself after a trip to New England—the same trip, no doubt, which had caused him to be recalled at the Arkham Historical Society.

This uncle had resembled her, and I had never liked him either. Something about the staring, unwinking expression of both of them had given me a vague, unaccountable uneasiness. My mother and Uncle Walter had not looked like that. They were like their father, though poor little cousin Lawrence—Walter's son—had been an almost perfect duplicate of his grandmother before his condition took him to the permanent seclusion of a sanitarium at Canton. I had not seen him in four years, but my uncle once implied that his state, both mental and physical, was very bad. This worry had probably been a major cause of his mother's death two years before.

My grandfather and his widowed son Walter now comprised the Cleveland household, but the memory of older times hung thickly over it. I still disliked the place, and tried to get my researches done as quickly as possible. Williamson records and traditions were supplied in abundance by my grandfather, though for Orne material I had to depend on my Uncle Walter, who put at my disposal the contents of all his files, including notes, letters, cuttings, heirlooms, photographs, and miniatures.

It was in going over the letters and pictures on the Orne side that I began to acquire a kind of terror of my own ancestry. As I have said, my grandmother and Uncle Douglas had always disturbed me. Now, years after their passing, I gazed at their pictured faces with a measurably brightened feeling of repulsion and alienation. I could not at first understand the change, but gradually a horrible sort of comparison began to obtrude itself on my unconscious mind despite the steady refusal of my consciousness to admit even the least suspicion of it. It was clear that the typical expression of these faces now suggested something it had not suggested before—something which would bring stark panic if too openly thought of.

The worst shock came when my uncle shewed me the Orne jewellery in a downtown safe-deposit vault. Some of the items were delicate and inspiring enough, but there was one box of strange old pieces descended from my mysterious great-grandmother which my uncle was almost reluctant to produce. They were, he said, of very grotesque and almost repulsive design, and had never to his knowledge been publicly worn, though my grandmother used to enjoy looking at them. Vague legends of bad luck clustered around them, and my great-grandmother's French governess had said they ought not to be worn in New England, though it would be quite safe to wear them in Europe.

As my uncle began slowly and grudgingly to unwrap the things he urged me not to be shocked by the strangeness and frequent hideousness of the designs. Artists and archaeologists who had seen them pronounced their workmanship superlatively and exotically exquisite, though no one seemed able to define their exact material or assign them to any specific art tradition. There were two armlets, a tiara, and a kind of pectoral, the latter having in high relief certain figures of almost unbearable extravagance.

During this description I had kept a tight rein on my emotions, but my face must have betrayed my mounting fears. My uncle looked concerned, and paused in his unwrapping to study my countenance. I motioned to him to continue, which he did with renewed signs of reluctance. He seemed to expect some demonstration when the first piece—the tiara—became visible, but I doubt if he expected quite what actually happened. I did not expect it, either, for I thought I was thoroughly forewarned regarding what the jewellery would turn out to be. What I did was to faint silently away, just as I had done in that brier-choked railway cut a year before.

From that day on my life has been a nightmare of brooding and apprehension, nor do I know how much is hideous truth and how much madness. My great-grandmother had been a Marsh of unknown source whose husband lived in Arkham—and did not old Zadok say that the daughter of Obed Marsh by a monstrous mother was married to an Arkham man through a trick? What was it the ancient toper had muttered about the likeness of my eyes to Captain Obed's? In Arkham, too, the curator had told me I had the true Marsh eyes. Was Obed Marsh my own great-great-grandfather? Who—or what—then, was my great-great-grandmother? But perhaps this was all madness. Those whitish-gold ornaments might easily have been bought from some Innsmouth sailor by the father of my great-grandmother, whoever he was. And that look in the staring-eyed faces of my grandmother and self-slain uncle might be sheer fancy on my part—sheer fancy, bolstered up by the Innsmouth shadow which had so darkly coloured my imagination. But why had my uncle killed himself after an ancestral quest in New England?

For more than two years I fought off these reflections with partial success. My father secured me a place in an insurance office, and I buried myself in routine as deeply as possible. In the winter of 1930-31, however, the dreams began. They were very sparse and insidious at first, but increased in frequency and vividness as the weeks went by. Great watery spaces opened out before me, and I seemed to wander through titanic sunken porticos and labyrinths of weedy cyclopean walls with grotesque fishes as my companions. Then the other shapes began to appear, filling me with nameless horror the moment I awoke. But during the dreams they did not horrify me at all—I was one with them, wearing their unhuman trappings, treading their aqueous ways, and praying monstrously at their evil sea-bottom temples.

There was much more than I could remember, but even what I did remember each morning would be enough to stamp me as a madman or a genius if ever I dared write it down. Some frightful influence, I felt, was seeking gradually to drag me out of the sane world of wholesome life into unnamable abysses of blackness and alienage, and the process told heavily on me. My health and appearance grew steadily worse, till finally I was forced to give up my position and adopt the static, scheduled life of an invalid. Some odd nervous affliction had me in its grip, and I found myself at times almost unable to shut my eyes.

It was then that I began to study the mirror with mounting alarm. The slow ravages of disease are not pleasant to watch, but in my case there was something subtler and more puzzling in the background. My father seemed to notice it, too, for he began looking at me curiously and almost affrightedly. What was taking place in me? Could it be that I was coming to resemble my grandmother and Uncle Douglas?

One night I had a frightful dream in which I met my grandmother under the sea. She lived in a phosphorescent palace of many terraces, with gardens of strange leprous corals and grotesque brachiate efflorescences, and welcomed me with a warmth that may have been sardonic. She had changed—as those who take to the water change—and told me she had never died. Instead, she had gone to a spot her dead son had learned about and had leaped to a realm whose wonders—destined for him as well—he had spurned with a smoking pistol. This was to be my realm, too—I could not escape it. I would never die, but would live with those who had lived since before man ever walked the earth.

I met also that which had been her grandmother. For eighty thousand years Pht'thya-l'yi had lived in Y'ha-nthlei, and thither she had gone back after Obed Marsh was dead. Y'ha-nthlei was not destroyed when the upper-earth men shot death into the sea. It was hurt, but not destroyed. The Deep

Ones could never be destroyed, even though the palaeogean magic of the forgotten Old Ones might sometimes check them. For the present they would rest; but some day, if they remembered, they would rise again for the tribute Great Cthulhu craved. It would be a city greater than Innsmouth next time. They had planned to spread, and had brought up that which would help them, but now they must wait once more. For bringing the upper-earth men's death I must do a penance, but that would not be heavy. This was the dream in which I saw a *shoggoth* for the first time, and the sight set me awake in a frenzy of screaming. That morning the mirror definitely told me I had acquired *the Innsmouth look*.

So far I have not shot myself as my Uncle Douglas did. I bought an automatic and almost took the step, but certain dreams deterred me. The tense extremes of horror are lessening, and I feel queerly drawn toward the unknown sea-deeps instead of fearing them. I hear and do strange things in sleep, and awake with a kind of exaltation instead of terror. I do not believe I need to wait for the full change as most have waited. If I did, my father would probably shut me up in a sanitarium as my poor little cousin is shut up. Stupendous and unheard-of splendours await me below, and I shall seek them soon. *Iä R'lyeh! Cthulhu fhtagn! Iä! Iä!* No, I shall not shoot myself—I cannot be made to shoot myself!

I shall plan my cousin's escape from that Canton madhouse, and together we shall go to marvel-shadowed Innsmouth. We shall swim out to that brooding reef in the sea and dive down through black abysses to cyclopean and many-columned Y'ha-nthlei, and in that lair of the Deep Ones we shall dwell amidst wonder and glory for ever.

About "The Deep Ones"

The late, great James Wade was a deliberate writer of period pieces. Keenly conscious of the "dated" character of Lovecraft's stories, he seems to have realized that the evident situation of a story in a definite sociohistorical context does not necessarily act as a lead weight, sinking the tale in the sea of the past, but rather as an integration point, incarnating the story's premise in an authentic life-world, if not the reader's own, then someone else's. In the latter case the story is not a mirror for ourselves (as Stephen King's major works were in the 1970's), but something more interesting: As Dilthey said, the tale becomes a monument of the culture of the past (in Wade's case, the recent past) and a window into it. Wade was in the habit of sketching scenes of the intrusion of the Mythos into the world of the 1960's and early 1970's, both in the stories included in this volume, as well as in "Planetfall on Yuggoth" (see *The Hastur Cycle*), which makes the space race catch up with Lovecraft, even as he anticipated at the end of "The Whisperer in Darkness", and in "The Silence of Erika Zann" (see Edward Paul Berglund, ed., *The Disciples of Cthulhu*).

"The Deep Ones" is a kind of (forgive me) Lovecraftian version of *Flipper*, a capitalizing on the 1960's interest in the remarkable intelligence of porpoises. Wade extrapolated this phenomenon in the same direction as the 1986 movie *Star Trek IV: The Voyage Home*, where we learn that intelligent life on Earth is to be found in the depths and that it has links, not vertically to us, as evolutionary prehuman ancestors, but laterally, to utterly unhuman species parallel or superior to us.

The cult leader is clearly modeled upon 1960's icon Timothy Leary, a veteran activist in "the politics of experience" (R. D. Laing). Like Leary and like the mad Arab, Dr. Alonzo Waite, precisely by being insane, is better calibrated to understand an insane Lovecraftian universe.

"The Deep Ones" appeared in the original edition of August Derleth's seminal anthology *Tales of the Cthulhu Mythos* (1969) but was inexplicably dropped in the 1990 edition. It must remain available. Here it is.

The Deep Ones

by James Wade

"Diviner than the dolphin is nothing yet created; for indeed they were afore-
time men, and lived in cities along with mortals."
—Oppian, *Halieutica* (A.D. 200)

I had never met Dr. Frederick Wilhelm before I went to work at his
Institute for Zoological Studies, located in a remote cove on the
California coast some miles north of San Simeon and Piedras Blancas,
not far from the Big Sur area; but of course I had heard of his studies. The
Sunday supplements picked Wilhelm up years ago, which was only natural:
What more potentially sensational subject could a journalist hope for than
the idea that man shared the Earth with another, older, and perhaps more
intelligent species; a species overlooked or ignored by modern science, but
with which communication might someday be established?

It wasn't a worn-out gambit like flying saucer people, or spiritualism,
or trolls hidden under the hills, of course. Wilhelm's subject was the dolphin, that ocean mammal glimpsed centuries ago by superstitious sailors
and transmogrified into myths of mermaids, sirens of the fabulous sea-
dwelling secret races of legend. Now it appeared the superstitions might not
be far wrong.

Preliminary tests had showed long ago that our ocean-going distant
cousins harbored a high degree of pure intelligence and potential for communication, unsuspected because of their watery habitat and their lack of
hands or any other prehensile apparatus for producing artifacts. Wilhelm's
researches had not been the first, but his speculations were certainly the
most daring, and he had parlayed his preoccupation into a career, attracting
both government and private foundation funds to set up the institute
toward which I found myself jogging in a rented jeep over rutted, sandy

roads beside the sinuous green Pacific one starkly sunlit afternoon in April a year ago.

Although I knew of Frederick Wilhelm and his institute, I wasn't sure just how or what he knew of me. In a sense, I could easily see how my field, extrasensory perception and telepathy, might tie in with his work; but his initial letters and wires to me had never spelled out in any detail what he expected of our collaboration. His messages, indeed, had seemed at once euphoric and evasive, confining themselves mostly to grandiloquent descriptions of his basic purposes and facilities, plus details on the financial aspects of our association.

I will admit that the amount of money Dr. Wilhelm offered was a strong factor in my accepting a job the exact nature of which remained unclear. As research coordinator of a small Eastern foundation devoted to parapsychological studies overlooked by the Rhine group at Duke, I had had my fill of skimped budgets and starvation wages. Wilhelm's offer had come as an opportunity golden in more ways than one, so I had lost little time in packing my bags for the trip to sunny California.

Actually, the location of Wilhelm's experiments gave me more pause than any of the other doubtful aspects of his offer. I confess that I have always had an antipathy to California, despite the little time I recall having spent there. Perhaps I had read too much in the works of mordant satirists like Waugh and Nathaniel West, but to me there had always seemed something decadent and even sinister about this self-eulogizing Pacific paradise.

The impression had not been allayed by my arrival via plane in gritty, galvanic Los Angeles, or by a stroll through that tiny downtown park where predatory homosexuals, drug derelicts, and demented fanatics of all kinds congregate under the bloated, twisted palms, like so many patients in the garden of Dr. Caligari's madhouse. To some, Gothic battlements of New England backwaters represent the apex of spiritual horror and decay; for me, the neon-lit, screaming depravity of Los Angeles filled the bill. As the comedian Fred Allen once remarked, California is a great place if you're an orange.

These thoughts and others tangled in my mind as I guided my jeep over the rough beachside path which, I had been assured by the jovial car rental agent in San Simeon, would take me unfailingly to the Institute for Zoological Studies. ("Ain't no place else the road goes, after you turn off left at the first orange juice stand—you know, the kind where the stand is built to look just like a great big orange. Jest keep on goin', and don't stop for hippies or high water till the road ends!")

As I glanced rather nervously around, I could see on my left a sort of encampment of bleached white tents and dark, darting figures down by the wavering lace of surf at water's edge. Were these the hippies my guide had referred to, those sardonic jesters on the periphery of our society, razzing and reviling all the standards and values of three thousand civilized years? Or had he been spoofing me—were these only a gaggle of middle-class youngsters out for an afternoon of beachside sun, sand, and sex as a respite from the abrasive grind of our precariously affluent society?

Even as these trite and puerile thoughts chased through my head, suddenly the vestigial road took a sharp turn over a rise and I found myself startlingly close up (a zoom lens effect) to what could only be the famous Institute for Zoological Studies.

II.

"What, actually, do you know about dolphins—or porpoises, as they are sometimes called?" queried Dr. Frederick Wilhelm, his eyes invisible behind thick lenses that caught the light from filtered globes under gold-tinted shades in his plush office. We had just settled down over a late afternoon cocktail, expertly crafted by Wilhelm himself, after my first rapid tour of the Institute, conducted by its director immediately after meeting my arriving jeep.

Wilhelm had been cordial and almost courtly, though it seemed a bit odd for him to start me off on a junket around his establishment before I had had a chance even to drop my luggage at my quarters and freshen up a bit after the long drive. I put it down to the vanity of a self-made scientific pioneer jockeying a cherished hobby horse down the home stretch in the big race.

The impression I'd received on the whirlwind tour was superficial and a bit bewildering: The long, low, white-plastered cement buildings straggling along the shoreline seemed crammed with more sound, lighting, recording, photographic, and less identifiable computerized equipment than would be needed to study the entire passenger list of Noah's ark, let alone one minor subspecies of marine mammal.

About Wilhelm himself there was nothing odd, though: A big, rumpled, graying penguin of a man, he moved and spoke with the disarming enthusiasm of a schoolboy just discovering that there is such a thing as science. As he hurried me from lab to lab at a breathless pace, he explained, "We'll see the dolphin pools tomorrow morning. Josephine—my research assistant, Josephine, is working there now; she'll join us later for drinks and dinner."

As I had learned from correspondence with Dr. Wilhelm, his senior staff (now totaling three, himself included, with my arrival) had quarters at the Institute, while the dozen or so technicians and laboratory assistants employed here made the trip to and from San Simeon billets in a Volkswagen microbus each day.

Now as I sat with Wilhelm in the dim, richly decorated office over an acridly enticing martini, I heard the bus pull away, and realized that I was alone in the sprawling complex of buildings with its director and the unsurmised Josephine.

"What do you actually know about dolphins?" Wilhelm was saying.

"About what any layman knows," I found myself replying frankly. "I know that research started back in the 1950's, and indicated that dolphin brain size and specialized adaptations made probable a high degree of intelligence, along with sensory equipment suggesting a possibility of communication with man. So far as I recall, up to date nothing conclusive has come of it all, despite a lot of effort. I bought Dr. Lilly's books on his research in the Virgin Islands, but all this has happened so fast I haven't gone very far into them, though I still have them with me, in my suitcase."

"Don't bother with Lilly," Dr. Wilhelm broke in, refilling my glass from a crystal shaker with the etched classical design of a boy riding a dolphin. "I can show you things here that Lilly never even dreamed of."

"But the big mystery to me," I had the temerity to mention, "is what I'm here for. Do you want me to try and hypnotize your dolphins, or read their minds?"

"Not exactly," Wilhelm answered. "At least, not at the present stage. The way I actually plan for you to begin is to hypnotize a human subject, to see whether such a person may become more sensitive to the thought patterns of the animal.

"We've done a lot of work, following up Lilly's leads, in recording and analyzing the sounds these beasts make, both under water and in the air: clicks, bleats, whistles, a wide gamut of noises—some of them above the sound spectrum audible to humans. We've taped these sounds, coded them, and fed them into computers, but no pattern of language has emerged, outside of certain very obvious signals for pain, distress, mating—signals many kinds of animals make, but which can't be called real language. And although dolphins will sometimes mimic human speech with a startling clarity, it usually seems to be mere parroting, without real understanding.

"Yet at the same time, our encephalographs show patterns of electrical output in dolphin brains similar to those that occur during human speech, and in parts of the brain analogous to our speech centers—all this while no vocalization of any kind is going on, subsonic or supersonic, airborne or waterborne.

"This led me to a theory that the basic means of dolphin communication may be telepathic, and the conviction that we'll never get in touch with them any other way."

I was somewhat taken aback. "Do you have a telepathically sensitive and experienced person on the staff, or are you going to hire such a person?" I queried.

"Even better than that," rapped Dr. Wilhelm triumphantly, his twin-moon spectacles jiggling with emphasis. "We have a person sensitive and experienced over many months with the animals themselves—someone who knows how dolphins think, feel, and react; someone who has lived with dolphins so closely that she might almost be accepted among them as a dolphin herself."

"He means me, Mr. Dorn." Through an open door leading to a dusky hallway stepped the lithe figure of a woman.

III.

Glancing sidelong at her across the candlelit dinner table an hour later, I decided that Josephine was striking but not beautiful. Fairly young, with a trim figure, she missed real distinction due to the muddy coloring and rather swarthy texture of her skin, and especially the staring protuberance of her eyes.

Nor was her manner entirely prepossessing. Her melodramatic entrance of Dr. Wilhelm's office that afternoon I could forgive, even with its implication that she had been listening outside for some time. In subsequent conversation she had proved as much a monomaniac as her employer on the subject of their experiments, and with far less sense of humor—a fitting Trilby to Wilhelm's benign, avuncular Svengali.

"But of course," she was addressing me over our coffee, "you know all the old Greek and Roman stories about dolphins, Mr. Dorn. How they herded fish to help fishermen, saved drowning persons, and sometimes even fell in love with attractive boys and carried them off to sea on their backs. There's a long history of friendly relations between our species, even though the latter type incident seems based on—shall we say, a misunderstanding?"

"I don't know about that, Miss Gilman," I riposted. "From what I've seen in California already, some of our modern youth would try anything once."

"Surf, sand, and sex," Dr. Wilhelm interjected, like a slogan. "I know what you mean. We have some of that type camped out down the beach right now, just south around the bend. Hippies, they call themselves these days. But to get back to dolphins, a more intelligent species. I'm not entirely sure that their good 'PR', so to speak, through the ages really rings true," Wilhelm continued. "Sometimes I even imagine it resembles the way superstitious people used to refer to the fairies and trolls as 'the Good Folk' to flatter them, out of fear of what they might do. So we get the modern nursery rhyme and Walt Disney-type of fairy instead of the hidden troll races, the menacing, stunted, displaced hill-dwellers that were their real origin."

Josephine picked up her coffee cup and daintily shrugged, as if to express disagreement.

"No, Jo, there's something to it," Wilhelm insisted, getting up and lumbering over to a big bookcase in the shadowed corner of the room. "Let me give you an example from a non-Western tradition." He searched for a book on one of the upper shelves.

"Sir Arthur Grimble was a colonial governor in the Gilbert Islands not so long ago. He visited an atoll called—what was it?—Butaritari, where there was supposed to be a man who could call dolphins." Wilhelm located the book he sought and fumbled it open.

"Grimble writes, let's see, here it is: 'His spirit went out of his body in a dream; it sought out the porpoise folk in their homes under the western horizon and invited them to a dance, with feasting, in Kuma village. If he spoke the words of the invitation aright (and very few had the secret of them) the porpoises would follow him with cries of joy to the surface.'

"Well, Grimble had him try it. The place was dead quiet that afternoon under the palm trees, the way he describes it, and the children had been gathered in under the thatches; the women were absorbed in plaiting garlands of flowers, and the men were silently polishing their ceremonial ornaments of shell. The makings of a feast lay ready in baskets. Suddenly—wait till I find it—'a strangled howl burst from the dreamer's hut. He dashed into the open and stood a while clawing at the air,' says Grimble, and 'whining on a queer high note like a puppy's. The words came out "Teiraki! Teiraki!", which means "Arise! Arise!" Our friends from the west .... Let us go down and greet them.'

"A roar went up from the village, and everyone rushed over to the beach on the atoll's ocean side. They strung themselves out and splashed through the shallows, all wearing the garlands woven that afternoon. Breast deep the porpoises appeared, 'gamboling toward us at a fine clip.' Everyone was screaming hard. When the porpoises reached the edge of the reef they slackened speed, spread out, and started cruising back and forth in front of the human line. Then suddenly they vanished."

Dr. Wilhelm brought the book to the table, sat down, and finished his remaining coffee. "Grimble thought they had gone away. But in a moment the dreamer pointed downward, muttering, 'The King out of the West comes to greet me.' There, not ten yards away, was the great shape of a porpoise, 'poised like a glimmering shadow in the glass-green water. Behind it followed a whole dusky flotilla of them.'

"The porpoises seemed to be hung in a trance. Their leader came slowly to the caller's legs. 'As we approached the emerald shallows, the keels of the creatures began to take the sand: They flapped gently, as if asking for help. The men leaned down to throw their arms around the great barrels and ease them over the ridges. They showed no sign of alarm. It was as if their single wish was to get to the beach.'

"'When the water stood only thigh deep, the men crowded around the porpoises, ten or more to each beast. Then "Lift!" shouted the dreamer, and the ponderous black shapes were half dragged, half carried, unresisting, to the lip of the tide. There they settled down, those beautiful, dignified shapes, utterly at peace, while all hell broke loose around them.'"

Wilhelm's glasses caught the twin candle flames from the table; his eyes were impossible to see. Was this wild account, I found myself wondering, the real basis for his belief in the possibility of man's telepathic communication with dolphins?

"Men, women, and children," he continued, "leaping and posturing with shrieks that tore the sky, stripped off their garlands and flung them around the still bodies, in a sudden and dreadful fury of boastfulness and derision. 'My mind,' says Grimble, 'still shrinks from that last scene—the raving humans, the beasts so triumphantly at rest.' There, what do you think of that?" He closed the book.

"It seems," I responded, "that the islanders made the dolphins the object of some sort of religious ritual, and that the dolphins enjoyed the proceedings. Sounds like something our hippie neighbors might go in for."

"You're wrong about that part," Josephine told me solemnly. "Those people out on the beach there hate the dolphins. Either that, or they're afraid of them."

IV.

The next morning dawned damp and cloudy. As I breakfasted in the glass-enclosed patio outside my quarters, which overlooked the surging gray-green waves of the Pacific across a narrow stretch of sand, I saw Dr. Wilhelm sauntering along the beach on what seemed a morning constitutional. Suddenly I was aware that he was not alone; slogging across the sand to meet him came a fantastic figure: a booted, bearded, fur-clad man with bulbous features and tangled masses of hair surmounted by a big, bright red beret—a coarse caricature, he appeared to me, of the well known bust of the composer Wagner. One of the hippies!

Some impulse, perhaps simple curiosity, moved me to bolt down the eggs and toast which the early-arriving housekeeper had brought me on a tray, and to rush out onto the beach through the storm door of my entryway and join that strange colloquy shaping up under the striated silver-gray clouds as Wilhelm closed with his odd visitor.

My employer's stance seemed brusque and unfriendly as he listened to whatever the bearded man was saying to him. I slowed and approached the pair, as if on a casual stroll; until I came up to them, all I could hear was the sibilance of surf hissing over the sand almost at our feet.

"Good morning, Mr. Dorn," Wilhelm snapped, obviously not pleased to see me. "Perhaps you ought to meet Mr. Alonzo Waite, since he's our neighbor. Mr. Waite is the high priest, or whatever he calls himself, of that hippie bunch down the way."

"I call myself nothing," the other responded quickly. "My disciples have awarded me the title of *guru*, or spiritual leader, since I have spent more time in mystic exercises than they. But I neither seek nor accept any preeminence among them. We are all fellow pilgrims on the sacred quest for truth." His voice was hollow, deep, strangely impressive; and his words, while eccentric, seemed more urbanely civilized than I had expected.

"All very well, perhaps," Wilhelm put in testily, "but your quest for truth seems determined to interfere with mine."

"I am simply warning you, as I have warned you before, that your work with the dolphins is potentially very dangerous, to yourselves and others. You should give up these studies and release the beasts before great harm results."

"And on what evidence do you base this remarkable prophecy?" Wilhelm inquired acidly. "Tell Mr. Dorn; I've heard all this before."

Waite's cavernous voice descended even deeper. "As you may know, the League for Spiritual Discovery has been working with mind-expanding substances—not drugs, in the proper sense—that produce intuitions and perceptions unattainable to the ordinary brain. We are not of that group, but we too claim that such states are true ecstatic trances, comparable or superior to those that have always played such a vital part in all the Eastern religions, and which modern science would do well to recognize and investigate."

"This is more Mr. Dorn's field than mine," Wilhelm said uneasily. "He's in parapsychology. I know nothing about such matters, but none of this sounds at all plausible to me."

"But what has all this to do with dolphins?" I asked the bearded *guru*.

"Our dreams and visions lately have been troubled by the presence of great, white, menacing shapes, cutting across and blocking out the sacred color patterns and animated mandalas that lead us to greater spiritual understanding," Waite boomed. "These are vibrations emanating from the creatures you have penned here, which you call dolphins, but which we know by an older name. These creatures are evil, strong and evil. As your experiments have progressed, so have the disturbing manifestations intensified. These vibrations are terribly destructive, not only mentally but physically. For your own good, I warn you to desist before it is too late."

"If what we're doing upsets your pipe dreams," Wilhelm remarked with ill-concealed contempt, "why don't you move elsewhere and get out of range?"

The tall, bearded man blinked and gazed into the distance. "We must remain and concentrate our psychic powers on combating the evil vibrations," he said quietly. "There are certain spiritual exercises and ceremonies we can undertake that may help curb or deflect the danger for a while. In fact, we are planning such a ceremony for tonight. But the only sure way to safety is for you to release these ancient, wickedly wise creatures, and to give up your experiment."

Waite stood solemnly staring out to sea, a grotesque, foreboding and somehow dignified figure in his oversized beret and flapping fur robe.

V.

"A scene right out of a Hollywood science fiction thriller," Wilhelm muttered angrily as he led me through the barn-like, high-ceilinged main laboratory and out a rear door. He couldn't seem to get the encounter on the beach out of his mind, and it bothered him more than I could well understand. As for me, I had put Waite down as just a typical California nut, though more intelligent than most, and doubted that we would have any real trouble with him.

"You've seen our sound recording equipment, both atmospheric and underwater," Wilhelm said, finally changing the subject. "Now you must see where most of it is used, and where your own work will be concentrated."

The back of the lab looked out over the beach; near the water's edge stood a smaller windowless structure—long, low, and plastered with white cement like the others. Wilhelm led the way to it and opened its single heavy metal door with a key from his pocket.

The inside was taken up mostly by a sunken tank that resembled a small indoor swimming pool. The narrow verge that surrounded the tank on three sides was cluttered with electrical control panels, head sets, and other paraphernalia connected with the main tape recording and computer banks in the big lab. The ocean side of the building consisted mostly of a sort of sea gate that could be opened on a cove communicating with the ocean itself, as I learned later, so that the water might be cleaned and freshened at need. Harsh fluorescent lamps played over the glittering surface of the pool, sending rippling whorls of reflected light into every corner of the room; there was a low hissing sound from the steam radiators run by thermostats that kept both the air and water temperatures constant and controllable.

None of this attracted my immediate attention, for here I was at last confronted with the subject of the experiment itself: A lithe, bulky, yet graceful shape—mottled gray above, dirty white below, with a long saw-toothed snout and deep-set, intelligent eyes—hung motionless in the shallow water on its slowly fanning flippers.

And not alone, for the dolphin shared its pool with Josephine, clad in a bright red bathing suit that set off her striking figure in an arresting manner. Indeed, I found myself staring more intently at Josephine than at her aquatic companion.

"Hi." Josephine's greeting was bland, but suggested a veiled irony, as if she were conscious of my covert gaze.

"Jo has been more or less living in this pool for the last two and a half months," Dr. Wilhelm explained. "The purpose is to get into complete rapport with Flip—that's the dolphin—and encourage any attempts at communication on his part."

"Flip," Josephine interjected, "is short for Flipper, of course, the dolphin hero of that old movie and TV series that was the first sign of popular awareness of the animal's intelligence."

Jo laughed, heaving herself adroitly onto the tiled edge of the pool. "The show was just a seagoing Lassie, of course." She reached out for and wrapped herself snugly within a heavy terrycloth towel. "Anybody for coffee? It's a bit chilly today for these early morning aquatics."

As Jo served coffee from a sideboard silex, Wilhelm was priming me with data on Flip.

"He's a prime specimen of *Tursiops truncata,* though a bit smaller than average—about six and a half feet, actually. The brain weighs an average of 1700 grams, 350 grams more than the human brain, with comparable density of cell count.

"We've had this fellow for over a year now, and though he'll make every noise they're noted for—barks, grunts, clicks and scrapes and whistles—and even mimic human speech, we can't dope out a language pattern. Yet they must talk to each other. My first interest in delphinology was aroused by a report on sonar charts that Navy boats made near Ponape in the South Pacific. The charts showed orderly discipline in their undersea movements over a distance amounting to miles, and something more: a pattern or formation of mathematically precise movements that suggests either elaborate play or some sort of ritual."

"Maybe," I interrupted facetiously, "they were practicing for the ceremony that so impressed Gov. Grimble."

"Anyway," said Jo, putting aside her cup and straightening a strap on her bathing suit, "in ten weeks I haven't gotten to first base with Flip here, and now you're supposed to get us onto the proper wave length. Also, you'll have to provide some hints about what to look for and concentrate on in telepathic communication attempts. Frankly, I don't put much faith in it, but if Fred wants to try, I'll cooperate with as few mental reservations as possible."

Remembering a passage from Dr. Lilly's pioneer book on dolphins, I asked Wilhelm, "Have you implanted electrodes in the beast's brain for pleasure-stimulus experiments?"

"We're beyond all that," Wilhelm replied impatiently. "It's been known for years that they'll learn the most complex reaction patterns almost immediately to achieve the stimulus, far beyond what any lower animal can manage. Besides, it's crude—a kind of electrical masturbation, or LSD, like our friends out there on the beach favor. It doesn't show a proper respect for our basic equality with the dolphin—or his superiority over us, as the case may be."

While this conversation progressed, my attention was gradually distracted by the animal itself, floating in the pool beside us. It was obviously following our talk, though I assumed without any degree of verbal comprehension. The single visible eye, set in a convoluted socket behind the rather menacing snout, moved from one to the other of us with lively interest. I even caught myself reading human expressions into it: proprietary interest when turned on Josephine, tolerant amusement in regard to Dr. Wilhelm, and toward myself, what? Resentment, animosity, jealousy? What fancies were these I was weaving, under the glaring lights of a scientific laboratory?

"You'll have to get better acquainted with Flip," Wilhelm was saying. "If you're to help us learn to interpret delphinese, you and he should become good friends."

There was a commotion in the water. Flip turned abruptly to his left and swam off semisubmerged, emitting as he did so the first dolphin sound I had ever heard: a shrill whistle of derision.

VI.

That evening after dinner, Josephine and I walked on the beach under a moon that shone only intermittently through scurrying clouds. Dr. Wilhelm was in his office writing up notes, and the housekeeper-cook, last to leave of the staff each evening, was just rattling off toward San Simeon in the Institute's Land Rover.

I found that I didn't know what to make of my feelings toward Jo. When I had seen her in the pool with the dolphin that morning, she had attracted me intensely, seeming in her proper element. But at dinner, in a frilly cocktail gown that somehow didn't suit her, she once more repelled me with her sallow skin, her bulging, humorless eyes.

"Tomorrow the hypnosis sessions are to begin," I reminded her as we paced slowly toward the surf's edge. "Are you sure you really want to undergo this? After all, you say you have no confidence in this approach, and that may inhibit your response to it."

"I'll do as Fred thinks best, and I'll assume what he assumes, temporarily at least. I've become quite good at that, within limits. Did you know he once wanted me to marry him? That's where I drew the line, though."

"No." I was embarrassed by her abrupt interjection of personal matters.

"I think it was for convenience, mostly. His first wife had died, we were working together, we shared the same interests—even the fact that we had to stay here together overnight, to watch over the work twenty-four hours a day when that was necessary—well, it would have made things easier, but I told him no."

"How did you first become interested in—delphinology, is that the word?" I sought to change the subject. We had reached the point beyond which the waves retreated, leaving streaks of hissing, iridescent foam half visible in the gloom.

"Actually, I've always been fascinated by the sea and things that live underwater. I used to spend half my time at the aquarium back home in Boston—either there or down at the harbor."

"Your family comes from Boston?"

"Not originally. My father was in the Navy, and we lived there a long time, ever since Mother died. His family came from a run-down seaport mill-town called Innsmouth, up past Marblehead. The Gilmans are an old family there. They were in whaling and the East Indies trade as far back as two hundred years ago, and I suppose that's where my oceanographic interests come from."

"Do you often go back there?"

"I've never been there, strange as it seems. The whole place almost burned to the ground back in the 1920's, before I was born. My father said it was a dead, depressing place, and made me promise years ago to keep away from it—I don't know exactly why. That was just after his last trip there, and on his next voyage he was lost overboard from a destroyer he commanded. No one ever knew how; it was calm weather."

"Weren't you ever curious about why he warned you away from—what was it, Innsville?" I faltered.

"Yes, especially after he died. I looked up the newspapers from around the time of the big fire—the Boston libraries had almost nothing else on Innsmouth—and found one story that might have had some bearing. It was full of preposterous hints about how the people of Innsmouth had brought back some sort of hybrid heathen savages with them from the South Seas years ago, and started a devil-worship cult that brought them sunken treasure and supernatural power over the weather. The story suggested that the men had interbred with their Polynesian priestesses or whatever, and that was one reason why people nearby shunned and hated them."

I thought of Josephine's swarthy skin and strange eyes, and wondered.

We had covered a mile or more from the Institute, and were suddenly aware that the darkness ahead was laced with a faint flickering, as of a fire on the beach to the south. At the same time, a sort of low mumble or glutinous chant became audible from the same direction. All at once, a high hysterical wail, reverberating in shocking ecstasy, burst forth on the night air, prolonging itself incredibly—now terror-stricken, now mockingly ironic, now mindlessly animal—rising and falling in a frenzy that suggested only delirium or insanity raised to the highest possible human—or inhuman—pitch.

Without thought or volition, Josephine and I found ourselves clinging together and kissing with an abandon that echoed the wild caterwauling down the beach.

The hippies, it seemed, were holding their promised ritual to exorcise the evil influence of the sinister creatures from the sea.

VII.

The next few days can most conveniently be summarized through extracts from the clinical journal which I began to keep from the outset of our attempt to establish telepathic contact with the dolphin Flip through hypnosis of a human subject:

April 20. This morning I placed Josephine under light hypnosis, finding her an almost ideally suggestible subject. I implanted posthypnotic commands intended to keep her alert and concentrating on the dolphin's mind to catch any message emanating from it. After I awakened her, she went back into the tank with Flip and spent the rest of the day there, playing the number games they have devised together. It is remarkable to observe how devoted the animal is to her, following her about the pool and protesting with loud barkings and bleatings whenever she leaves it. Flip will accept his food, raw whole fish, only from her hands.

I asked Dr. Wilhelm whether there was any danger from those wicked-looking hundred-toothed jaws, which snap down on the fish like a huge, lethal pair of shears. He said no; in neither history nor legend has there ever been a report of a dolphin attacking or even accidentally injuring a human. Then he quoted something from Plutarch—his erudition is profound, if one-sided—which I looked up in the library later. Here it is:

"To the dolphin alone, beyond all others, Nature has granted what the best philosophers seek: friendship for no advantage." ...

April 22. Still no results. Wilhelm wants me to try deeper hypnosis and stronger suggestion. In fact, he proposed leaving

Josephine in a trance for periods of a day or more, with just enough volition to keep her head above water in the tank. When I protested that this was dangerous, since in such a state she might well drown inadvertently, Wilhelm gave me an odd look and said, "Flip wouldn't let her." ...

April 25. Today, in the absence of any progress whatsoever, I agreed to try Wilhelm's second-stage plan, since Jo agrees. I put her to sleep by the pool's edge while Flip watched curiously. (I don't think this dolphin likes me, although I've had no trouble making friends with the others in the bigger tank up on the north beach.) After implanting in her subconscious the strongest admonitions to be careful in the water, I let her reenter the pool for a few hours. Her demeanor, of course, is that of a sleep walker or a comatose person. She sits on the lip of the pool or wades about in it abstractedly. Flip seems puzzled and resentful that she won't play their usual games with him.

When I was helping Jo out of the pool after an hour or so of this, the dolphin zoomed past at terrific speed, and I was sure he was about to snap at my arm, thus making me the first dolphin-bitten human in history; but he apparently changed his mind at the last moment and veered away, quacking and creaking angrily, his single visible eye glaring balefully. ...

April 27. Dr. Wilhelm wants to increase the period with Jo in the pool under hypnosis. This is because when she woke up yesterday she said she remembered vague, strange impressions that might be telepathic images or messages. I'm almost certain that these are pseudomemories, created by her subconscious to please Dr. Wilhelm, and I have strongly protested any intensification of this phase of the experiment.

Those hippie orgies on the beach south of here go on almost every night till all hours. The three of us are losing sleep and getting on edge, especially Jo, who tires easily after the longer periods under hypnosis.

April 28. Jo had an especially vivid impression of some sort of scenes or pictures transmitted to her during hypnosis after I brought her out of the trance this afternoon. At Wilhelm's suggestion I put her under again to help her remember, and we taped some inconclusive question-and-answer exchanges. She spoke of a ruined stone city under the sea, with weedy arches and domes and spires, and of sea creatures moving through the sunken streets. Over and over she repeated a word that sounded like "Arlyah." It's all imagination, I'm sure, plus memories of poems by Poe or cheap horror fiction—maybe even the story Wilhelm read us about the Gilbert Island porpoises and their "King out of the West." Yet Wilhelm was excited, and so was Josephine when she woke up and heard the tape played back. Both of them want me to put her in a deep trance and leave her in the pool around the clock. I consider this to be a nonsensical idea and told them so.

April 29. This morning Wilhelm pressed me again. I told him I couldn't be responsible for what might happen, and he answered, "No, of course not; I am responsible for whatever goes on at this Institute myself." Then he showed me a kind of canvas harness or breeches buoy affair he'd rigged up in the pool, securely anchored to the verge, where Jo could be strapped and still move around without any danger of drowning under hypnosis. I gave in and agreed to try the idea for a while.

April 30. Everything went off without any difficulty, and at least Jo and Wilhelm are convinced that what they call her "messages" are getting sharper and more concrete. To me, what she recalls under light hypnosis is just nonsense or fantasy, mixed in perhaps with those odd rumors concerning her father's home town Innsmouth, which she told me about earlier. Nevertheless, the two of them want to keep it up another day or so, and I agreed since there seems to be no actual danger involved.

VIII.

"No danger involved!" If, when I wrote those words, I had had even an inkling of what I know now, I would have halted the experiment immediately; either that or left this oceanside outpost on the edge of the unknown, threatened by fanatic superstition from the outside and a stiff-necked scientific *hubris* from within. Though the hints were there, recognizable in hindsight, still at the time I saw nothing, felt nothing but a vague, unplaceable malaise, and so did nothing; and thus I must share the guilt for what happened.

Late on the evening of April 30, soon after I had written the journal entry quoted above, Dr. Wilhelm and I were roused from our rooms by the sound of a scream which, though faint and muffled by distance, we at once recognized as Jo's voice, not the subhuman caterwauling of our drug-debauched neighbors.

Ask me now why we had left Jo alone in the dolphin's tank that evening and I must admit that it appears to be criminal negligence or inexcusable folly. But Wilhelm and I had stood watch over her alternately the night before as she hung half-submerged in her canvas harness and dreamed her strange dreams under the glare of the fluorescent tubes. The harness held her head and thorax well clear of the water; and Flip, lolling quiescent in the tank, seemed to drowse too (though dolphins never sleep, since they must keep surfacing to breathe, like whales). Thus this second night, at her own prior urging, Wilhelm and I had retired for dinner and then sought some relaxation in our rooms.

The scream, which jolted us both out of a vague torpor induced by a loss of sleep, came at about 10 p.m. Dr. Wilhelm's room was nearer the main lab than mine; thus, despite his greater age and bulk, he was ahead of me in reaching the heavy iron door of the beachside aquarium. As I approached the building, I could see him fumbling with the lock, his hands trembling. I was taken aback when he wheezed breathlessly at me over his shoulder: "Wait here!"

I had no choice, for he slipped inside and clanged the door shut behind him. The lock operated automatically, and since only Wilhelm and the chief lab technician—now miles away in San Simeon—had keys, I was forced to obey.

I can recall and relive in minute detail the agony and apprehension of that vigil, while the sibilant surf piled up only yards away under a freshening wind, and the half-full moon shone down with an ironic tranquility upon that silent, windowless, spectrally white structure.

I had glanced at my watch as I ran along the beach, and can verify that it was almost exactly ten minutes after Wilhelm had slammed the door that he again opened it—slowly, gratingly, the aperture framing, as always, a rectangle of harsh, glaring light.

"Help me with her," Wilhelm muttered from within, and turned away.

I stepped inside. He had removed Jo Gilman's limp form from the water and had wrapped it in several of the capacious beach robes that were always at hand near the tank. Glancing beyond the inert figure, I was startled to see Jo's canvass harness strung out dismembered across the winking surface of the water, and even part of her bright red bathing suit, which seemed entangled with the shredded canvas. The shadowy shape of the dolphin Flip I glimpsed too, fully submerged and strangely immobile in a far corner of the pool.

"To her room," Wilhelm murmured as we lifted Jo. Somehow, staggering and sliding in the shifting sand, we gained the dormitory building, groped open the door, and stumbled through Jo's apartment (I had never been inside, but Wilhelm seemed to know his way), finally dropping her muffled body unceremoniously onto the narrow folding bed.

"I'll call a doctor," I mumbled, lurching toward the door.

"No, don't!" Wilhelm rapped, adjusting the dim bedside lamp. "She's not really hurt—as a zoologist, I'm doctor enough myself to know that. Bring a tape recorder from the lab. I think she's still hypnotized, and she may be able to tell us what happened."

"But you saw—" I began breathlessly.

"I saw only what you saw," he grated, glaring at me through lenses that picked up the muted glow of the bed lamp. "She was clinging to the edge of the pool when I went in there, only partly conscious, out of her harness, and—get the tape machine, man!"

Why I obeyed blindly I still do not understand, but I found myself again blundering along the beach, Wilhelm's key ring in my hand, and then fumbling a portable tape recorder from the orderly storage cabinets of the main laboratory.

When I lugged the machine back to Josephine's room, I found that Dr. Wilhelm had somehow maneuvered her into an incongruous frilly lounging robe and gotten her under the bed covers. He was massaging her wrists with a mechanical motion, and scanning her face anxiously. Her eyes were still closed, her breathing harsh and irregular.

"Is she in hypnosis or shock?" he inquired edgily.

"Either, or perhaps both," I shot back. "At this point, the symptoms would be similar."

"Then set up the machine."

It soon appeared that the deep mesmeric state into which I had placed Jo that morning still held. I was able to elicit responses from her by employing the key words that I used to trigger the state of trance, so easily invoked these days as to be almost disconcerting.

"Jo, can you hear me? Tell us what happened to you," I urged her gently. The color began to return to her face; she sighed deeply and twisted under the bed clothes. For what happened next, I have the evidence not only of my own recollections, but a transcription typed up the next day from the tape machine, whose microphone Dr. Wilhelm now held beside her pillow with tense expectancy. This is a summary—omitting some of her repetitions, and the urgings on our part—of what we heard muttered by the bruised lips of that comatose woman writhing uneasily on her cot in a dimly lit room beside the glittering, moon-drenched Pacific, close on to midnight of May Eve:

"Must get out ... must get out and unify the forces. Those who wait in watery Arlyah (Sp.?), those who walk the snowy wastes of Leng, whistlers and lurkers of sullen Kadath—all shall rise, all shall join once more in praise of Great Clooloo (Sp.?), of Shub-Niggurath, of Him Who is not to be Named. ...

"You will help me, fellow breather of air, fellow holder of warmth, storer of seed for the last sowing and the endless harvest. ... (Unpronounceable name, possibly Y'ha-nthlei) shall celebrate our nuptials, the weedy labyrinths shall hold our couch, the silent strutters in darkness will welcome us with high debauch and dances upon their many-segmented legs ... their ancient, glittering eyes are gay. ... And we shall dwell amidst wonder and glory for ever. ..."

The speaker gasped and seemed to struggle to awaken. My apprehensions had crystallized into certainty: "She's hysterical," I whispered.

"No—no, she's not hysterical," Dr. Wilhelm hissed, trying in his elation to keep his voice subdued. "Not hysterical. She's broken through. Don't you see what this is? Don't you see that she's echoing ideas and images that have been projected to her? Can't you understand? What we've just heard is her attempt to verbalize in English what she's experienced today—the most astonishing thing any human being has ever experienced: communication from another intelligent species!"

IX.

Of the rest of that night I remember little. The twin shocks of Jo Gilman's hysterical seizure—for so I interpreted not only her unconscious ranting but also the initial scream, and her struggle out of the restraining apparatus—plus the unreasoning interpretation placed upon these events by my employer, served to unnerve me to the extent that when Jo sank gradually into normal slumber, I excused myself to Dr. Wilhelm and reeled off to my own room a little before midnight, for ten hours of uninterrupted—if not undisturbed—sleep.

It was a distinct surprise to me when I joined the others at staff luncheon the next day to find that a reticence amounting almost to a conspiracy of silence had already grown up in regard to the events of the preceding night. Jo, although pale and shaken, referred to what had happened as her "LSD trip" before the other staff members, and Dr. Wilhelm merely spoke of an abortive phase of "Operation Dolphin" which had been given up.

In any event, Jo completely abandoned her previous intimacy with Flip. Indeed, I never once saw her in the aquarium building again; at least, not until a certain climactic occasion, the facts about which I almost hesitate to affirm, even at this juncture.

Suddenly, all research efforts seemed to be shifted hastily to the crowded pens of young dolphins on the north beach, and I was called upon to interpret sonar charts and graphs recording patterns of underwater movement that might—or might not—indicate a telepathic herd-communion between individuals and groups of animals, both free and in captivity.

This, although a plausibly rational shift in experimental emphasis, somehow failed to convince me; it seemed merely a cover-up (on the part of Josephine as well as Wilhelm), masking a fear, an uncertainty, or some unsurmised preoccupation I failed to grasp. Perhaps these further extracts from my journal will make clear my uneasiness during this period:

May 7. Jo is still distant and evasive with me. Today as we worked together coding patterns of dolphin movement for the computer, she suddenly fell silent, stopped work, and began to stare straight ahead. When I passed my hand in front of her face, I confirmed that her stare was unfocused and that she had actually fallen into a trance again, from which I was able to awaken her with the same key words we used when she was regularly under hypnosis.

I was horrified, for such involuntary trances may well be a symptom of deep psychic disturbance, over which I can only blame myself for giving in to Dr. Wilhelm's rash obstinacy. When she woke up, however, she would admit only to having a headache and dozing off for a moment. I did not press the issue then.

May 8. The above entry was written in the late afternoon. Since Jo seemed herself at dinner, I determined to go to her room later for a serious talk about the dangerous state into which she has fallen. When I reached the door of her apartment I was surprised to hear voices, as it seemed, in muttered conversation inside.

I stood there for a few moments, irresolute whether to knock or not. Suddenly I realized that although what I heard was divided into the usual give-and-take exchanges of conversation, with pauses and variations in the rhythm and tempo of the participating voices, in actuality the timbre was that of only one speaker: Josephine herself.

I was shocked—has her state deteriorated into schizophrenia? Might she indeed be picking up telepathic messages; if so, from whom? I could distinguish no words in the muttered stream of speech. Cautiously I tried the door. It was locked, and I tiptoed away along the outer corridor as if I were a thief, or an ordinary eavesdropper. ...

May 10. I still cannot believe that what Jo said on the tape after her so-called hysterical seizure was really a remembered telepathic transmission from Flip; despite what Dr. Wilhelm said that night, I don't know whether he still believes it either. I have studied the transcript over and over, and think I have found a clue. Something about one of the phrases she spoke seemed hauntingly familiar: "Their ancient, glittering eyes are gay."

Recalling Wilhelm's remarkable memory, I mentioned it to him, and he agreed immediately: "Yes, it's from Yeats. I recognized that almost at once."

"But that means the so-called message, or part of it at least, must have come from her own subconscious memory of a poem."

"Perhaps. But after all, it was Yeats who wrote the line about 'that dolphin-torn, that gong-tormented sea.' Perhaps he's their favorite poet."

This flippancy irritated me. "Dr. Wilhelm," I answered angrily, "do you really believe that the tape was a telepathic transmission from Flip?"

He sobered. "I don't know, Dorn. Maybe we'll never know. I thought so at first, but perhaps I was carried away. I almost hope so—it was a pretty unsettling experience. But one thing I do know: You were right; that particular line of approach is too dangerous, at least with a subject as highly strung as Jo. Perhaps we can devise a safer way to resume the research with hypnosis later, but just now I don't see how. We're only lucky that she didn't suffer any real harm."

"We don't know that, either," I replied. "She's started hypnotizing herself."

Wilhelm didn't answer. ...

May 20. For over a week, I have not observed Jo fall into one of her trances in the daytime. However, she always retires early, pleading exhaustion, so we don't know what may go on at night. Several times I have deliberately paused outside her door during the evening, and once I thought I heard that strange muffled conversation again, but softer or more distant.

The research is now mechanical and curiously artificial; I don't see that we're accomplishing anything, nor is there any special need for me to be here at all. The old enthusiasm and vigor seem to have gone out of Wilhelm, too. He has lost weight and appears older, apprehensive, as if waiting for something. ...

May 24. I sat late on the patio last night, looking out toward the ocean, which was invisible, since there was no moon. At about nine o'clock I thought I saw something white moving down by the water's edge, proceeding south in the general direction of the main lab. Curiously disturbed, I followed.

It was Jo of course, either under hypnosis or walking in her sleep. (Here indeed was a scene from a horror film for Wilhelm to snort at!) I took her arm and was able to guide her back to the dormitory building. The door to her apartment was open, and I put her to bed without resistance. However, when I tried to awaken her by the usual mesmeric methods, I failed. After a while, though, she seemed to fall into ordinary slumber, and I left, setting the lock on the hall door to catch automatically.

Wilhelm was working late in his study, but I could see no reason to tell him about this incident. I shall probably not tell Jo either, since it might upset her nerves even more. I realize that I have become extremely fond of her since her "LSD trip", in a tender, protective way unlike my initial physical attraction for her. This knowledge makes me recognize, too, that something must be done to help her. All I can think of is to call in a psychiatrist, but Wilhelm has already denied the need for this, and I know Jo will follow his lead.

I must keep alert for more evidence to convince the pair of them that such a step is urgently indicated.

For the past few weeks our hippies have abated their nocturnal ceremonies, but last night after I left Jo's room I could hear that inhuman chanting and shouting start up, and see from my patio the reflections from their distant fire on the beach.

Again I did not sleep well.

X.

It was past mid-June, with no change in the tense but tenuous situation at the Institute, when I had my momentous interview with the hippie *guru,* Alonzo Waite.

The moon shone brightly that evening, and I sat as usual on my glass-fronted patio, nursing a last brandy and trying to put my thoughts and ideas into some sort of order for the hundredth time. Jo had as usual retired early, and Dr. Wilhelm had driven into town for some sort of needed supplies, so I was in effect alone in the Institute. Perhaps Waite knew this somehow, for he came unerringly up the beach to my door, his fur cloak flapping dejectedly around his shanks, even though my apartment showed no light. I rose somewhat hesitatingly to admit him.

He seated himself in a canvas chair, refused brandy, and abstractedly removed the soiled red beret from his unshorn locks. In the faint glow of the hurricane lamp I had lit, his dark eyes were distant and withdrawn; I wondered whether he were under the influence of drugs.

"Mr. Dorn," my visitor began, in the resonant tones I well remembered, "I know that you as a man of science cannot approve or understand what my companions and I are trying to do. Yet because your field is explo-

ration of the lesser known aspects of the human mind, I have hopes that you
may give me a more sympathetic hearing than Dr. Wilhelm has done.

"I, too, am a scientist, or was—don't smile! A few years ago, I was
assistant professor in clinical psychology at a small school in Massachusetts
called Miskatonic University, a place you've possibly never even heard of. It's
in an old colonial town called Arkham, quite a backwater, but better known
in the days of the Salem witch trials.

"Now, extravagant as the coincidence may seem—if it is really a coincidence—I knew your coworker Josephine by sight when she was a student
there, though she would certainly not recognize me, or even recall my name
perhaps, in the guise I have now adopted." He shrugged slightly and
glanced down at his eccentric get-up, then continued.

"You probably don't remember the scandal that resulted in my leaving
my post, since it was hushed up, and only a few sensational newspapers carried the item. I was one of those early martyrs to science—or to superstition, if you like; but whose superstition?—fired for drug experiments with
students in the early days of LSD research. Like others who became better
known, and who sometimes exploited their discoveries for personal profit or
notoriety, I was convinced that the mind-expanding drugs gave humanity
an opening into a whole new world of psychic and religious experience. I
never stopped to wonder in those days whether the experience would
involve beauty alone, or also encompass terror. I was a pure scientist then, I
liked to think, and to me whatever was was good—or at least neutral raw
material for the advancement of human understanding. I had much to learn.

"The drug underground at Miskatonic University was a little special.
The school has one of the most outstanding collections of old books on out-
of-the-way religious practices now extant. If I mention the medieval Arab
treatise called the *Necronomicon* in its Latin version, you won't have heard of
it; yet the Miskatonic copy is priceless, one of only three acknowledged still
to exist—the others are in the Harvard and Paris libraries.

"These books tell of an ancient secret society or cult that believes the
Earth and all the known universe were once ruled by vast alien invaders
from outside space and time, long before man evolved on this planet. These
entities were so completely foreign to molecular matter and protoplasmic
life that for all intents and purposes they were supernatural—supernatural
and evil."

Waite may once have been a college professor, I reflected, but judging
by his portentous word choice and delivery, he would have made an even
better old-time Shakespearean actor or revival preacher. His costume helped
the effect, too.

"At some point," the bearded *guru* continued, "these usurpers were
defeated and banished by even stronger cosmic opponents who, at least

from our limited viewpoint, would appear benevolent. However, the defeated Old Ones could not be killed, nor even permanently thwarted. They live on, imprisoned, but always seeking to return and resume their sway over the space-time universe, pursuing their immemorial and completely unknowable purposes.

"These old books record the lore that has been passed on to man from human and prehuman priesthoods that served these imprisoned deities, who constantly strive to mold and sway the thoughts of men by dreams; moving them to perform the rites and ceremonies by means of which the alien entities may be preserved, strengthened, and at last released from their hated bondage.

"All this goes on even today, and has influenced half the history of human science and religion in unacknowledged ways. Of course, there are rival cults that seek to prevent the return of the Old Ones, and to stymie the efforts of their minions.

"To be brief, the visions induced by LSD in the Miskatonic students, together with the results of certain experiments and ceremonies we learned from the old books, confirmed the reality of this fantastic mythology in a very terrible way. Even now I could not be persuaded to tell any living person some of the things I have seen in my visions, nor even to hint at the places my spirit has journeyed during periods of astral detachment. There were several disappearances of group members who dared too much, and several mental breakdowns, accompanied by certain physical changes that necessitated placing the victim in permanent seclusion. These occurrences, I assure you, were not due to any human agency whatever, no matter what the authorities may have chosen to believe.

"Though there was no evidence of foul play, the group was discovered and expelled, and I lost my job. After that some of us came here and formed a community dedicated to thwarting the efforts of evil cultists to free the Great Old Ones, which would mean in effect the death or degradation of all men not sworn to serve them. This is the aim of our present efforts to achieve spiritual knowledge and discipline through controlled use of hallucinogenic agents. Believe me, we have seen more than enough of the horrors connected with these matters, and our sympathies are all on the other side. Unfortunately, there are opposing groups, some of them right here in California, working in parallel ways to effect directly contrary results."

"An interesting story," I put in impatiently, disgusted by what I regarded as insane ramblings, "but what has all this to do with our research here, and the fact that you knew Miss Gilman as a college student?"

"Josephine's family comes from Innsmouth," Waite rumbled forebodingly. "That blighted town was once one of the centers of this cosmic conspiracy. Before the Civil War, mariners from Innsmouth brought back strange beliefs from their South Pacific trading voyages—strange beliefs, strange powers, and strange, deformed Polynesian women as their brides. Later, still stranger things came out of the sea itself in response to certain ceremonies and sacrifices.

"These creatures, half human and half amphibian of unknown batrachian strains, lived in the town and interbred with the people there, producing monstrous hybrids. Almost all the Innsmouth people became tainted with this unhuman heritage, and as they grew older many went to live underwater in the vast stone cities built there by the races that serve Great Cthulhu."

I repeated the strange name falteringly; somehow it rang a bell in my memory. All this was oddly reminiscent, both of what Jo had told me and of her delirious words on the tape, which Wilhelm half-believed represented a message from the mind of an undersea race.

"Cthulhu," Waite repeated sepulchrally, "is the demonic deity imprisoned in his citadel amidst the prehuman city of R'lyeh, sunken somewhere in the mid-Pacific by the power of his enemies aeons ago; asleep but dreaming forever of the day of release, when he will resume sway over the earth. And his dreams over the centuries have created and controlled those undersea races of evil intelligence who are his servants."

"You can't mean the dolphins!" I exclaimed.

"These and others—some of such aspect that only delirious castaways have ever seen them and lived. These are the sources of the legendary hydras and harpies, Medusa and mermaids, Scylla and Circe, which have terrified human beings from the dawn of civilization, and before.

"Now you can guess why I have constantly warned Dr. Wilhelm to give up his work, even though he is nearer success than he realizes. He is meddling in things more terrible than he can well imagine when he seeks communication with these Deep Ones, these minions of the blasphemous horror known as Cthulhu.

"More than this—the girl through whom he seeks this communication is one of the Innsmouth Gilmans. No, don't interrupt me! I knew it as soon as I saw her at the university; the signs are unmistakable, though not far advanced yet: the bulging, ichthyic eyes, the rough skin around the neck where incipient gill openings will gradually develop with age. Some day, like her ancestors, she will leave the land and live underwater as an ageless amphibian in the weedy cities of the Deep Ones, which I glimpse almost daily, in my visions and in my nightmares alike.

"This cannot be coincidence—there is manipulation somewhere in bringing this girl, almost wholly ignorant of her awful heritage, into intimate, unholy contact with a creature that can end what slim chances she may ever have had of escaping her monstrous genetic destiny!"

XI.

Although I did my best to calm Alonzo Waite by assuring him that all attempts to establish hypnotic rapport between Jo and Flip had ended, and that the girl had even taken an aversion to the animal, I did not tell him any of the other puzzling aspects of the matter, some of which seemed to fit in strangely with the outlandish farrago of superstition and hallucination that he had been trying to foist upon me.

Waite did not seem much convinced by my protestations, but I wanted to get rid of him and think matters over again. Obviously the whole of his story was absurd, but just as obviously he believed it. If others believed it too, as he claimed, then this might explain in some measure the odd coincidences and the semiconsistent patterns that seemed to string together so many irrelevancies and ambiguities.

After Waite left, I decided that there were still pieces missing from the puzzle. Thus when Jo knocked on my door a little before 11:00 o'clock, I was not only surprised (she never came out at night any more, since her sleep-walking episode), but glad of the opportunity to ask her some questions.

"I couldn't sleep and felt like talking," Jo explained, with an air of rather strained nonchalance, as she settled in the same chair Waite had used. "I hope I'm not disturbing you." She accepted a brandy and soda, and lit a cigarette. I had a sudden, detached flash of vision that saw this scene as a decidedly familiar one: drinks and cigarettes, a girl in a dressing gown in the beachside apartment of a bachelor. But our conversation didn't fall into the cliché pattern—we talked of sonar graphs and neuron density, of supersonic vibrations, computer tapes, and the influence of water temperature on dolphin mating habits.

I watched Jo carefully for any signs of falling into that autohypnotic state in which she held conversations with herself, but could see none; she seemed closer to normal than had been the case for many weeks. At the same time, I was annoyed to realize that I had become more conscious than before of the physical peculiarities which that idiot Waite had attributed to a biologically impossible strain in her ancestry.

The conversation had been entirely prosaic until I seized the opportunity of a short silence to ask one of the questions that had begun to intrigue me: "When did you first hear about Dr. Wilhelm's studies, and how did you happen to come to work for him?"

"It was right after my father was drowned. I had to drop out of graduate school back in Massachusetts and start making my own living. I had heard about Fred's research, and of course I was fascinated from the start, but I never thought of applying for a job here until my Uncle Joseph suggested it."

"Your father's brother?"

"Yes, a funny little old fellow; I always thought when I was a child that he looked just like a frog. He spends about half the year at the old family place in Innsmouth and half in Boston. He seems to have all the money he needs, though I've never seen any of it. My father once asked him jokingly what he did for a living, and Uncle Joe just laughed and said he dove for Spanish doubloons.

"Anyway, a few weeks after I left school and came back to Boston, Uncle Joe showed me a story about Dr. Wilhelm's work with the del-phinidae—I think it was in the *Scientific American*. Joe knew of my studies in oceanography, of course, and he said he knew an authority in the field who would write me a good recommendation. It must have been a good one, all right, because in less than six weeks here I was. That was over two years ago now."

If Alonzo Waite needed a further link in his wild theory of conspiracy, here was perfect raw material!

"You know," Jo went on with apparently casual lightness, "I told you a long time ago that Dr. Wilhelm asked me to marry him. That was over six months ago. At the time I thought it was a bad idea, but now I rather wish I had taken him up on it."

"Why? Afraid of becoming an old maid? I might have something to say about that one of these days."

"No." Her voice remained as calm and casual as before. "The reason is that—dating from right around the time that Fred Wilhelm rescued me from my LSD trip in that dolphin tank—I've been pregnant. At least, that's the timetable that the doctor in San Simeon has figured."

XII.

"Then it's Fred?" My remark sounded stupid, clumsy, like something that hypothetical beachside couple I had imagined might be discussing in some tawdry charade illustrating California's vaunted "New Morality."

"Figure it out for yourself," Jo answered with a nervous laugh. "It's either you or Fred. I don't remember a thing until I woke the next morning feeling like a used punching bag."

"Wilhelm was alone with you for at least ten minutes before he let me in to the aquarium. And he was alone with you in your apartment after I went to bed three hours later. I never was alone with you that evening."

"That's what I assumed from what you both told me the next day. Besides, I never turned you down—maybe only because you didn't ask me."

"Jo," I said, getting out of my chair, and didn't know what to say next.

"No, whatever it is, forget it," she murmured. "Whatever you were going to say, it's too late. I've got to think in an entirely different frame of reference now."

"What are you going to do?"

"I think I'm going to marry Fred—that is, if he's still interested. From there we'll see. There's more now than just me to worry about, and that seems the right move—the only move—to start with."

We didn't say much more. Jo felt drowsy all of a sudden and I walked her back to her apartment. Afterward, I strolled on the beach. A brisk wind arose around midnight, and clouds covered what moon there was. I felt numb; I hadn't known, or anyway admitted to myself, how I felt about Jo until now. I loved her too. But if Wilhelm, the old satyr, had made her pregnant while she was under hypnosis, then what she planned was probably best for all concerned. But how unlike Wilhelm such an act appeared! The gentlemanly, scholarly enthusiast, with his grandfatherly gray hair and amusing penguin shape—he might become infatuated with and propose to a young woman, especially someone who shared his enthusiasms. That was in character. But a dastardly attack like the one Jo suspected? He must be insane.

I heard the Land Rover chugging up the sandy mud. Dr. Wilhelm was returning. I'd find it hard to face him tomorrow. In fact, that might just be the best time for me to offer him my resignation, although I had no future prospects. Maybe I could get my old job back. At any rate, nobody needed me around here any more, that much was crystal clear.

I went back to my room and had several more brandies. Before I fell asleep, I became aware that the hippies were launching one of their wild orgies down on the south beach. From what Waite had said, they were holding ceremonies to keep the nice, normal, sane world safe for nice, normal, sane people.

If there were any left these days.

XIII.

I don't think I had slept as much as an hour when something sent me bolt upright in bed, wide awake. It may have been a sound, or it may have been some sort of mental message (ironic, since this was my field of study, that I had never observed, much less experienced, a fully convincing instance of telepathic communication).

In any case, something was wrong, I was sure of that; and if my premonition proved right, I knew where to go to find it: the beach by the main laboratory. I dressed hurriedly and dashed out on the shifting sands.

The wind, now near gale force, had swept the clouds away from the sickle moon, which shone starkly on the beach and glared upon an ocean of crinkled tinfoil. I could see two figures moving toward the windowless building at the water's edge where Flip, the neglected subject of our old experiment, was still kept in isolation. They converged and entered the building together, after a moment's hesitation over the locks.

As I dashed in pursuit, the gusty wind brought me snatches of the hippie ceremony. I made out drums and cymbals beaten wildly, as well as that same muffled chanting and the high, floating wail of ecstasy or terror, or both.

The harsh white light of fluorescent tubes now streamed through the open door leading to the dolphin tank, and I heard another sound inside as I approached: the clank of machinery and the hum of an electric motor. Dr. Wilhelm was raising the sea gate on the ocean side of the building, the gate that was sometimes used to change the water in the tank while Flip was held under restraint by the daytime lab assistants. No one could be holding him now; was Wilhelm about to release the animal, to satisfy some vague, belated qualm of conscience?

As I panted up to the open door, I realized that more than this was afoot. In a momentary glimpse just before the storm cut out our power lines, I took in the whole unbelievable scene: the massive sea gate was fully raised now, allowing turbulent waves to surge into the floodlighted pool and even to splash violently over its rim, inundating the observation deck and its elaborate equipment.

The dolphin, pitting his powerful muscles against the force of the incoming water, was relentlessly beating his way out to sea. Of Dr. Wilhelm there was no sign; but, perched on the broad, smooth back of the great sea beast itself, her naked body covered by her soaked, streaming hair, sat Josephine, bolt upright, bestriding her strange mount like the old Grecian design of the boy on the dolphin, that enigmatic emblem of the marriage of earth to ocean.

Then the lights failed, but the waves pounded on, and the distant delirious chanting reached a peak of hysteria that sustained itself incredibly, unendingly.

I can recall no more.

XIV.

Josephine's body was never found, nor was there any reason that I should ever have expected that it would be. When the lab crew arrived next morning, they repaired the power line and raised the sea gate again. Dr. Wilhelm's mangled body was caught beneath it. The gate had fallen when the power failed, and had crushed Wilhelm as he attempted to follow the fantastic pair he had liberated into the open sea.

On the neat desk in Dr. Wilhelm's office, where I had first met Josephine on the evening of my arrival, lay a manila envelope addressed to me. It contained a typed letter and a roll of recording tape. I found the envelope myself, and I have not shown it to the police, who seem to believe my story that Wilhelm and Josephine were swept out to sea when the gate was accidentally raised during an experiment.

This is what the letter said:

Dear Dorn:

When you read this I shall be dead, if I am lucky. I must release the two of them to go back to the ocean depths where they belong. For you see, I now believe everything that grotesque person Alonzo Waite told me.

I lied to you once when you asked me whether I had implanted electrodes in the brain of the test dolphin. I did implant one electrode at an earlier stage of my work, when I was doing some studies on the mechanism of sexual stimulation in the animal. When our experiments in telepathic communication seemed to be inconclusive, I was criminally foolish enough to broadcast a remote signal to activate that stimulus, in a misguided attempt to increase the rapport between the subject and the animal.

This was on the afternoon of April 30, and you can guess— reluctantly enough—what happened that evening. I assume full responsibility and guilt, which I will expiate in the only way that seems appropriate.

When I got to the pool ahead of you on that awful night, I saw at a glance what must have just occurred. Josephine had been ripped from her canvas sling, still hypnotized, and badly mauled. Her suit was torn almost off her, but I wrapped her in a robe and somehow got her into bed without your guessing what had really happened. The hypnosis held, and she never realized either. From then on, though, she was increasingly under telepathic contact and even control by that beast in the pool, even though she consciously and purposely avoided him.

Tonight when I got back from town she told me about her pregnancy, but in the middle of talking she fell into the usual trance and started to walk out on the beach. I locked her in her room and sat down to write this, since you have a right to know the truth, although there is nothing more that can be done after tonight.

I think we each loved Josephine in our own way, but now it is too late. I must let her out to join her own—she was changing—and when the baby is born—well, you can imagine the rest.

I myself would never have believed any of this, except for the tape. Play it and you'll understand everything. I didn't even think of it for a couple of weeks, fool that I was. Then I remembered that all during the time Jo spent hypnotized in the pool with the dolphin, I had ordered the microphones left open to record whatever might happen. The tapes were routinely filed by date the next day, and had never been monitored. I found the reel for April 30 and copied the part that I enclose with this letter.

Goodbye—and I'm sorry.

Frederick C. Wilhelm

* * * *

Many hours passed—hours of stunned sorrow and disbelief—before I dared bring a tape machine to my room and listen to the recording Wilhelm had left for me. I debated destroying the reel unheard; afterward I did erase the master tape stored in the main laboratory.

But the need to know the truth—a scientific virtue that is sometimes a human failing—forced me to listen to the accursed thing. It meant the end for me of any peace of mind or security in this life. I hope that Jo and Flip have found some measure of satisfaction in that strange, alien world so forebodingly described by the *guru* Waite, and that Frederick Wilhelm has found peace. I can neither look for nor expect either.

This is what I transcribed from that tape after many agonizing hours of replaying. The time code indicates that it was recorded at about 9:35 on the evening of April 30, a scant few minutes before Josephine's agonized scream sent Wilhelm and me dashing belatedly to rescue her from that garishly illuminated chamber where the ultimate horror took place:

"My beloved, my betrothed, you must help me. I must get out and unify the forces. Those who wait in watery R'lyeh, those who walk the snowy wastes of Leng, whistlers and lurkers of sullen Kadath—all shall rise, all shall join once more in praise of great Cthulhu, of Shub-Niggurath, of Him Who is not to be Named. You shall help me, fellow breather of air, fellow holder of warmth, another storer of seed for the last sowing and the endless harvest. Y'ha-nthlei shall celebrate our nuptials, the weedy labyrinths shall hold our couch, the silent strutters in the darkness will welcome us with high debauch and dances upon their many-segmented legs ... their ancient, glittering eyes are gay. And we shall dwell amidst wonder and glory forever."

Merely a repetition, you say—merely an earlier version of that meaningless rant that Josephine repeated an hour later under hypnosis in her bedroom, a garbled outpouring of suppressed fragments and fears from the subconscious mind of one who unreasoningly dreaded her family background in a shunned, decadent seaport a continent away?

I wish I could believe that too, but I cannot. For these wild words were spoken, not by a mentally unbalanced woman in deep hypnotic trance, *but in the quacking, bleating, inhuman tones that are the unmistakable voice of the dolphin itself, alien servant of still more alien masters; the Deep Ones of legend, prehuman (and perhaps soon posthuman) intelligences behind whose bland, benign exterior lurks a threat to man which not all man's destructive ingenuity can equal, or avert.*

About "A Darker Shadow over Innsmouth"

It is a revealing paradox that, while Wade here uses the Cthulhu Mythos as a foil against which to display a far more ominous horror, that of nuclear destruction, the atomic specter is perfectly represented by the metaphor of the Mythos: mere human beings perversely tampering with the terrible secrets of ultimate entity.

The "Pickman Nuclear Lab" is admittedly parodic, but don't miss the serious element. In the same way, some readers find Brian Lumley's demythologizing of Azathoth as nuclear energy (*The Burrowers Beneath*, *The Transition of Titus Crow*) unwittingly self-satirical. Yet what are Wade and Lumley doing but facing unflinchingly Lovecraft's revelation that science is the true horror, the true threat to human self-importance? We would like there to be a divine plan, at least an intelligible logos-structure, to life and the universe, but Lovecraft casts in our teeth the vision of a "monstrous nuclear chaos" at the center of all things, whose groggy mutterings "give each frail cosmos its eternal law."

"A Darker Shadow over Innsmouth" first appeared in *The Arkham Collector* #5, Summer 1969.

A Darker Shadow over Innsmouth

by James Wade

> The figure turned to meet my gaze;
> A woman's cold, translucent form
> Stood wrapped in early dawning rays,
> While on its mouth the blood was warm.
> Then in the east the sky turned red,
> The phantom sought the grave it knew;
> I clutched the stake with hand of lead,
> And from my box the hammer drew.
>
> —Wade Wellman

A s I boarded the wheezing, rattling bus bound for Innsmouth there at the station next to a bustling supermarket in Newburyport, I could not suppress a shudder at the thought that now, at last, I was bound for that ancient, decadent, shadow-blighted Massachusetts seaport of which so many repellent legends are whispered. I had read all the Lovecraft stories, of course, and those of his numerous successors, which chronicle how rapacious voyagers of the past century brought horror and calamity upon the town through their impious trafficking with blasphemous humanoid sea-dwellers—creatures who fetched them treasure from weed-grown, cyclopean ocean-bottom cities, but who in turn insisted upon not only the townsmen's worship of frightful alien deities like Dagon and Great Cthulhu, but even upon the unholy mating of human and amphibian, producing a hideous hybrid of half-reptilian, fish-like abnormalities who inhabited the town until they "changed" sufficiently to take up an immortal existence at the bottom of the sea.

Of course, I knew too that the town had been hard hit by federal raids over forty years ago, according to Lovecraft's informants; but I realized:

"That is not dead which can eternal lie,
And with strange aeons, even death may die",

in the words of a fortune-cookie verse I once nearly choked on—a cookie served me, strangely enough, at an Arabian restaurant in Osaka.

Now I was at last on my way to see for myself these eldritch, unholy entities and enclaves, and to join in the bestial rites therewith associated— that is, if my credentials were all in order. (My Order of Dagon card was signed by August Derleth, but a report had reached me that Colin Wilson had taken over the high priesthood in a daring palace coup.)

As we approached ill-rumored Innsmouth along the desolate Rowley road, I knew I would not be disappointed—here were the rotting, fishy-smelling wharves; the blear-paned ancient houses; the massive, obscurely terrifying warehouses, holding impassively the secrets of outer arcana; the crumbling, desecrated churches devoted to what hideous ceremonies the sane mind could only shudder to imagine.

As I alighted from the bus at Town Square in front of the sinister and horror-infested fabric of the Gilman House hotel, with its tattered Diners' Club sticker, the only person in sight was a slatternly girl with bulging, unwinking eyes and rough, crinkly skin around the sides of her neck. I struck up an acquaintance with this unprepossessing creature—whose name, I learned, was Nella Kodaz—on the pretext of being a stranger in need of guidance, and we strolled down to a deserted wharf where the sibilant and immemorial sea came sliding and hissing out of the mist.

"Tell me, Nella," I queried, "I know there is more in Innsmouth than meets the eye. How can I arrange to see the forbidden things secreted in those dilapidated warehouses and hidden away in the ancient boarded-up dwellings here?"

"Better get a CIA clearance first," she replied.

"CIA? Don't you mean Esoteric Order of Dagon?"

"That Dagon jazz is all washed up. After the Navy raids here in 1928, they say, the government kept a close eye on any funny business. During World War II there was a commando school here, and since then it's been used mostly as a hush-hush Defense Department experimental and training station. That's why everything's under cover and visitors aren't welcome. I thought you knew, from the way you talked."

I was flabbergasted. "But what about the monstrous batrachian sea-creatures out beyond Devil Reef? The blasphemous fish-frogs that always dominated Innsmouth and extracted their unholy tribute?"

"Well, every few weeks the Navy people dump a few crates of shark-repellent into the deep water off the reef. If there's any boogie-men around, that seems to hold them."

"You must excuse me, Nella—but it seems to me you yourself exemplify what is referred to as 'the Innsmouth look', those peculiarities of personal appearance shown by people descended from human matings with the Deep Ones—people who will some day dive down to live forever in the sea-bottom citadel of Y'ha-nthlei."

"Wrong again. I got an overdose of radiation, just a slight one, when I was working as a lab tech at the atomic reactor where they're making defoliants. The insurance paid through the nose, and I'm due for some free plastic surgery in a few months."

"But what about those older inhabitants of Innsmouth who did have an amphibian strain in their ancestry?"

"The ones who are left come under Medicare now. Mostly their relatives committed them years ago, and they're in protective custody at a big aquarium down near Marineland. It's sort of like Disneyland—people pay to see the Creatures from the Black Lagoon, only they think it's a fake."

"Then what's hidden in all those huddled, leering old houses and sealed, sagging warehouses?"

"Oh, all sorts of things—antipersonnel bombs, defoliant, infiltration training set-ups, secret courses on karate and winning the hearts and minds of the people. Professors from Miskatonic University come out twice a week to teach counterinsurgency tactics."

"Not the famous Miskatonic University?"

"Yes, in Arkham—where the new napalm plant is going up. Miskatonic U. got a big government contract, so they tore down their library, threw out all those moldy old books on sorcery, and built the biggest Pacification and Incineration Training Center in the country."

Suddenly, with a numbing shock, I saw a hideous form emerging from the foaming breakers—a dark, glistening shape, its skin a squamous green—vaguely humanoid in outline, but surmounted by a flat, bestial head with bulging, glassy eyes.

"Run for your life!" I shouted. "They've seen us! The Deep Ones! The monstrous, frog-like minions of—"

"Calm down," Nella interrupted in a bored tone. "It's a frog-man, all right—just part of the underwater demolition school for Special Forces. Why, it's Elvis Whateley from Dunwich Acres. Hi, there! Dry off and let's all go downtown and slug back a few beers."

So we did.

Now I have been in Innsmouth over six weeks. More and more I admire the quaint but swinging old town; more and more I enjoy my job packing defoliant from the atomic reactor; more and more I love my new wife, Nella Kodaz, with her soulful staring eyes and intriguing wattled neck. And in just eight months, a little stranger will join us!

I'm taking a night course in karate at Miskatonic, and angling for a job at the napalm factory when it's finished. I may even quit the Order of Dagon and join the Green Berets.

Yes, I'm a happy, fulfilled person. I came to Innsmouth seeking the cosmically evil—looking for sin on a supernatural scale, for horrors beyond the imagination of mere mortal man.

And I've found them. Lovecraft and the Great Old Ones don't hold a candle. Give me the crusade to protect peace and freedom any day.

About "The Innsmouth Head"

Why do hunters have the heads of animals stuffed and mounted? It is to display their prowess as a mightier killer than the creature whose head is a trophy on the wall. (In the case of the meek deer, it is an empty boast.) But every stuffed trophy-head is, in Brian Lumley's phrase, "an item of supporting evidence." It is a tangible vestige of a tale told by the fireside above which our mounted trophy hangs. It recalls and invokes a more adventurous series of events which creeps up to the edge of, but does not threaten, the comfortable set of events in which we currently sit. This is all the more evident in a case like mine, in which a bristled, tusked, flaring-nostriled boar's head emerges from the wall above my mantel clock. I did not kill the boar and do not mean to deceive anyone into believing that I did. No, I and my boar's head are removed yet another stage. The imaginary narrative I mean to invoke is that of scholarly characters from literature. It is just a stage prop.

The stuffed and mounted head is the proverbial tip of the iceberg. One knows there was more to it, and one is left to imagine what. The hunter who bagged it has a tale to tell about the rest of it, but who knows if it will be the truth? Like the dead youth's head that Simon Magus caused to speak demonic oracles, a relic head speaks silent volumes of implication by its sheer mute presence.

If a first view of an Innsmouth tiara in "The Shadow over Innsmouth" involves the "unknown arcana of upper air", how much more would the glimpse of a stuffed noggin of a fish-man by itself plunge us beyond all possible doubt into a world we had not suspected—just like the initial discovery of the skeletal arm of a gill man at the beginning of *The Creature from the Black Lagoon*.

An earlier version of "The Innsmouth Head" appeared in *The Dark Messenger Reader* #1, 1975.

The Innsmouth Head

by Franklyn Searight

I should have suspected something was amiss that Saturday morning when Morley Hart, proprietor of the Hart Taxidermy Shop and long-time acquaintance, called to let me know the head was ready. The preparation of the magnificent specimen had been completed two weeks earlier than expected and would soon be delivered. This alone should have triggered my suspicions into instantaneous arousal, but it merely stirred a slight curiosity on my part, not enough to make me inquire why the job had been so swiftly completed.

I was soon to learn.

Morley had simply wanted that monstrosity out of his shop as soon as possible.

Long and unruly grass in my front yard, growing so closely to the fence that the lawn mower was unable to shred it, needed my immediate attention. So it was that I chanced to be outdoors that early afternoon, happily clipping away with my trimming shears, when a delivery van pulled onto the side drive. A prominent sign along its side identified it as belonging to the Hart concern. Carelessly, in my excitement at last to view the finished trophy, I ripped a jagged hole in the faded slacks I wore as I hurried over to greet the driver.

"You Mr. Trumbell?" he asked, his voice somewhat crude and abrasive as he opened the door and squeezed his husky body out onto the drive.

"Yes. You have a package for me?"

He nodded, the fleshy lumps beneath his eyes quivering. "I sure do. And I'm damned glad to be gettin' rid of it!"

With that grim pronouncement almost anyone would have been warned that all was not quite as it should be. But not me. I was simply too anxious to think of anything but the cargo he was delivering. Had I known then what I know now, I would have politely but firmly requested that he drive the short distance to the Miskatonic River and sink the package to its murky bottom where it would never again be seen.

I followed the driver's broad, muscular back as he walked around to the back of his vehicle and opened the swinging doors. Nearby, where he could quickly retrieve it, reposed a large box which he grabbed with two meaty hands and handed to me in one swift motion. I was startled at the haste with which he thrust it at me.

"Here," he muttered, his facial muscles visibly relaxing as though he had just relieved himself of a straining python or some equally objectionable burden. "It's all yours, Mr. Trumbell."

Before I could invite him to enjoy a tall glass of iced tea or frosted brew under the cool sycamores that shade my lawn, he turned his brawny frame again and returned to the driver's side of the van. I was somewhat startled, I must admit, by the abruptness of his departure. Wasting no time with good-byes, he entered, turned on the ignition, and started to back the vehicle out of my drive.

But he slowed and stopped as he came abreast of me, and a curious expression contorted his ruddy face as he looked down at me holding the box securely in both hands.

"I hope you like it, Mr. Trumbell," he ventured, "but I doubt if you will—even though Morley did as fine a job on it as he's ever done before; said it was quite a challenge for him. But there's something about that thing—don't ask me what, nobody seems to know—that's had everyone in the shop jittery and nervous ever since you dropped it off. We're betting that you get rid of it pretty damn quick!"

With that he revved the engine and departed, backing his vehicle rapidly onto the street with the skilled precision of his trade. He was gone before I could ask the questions that were mounting in my mind, even before I could close my mouth, which had frozen open in surprise.

Strange man, I reflected, momentarily watching his van make its way down the street. I shrugged my shoulders in wonder, somewhat amazed that such a large and strident person should feel at all squeamish at the wonderful trophy he had delivered which I would soon display with anticipated pride.

After all, it was only a head.

I made my way into the house. It would be unwise to open the package on the lawn, I felt, imagining with a smile the initial curious and then frantic reactions of my neighbors if they should happen to see the contents without proper explanation.

So, temporarily quelling my curiosity, I proceeded to the living room and set the package on the couch. There I briefly examined the wrapping, savoring each moment of anticipation, for there is a certain delight in the keen expectations that precede an activity you are certain you will enjoy. That's what I thought at first as I carefully examined the plain wrapping paper and brown cord which secured it tightly, until it occurred to me that I was simply delaying the actual moment when I would view the thing now professionally prepared for my wall.

Just why I should procrastinate in this manner was something I could not answer at the moment, although now I can, and I readily admit to a far greater respect for the subconscious mind with its incredible insight which frivolous mankind so seldom heeds. I know now that a part of me recognized or at the least suspected the nature of the incredible evil that nestled within the box and was attempting to protect me.

At last I could delay no longer.

With trembling fingers—yes, *trembling fingers,* although I was truly looking forward to the revelation with happy excitement and there should be no reason for any nervousness—I cut the cord that bound the package. Moments later the wrapping paper had been pulled aside to reveal a plain cardboard box which I also hastened to open. Inside was a quantity of stuffing to protect the trophy from any undue bumps and jolts, which I awkwardly removed with quivering fingers that I could barely control.

Moments later It *was looking up at me with huge round eyes that seemed to stare accusingly into my own!*

And for a moment I froze.

It seemed so alive!

It was dead, of course. I knew it was dead. It had to be dead. I had seen to that myself—along with my friend Alan—after catching it off the dark coast of Innsmouth. Why did it now seem so *vital?* There was no movement on its part—the *aliveness* came from the eyes, those cold, frog-like orbs of unhealthy whiteness that peered steadily into my own.

An inexplicable and uncontrollable shudder passed through me as I lifted the head, now securely fastened to a mounting board of polished oak, and studied its repellent features. The prize was precisely as I had imagined it would be. My friend Morley had certainly done a magnificent job in restoring and preserving its original features, and I resolved to phone him sometime soon to tell him so.

And what a head it was!

It was magnificent, the likes of which probably no one else had ever possessed, with features so obscenely revolting that they might have emerged from some hellish nightmare. That, I suppose, was what attracted me so strongly. Like most people, I admire loveliness, but, unlike most, I am also able to enjoy its opposite. My new acquisition, hideously appalling, was such a contrast to anything beautiful that my appreciation of it was greatly enhanced.

One could think of many adjectives to describe the thing and still fail to approach even an accurate description. It was a marine animal, there was little doubt of that, but it did not look like a fish except for its gills and scaly skin. It was also somewhat amphibious or froggish in aspect, but only because of the bulging contours of the hideous face and its enormous eyes. It appeared to be, I reflected, a combination of the two.

What I can say with some degree of conviction is that it was a one-of-a-kind trophy; certainly, I had never seen or even heard of anything that came close to resembling it, unless one considered fictional creatures such as might appear on the movie screen.

It was too bad I couldn't have also kept the body, but that simply had not been practical. My friend Alan Hasrad, a journalist on the staff of the *Arkham Daily News,* had been with me when I caught it. He had argued forcefully in favor of discarding the entire carcass, but conceded that if I had to preserve something I should limit it to the head. People, he insisted, would simply be too shocked and be unable to deal with its *two arms and legs, with fingers and toes incredibly webbed and yet outlandishly humanoid.* I finally had to agree, with considerable reluctance, that the body should be disposed of, that people would simply not accept the existence of such a monstrosity. It would be hard enough for them to accept the head, but I was fairly certain that would create no unsolvable problem.

So ... I proceeded to hang the prize in my library. I must say it looked magnificently unique, hanging on the wall overlooking my desk, directly across from my favorite Picasso reproduction. There they could endlessly stare across at each other, direct extremes of ugliness and beauty, stunning contrasts that my finer sense would truly appreciate.

Fortunately, my wife Martha was out of town visiting relatives, so there was little need to fret, at least not for a while, about that moment when she viewed it for the very first time. She would probably not like it, I suspected, but she was reasonably flexible and understanding and might even get used to it in a short while.

I had related to Martha a portion of the story of how I had caught it, omitting how furiously it had squirmed on the deck of the fishing boat Alan had rented. Nor did I tell her how it had risen to its feet with the obvious intent of attacking us when the .30-30 we carried to chase off sharks had brought it down to the deck, great gouts of crimson staining its dark green, scaly chest.

I had told her, of course, a little of its appearance, so she had some idea of what to expect, but deliberately withheld my own initial impressions when viewing it alive for the first time. That it looked, at first glance, somewhat like the fictional monstrosity featured in *The Creature from the Black Lagoon,* popularized in past movies, was a judgment I decided not to share with her. The biggest difference, of course, was that there was no seam to provide entrance for a human to get into and out of an obvious costume. I was quite hopeful there would be no harsh words before Martha conceded my right to have it in the house.

Having admired the head long enough, I strolled to the kitchen and disposed of the container. As I prepared myself a late afternoon drink, I glanced casually at the clock over the sink and was startled to learn that I had spent nearly two hours in my study. *How*, I pondered, *had so much time elapsed without my knowledge?* I would have guessed that no more than half an hour had passed. From there I proceeded to the chaise lounge in the back yard, bruising the shards of ice as I swirled the Scotch and soda which I carried.

The moment I left the house I experienced a sudden relaxation of muscles which occurred so abruptly that I found myself swaying as though in a drunken stupor, nearly falling to the recently manicured lawn before I could steady myself. *Now what*, I wondered, easing into the chair, *had brought that on?* Unknown to myself at the time, every muscle in my body had seemingly been tense and strangely contracted until I had left the house.

Could this be what the truck driver had referred to?

Presently, seated in the lounge chair sipping my drink, I allowed my thoughts to roam at will and was not at all surprised to find myself recalling the incidents of my spectacular catch.

Alan and I had spent the entire day trolling for big fish off the Massachusetts coast, as we occasionally do on weekends, lazily sipping our favorite libations and enjoying each other's companionship. For some reason we had chosen this day to investigate new waters, and had traveled down the coast farther than we had ever gone before, until we sighted the brooding features of the shadow-cursed town of Innsmouth.

What a filthy, rotting sight it was, nearly abandoned, with most of its buildings already fallen into a desolate ruin. That sunny day it appeared to be nothing more than a near-deserted, ravaged fishing village, but both Alan and I were well aware of the dark rumors which concerned it—darkly whispered descriptions of things which supposedly had occurred there. We had laughed at them, as did most others, although Alan seemed to be certain that some strange things probably had taken place there in years past.

I recalled tales my father had related to me of the federal agents that had moved into festering Innsmouth in the winter of 1928—close-mouthed emissaries of our government who had torched many of the buildings and torpedoed the depths about Devil Reef; rock-jawed officers who refused comment to the newspapers about what they had witnessed or the nature of the Innsmouth people who had been locked away, never to be seen again.

I had laughed lightly at the strange legends concerning the area, even though Alan had not quite shared in what I had taken to be only amusing anecdotes. It was at my bidding that we moved closer to Devil Reef, where the fishing had at one time been notoriously phenomenal. Once there, Alan hinted darkly that the region had been the legendary site of Y'ha-nthlei, an ancient underwater city, and suggested we limit our stay to no longer than an hour.

That was just about how long we idly circled the black fangs of rock that poked above the swelling ocean, wondering why no fish were attracted to our lures in what had once been sensational fishing waters.

And then it struck!

With an attack that nearly wrenched me from the boat, *it* began a fight that was to last for nearly two exhaustive hours. But I kept the steel line taut throughout the long minutes, even though at times the deep-sea rod threatened to break in two, thinking for quite some time that a shark had been snared. When at last *it* surfaced, I knew immediately that I had linked with a specimen which I had never seen before. With frantic barking noises it rushed the boat, then retreated out into open water.

Fascinated, we watched webbed hands futilely attempt to snap the steel line or pull the lure from its mouth. But the rod stood the strain, and the line, designed to bring in fish weighing up to several hundred pounds, remained unbroken. Possibly the creature had swallowed the bait whole and the hook had become firmly embedded in its stomach. This would explain why it was unable to disgorge it despite the desperate, anguished efforts it made.

As already mentioned, it took about two hours. At last, greatly fatigued and unable to continue resisting my unrelenting attempts to pull it to the boat, it feebly swam alongside, looking up with a monstrous visage that blasted us with incarnate hatred. It thrashed about in the water again as Alan reached for it with the long gaff hook, but could not elude his practiced eye and arm as he embedded the sharp point in its gills. Together we heaved until we had brought the hulking fish-thing clumsily over the side of the boat.

There it lay in a pool of water, the gaff hook removed from its gills, panting heavily after the exertion of its fight. I, too, was exhausted, and my hands were practically numb from the constant strain. Together, Alan and I stood over the specimen. The proud glow of supreme accomplishment must have blazed in my eyes as we viewed the thing, which was now beginning to stir with growing animation.

For several minutes we gazed upon the chilly grayness of that rough-skinned, scaly body, marveling at the powerful arms and legs which ended curiously in webbed fingers and toes, and at that hideous face so much more like a frog than a fish, with fiercely glaring eyes that hinted at a malign intelligence.

After a while it stopped its feeble squirming and began to rise, placing one knee unsteadily on the deck of the boat. A moment later, madness in its huge, frosted eyes, it lunged to its feet and hurled itself toward us. Fortunately, I had earlier secured the rifle we carried to ward off mischievous sharks interested in our activity, for the creature surely would have ravaged the two of us within moments.

I emptied three rounds from the rifle into its chest and would probably have continued had not Alan stopped me.

The struggle was over. Whatever it was, it collapsed in a scarlet pool of spreading blood and water that stained the deck.

"What we should have done," Alan speculated, as he looked for some movement that might suggest it was still alive, "we should have cut the line and let it go. As it is, we'll just have to toss it overboard now anyway."

"*Are you crazy?*" I cried, spinning to face him with an unaccustomed belligerence. "After *that struggle?* Throw away *this?*"

Alan nodded soberly.

"Exactly. How can you keep it? This is intelligent life, Larry—or was. Do you doubt it? Its very appearance would scare most people out of their wits. Years ago the authorities hushed up the existence of these things. Don't you know what it is?"

I stared at him dumbly.

"It's a deep one from the ocean depths," Alan stated simply.

"You mean—"

"Yes. And I'm very serious, Larry. Since childhood you've belittled the stories of Innsmouth and its strange looking people, but you must have known there was at least a spark of truth to them. And, Larry—I've seen such creatures as this before. Without a doubt it's a deep one, one of the servants of Great Cthulhu who lies sleeping in his house in R'lyeh on the ocean floor—a mighty cosmic being who is expected to one day awake when the stars are right and seize control of our world."

Say again?

My immediate reaction was to wonder why Alan was vocalizing such absurdities. My next response was silently to consider his words and wonder if he might be right. I would certainly dismiss, and quickly, such notions coming from anyone else, but I knew Alan to be a keen student of the occult, an authority on the myths and legends that pervade the New England coast. So I listened to him, although with a degree of respect perhaps tempered by my desire to keep a splendid trophy—and then a thought occurred to me.

"Well ... then how about the head, Alan? It's as monstrous as you say only because it has arms and legs somewhat like a human being; but suppose we dispose of everything but the head. Wouldn't that be all right?"

He thought for a while, considering. "Perhaps. The head is plenty bad enough, but without the body to accompany it, maybe it would be okay. But what would you possibly do with it?"

"Mount it, of course!" was my exultant response. "Put it on my wall, possibly next to that elk's head I brought back a few years ago from Colorado."

"I see." Alan stroked his chin, considering the idea as he slowly relented. "Well, it's an interesting thought—maybe it would be okay."

And that, as you can well imagine, brought a smile to my tired features. The head, a souvenir of this triumphant contest, would certainly be better than nothing.

Using a very sharp filleting knife, I proceeded to sever the muscles and tendons, arteries and veins, and assorted bones that connected the head to the body. When finished, Alan and I returned the remainder of the carcass to the water, and I placed the head in the ice chest we kept on hand to hold our catch of fish.

The sudden thought that there might be more such creatures about— others who had noted my indiscriminate deed and might seek reprisal— prompted us to leave those waters as soon as possible. I suspect now, seeing that no such retribution came our way, that this had been a solitary traveler, perhaps there on its own to view again the watery element where it might have lived years ago when Innsmouth was a thriving seaport.

And so this extraordinary incident had ended. Once back in the city I contacted the Hart Taxidermy Shop and made arrangements for the head to be preserved as a memento of this strange and exciting episode.

Now the head was mounted in my library, and I was satisfied and happy. But upon returning later to the house, my muscles again began strangely and strongly to contract, as though subtly warning me of a danger I had yet to recognize. Quickly, I prepared another drink, a bit more potent this time, and returned to the back yard. As I sat down for another period of relaxation and reflection, the tension that had been building up within me slowly dissipated away.

Too bad Alan was unable to be here with me to view the specimen, I reflected, but as a reporter for the *Arkham Daily News* he was out of town chasing a story that would probably keep him away for at least another day or two. He would no doubt be surprised to learn that preservation of the head had been finished earlier than expected and that it was even now suspended in its place.

The remainder of my day was devoted to further attention to the yard and other moments of just relaxing and considering the head. It occurred to me after a while that, for some reason, I was developing a strange reluctance to enter my house, staying in the back yard except when the time came to prepare my supper. Not surprisingly, I chose to eat on the patio, where a cool breeze made my repast quite pleasant.

At last twilight blended into darkness, and I retreated again into the house, there to spend the night by myself—alone except for the strange head.

As the hours passed I became more and more uneasy, watching television and switching from channel to channel. Presently the notion occurred to me that perhaps the head itself was exerting some sort of an inimical influence over me. Bedtime found me apprehensive, and I remembered the curious trepidation of the driver who had delivered my wall decoration and the haste with which Morley Hart had processed it and had it removed from his shop.

Despite the mounting uneasiness and tension I experienced during those evening hours, I had little difficulty in falling asleep when at last I turned off the tube and went to bed. Only a minute or two after my head touched the pillow I was fast asleep.

Not surprisingly, I dreamed.

And it was truly a wretched night I suffered, tortured by visions of a strange submerged city, the aspect of which was surely beyond the normal scope of man's imagination.

In my dreams, I found myself at what I sensed to be an incredible depth below the surface of a vast body of water. A sunken city sprawled fantastically before me, vaguely lit by an unknown source of illumination that shed a lambent glow about its ancient parapets. Resist though I tried, I found myself unable to detour from a course that brought me to the only apparent entrance, an opening in the ancient, slime-covered wall that appeared to encircle the city.

I entered that dim metropolis, passing curious columns and stone statues of an awesome marine nature, my mind overpowered by a dreadful apprehension. It was not trepidation that resulted from what I could see, however, but rather from something which I could only sense through an unsuspected faculty I had never experienced before. Something overwhelmingly malignant, abhorrently evil, seemed to exude from the shadowy structures that climbed above me.

It was at this point that the vision thankfully ended and I found myself instantly awake with face and limbs dripping with perspiration. My first thought was that perhaps somehow the heat had been accidentally turned on, causing me to sweat profusely and dream those visions of vast watery depths. A quick glance, however, assured me the bedroom window was open wide; further, the nighttime air was cool and comforting. I had barely started to consider this, however, when I dropped back to sleep. My slumber continued unbroken throughout the remainder of the night, although accompanied by strangely disturbing dreams which I failed to remember when I later awoke.

In the morning I was able to recall clearly the dream sequence regarding that submerged city, and was unable to dispel the notion that the illusions had been caused by *something* that had seized my mind, binding it in a tenacious grip which could not be broken.

Was I going crazy?

To validate this notion, at varying intervals throughout the day I imagined that I was receiving the indistinct postulates of some *outré* cosmic being. These blasphemous thoughts, many so obscure as to defy human understanding, I knew to be intimately connected with the experiences in my dream state of the previous night. They were arcanely accompanied by weird ululation-like sounds, terrifyingly bizarre noises that rose and fell with an insistent, primordial rhythm, but which were heard, I am certain, only in my mind.

Of course, it had only been a dream last night—and yet—and yet something much, much more.

The new day was spent in a nebulous daze, and I'm unclear now as to precisely how I occupied my time. I know I drank much more than usual to dull the alien influences throbbing in my head, and passed the hours in growing dread of the time that I would sleep and experience again the visions of the night before. With an unassailable conviction, I was certain they would return to haunt me once again.

My apprehensions proved to be well founded.

I delayed going to bed that night as long as possible, but after the ten o'clock news I was barely able to keep my eyes open, so off to bed I stumbled. After falling asleep, I found myself again far beneath the surface of a vast expanse of water, standing at the gateway to the submerged city I had dreamed about the previous night. As before, unable to flee and powerless to control my movements, I stepped through the towering basalt portals into the shadow-infested domain of unknown, unseen presences.

For a time I walked along a weed-grown avenue, passing great monolithic structures with filth-encrusted walls. Shadowy forms darted about in the distance, too far away for me to determine any features, but as I drew nearer they resolved themselves into an array of strange batrachian creatures. Now and then they entered or emerged through the high, gloomy openings in the towering structures where perhaps they lived.

A short time later I was able to recognize them and knew them to be of the same species as that creature I had caught off Innsmouth, whose head even now adorned my library wall!

Those awful entities, with scaly hides and obscenely pulsating gills, were apparently unaware of me, for they took no notice of my presence. They continued to propel themselves through the shadows with webbed hands and feet that were so suitably shaped for underwater travel. I was unable to repress the grip of raw, brain-searing horror that inched along my spine when I first saw more distinctly their features, for from a short distance away these frog-like creatures appeared to be grotesquely human.

Perhaps it was my mind reacting to the horror that awakened me. I cannot be certain. But I suddenly sat up in bed to note that it was still dark outside and quiet—very quiet. My face was wet, as though a huge saturated sponge had been held above it and squeezed, although the air in the bedroom was pleasantly cool. Still tired as I was, my eyes presently closed and I spent the remainder of the night in restless slumber.

The following morning I awoke limp and weak, unable to explain the exhaustion I felt, as though I had actually spent the night swimming endlessly in the murky depths about which I had dreamed. I called my employer to tell her I was feeling ill and would not be in for work. There was no problem in this, as my days off thus far this year had been quite few and distantly spaced. Encouraged to relax and get well soon, I rang off and began the day in fearful anticipation of the night.

During the following hours those weird ululations and cosmic-oriented thoughts continued to invade the sanctuary of my mind. At one point came the odd realization that the nighttime visions had not been entirely dreams at all, but were, in a sense, actual experiences; that while my body had slumbered on the bed, another part of me—my spiritual essence, perhaps—had actually transcended space and the fathoms of water which covered the hidden city.

I knew then, with a soul-damning realization and intense conviction, that the phantasmagoria had not been a dream nor merely impressions received from some otherworldly mind—*but that an actual part of me had visited that blasphemous city beneath the waves!*

Quietly came to me the unassailable knowledge that it was the mounted head which must have been the focal point of my nightmare horrors, being used by some inexplicable force to reach across great spaces insidiously to invade and control my mind. With that enlightenment came the certain knowledge that there was nothing I could do to prevent it. Already my mind was totally captive to an incomprehensible power which I could not overcome.

Perhaps if I could rid myself of the fantastic head that glared malefi-
cally above my desk I might bring an end to these nightly visions and return
to a sane and normal life. But free myself of that awful malignancy I was
unable to do. No longer could I touch the hideous head itself, nor could I
even bring myself to handle the oaken mount upon which it was attached.
Not surprisingly, my attempt later in the day to leave the house proved also
to be an impossible task.

I did not relax. I did not get well. The knots in my stomach doubled
and tripled and swelled and threatened to erupt and split me apart.

What will Martha think, I speculated, *when she returns home in a few days?*

It was past noon when I began to doze on the couch, utterly debilitat-
ed, my brain soaked from the fumes of Scotch. I had been drinking straight
from the bottle with the hope it might end or at least partially ease the
awful thoughts that were now almost constantly blasting my brain.

On a nearby table were strewn several books about the occult, through
which I had feverishly hunted for some clue as to what was happening. Nor
had my search been in vain, for the nature of the spectral city was no longer
a mystery to me as it first had been. One of the books, a fairly thick volume
recently lent to me by Alan, had contained various excerpts from such hidden volumes as the *Necronomicon,* the *Pnakotic Manuscripts,* the *Eltdown
Shards,* and other ancient writings of a similar nature.

*From them I learned that the location of my nightly excursions had been the
myth-shrouded, half-cosmic city of R'lyeh, the domain of once-mighty Cthulhu.*

Great Cthulhu, banished by the Elder Gods to dwell within a vault
buried beneath the sunken city of R'lyeh, was now subdued in a death-like
sleep. But one day he would awake, hinted the hoary writings, when the
Elder Sign was lifted, to regain his dominion over Earth and those who peo-
pled it. The hideous batrachian creatures that had so terrified me at first I
knew to be deep ones, just as my friend Alan had asserted, amphibious entities who awaited the day Great Cthulhu would arise that they might serve
him as they had in millennia past.

Fatigued from the previous nerve-shattering nights, my senses dead-
ened by excessively large quantities of alcohol ingested into my system, I
was unable to stop myself from falling asleep. I knew, even as that black curtain descended, that even though it was still afternoon I would probably
continue further through the labyrinth of avenues, deeper and deeper into
the arcane submerged city. And there I would view new revelations of marvels and horrors hidden mercifully from the sight and mind of mankind.

My expectations were well founded.

This time I reached what I believe to be the center of the city, and here
the blighted buildings ceased near a steeply ascending mound that appeared

to cover several acres. This I climbed, hoisting myself over ancient stairs certainly not meant for man, finally reaching the top after a difficult climb.

It was at the highest point, where the rock leveled off, that I discovered a curious star-shaped design of five radiating points deeply engraved into a huge slab of grayish stone. Directly in the center of this unusual pattern were the discernible outlines of an open-ended oval in which was set a tower of cascading flame. Beneath the sign, faintly perceptible, were the words *Ph'nglui mglw'nafh Cthulhu R'lyeh wgah'nagl fhtagn*, which I had seen translated in an excerpt from *The R'lyeh Text* as meaning: "In his house at R'lyeh dead Cthulhu waits dreaming."

There was no doubt to my slumbering mind that this five-pointed star was the Elder Sign, set there by the Elder Gods to seal the crypt of Cthulhu, nor was there any doubt that beneath the slab at my feet reposed the titanic colossus that patiently awaited its moment of freedom.

Something was searing into my mind the irresistible desire to efface the star engraved upon that cold slab. Mechanically, without conscious involvement on my part, I found a large jagged rock that fit the contours of my hand and which would enable me to scratch and gouge until that pattern was no more. I returned to the slab and with a chilling dread, mixed with a strange and joyful exultation and exhilaration, my hand reached forth to mutilate the star beyond recognition.

As I did so, I stumbled, lost my footing, and began to fall. The block was but a vague blur that rose to meet me, offering no resistance. Unexpectedly, as though it had been but a shadow, I plunged through it, falling into an incredibly deep abyss. Long minutes later, it seemed, my descent was interrupted and I hovered over a titanic form which reposed beneath me.

My first impression, vague though it was, was of a semiamorphous mass; gradually, its dim pulsing outline could be better seen—*and the features of that hideous cephalopod head burned its way into my brain!* The conviction came to me that it was this entity which was the source of those infernal thoughts that had invaded my mind during the daylight hours.

A series of shudders racked my being when a long tentacle or feeler, far thicker than the hawser of an ocean-going freighter, began to move and stretch toward me. With a scream, I fought my way to the edge of consciousness.

Someone was pounding at my front door!

The thud … thud … thud of a heavy fist assaulting the panels was my first impression as I awoke, and I suspected later it was that which had also caused me to stumble when on the verge of releasing a nightmare on the world!

Slowly, I made my way from the couch, slightly staggering, blindly striving to answer the insistent summons. At last I reached the door and threw it open.

Alan Hasrad stood before me.

His hand was poised for another resounding onslaught. "Thank God," he cried. "You gave me an awful fright!"

I nodded and muttered, running shaky fingers through my damp, tangled hair as I came out onto the porch. "Don't come in here, Alan. God knows, it would get you, too!"

"What's that supposed to mean, Larry?" Alan sternly demanded, eyeing me with a concerned, critical look. "What's happened to you? What would get me? You look as though you've just stepped from the grave!"

"Exactly how I feel. But let's find another place to talk—anywhere but inside the house."

"Okay with me," Alan agreed, relief in his voice, lending a hand to help me off the porch. Together we walked around the house to the patio, where several chairs and a table were arrayed under towering trees.

"I rang your doorbell for nearly five minutes," he explained. "I was pretty sure you were home because I phoned you at work earlier and someone told me you weren't coming in today. Also, your car is in the drive. When you wouldn't answer the bell, I peeked through the window and saw you on the couch, squirming and thrashing your arms about. I thought I might have to break down the door. What's been happening?"

Slowly I lowered myself onto one of the lawn chairs while Alan took another one nearby. "I can only guess, but I'll be all right now—at least for a while ... at least until ...."

In truth, I *was* beginning to feel better already. My voice steadied, and I began to relax; my fingers ceased their trembling.

"Sooner or later, though, I'll have to go into the house again and see *it* again and *sleep* again." I lowered my head and pressed the palms of my hands to my face, rubbing my eyes and shutting out the sunlight, wincing at the anticipating of what I knew I would be unable to resist doing.

"You must think I'm crazy, Alan."

"Nonsense, Larry," Alan returned steady and calmly. "Now tell me about it."

I nodded my head. "First, go into the house and into the library. You'll see *it* over my desk. But don't stay! God, don't stay for longer than a few seconds, Alan. I think you'll begin to understand."

Alan stayed longer than a few seconds. Nearly five minutes passed before he returned, concern etched even more deeply on his features. He resumed his seat.

"Well, I saw it—ugly thing—tell me—"

I told him everything, all that had occurred since the head had been delivered, and he listened silently, attentively, nodding encouragingly, not interrupting when others would have loudly questioned my sanity.

His words, when I finished, were carefully chosen, but blunt and forceful.

"I'm sure you know I have some knowledge of these matters, Larry; otherwise I would pronounce you a hopeless drunk or outright loony. But I've experienced some pretty extraordinary things—they seem somehow to seek me out—and the very existence of that head is all the proof I need to believe every word you've said!"

I nodded, my tormented senses flooding with relief, and he continued.

"But this is more serious than you might realize—*far more serious!*" He looked me straight in the eyes. "Larry, you can't sleep again as long as this influence is upon you—"

"I know, Alan! I know!" I cried, my voice breaking.

"—for if you do," he continued, "the very worst that could happen surely would. The minions of Cthulhu are unable to remove the sign that confines their master to his watery crypt—someone not affected by the potency of the Elder Sign must perform that task. *And that someone is you!*"

"I know it, Alan," I repeated. "God, how I *know it!* And once I destroy that symbol I also know what horror will be freed to stalk the Earth! I dare not sleep again—not *ever* again. You've got to help me, Alan. The rifle in my closet and a bullet to my brain will solve this matter once and for all."

Alan shook his head firmly.

"Not that. Not yet." He pondered for a time. "There's still a chance— a good chance, perhaps—that we can fight this together."

"You—you really think so?"

He nodded somberly. "We'll begin with a fire. Perhaps by destroying the focal point we can destroy the insidious influence. Fire is the universal, age-old cleanser."

Hope! With those words from my staunch ally hope was kindled within me, and a blessed relief began to banish the despair that had seized my very soul.

"You really think so?" I said again. "Certainly, it's worth a try."

Together we gathered armloads of branches and assorted debris that we set near the back fence. Spread beneath was a section of newspaper that had littered a corner of the yard. With a single match Alan ignited the combustible fuel and a small blaze began that, within a short time, roared into a fiery conflagration. Scarlet fingers reached toward the sky and radiating waves of heat sent us scurrying back.

Alan retreated into the house and reappeared a minute later carrying something in his hand. I knew instinctively what it was and turned so as not to see the head again.

But I could not help myself, and spun about to watch as helplessly as a puppet on strings while he heaved that mounted abnormality into the surging flames. Hungrily they licked about the hideous features, searing, reddening, and finally blackening them beyond any recognition while an appalling stench arose that drove us further away. Charred flesh parted from bone and cartilage as greedy tongues of red and yellow incinerated the oaken mount and all that had been attached to it.

Relief!

A soul-stirring relief was precisely what I felt when it was over, when the head had been reduced to dusky ashes and the kindling to nothing more than glowing embers that finally dimmed and winked out.

As though I had removed my throbbing head from a slowly squeezing vice, great feelings of comfort swept over me and I knew for a certainty what had happened.

"It's gone, Alan," I exclaimed with a sense of heightened elation I had never experienced before. "That maddening influence is gone! I can *feel* its absence!" My voice shook and the sobs began. "Alan, I'm myself again!"

My good friend nodded and smiled and laid a reassuring hand upon my shoulder. A twinkle danced in his eyes as he observed, "What you need, Larry, is time to relax. A short vacation, perhaps. Suppose we take a few days off and enjoy a leisurely fishing trip ...."

About "Innsmouth Gold"

This has got to be one of the most controversial small press horror tales ever penned. The ensuing brouhaha proved to be almost as horrifying and entertaining as the story itself. "Innsmouth Gold" appeared in *Chronicles of the Cthulhu Codex* #2, 1985. It came in for brief criticism, along with the whole subgenre to which it belonged, in a review essay by Stefan Dziemianowicz ("New Tales of the Marvelous and the Ridiculous", *Crypt of Cthulhu* #40, St. John's Eve, 1986, 55). He chided the story for having "forsaken the subtlety of the slow buildup" and lambasted how it "use[s] physical description in an attempt to ram the horror home. This overstatement of detail supersedes the power of suggestion."

Readers rushed to Vester's defense: "This story had vitality and sincerity. ... Vester writes well, and 'Innsmouth Gold' is a fine tribute to HPL as well as an entertaining horror tale" (Wilum Pugmire, letter to the editor, *Crypt of Cthulhu* #42, Michaelmas 1986, 50, 58). "I believe Henry Vester conveyed the utter alienness of the Innsmouth people's culture" (Tani Jantsang, *ibid.*, 58). "It is not that G'thuga is like Rodan or Godzilla; the subtlety is that the 'man' listening to Beethoven next door, shaking your hand, looking you in the eye, does not have a human consciousness whatsoever" (Phil Marsh, *ibid.*).

Dziemianowicz stood his ground. While admitting that "Vester's story is better written than many attempts at Mythos stories", he still faulted "Innsmouth Gold" for a lack of Lovecraftian cosmicism and the fact that "Vester's story never gets beyond the immediacy of physical revulsion" ("'Innsmouth Gold' Revisited", *Crypt of Cthulhu* #47, Roodmas 1987, 61, 62). For his part, Vester confessed himself astonished that his story should have generated this much debate. I dare say many more readers were conversant with the debate about the story than had ever had the opportunity to read the story itself (until now).

Innsmouth Gold

by Henry J. Vester III

I

I'm too close here—much too close. Even at Oakridge in Santa Rosa I could sometimes smell the sea when the wind was right. But here, not a mile from the coast, the air reeks day and night with salt spray and seaweed. And although they tell me it's impossible here in the inner wards, I swear I can hear the breakers on the rocks every day at sundown. I don't know what I'll do. My only safety is in death, but I have neither the nerve for suicide nor the means. God help me. God in Heaven help me.

The staff here are decent people. They'd help me if they could, but why should they believe me any more than the others at Oakridge did? Perhaps I am crazy after all, but even if that's true it doesn't mean they're not out there anyway. And who wouldn't be a little mad after carrying my memories for more than half a century? Maybe if I can write it all out I can find some way to convince them of the truth, or at least to move me to some place further inland. Maybe then I wouldn't have the dreams.

My name is Thaddeus Miller Hess. I was born in Newburyport, Massachusetts, in 1903. I am 82 years of age. I am currently being detained at Bodega State Hospital on the California coast, about an hour's drive north of San Francisco. If the doctors do not consent to move me further inland, I fully expect to die here. But now that *they* know where I am it probably wouldn't make any difference even if I went back to Kansas. But I'm getting ahead of myself. I must try, above all, to compose a coherent statement of my experience.

The events of my life up until my twenty-third birthday were altogether prosaic and mundane. My paternal grandfather, a German immigrant, had gained a respectable fortune through the importation of teas and spices. My father, a lawyer, had increased his inheritance substantially by various judicious investments. My mother, the final member of an honored Hampton family, added her properties to those of my father when they married in 1901. Thus, when both of my parents were drowned in a boating accident in 1924, I, their only child, inherited a sizable estate whose holdings made it unnecessary for me to obtain conventional employment. I withdrew from my studies of law and returned home to Newburyport in order to manage the estate's properties and investments. I was very close to both of my parents and their loss affected me deeply. So much so, in fact, that my few friends suggested that I was becoming a bit too much the dreamer and recluse, and gradually fell away from me in favor of more gregarious and pragmatic companions. I was thus left with a very great deal of time on my hands, as I had arranged my properties such that they required very little of my personal attention.

In search of ways to occupy my time I had purchased a set of telescopes with which to pursue my old interest in astronomy. During the day, while the stars and planets were invisible to me, I frequently used a low-powered telescope to survey the activities of the town and the traffic in the bay and up and down the Merrimack River. I had spent many days in this idle pursuit before I happened to catch sight of Sargent's disreputable motor-coach pulling into town one morning on the Ipswich road. The old bus smoked along High Street, made a right turn onto State, and thence into Market Square, where it halted in front of a pharmacy. I had seen the decrepit vehicle a few times previously, but had never felt anything akin to curiosity regarding its route or clientele. The attitude in town, held by all regardless of birth or station, was that anything originating in Innsmouth had a taint about it and was best left alone by "decent" folks. But now, with so little else to occupy my mind, this bus and its odd driver took on new fascination for me. I had never seen Sargent except from a distance, and I suddenly developed an interest to do so at much closer range.

I rushed downstairs, threw on my hat and coat, and drove my father's old Ford the mile or so to Hammond's Drug Store. I parked across the street from the establishment and, in the hope that Sargent might also be there, entered on the pretext of purchasing some patent remedy. Jedediah Hammond, the proprietor, had once mentioned to my father that Sargent purchased medicines and sundries in Newburyport because Innsmouth had had no druggist for almost a decade. In point of fact, the town had but a single physician, and Hammond's gossip indicated that this individual kept himself drunk most of the time since the unexplained disappearance of his wife and their small son a few months earlier. Hammond seemed surprised to see me in the store and examined me a bit quizzically, I thought, when I placed my order with him. I supposed this to be due to the fact that townsfolk generally kept their distance from the Innsmouth bus, and especially from the residents of that crumbling town. Loungers and idlers always seemed to be somewhere else when the bus was due to arrive, and few and far between were the times I had heard of townsfolk actually boarding it. A train ran from Newburyport through Rowley, Ipswich, and Wenham, all the way through Arkham to Boston. So there was no need to use Sargent's vehicle unless one's business made a visit to Innsmouth unavoidable. In such a case this bus was the only option for public transportation, since none of the other bus lines ran through Innsmouth, and none of Newburyport's taxi drivers would accept a fare to that shadowed village. It seemed, therefore, that Sargent operated his private bus line for the sole convenience of Innsmouth residents. That being the case, it was little short of remarkable that he was able to stay in business, since there were never more than a few passengers aboard, and not infrequently the bus entered and left Newburyport without a single rider.

Such recollections as these crowded my thoughts as I strolled up and down the aisles of Hammond's establishment, appearing to browse while actually searching to see if Sargent was in the store. After a few moments I spotted his tattered brown cap bobbing along a few aisles distant from where I stood. He appeared to be moving toward the back counter where pharmaceutical orders were filled, so I unobtrusively made my way in the same direction, for I had not yet been given the medication I had requested and this seemed a likely opportunity for a closer examination of this reportedly unsavory individual. The bus driver was already standing at the counter by the time I arrived there, and appeared not to notice me in the least as I took a seat on a waiting bench, picked up a magazine, and began leafing through it. As I was seated behind him and a bit to Sargent's right, I was able to look him over with relative impunity as I continued to flip the pages of the periodical. What I observed merely served to reinforce the whispered stories of the air of repellence which seemed to hover about most of the residents of Innsmouth.

The man was thin and slope-shouldered, perhaps six feet in height. His clothing was shabby and nondescript, except for his shoes. These I saw to be abnormally long and strangely wide at the toes. My vision was very good in my youth, and I perceived that these shoes had been rather crudely hand-sewn. The man's skull seemed somehow misshapen, as though with a congenital deformity, for it was very narrow and seemed to taper oddly toward the crown. I found myself wishing that he would remove his cap, and at the same time grateful that he did not. This apparent deformity was accentuated by the weak, almost nonexistent chin, the flat nose, and the radically sloping forehead which caused his cap to slip down so that it rested just above his eyebrows. But undoubtedly the most disquieting feature I noticed was the appearance of the man's skin, which was heavily pitted and blotched with dull gray patches, as though from exceedingly poor circulation. It seemed oddly tufted and wrinkled in spots, especially on the neck under each ear. These characteristics strengthened in my mind the belief that Sargent was a victim of some form of genetic defect, possibly due to the inbreeding which was rumored to have strangely affected so many Innsmouth families. As if these physical aberrations were not sufficient to engender a sense of disgust, the man's clothing exuded a most unpleasant odor, as though he carried a dead fish in his pocket. I knew that fishing was Innsmouth's principal industry, and it occurred to me that perhaps Sargent augmented his meager income by working in one of the fish processing plants which were still operating. If that was the cause of this foul odor, then God alone knew when Sargent had last washed these clothes.

Hammond finished boxing the supplies which Sargent had requested and received payment. As the man turned to leave he looked full upon me with those eyes which I had not yet seen. They were hugely round and protruding, and seemed to have about them an alien quality which I could define only by the utter lack of expression in them. The duration of his glance could have been no more than a second or two, and yet in so brief a time I came to understand why people avoided even so much as the mention of Innsmouth, and why the very name had become synonymous with decay, disgrace, and alienation. It was Hammond's voice which brought me from Innsmouth back to safe and familiar Newburyport.

"I asked which size of bromo you wanted," he repeated in his piping voice.

"Oh, the small bottle will do," I replied, still watching through the front window as Sargent boarded his contraption. Somewhere in the distance a dog barked furiously. "Say, how long has Sargent's bus run through Newburyport?" I asked in as casual a manner as I could manage.

"Must be seven or eight years now," Hammond returned. "Started soon after the other lines, the Lawrence and the Atlantic, quit running to Innsmouth. They said it was because there were too few passengers to make it worthwhile, but my wife's brother used to be a mechanic for the Lawrence Company, and he told her it was because sooner or later every driver refused to go out there. They fired a few men over it, but nobody budged. Finally, they just up and quit service east of High Street. Pretty soon that old thing started wheezing into town. Nobody here liked it but there was no legal reason not to allow it. You wouldn't think to look at Sargent that he'd even be able to tell time, let alone keep a schedule. But he's always on time—ten a.m. and seven p.m., every day except Sundays and twice a year during the—'holidays' I guess you'd call them, that they have at the old Masonic Hall."

"Masons in Innsmouth?" I asked with amazement. "I had understood them to be completely inactive there since before the turn of the century!'

"There's not a Mason in this state as would set foot in that town," the druggist affirmed. "I didn't mean that Sargent is a Mason, God forbid. I'm sure he's a member of that group which took over the Hall 'round about '45, I think it was. 'Esoteric Order of Dagon' they call themselves, and from what the doc out there tells, they're as strong in members now as they've ever been. Maybe stronger. Seems they've forgotten all about Christian ideas and worship this Dagon and his kin. Supposed to be an ancient Philistine fertility god, with power over sea animals, or such. All the churches there were either boarded up or converted to heathen worship by the time of the Civil War. 'Course they keep strictly to themselves and don't abide curious visitors, so there's just the rumors to go on. Suits me just fine. I know more than I care to as it is, and I'm doing more talking about those people than I really want. But I've known you all your life, Thaddeus, and it's right that you should know at least that much—enough to steer you clear of any involvement with those folks. Sargent's never done anything for me to point a finger at, but I swear I feel like washing my hands every time he comes in here. And maybe I'm going blind, but it seems to me he's gotten a sight uglier since he started coming through here those years ago."

So saying, he shook his head and accepted the price of the remedy I had requested. I left the store with my purchase just as Sargent's bus coughed into life and, with a grinding of gears, pulled away from the curb and down the empty street. I sat in my auto and watched the bus disappear around the corner of the square to begin its return to that ill-rumored village.

In the days which followed I tried to turn my attentions to more practical concerns of business and away from my admittedly morbid interest in the decline and decay of the once healthy and prosperous coastal town. Although I was rewarded with some slight improvement in my financial affairs as a result of this attention, I could by no means suppress my fascination with Innsmouth and its aversive bus driver. I took to watching through my spyglass every day in the morning and evening to see that fuming, rattling conveyance pull up in front of Hammond's, discharge or pick up its infrequent passengers, and then clatter out of town. I found that by ascending to the cupola of my house, I could observe the bus for quite some distance as it made its way South along High Street, passed Old Town and Parker River, and finally disappeared as it swung East off of High Street toward the Manuxet River and Innsmouth. Except on those rare instances when I was away from home on business, I was as punctual as Sargent himself as I waited in my cupola each day, trying to observe every detail of his comings and goings in the hope of learning something new about this strangely compelling individual.

I followed this regimen faithfully for several weeks without learning anything of material interest. Then one evening late in the spring of 1925, I sat watching the familiar tableau of that decrepit vehicle as it left Market Square and made its way south on High Street. What was unusual about this instance, however, was that instead of proceeding along the highway toward Innsmouth, Sargent pulled his bus off the main road at Newburyport and proceeded east toward the coast. Even so mundane a difference as a change in route was intensely interesting to me and I was delighted that I was able to follow the progress of the vehicle as it continued all the way to the beach road and halted near the shore. The coach sat for perhaps a minute with no sign of activity. Then I saw Sargent descend from the vehicle and walk toward the water, wending his way between the many sand dunes which characterized that part of the coast. Although I had, by this time, switched to a more powerful telescope, the distance was too great to allow for detail. It seemed to me, however, that Sargent was carrying something heavy, for he walked in a very stiff and awkward gait. I lost sight of him as he passed behind a large, red-feathered dune, and my frustration at not being able to observe his activities increased with each passing moment. He re-emerged after several seconds, apparently having deposited his burden, for his gait had resumed the odd lurching shuffle with which I had become so familiar. Even at so great a distance I knew it when Sargent had started the bus's engine again, thanks to the cloud of gray smoke which it always released like an escaping djinn.

As soon as I had ascertained that the vehicle was indeed retracing its course westward, I rushed downstairs, backed my car out of the garage, and headed south on High Street. My curiosity was a compelling force, and I did not even attempt to resist it. It seemed to me to be the most reasonable thing in the world that I expend every effort to discover what Sargent had sequestered in the sand. As I drove, I became conscious of the fact that I might well meet Sargent's coach coming toward High Street if I made the turn onto the coast road before he regained the main highway. In order to prevent arousing his suspicions, therefore, I pulled my car off to the side of the thoroughfare just before reaching the coast road and parked behind a copse of trees which would somewhat obscure my vehicle while affording me a satisfactory view of the juncture of the two highways. I had not waited long before I heard the wheeze and rattle of the dilapidated machine as it approached the intersection. Sargent slowed but did not stop his bus at the junction, turned south on High Street, and clattered off into the incoming fog without appearing to have noticed the presence of my vehicle. As soon as the coach had disappeared into the mist, I started my engine and proceeded east down the coast road toward the shore. I found without difficulty the spot where Sargent had parked, and began following his unmistakable footprints out between the spray-swept dunes and toward the water line. As I proceeded I felt it was wise to exercise caution in my movements. I tried to set this uneasiness down to the effects which the rising fog was having upon my imagination, but continued to maintain a certain vigilance as I made my way along.

A light but chilling wind continued to bring the vapor in from seaward, obscuring the details of the landscape like a close-lying shroud. A gull descended noiselessly from the overcast sky and landed upon a low hillock several feet to my right, to be joined almost immediately by two more. The birds gave not the slightest sound, but appeared to be observing my passage with rapt interest. As I continued to follow Sargent's tracks, more sea birds dropped silently to the sands all about me. Even in my haste I noted the very unusual behavior of these creatures. Gulls, terns, cormorants, and even several of the little sandpipers seemed simply to sit and stare at me, as though in some sort of challenge to my presence there. It occurred to me that I might have wandered into one of their nesting habitats, and so had provoked this resentful scrutiny. I paid them scant attention after that, although I was not unaware that newcomers continued to swell their population minute by minute, each cocking a tiny black diamond of an eye upon my every step and movement. The prints which I followed led steadily down toward the water line, and as I rounded the last low dune I spied, through the restless arms of the fog, a dark object in the sand, perhaps twenty-five yards from where I stood. Sargent's prints led directly to that object. I hurried across the intervening distance and knelt in the sand beside my discovery.

It appeared to be a small chest of some sort, about twenty inches long and perhaps ten in width and depth. Its corners were quite rounded and the entire thing was constructed of materials which, to this day, I have been unable to identify. A jetty black it was, and seemed to possess properties of metal, wood, and even of some incredibly hard rubber or plastic. I knocked upon it with my knuckles and listened to the strange resonances which seemed to echo back and forth within it, as though across impossibly great distances. The chest was so expertly crafted that only by the closest scrutiny could I discern the merest hint of a seam where the upper and lower halves met. There was no way to know which was the front and which the back side of the case, for there were no hinges anywhere upon its surface. Four gleaming handles extended from the receptacle, one from each side. At first I took them to be of some alloy of gold, for their color seemed unmistakable. But as I curled my fingers beneath one of these grips I was astounded to be able to see my fingers, however dimly, through the aureate material. In my astonishment and perplexity I stood to my feet, scattering several of the shore birds which had landed in my proximity while I had been so deeply engrossed. All these, too, simply sat and gazed upon me with what appeared to be an interested indifference, as one might idly observe the tiny scurriers upon an ant hill. Being thus apprised of their presence, I took no further note of them. As I stood pondering my next move, I perceived by the increasing salt spray that the tide was coming in rapidly. I don't believe that I had ever, or have ever since, seen so rapid a tidal movement. With each incoming wave the sea gained perceptible conquest of the land. I have wondered, since that day, whether the beaches of the world belong more truly to the solid earth or to the ancient, unknowable sea? Even now I am alarmed for their safety when I see children cavorting on the ocean sands at Salmon Creek, or see lovers strolling along the cliffs at Bodega Head. The sea has its dolorous secrets to tell, and tell them it does, in the evening, at sunset. It whispers its primal lore in the crashing of the breakers on the rocks and cliffs at the setting of the sun, and mutters its riddles in the swirling waters of the tide pools at midnight. But on that evening of more than fifty years ago I stood calmly before the incoming tide and realized that I had but a single decision to make, and that very quickly. Was I to leave this remarkable casket where it lay for the waters to engulf and hide forever, or should I take it with me back to Newburyport for further study?

The question had no sooner formed itself in my mind than I knew the obvious, the only possible, course of action. Regardless of its legal ownership or of Sargent's mysterious intentions for this extraordinary object, I must and would rescue it from the sand and continue my investigations of its properties and possible contents in the comfort and security of my home. I bent, grasped one of the golden handles, and lifted the heavy case from the dampened sands. The instant I did so, the innumerable birds which had continued to arrive and to group themselves about me gave voice to a single horrendous screeching cry, as of a thousand souls deposited en masse onto the white-hot floor of Hell and, as one, threw themselves upward and disappeared silently into the eastern fog. Not a solitary bird remained anywhere upon the beach. Amazed and more than a little shaken, I could only stand gaping, my eyes unable to move from the spot where I had seen the last of the birds disappear into the approaching mist.

II

It was the splash of water about my shoes which brought me back to the present moment, for the tide now appeared to be moving in faster even than before. Stepping backward out of the water, I wasted no time in retracing my footprints through the damp sand and back to the roadside where I had parked my car. Depositing my prize on the back seat, I started the engine and drove back to town without incident, save that the fog was by now so thick that I was unable to exceed a speed of twenty miles per hour for the entirety of the short drive. As I drove, I pondered the inexplicable behavior of the birds. They had seemed completely fearless of my presence during the entire time that I was intruding upon their domain, so it was inconceivable to me that my act of picking up the chest had so terrified them. I finally settled upon the belief that the creatures must have reacted to some noise which had been beyond the range of human audition, although I could not imagine what the source of such a sound might have been.

The lowering sky was nearly dark by the time I drove into the garage beside my house, and the heavy layer of clouds and mist accentuated that darkness with a subtle sense of intangible imprisonment. I was glad to finally get inside my study, where I turned on several lamps and began more closely to examine the singular ebon casket. Although I searched painstakingly for some method of opening the chest, it proved to be completely smooth and without markings of any sort. The two halves of the case were so tightly sealed that not even a knife blade could be slipped between them. Having thus failed to discover any possible contents, I turned my attention toward another avenue of inquiry. As an amateur chemist I was not unfamiliar with the various means of testing an unknown material, and had at my disposal several of the more commonly used acids and reagents. Try as I might I was unable to chip a piece from the case for testing, and so was forced to apply the different vitriolic substances directly to the casket itself. My acids were so ineffectual that I thought they might have lost their potency over time. A test with a match stick (which was readily dissolved) dispelled that notion. Only some light grayish spots indicated the areas which I had tested with the acids, and no pitting of the material was visible even beneath a powerful magnifying lens. Fire had absolutely no visible effect whatever, and the rapidity with which the material dissipated applied heat was utterly without precedent in my experience. The only success achieved through all my efforts lay in confirmation of the belief that the substance of the remarkable chest was altogether unknown and, by the methods available to me, undiscoverable.

By this time I was very tired and immensely frustrated. I wanted nothing more than to forget the whole matter for the balance of the evening and try to get some sleep. I placed the palm of my hand on one of the semi-translucent grips and, with some force, pushed the case away from me and against a heavy stack of chemistry texts. When the handle on the opposite side struck the stack of books, I was amazed to feel the grip under my palm recede into the case a fraction of an inch, and to see the upper half of the container spring open to about the width of a finger. For a few seconds I was too surprised to act, but quickly recovered and inserted a pencil into the opening to prevent its accidental reclosure. I pulled the case toward me and turned it so that the light from my desk lamp would fall full upon its contents when the lid was drawn back. I drew a short breath, held it, and opened the cover so that it rested flat upon the desk top.

The object which lay within was both exquisitely beautiful and utterly alien. Pocketed between cushions of an unknown, neutral-colored fiber which lined each half of the casket lay the most extraordinary example of the goldsmith's art which I had ever seen. The piece was obviously an ornament of some sort, although its bizarre configuration made its application anything but obvious. Its identification as a tiara or coronet would have been simple enough had it not been for the thing's oddity of proportion, for it consisted of a continuous band of a lustrous golden alloy which supported at its front eight fantastic jewels. The strange proportion to which I refer lay in the outlandishly elliptical shape of the headband itself which, although only about eight inches across at its widest point, was at least sixteen inches long from front to back! An instant numbing shock accompanied my realization that no human head, regardless of possible cranial abnormality, could conceivably support such an ornament. I then recalled a bit of my old anthropological studies and remembered that several cultures of the Far East often decorated their religious statuary with adornments of precious gems and metals. Although I could recollect no deity or demon of any religion which might be graced with such a peculiarly shaped embellishment, I was certain that I had hit upon the only possible explanation.

I was less startled but no less puzzled as I began to examine the gems themselves. Four rubescent, spherical stones sat atop four thin golden spindles, two on the right and two on the left side of the tiara. Each rear spindle was two or three inches taller than the one in front. At first I took these stones to be rubies, but upon closer inspection I discerned minuscule silvery glints of light in each of the gems, ruling out the possibility of their having any familiar identity. In the center of the headpiece, between the four sanguine jewels, rose three successively higher spindles, wider at their bases than the other four but of approximately equal thickness. At the top of each of these miniature spires sat what could only have been a black pearl of the most perfect color, texture, and shape imaginable. Their worth must have been all but incalculable, and I must confess to a slight trembling of my hands as I bent to examine the stone which I had reserved for my final scrutiny. In the front and center of the coronet, so as to be in position over the forehead of its wearer, rested in its setting a huge ovoid gem about four inches long and perhaps three wide.

As baffled as I had been in trying to identify the four crimson jewels, I was doubly mystified, even vaguely alarmed, by this inexplicable stone. A very dark green in color, it was veined throughout with tiny black filaments suggestive of a network of blood vessels. In and among the branches of these fibrils I could make out what appeared to be tiny flecks of gold or a gold-like metal. The mineral was clearly not jade or emerald but metal belonging to some lapidary classification with which I was totally unfamiliar. What I found most disquieting about this gem, however, had nothing to do with its strange composition and coloring. In examination of the texture of the thing I ran my finger across its surface and was astonished to feel it to be wet and extremely slick, almost as though the stone had a thin coating of oil over its exterior. When I looked at my finger under the light of the lamp, I found it to be perfectly dry. I repeated the test with identical results. I had dabbled in most of the physical sciences in my younger days, including geology and a smattering of lapidary, but nothing in my experience offered a parallel to this anomalous mineral. More than a little disturbed at my inability to identify even the geologic family to which this stone belonged, I determined to take the tiara to a jeweler the following day for his analysis of its many confounding properties before I turned it over to the police. Having recalled reports of similar jewelry having come out of Innsmouth and rumors of old-time smuggling, I thought it not impossible that Joe Sargent might have been involved in some illegal enterprise. His leaving of so valuable an object as this weird headpiece on a deserted beach was certainly a behavior which prompted suspicion, and it seemed more than likely that the police would want to question him in its regard.

In addition to the remarkable gems which I have described, the piece was also decorated with a series of humanoid characters in bas relief of the most excellent workmanship and detail. These appeared to be the water-demons of some Far Eastern mythology, for the artist had endowed the creatures with as many ichthyic characteristics as human, even to the extent of carving tiny gills on each side of their necks. Most of these figures embellished the headband itself, and were poised in positions of swimming—more in the manner of frogs than of humans. A few of these figures, however, I saw to be in attitudes of worship or supplication. This suggested to me that perhaps these were not the creatures worshiped by the coronet's artisans. For more clues as to its possible origin I resigned myself to wait until I was able to consult others more learned in these matters than I.

Glancing at the mantle timepiece, I saw that it was almost ten o'clock and remembered that in the evening's excitement I had neglected to prepare so much as a sandwich for supper. As I pushed back my chair from the desk and stood to stretch, I distinctly heard a scraping noise against the pane of one of the study's windows. As a man of independent means I was not unaware of the danger of burglary, although such occurrences were admittedly rare in quiet Newburyport. I furtively unlocked the drawer of my desk and withdrew my father's old but trustworthy Webley revolver. Crossing the room swiftly, I threw open the curtains. There, preening itself on the window sill, was a rather large seagull. It cocked its head, eyed me unconcernedly, and continued its grooming. I laughed aloud at my unwonted nervousness and left the room to prepare a quick meal before retiring. As I pushed the button to turn on the kitchen lights, I was jolted again by a flurry of motion at the window over the sink. Had my perceptions been an instant slower I would most certainly have shot the little sandpiper which sat upon the sill. Realizing then that I was far too jittery to handle a firearm responsibly that evening, I shut it in a cupboard and decided to leave it there until morning.

I prepared a cold supper, rinsed the dishes, and went upstairs for some badly needed sleep. Gaining my bed, I tried for perhaps an hour to relax before I gave it up as a lost cause and arose to sit in the rocker at my bedroom window, as was my habit when troubled with insomnia. The fog had continued to roll in all evening so that by this time, around midnight, I could just barely see the houses across the street by the muted glare of the few street lamps which lined the road.

As I sat rocking, perhaps almost dozing, I was snapped awake by the sight of a shadow stirring in the yard below the bedroom window. It moved again just a bit, and I was relieved to see that the creeper, whatever it was, was far too small to have been any human threat. Probably one of the many elegant and courtly felines which graced the neighborhood, I surmised. Purely for curiosity's sake, I took a flashlight out of my nightstand and shone its yellow beam down at the spot where I had seen the movement. In the circumference of its glow I saw a tern sitting on my lawn. I swept the light across the yard and discovered at least fifty of the sea birds at rest on the grass. I thought this to be not terribly unusual, since coastal birds often come inland shortly before a spell of rough weather, although I had not been aware of any approaching storm. I shone my light through the mist and across the street and was surprised to see not a single bird upon any neighbor's lawn. Up and down the street I peered, as far as the light's beam could penetrate, and saw that mine was the only property to host such an assemblage. I switched off the light and rocked in darkness, pondering a natural explanation for this phenomenon. The more I considered the question, the more disconcerted I seemed to become.

It was then that I decided that a whiskey and soda would go a long way toward quieting my nerves. I slipped on my robe and went downstairs toward the parlor for the beverage's ingredients. As I passed the kitchen door I was arrested by a muffled scraping noise, all but inaudible, coming from the direction of the cellar. I crossed the kitchen floor to the door of the cellar, remembered where I had secreted my revolver, and retrieved it. Listening at the door I heard nothing, but soon began to smell a disquietingly familiar odor. Wafting from beneath the cellar door, magnified ten-

fold, was the same fishy redolence which, from the day I met him, I forever
afterward associated with the repellent Joe Sargent. Fortunately, the switch
to the light above the cellar stairs was beside the door and near at hand. At
the same instant, I threw open the door and shoved the light button, gun
extended at the top stairs. I saw nothing but the steps leading down into
the veiling shadows. I was about to shut the door upon the increasingly
strong piscine reek when I noticed with a shock of fear that the shadows on
the stairs were not still! The light bulb, suspended from the ceiling on its
cord, was swaying gently from side to side! There had been an intruder after
all! I considered going down into the cellar to investigate but, judging dis-
cretion to be the more intelligent alternative, I closed and locked the door
and began making my way down the hall toward the telephone in order to
summon the police. I was somewhat surprised to find the fishy odor to have
penetrated all the way to the vestibule where the phone was located, but
decided to postpone going back to close the kitchen door until after I had
made the call. A slight scuffling sound behind me was all the warning of
danger I had before my arms were pinned from behind and a filthy rag
clamped over my face. The gun was struck from my hand and I struggled
briefly but ineffectually. The last sensation I experienced before lapsing into
insentience was the choking pungency of ether mingled with the stench of
rotting fish.

III

Awareness returned not by degrees but with a single gut-wrenching heave.
Had I not been lying on my side I might well have been asphyxiated on my
own bile. I spat the foulness from my mouth and breathed great gulps of
fetid air. I lay upon a stone floor with my hands and feet tightly trussed. The
only illumination in the small, rock-walled chamber in which I had been left
was an ancient kerosene lantern hung from a hook in one of the heavy
wooden beams which supported the ceiling. By its dim light I saw that the
room's only entrance appeared to be a door at the top of a set of stairs in a
far corner of the room. I had no idea where I was, other than the scant information which the sound of distant breakers suggested. I was completely at
a loss regarding the reason for my abduction, but I realized that I might
never have the time to speculate upon these matters if I did not make an
attempt at escape while the opportunity afforded itself. I tore at the bonds
which pinioned my hands behind my back, but succeeded only in bloodying my fingers with the effort. Bracing my back against a damp wall, I
brought myself to an upright position and began hopping about the room
in search of any sharp projection upon which I might scrape my bonds. I
located what appeared to be the sharpest edge I could reach upon one of the

great stones in the walls, and had just begun to work the cords back and forth on this prominence when I heard voices at the top of the stairs. I had just resumed my seated position when the door opened and two figures descended toward me. As the men entered the dim halo of light from the lantern, I saw that one of them was a middle-aged, haggard, though otherwise nondescript-looking gentleman. What struck me most pointedly about this man was that he appeared to be weary to the depth of his soul.

I thought momentarily that the other man was Joe Sargent, but then saw that this individual was even more grotesquely misshapen than the revolting bus driver, and gave off an even more nauseating odor. He wore no cap, and the terrible deformation of his hairless skull was a thing shocking to behold. From the vertical center of his face, the skull sloped sharply back to such a radical extent that the orbits of his huge, unblinking eyes were located on opposite sides of his head. His hands were clearly webbed to his fingers' middle joints, and his feet, clad in slippers of soft felt, were easily the size of Sargent's own. The creature's skin could hardly be called such for it was a dull, dead gray in color and bore plain evidence of the formation of scales just below its surface. The nose and chin were so atrophied that they were only a mocking parody of normal features. His breath seemed quite labored and his throat, hidden beneath swaths wound about his neck, swelled visibly with each rasping inhalation. His malformation plainly extended to his vocal cords, for speech came only with some effort and sounded, to my ears, more like the gurgling of water through a pipe than anything akin to a human voice.

"Mr. Hess, how kind of you to join us," he said jeeringly. "I hope that you are not too greatly inconvenienced, but your participation in our— activities here this morning will be deeply appreciated by all. On that you have my solemn word!"

"If it's ransom you're after," I replied with sham truculence, "only I have access to my accounts, and I can't very well meet your demands if I am kept a prisoner here, can I?"

"Oh, you will most certainly meet our demands, Mr. Hess," he returned with contempt in his loathsome voice, "but your heirs may keep your money. It is your blood which G'thuga wishes!" he announced with an ululation which no sane mind would have identified as laughter. "He is your responsibility, Dr. Kentfield," he announced as he moved, in his awkward gait, toward stairway. "Make certain that he remains in good health until the ceremony. Any deviation from your instructions will result in— well, you remember our agreement!" he gurgled invidiously. The door slammed behind him and his shuffling footsteps receded from my hearing.

Kentfield moved to the nearest wall and sank to a seated position, his back against its mildewed surface. After he had sat thus, with his head in his hands, for a minute or so, I ventured to speak.

"Are you a physician?" I inquired. His nod served as reply. "Will you tell me where I am, and what that maniac was talking about?" After several seconds the man raised his head and stared steadily at the glowing lantern.

"Maniac. I wish to Heaven he was only a raving maniac," he muttered. "That was Barnabas Marsh, Exalted Priest of the Esoteric Order of Dagon. He isn't human anymore," he stated matter-of-factly. "Never was, I guess. I'm George Kentfield, the only physician Innsmouth has had for God knows how long."

"This is Innsmouth, then?" I asked with a chill of apprehension. He nodded. "What do they want with me? What's that thing Marsh said wants my blood?"

"G'thuga. I've seen her only once, and that by accident. God spare any sane man from such an accident! I don't know how to tell you what she is except by comparison. You saw Marsh. He appears to be about half human, half ... other. G'thuga is a huge female of the race. I suppose she looked about the same as Marsh at one time, maybe forty or fifty years ago. There's nothing even faintly human about her anymore. There's no time to explain all of it except to say that the Innsmouth 'taint' or 'look' that has become so shunned in this area is the result of the interbreeding of the families of Innsmouth with inhuman amphibious creatures originally from somewhere in the South Seas. Obed Marsh, Barnabas' ancestor, introduced them here almost a hundred years ago. Many resisted and were slaughtered. Not many pure-blooded humans left here, and most of them deranged. Like old Zadok Allen, who told me only too recently the story I'm telling you. I started my practice here about a year ago—felt it was my duty, since no other physician would work here. I thought it was due to simple prejudice. Now that I know the truth, it's too late!" He buried his face in his hands and began to sob.

I realized with a start that this must be the doctor whose wife and son had vanished. Their disappearance now took on a fearsomely sinister cast. Kentfield recovered himself somewhat, took a deep breath, and continued his narrative.

"My wife and little boy were out walking on the beach about three months ago. They never came home. The sheriff made inquiries but had nothing tangible to pursue. They were supposed drowned but their bodies were never recovered. Soon afterward, Marsh, whom I had never before seen, came to my house and told me that my wife and son were being held by the Order of Dagon, and that they would be freed unharmed only if I cooperated with their demands."

He lapsed again into silence, and I considered the content of his fantastic tale. Although his story explained much about the history of this town which had been only mystery before, even so I would have dismissed Kentfield's tale as the phantasm of a brain too long soaked in alcohol had I not seen the abhorrent Marsh with my own eyes. But seen him I had, and I found myself accepting the doctor's story with full confidence. He spoke again.

"Since that day I've procured little-known drugs for them, performed abominable surgeries, signed a vast number of death certificates for patients I've never seen, and done some things about which I shall never speak. Even the ether they used on you last night came from my office. Marsh continues to give me his word that my wife and boy are alive and unharmed, but he will not let me see them. And now you—" he ended with a great sigh.

"Yes, what about me?" I demanded. "I'm certainly sympathetic to your troubles and I'd help you any way that I could, but I seem to have a serious problem of my own just now. Why have they kidnapped me, and what do they want? What's this about my blood?"

"Yesterday you found a strange chest on the beach and took it home, right? You opened it and found a strange golden headpiece. That headpiece is called the Crown of Hydra—one of the gods these creatures worship and serve. In a very short while G'thuga is to be honored, becoming a Daughter of Dagon, the male counterpart of Hydra. As such, she will become handmaiden of the supreme deity of her race, a thing of titanic size and power they call Kithoolhew. Yesterday, when Sargent put the Crown of Hydra down on the beach, it was supposed to have been retrieved by one of their undersea priests for a special blessing in a hidden temple they have on the ocean bottom not far from where you found it. The ceremony was scheduled for last night, and when you took it you upset their timetable. Your town is lucky that their agents found you. They would have leveled Newburyport to find the Crown, if they'd had to. And now, according to their religion, you've defiled the Crown. It's probably being ritually purified in that temple right now. And in recompense for her inconvenience in having to wait for her coronation, G'thuga is to be permitted to—" He looked me full in the eyes. "Do I have to say it?"

"I think that will be unnecessary, doctor," bubbled a hatefully familiar voice from the head of the stairs. "I feel certain that Mr. Hess understands his position with admirable clarity." Marsh began to descend the stairs, taking great care not to lose his balance on steps designed for human feet.

"Be assured," he continued, "that everything the good doctor has seen fit to tell you is true. It is his good fortune that you will not be able to use this information against us. The Crown of Hydra has indeed been cleansed of your profaning touch, Mr. Hess," he rasped, halting before me where I sat, still bound, against the wall. "The ceremony is being readied for the crowning of the Daughter of Dagon, handmaiden to glorious Cthulhu himself. As such, she will be Innsmouth's emissary to The Master, and will gain much honor for his servants in this far realm. Now we must go, but never fear. We will not begin the festivities without you, landwalker! Come, doctor. We will leave Mr. Hess to make his peace with his own paltry gods."

The doctor rose and, without a backward glance, followed Marsh up the stairs and shut the door behind him. As soon as I heard the click of the door latch, I arose frantically and began scraping my wrist bonds against the sharp outcropping of rock which I had found earlier. I must have been at this for the better part of an hour without tangible result when the door again opened and the doctor, alone this time, descended the stairs carrying a kerosene lantern. He moved swiftly to my side and whispered frantically in my ear, his voice quavering in his agitation.

"We're escaping—both of us. We'll have to pretend you're still a prisoner, but I'm reasonably sure we can get out of town. We have nothing to lose in trying."

"But—your family—" I began.

"Dead," he replied with a sob of grief and rage. "Zadok Allen told me. He and I have gotten drunk together dozens of times, and I guess he just found out what really happened to my wife and son. They were killed—murdered—when they came upon something on the beach they shouldn't have seen. Allen wouldn't say what it was, but just said there was nothing to hold me here anymore, and that I should get out fast. It seems I'm becoming more of a liability than an asset to their plans, and I'm scheduled to join you as part of this morning's show. I'll explain more as we go, but we've got to move fast. I'll cut your bonds on your feet, but we'd better leave your hands tied for a while yet." I insisted, however, that he cut those too, so I proposed to hold my wrists against my stomach to keep the loosened ropes in place.

Kentfield informed me that the stone chamber in which we stood was one of many similar rooms situated beneath the Hall of the Esoteric Order of Dagon, and that the ceremony marking the coronation of the ichthyic monstrosity called G'thuga was to begin at any moment. Indeed, I could already hear the beginning strains of some alien litany being sung somewhere above our heads. I use the word "sung" here with serious reservations, for the voices which I heard that day held at least as much of an animal quality as human. I may use words such as barking, bleating, honking, braying, and howling in an attempt to convey the dissonance of the ever-increasing cacophony, and these might suffice in the description of the noises of familiar beasts. But when such sounds as these are employed in the formation of distinct words—and even in the chanting of a reprehensible liturgy—then my poor powers of depiction must fail. It is beyond me to communicate the depth of horror and disgust which were engendered in me by that demonic uproar. I wanted only to be gone from that temple of Hell-on-Earth with all possible speed.

The doctor explained that he had left his auto parked, keys in the ignition, just outside the Hall on the street beyond the door which was to be our exit from the building. There were two guards at the top of the stairs, but he felt fairly sure that he could bluff our way through them, since they could not know that he no longer feared for his wife and child. He opened his coat and showed me a heavy, short-barreled revolver stuck in his waistband. He said that it might not only provide us with an advantage during our escape, but that it was his personal insurance against being taken prisoner should our desperate efforts fail. As he explained his plan of escape, I noted that the caricature of singing above us was increasing in volume and pitch, and that a far deeper and louder voice had been added to the general clamor—one which seemed to echo all the voices which had ever sounded beneath the waves of the unsleeping sea. Kentfield blanched when he heard it.

"That's G'thuga," he told me. "They're probably crowning her right now. If we don't go now, we'll never stand a chance."

As we had agreed, I preceded him and he held the lantern in one hand and the gun to my back, as though I was still his prisoner. As we ascended the stairs toward the door I could hear the chanting in the main part of the building with frightful clarity:

"Cthulhu fhtagn—G'thuga w'gah! Ng'goka y'gotha ooboshu R'lyeh! Cthulhu fhtagn! Fhtagn!"

This they repeated over and over again with increasing fervor. I hear it still in my dreams. I paused and took a deep breath at the top of the stairs, and Kentfield nodded for me to proceed. I opened the door and stepped out into what appeared to be a storage room, dimly lit by electric bulbs. I was surprised to see that the two guards which the doctor had mentioned appeared to be completely human, one apparently a lascar and the other of Malaysian extraction. The lascar spoke.

"Where you go?" he challenged Kentfield with menace in his voice. "Priest say he come for this man."

"Marsh told me he wanted the prisoner brought into the Hall by the front entrance," the doctor replied. "He said that's how G'thuga wants it done."

I merely stood with my head bowed as though drugged or exhausted, inwardly praying with every fiber of my being. The brutish guards fidgeted and whispered nervously to one another, not wishing to make this decision but fearing evil consequences should their detainment of us run afoul of the wishes of Marsh and his monstrous companion. The two men appeared to reach an agreement, and the lascar pulled a wicked-looking dirk from its sheath while the Malaysian hurried from the room.

"Tibo goes to ask. We all stay here," he announced with a leer, making a great show of cleaning his filthy fingernails with the knife.

"Well, I guess there's nothing for it," Kentfield said resignedly. In one swift motion he drew the revolver, aimed the weapon, and blew the lascar's brains out the back of his head. Galvanized to instant action, the doctor pushed me toward a door in the outer wall, thrusting the lantern into my hand. Once through the door and outside, I saw the doctor's auto at the curb in the light of the dawn sun. We were only halfway to the car when we were beset by three Innsmouth residents in varying degrees of metamorphosis. I dropped my antagonist with the knife I had snatched up from the lascar's dead hand and turned back to help the doctor.

"No!" he shouted. "Start the engine!"

I finished the distance to the car and started the engine without difficulty. With the motor thus running, I started back to lend what assistance I could when I saw Kentfield shoot one of his assailants in the chest, leaving but one to deal with. This one turned and ran back toward the front of the Hall to be met by a vast surge of worshipers from within the structure, summoned forth by the pistol shots and commotion. Some appeared to be human, but most were clearly tainted with the same ichthyic characteristics which Barnabas Marsh so markedly displayed, and which I had seen in bas relief upon the tiara. I expected them to rush us en masse but, inexplicably, they stopped several yards away from us and seemed to be peering behind us expectantly. Then, perhaps twenty yards to our rear, Marsh descended the rear steps of Dagon Hall, resplendent in ceremonial robes and wearing a smaller version of the coronet which I had found. Behind him, with a shuffling, hopping parody of ambulation, followed the creature whose appetite I had been ordained to satisfy. This was G'thuga—a tremendous semianthropoid abomination which could only have been conceived in the nightmare pits of Hell. Fully seven feet tall, the thing must have weighed at least five hundred pounds. Its gray-green scales glistened with slime in the morning sun and its webbed, taloned claws opened and shut continually. A ridge of bony spines began at the base of its hunched neck and ran the length of its back and ended at the tip of its vertically flattened tail. Its head was massive, with features at once piscine and batrachian, and upon that highridged brow rested that terrible tiara, its gems flashing brilliantly in the rising sun—the Crown of Hydra! As horrendous as such a beast must have appeared under any circumstances, it was doubly shocking for me to see reflected in its rheumy, red-rimmed eyes the unmistakable glint of a fiendish intelligence—an intelligence aflame with hatred and the desire to rend and to feed!

Marsh neither spoke nor gestured but merely stepped to one side, affording the behemoth unobstructed passage to us. With its first lumbering step toward us Kentfield raised his revolver and emptied his last four bullets into the thing. Rather than stopping or even slowing the monstrosity, the pain of its little wounds seemed only to infuriate it to swifter action. With a speed I would not have thought possible, it leaped the remaining distance separating us, grasped my companion by the shoulders, and lifted him off his feet. Engulfing his head in her steaming maw, she clamped shut her jaws and shook her head violently from side to side. I shall not describe what fell to the dead and brittle grass when she turned to face me. I turned and ran a few paces but saw my way blocked by well over a hundred worshipers of Cthulhu. They kept a very respectful distance from the tiaraed thing, but were equally intent on preventing my escape. Spinning around again to face the sea-demon, I was momentarily thrown off-balance by the weight of the full kerosene lantern which Kentfield had shoved into my hand back in the storage room. The creature advanced upon me, Kentfield's blood still running in rivulets from its champing jaws. As it extended its front claws and crouched for the leap which would hideously end my life, I drew back the lantern and pitched it full in the face of the shambling horror. The beast threw up its claw and shattered the vessel to bits, releasing a deluge of flaming kerosene which rained down over the monster's bulk.

With a bellow of fear and rage which must have been audible in Arkham, Dagon's daughter raced blindly toward the crowd of terror-stricken residents which had blocked my escape, spattering many of them with the burning fluid and batting and trampling others out of its path as it disappeared around the corner of Dagon Hall and toward the sea. As the members of the throng scattered in their panic, I raced toward the still-idling auto. Marsh made a clumsy attempt to stop me, but his legs and feet were no longer suitable for running, and his voluminous robes encumbered him greatly. I gained the vehicle without mishap and drove off in the direction which I hoped corresponded to the one Kentfield had said we would take out of town. By accident or by a merciful Providence I was able to reach the main highway out to Clipper Street before my pursuers had a chance to locate me in their own autos. I knew that I dared not go back to Newburyport, so I followed Clipper Street to Essex Road and didn't slow the vehicle until I had reached the outskirts of Ipswich.

IV

After wiring my bank for funds, I obtained a ticket that very day at Arkham North Station and made for Wichita, my sole aim to be as far from the sea as possible. I made anonymous reports of my experience by phone and by mail to the Massachusetts State Police, but made no further inquiries about the matter. I heard rumors a few years later about a full-scale government investigation of the goings-on in Innsmouth, and even of the use of explosives in destroying certain structures both in the town itself and a short distance offshore. I never knew whether my reports had instigated that investigation, but I hoped that I had been in some measure responsible.

I had a real estate agent sell my house and had my belongings and accounts transferred to Kansas, and made that state my permanent residence. In time I married and my wife bore two children, a boy and a girl, both of whom moved out to California shortly after her death from cancer in 1979. I soon grew very lonesome for their company and decided to move to California, even though their homes in the Santa Rosa area were rather nearer the ocean than I liked. I reasoned, however, that over fifty years had passed since the incident at Innsmouth and that all of my enemies from that corrupted village must by now have been long dead. Besides, three thousand miles separated Innsmouth from Santa Rosa—it would take more years than I had remaining to me for them to find me. And so I made the journey with scant apprehension, and took up residence in the lovely hills east of Santa Rosa. All went very well for a time, and my children's families welcomed me with a degree of warmth which met my fondest hopes.

Then I began to see them. First, a register clerk at a supermarket— her great, staring eyes boring into my own with a spark of recognition. Then, in my own neighborhood, I noticed that the man who delivered bottled water to my neighbor had oddly tufted skin at each side of his neck and under his ears. His mouth seemed to open very wide as he wished me a good morning.

My "breakdown" came when I was taking a meal at a local steak house. I had placed my order of prime rib, but when the waitress arrived she set before me the seafood platter. I looked up at her to protest the mistake, but the words froze in my throat. Her wide, glassy eyes opened just a trifle further and seemed to exhume from the depths of my memory all the horror and loathing of a morning in Innsmouth more than half a century before. I don't know what happened next. The doctors at Oakridge told me that I attacked her with a steak knife, screaming about demons and kerosene. She did not die, but they have kept me locked up ever since, first at Oakridge and now here, not a mile from the sea. Are they out there even now? Does the thing called Barnabas Marsh hold blasphemous sacrament in some watery temple off the Northern California coast? God help me—I believe it is true. The dreams tell me so. They bring me visions of weed-flowing spires deep below the waves, and of maledictions chanted in aqueous chambers litten by phosphorescent marine fungi. The dreams bring sounds, too—voices from the past. I know they will find me. I know they have already found me, for the chanting tells me that all things are now ready. How they will reach me I do not know, but reach me they shall. I shall not struggle, for I realize now that hope is but a cruel self-deception. Every night now the chanting haunts my sleep:

> "*Cthulhu fhtagn—G'thuga w'gah!*
> *Ng'goka y'gotha ooboshu R'lyeh!*
> *Cthulhu fhtagn! Fhtagn!*"

I shall be glad to see it end.

About "Custos Sanctorum"

Roger Johnson is best known as one of the *Ghosts & Scholars* gang, a torchbearer for the noble tradition of M. R. Jamesian spectral fiction. But he is a Lovecraftian, too. Perhaps it is the osmosis ecclesiasticalism that sooner or later rubs off on Jamesians that makes Johnson more sensitive than many Innsmouthers to the absolutely crucial dimension of ritual and initiation that lies at the heart of "The Shadow over Innsmouth" (see my introduction to this volume). "Custos Sanctorum" may be the only Innsmouth pastiche/sequel to grant the appropriate centrality to this feature of the Innsmouth mythos.

"Custos Sanctorum" originally appeared in Johnson's collection *Deep Things Out of Darkness* (Garrie Hall: 1987).

Custos Sanctorum

by Roger Johnson

Wrabsey
Nr Maldon
Essex
13th Nov. 1832
to Mr. Salter,
Wyvern.
Cousin,

You have asked me about the coming of a stranger to this town, of whose visit rumour only has reached you. One, as you have heard, claiming kinship with us of the Blood. Be sure, then, that none save Those who guard us may know the full truth, but that I, Their servant, can tell as much as any man. From me you shall learn what befell.

It was upon the second Saturday of last month that the man came to Wrabsey. His appearance should have been instantly noted, for strangers are few and unwelcome, as you will appreciate, in this small town, whose days of market and fair are long vanished. Nevertheless, he was not remarked, it seems, until he presented himself within my office in Fish Street and asked to have word with me. I saw a person of middling height, slim but stooping slightly, plainly dressed, and with dark hair receding somewhat from a scalp whose greyish pallor matched that of his face and hands. His age, I suppose, was about thirty, but there was such a set of wrinkles upon his face, and his pale eyes bulged so hugely, that I could not be sure. In short, you see, he had about him that look which distinguishes us from the common rank of man.

His greeting was fair, but brief. "Mr. Martyr," said he, "I know that you are the leader of the people in this town." I replied, somewhat wary, that to see the leader he should enquire for Amos Luckin, the Deputy, at the Moot Hall. "I know of the Deputy," he said, "and am persuaded that you, and not he, are the man I seek. Let me make myself known. My name is Walter Garlick, and I have come here from Gate's Quay, on the rocky coast of Dorset. My home, if not my family, must be known to you."

The name of Gate's Quay was, of course, familiar to me, as it is to you, cousin. "Then you come in the service," said I, "of Those whom we serve?" I spoke with caution, for one does not carelessly utter the names of power, but my mind was set easy—in part, at least—by the instant assurance that Mr. Garlick was a faithful adherent of C———. He had, he claimed, a mind to settle here in Wrabsey, and so forge stronger links of friendship between two enclaves indissolubly bound by ties of blood and allegiance.

For the moment nothing further could profitably be said on so important a matter. I resolved to call as quickly as might be a meeting extraordinary of the Elect, and meanwhile to show all courtesy to this unbidden guest. Over a glass of good port wine, I commended to him the facilities of the *Dolphin* Inn, under the ownership of my good friend Silas Choate, while he sought for a proper dwelling in the town. "And I myself," said I, "may be of service to you there, for my small practice has mainly to do with property. A man must live in this world, you know, even while preparing himself for that other that we know of. There is a house but recently empty upon Murrell Hill belonging to Thomas Warden, who is of high rank in the Elect. Surely he would be glad to see it occupied by a kinsman such as you."

After some further talk of this nature, I asked him how matters stood in his native town—for you know, cousin, that I am of an enquiring mind, and hold that we who are so encompassed upon all sides by mere humanity do need to keep aware of the doings of our brethren, that we may better serve our Masters. To my questions he answered in straight but general terms, telling me nothing that I did not already know, but revealing a knowledge of Gate's Quay that certainly seemed authentic. It was a pleasant conversation, though necessarily guarded upon one side at least, for Walter Garlick, whatever else he might be, was an intelligent man and educated. At last, bidding my clerk to oversee the office until I should return, I conducted Mr. Garlick out into Fish Street and thence by way of Salt Street and Church Lane to The

Hythe, where stands the *Dolphin*. As we passed St. Mary's
Church, he looked with an appraising eye and remarked, "It
seems in good repair, friend."

"To be sure," said I, "for there are still in Wrabsey many of the
common sort of humanity who cling to their fathers' faith."

"As we to ours," said he, "and with solid reason. But do you not
find dissension between the men who attend upon Christ and the
Chosen who swell the congregation of Dagon?"

"There has long been unease," I admitted, "but you may find
this country somewhat different from your own. These marshlands, bare and bleak, that sever us from the rest of Essex, breed
men to suit them. In this land that is not quite land, nor yet
quite sea, the people are accustomed to uncover the secrets of
both. They are, you may say, amphibious. Wrabsey is in England,
but it is no more *of* England than is Gate's Quay, or Wyvern, or
that place of wonders where our fathers dwell. No, the church is
under the care of the Vicar of Tolleshunt D'Arcy, but those who
attend know enough to keep their beliefs to themselves. They
know that we, and not he, are their kin. Will it surprise you to
learn that some of them—one a warden—are faithful servants of
the Council of the Elect?"

Surprised he was, none the less. "It is not so in Gates Quay!
Spies, are they?"

"It would be wrong to call them so. They are but men. Men who
know which way this world tends, and suspect to whom it truly
belongs. It is not from within that danger comes, but from without—ah! But here is The Hythe, and yonder the inn. Good day
to you, friend. You shall be summoned as soon as may be to
meet us formally and, I trust, to be admitted to the mysteries of
the town."

* * *

Things are not done hastily among us, who have a sacred end in
view. None the less, upon the very next evening, the Sunday, the
Inner Council of the Elect was gathered within the great Hall of
Dagon, upon Murrell Hill, ready to receive and appraise the
newcomer. If I name names, it is so that you, cousin, may appreciate the utter trust which I repose in you, as a blood-kinsman of
like rank within the Chosen. Present, then, were the senior members, as yet untranslated, of the senior families of Wrabsey—
those who, between them, two centuries ago, had brought destiny from the East and from the Sea. Aye, destiny and glory and

fear! In full, the Council numbers twelve, but the Inner Conclave only four, viz. Silas Choate, Enoch Warden, Rahab Martyr, and myself, Israel Martyr, as Principal. On so solemn an occasion, naturally, we were garbed in the panoply of office bequeathed us by our fathers beneath the waters—such robes as would make the recognised Deputy of the town sweat with envy and fear.

While Walter Garlick sat in the antechamber, we four deliberated upon his fate. I had not spoken idly in asserting that danger might be expected from without our ranks, and what was he, if not an outsider? Still, his claim was to ties of blood and allegiance (allegiance to the Great Ones that we know of), and truly he had that look about him that spoke of such. Nothing must be done in such haste that we would regret it, though to be sure there remained one final test or protection that should make all plain. We in mortal state may be fallible, but our fathers who have undergone translation and who dwell in that other world (to which, C——— grant, you and I are bound) are far from such. On their powers we may rely utterly.

At length it was decided to take the man Garlick, to appearances at least, upon his own word, and Silas Choate was dispatched to the anteroom to bring him before the Council.

This I must say in his favour: Upon entering from the severe blankness of the anteroom into the gorgeousness of the great hall he showed not the smallest sign of surprise. Even our own younger Brethren have been known to exclaim in wonder at first seeing the barbarous magnificence of the mural hangings (predominantly green, purple, and gold) which everywhere catch the eye, telling to those who have the knowledge and the intelligence of the wonders of that subaquarian world whence our fathers came to glorify mere mankind, and of that other, nearer realm where they now serve, awaiting the return of the great Dagon and his greater masters. And if Walter Garlick did not blink at this (but with such eyes, after all, he could not blink), how much more telling that he gave no start at seeing the four judges (for such we surely were) who sat before him! Our garments of green and gold, woven with fantastic designs, our diadems, whose richness the King of England himself could not but envy—these alone must have bewildered mere humanity. But what could mere man think when confronted with our own selves? Silas Choate and I have still some years—even decades—to go, but Enoch Warden is fast approaching the Change, and so must appear most monstrous to men, while Rahab Martyr (rep-

resenting the cadet branch of that same ineffable family of which
I am head) was so perilously close that she could not long bear to
be away from the salt water. There was little left in her of the
corruptible flesh of humankind, and even in this haven she was
then rarely to be seen abroad in the daylight hours.

No sign of surprise showed upon the face of our postulant (if so I
may call him), but only, if Silas interpreted correctly, the slightest
expression of satisfaction. Here was one who had in part achieved
his goal. Very good, then. Let us know whether he were fit to
achieve it fully.

Yourself being a fully professed adherent of Dagon to the Third
Degree will be aware of such questions as we thought it good to
put. Had this Garlick subscribed to the first Oath, and could he
repeat that Oath in full? He could, but so can many who are not
of the Blood. Satisfactorily, too, he repeated the second Oath, but
what of that? The supreme test would be the third and greatest
Oath, and this test, also, he passed.

Supreme, did I say? In some places that would be so: in Gate's
Quay, perhaps, and even in Wyvern. But here in Wrabsey we
have yet a further ordeal, and of a very different kind, a kind
that should not be revealed to the postulant immediately, for it
occurred to us four (Rahab uttering thought in those indescribable tones that have already replaced mere human speech in her)
that within three weeks, upon the last day of October, would be
celebrated one of the two great Festivals of the Order, and that
this occasion, no other, should prove the making or breaking of
Walter Garlick.

In the meanwhile, we thought it well to tell him something of
the history of our People in this place, and of their practices.
From him, too, we might learn of how things were done in
Gate's Quay. Similarities there must be, for our greatness all
derives from a common blood and a common revelation, but for
the rest we have also humankindness in our veins and are prone
to fallibility and change.

We discoursed, therefore, of that great voyage of Jabez Martyr
(my own great-great-grandfather) to the Indies and beyond,
where he encountered those strange dwellers upon unknown isles
and in unknown seas, whose form was not as the form of men
and whose worship was not as the worship of men. Of how Jabez
and his fellows (Ambrose Choate and Marcus Warden among
them) embraced wholeheartedly the wealth of gold and fish that

the strangers offered, and with them the new faith (new but aeon-old) that was demanded in return. Of how, in 1629, the ship *Sea-Unicorn* returned to Wrabsey, with but half her crew on board, and that half having taken wives from those lands beyond the Indies. Of the treasure brought as dowry by those wives, and of the Charter of Regulation that Jabez had drawn up upon the instruction of his own wife, the Charter which for two centuries, in despite of the Deputy and his officers, has truly been the pattern for life in this town.

"On the thirty-first of the month, friend Walter," said I, "on that eve that the Christians call Hallowmass, the Chosen of Wrabsey will meet in full. Supplications will be made and sacrifices offered. Doubtless you have attended such gatherings in your own native place, and as a full member of the Order of Dagon. Here, we shall be pleased to welcome you as such. Until that time, you may come and go freely as you will, provided only that you stay within the town. You have our full permission to converse with the People of the Blood, but do bear in mind that they may not wish to converse with you until they know you fully. You may also converse with those townsfolk who are not of our kind, but you will, of course, refrain from speaking of matters which do not pertain to them. Go in peace now, and return upon the appointed day."

* * *

I saw but little of Walter Garlick during the days that followed, though twice he called into my office to pass an hour or so in the most innocuous fashion. For the rest, I have heard that he was betimes to be seen wandering down by the waterfront, among the boatyards, the cocklesheds, and the fishermen's huts. If the odour offended his nostrils (as I have heard that some men complain) he gave no sign of it. Altogether, he seems to have conducted himself with great circumspection, speaking but little to any of the townspeople, of whatever sort, and apparently neither prying where he should not, nor asking importunate questions. Of his behaviour, save for the long hours during which he confined himself to his rooms at the *Dolphin,* I have some measure of certainty, for I had taken pains to have him watched. If he did not spy, at least he was spied upon, both by some more agile members of our Order and by some of those faithful servants whom I mentioned before.

His thought, as I should judge, was simply to let himself be seen,
so that the folk of Wrabsey might come to recognise him and
become accustomed to the fact of his presence. They might, so
insular are the men of these marshlands, forever scorn him as a
foreigner, but should he prove true—should he actually settle
and marry here—then his position would be secure. I could only
admire the soundness of the ploy. And in the meanwhile the execution of it gave me no cause for worry. Besides, the eve of the
Festival would tell all.

Time came, and with it Walter Garlick. He took without demur
the seat specified for him among the congregation in the Hall of
Dagon, as one who has no reason to keep within the shadows.
And if he showed some hesitation in response and gesture, what
of that? The end may be the same, but doubtless the form differs
somewhat between Wrabsey and Gate's Quay. Not even our
most respected Elders can claim perfection this side of the Water.

It is said that spies before now have betrayed themselves at our
great ceremonies by their reaction at the moment of sacrifice, but
that night Walter Garlick's face and posture remained utterly
calm and inscrutable. Even when our congregation was blessedly
swelled by the presence of two of our Fathers from the Sea, now
grown quite beyond human semblance, I could read in his face
neither fear nor horror, but only wonder. Here, said I to myself,
is surely a true Brother of the Blood. There remained but the one
final test.

The symbolic feast concluded the ceremony, after which, with
the golden wand bequeathed to us from the Indies, I made the
sign of the Sun Wheel in true blessing, and gave permission for
those who could to make their way out into the salt waters, there
to commune with those who had gone before. For Rahab, my
cousin, this was, indeed, to be her last farewell upon land.
Henceforth we would meet only in our natural and final element. I was greatly touched, not with sadness, but with the hope
that but few more years might pass before I should join her. In
spirits high but tranquil, then, I summoned Walter Garlick to
remain within the hall, and to join the members of the Inner
Council upon the dais. (Knowing that Rahab was so soon to
leave us, we had already appointed her younger sister, Zillah, so
that our number remained at four.)

"Friend Walter," I said, "the final stage of your initiation into the
mysteries of Wrabsey will be conducted shortly. I shall not ask

whether you wish to proceed, for you must do so. Your choice, as
you will recognise, is to proceed or die. Perhaps to proceed *and*
die, but if so the matter is not within our hands. Very well.
Before we withdraw to the Inner Chamber—to what I may call
the *Sanctum Sanctorum* of this our Temple—you must know the
history and the purpose of this final stage.

"Learn, then, that this Hall of Dagon in which we sit was build-
ed nearly a century and a half ago by my own great-grandfather
Japhet Martyr, son of that Jabez of whom you have heard. There
had been a house, among other houses, here upon the hill, where
dwelt Jabez and his wife from the sea, and their children also.
But in time a wonder occurred, for the wife lost her human semblance to take on that of the very gods whom Jabez and his fellows had learned to serve. Who can tell what emotions were in
the old sea-captain's breast as he realised that the same divine
blood ran in the veins of his children, and not in his own?
Doubtless he conferred much with the men who had returned
with him from that fateful voyage. Some, we know, perfidiously
foreswore their solemn covenant, but what became of them we
know not, only that their wives and children survived. Jabez
himself remained faithful and was admitted to full counsel with
those of the Blood. Truly he could never be of their kind, but he
had been the willing means of bringing them to this land.

"And so, being merely mortal, Jabez Martyr died, having seen
with joy his wife return to the sea, which was her first and last
home. Full of years and honour, he was buried in the churchyard
of St. Mary's. His children, meanwhile, and those of his crew
members, were grown to adulthood, and in their features could
clearly be discerned the mark of their mothers. Numerous they
were, and glorious, strong enough already to resist any bar raised
against them by the children of men. And they coupled, with
each other or with the townsfolk, for the Blood is not made less
strong thereby. Not wishing to draw the attention of the world
to this little town, they made no interference with the
Corporation, and since then the office of Deputy has never been
held by one of the Chosen. But it was by that generation that
the Council of the Elect was fully established, which is the inner
life of Wrabsey. And being an organised body, the Council needed a meeting place of proper dignity. Hence this hall.

"The design was laid down by Japhet himself, and was inspired,
so I understand, by that of one of the London churches. Myself, I
have never travelled so far inland, so cannot tell, but I think you

will admit the majesty of that Doric facade, whose pediment
bears the name of Dagon in letters both discreet and imposing.
You must confess too the very striking nature of this great chamber of worship, but there is more to the hall than this, for, acting
upon the commands of his mother, Japhet constructed also an
inner chamber, a Holy Place. Thus far, friend, the story will be
familiar to you, for surely the Chosen of Gate's Quay have also a
hall of worship, but of such a Sanctum Sanctorum I have never
heard tell elsewhere. It is protected, friend Walter, guarded by
one who is beyond fear or corruption.

"None may guess with what anguish Japhet Martyr laid the first
stone of the Holy Room, for below it he had interred the small
body of his own first-born child, slaughtered in most decorous
and ritual fashion by himself at the stern decree of his mother.
Think! A child that should have grown to be a prince among the
People of the Sea, and yet who now serves in a different fashion
Him Who is to Come, for it is the soul—the essence—of that
child that is the supreme guardian of the Faithful of Wrabsey.

"There may enter the Sanctum in safety only those of true Blood
and true Allegiance. All the Elect of the town, upon coming of
age, must pass the test of that room, and since you, Walter
Garlick, desire acceptance among the Elect, then you also must
pass the test. Are you prepared for the ordeal?"

No sign of fear showed upon that impassive face, but he ventured a question: "Of what manner, Master, is this ordeal?"

"Alas. Of that I may not speak." And nor, indeed, could I, for
within my own long lifetime none had failed to enter the room
with utmost safety, though I had heard of one in my father's time,
a faithful servant but not of the Blood, who had reasoned to herself thus: I have sworn to the highest Oath of this Order and am
as true an adherent of C——— as any in this town; why may not
I with impunity enter the Holy Room? And against dissuasion
she entered in. What became of her, my father declined to tell.
Certain it is that she did not return alive, although no man laid
hands upon her. But of this I did not speak to Walter Garlick.

"I am prepared," said he, at length, and at my sign Silas Choate
drew back the great and gorgeous curtain that hung behind the
dais. It is fitting, cousin, that this curtain should conceal the
entrance to the Sanctum, for upon it is depicted in most fearful
majesty the image of Him who lies dreaming, and whose coming
we are destined to precipitate.

With that key that hangs always upon a chain around my neck,
I unlocked the great door and pulled it open. "Come, brother," I
said. "Stand here at the portal with me and tell me what you
see within."

Still his features showed no emotion other than calm self-assur-
ance as he gazed steadily through the doorway into the chamber.
Instead, it was I who felt an insidious unease as I heard his pronouncement: "Why, Master, I see naught but darkness. No—
darkness and water! Master—" (he turned his face to me for a
moment, and at last there was true expression there, of joy and
wonder) "—this is indeed a great mystery! For surely within this
room, within this hall, situated as it is upon a hill, is the sea!"

I trust that my own face betrayed nothing, though my heart
within me was heavy, as I said, "Very good, brother. Now, do you
remain here while we enter the chamber, and then you shall join
us, no man forcing you."

"Oh, willingly!" said he. And at that my heart sank further, for it
seemed, to his own loss and ours, that he was in all things sincere.
But the Charter must not be transgressed, and the farce must be
played out. Together, then, Silas Choate, Enoch Warden, Zillah
Martyr, and I entered, as we had done many times before, the
room which we knew and saw to be a plain, square, unfurnished
chamber. It measures fifteen feet in each direction, the walls and
ceiling being quite bare, and the floor set with marble squares of
green and gold, in a pattern that will be known to you.

Having reached the farther wall, we turned, and I said, not loudly, "Brother Walter, you may enter now."

Each of us bore a lantern, and the light fell full upon him, yet his
expression was that of a man in darkness. He peered this way
and that, and called out with some attempt at his former confidence, "Master, I can scarce hear you!"

Again, I summoned him, but more loudly. His own reply sounded very loud to my ears: "Enter, Master? Oh, yes, I shall enter.
But oh! this is a terror and a wonder! In the name of our fathers,
if only I could see you!"

My heart a stone in my body, I watched him, plainly gathering
his courage and then taking a bold step into the room. Then I
saw happen what I suppose my father must have seen all those
years ago, and what I hope never to see again. He was throughout like a man blinded, stretching his hands before him to feel
his way (in that bare and well lit room!) and, cousin, I swear to

you that as he progressed the sound of his voice grew fainter—
and as for his *footsteps*—

He approached us for perhaps four feet and was then brought up
sharply by some obstacle invisible (and indeed intangible) to us. I
heard him mutter, "Most strange!", as he felt with his hands this
apparent wall, up, down, to left and right. At last he turned to
his left, feeling the wall along his right hand, until he encountered a wall that was indeed visible to us, for it was the north-
ernmost wall of the room. At that he paused, considering, and
then retraced his path, keeping the invisible obstruction now
upon his left. A little more than two thirds of the way across the
room, his outstretched left hand suddenly encountered—nothing. Either this putative wall took a turn here, or else there was a
gap. Walter Garlick made some small hesitation here, and then
plunged boldly forward.

My account now must retain its utter precision, for all that it
resembles the merest fantasy. Cousin, within two or three steps
Walter Garlick's path began to *descend*—and this on a level stone
floor. I cannot explain it, but only marvel at the subtlety and
efficacy of our protector. It was not at first noticeable, for my
attention was fixed upon his face, and plainly he felt nothing
more strange than his already strange experience. It was Zillah
who grasped my arm and pointed wordlessly to Walter's feet—or
rather, to the floor where his feet should have been visible. They
were not. In macabre fashion, he seemed to stand upon the
stumps of his ankles. And then we saw one foot raised, as it
seemed, through the solid stone of the flooring. Gradually he
proceeded and descended, his steps becoming more and more
laboured, as if he were in truth wading through salt water. Not
once did he come near to any of the walls that we could see; his
way took him this way and that within the room, often moving
where he had moved before, but ever descending, until at last
only his head remained visible above the stones, the eyes bright
with fear and wonder. And never, though at the last we could
distinguish no words, did he cease to speak: "This is a great and
holy thing!" "I am daring much to be accounted worthy!"
"Master, shall I be with you soon?"—and the like. And at last he
was gone, with never a sign in the room to show that he had
ever been.

It was with most solemn hearts and minds that we four left the
Holy Chamber, and with no obstacle (need I say?) to bar our way.
No word was spoken as we closed and locked the door, redrew

the curtain, and departed the hall, each to our separate home, but I know that we thought to see no more of Walter Garlick.

In that we were mistaken, however, for upon the following morning I was woken early by that churchwarden of whom I have spoken, a bearer of strange news. The body of Walter Garlick had been found lying dead within the churchyard of St. Mary's, beside the grave of my own ancestor and founder of the town's fortunes, Jabez Martyr. There was an ironic appropriateness in that, I suppose. But stranger still, examination proved him to have died of drowning—which is all but unheard of in people of our kind. And, yes, cousin, I have to report that examination proved beyond a doubt that he was indeed of the Blood. (Naturally, I ensured that the matter was taken in hand entirely by my own office, so that knowledge should be confined to those who ought to know.)

Questions no doubt occur to you, as they occurred to me—and, alas, I cannot answer them. If Walter Garlick was of the true Blood, why did he fail the final ordeal? Was he, perhaps, apostate—that danger from without of which I have spoken? Or could it be that the Guardian accepts only those born of the faithful of Wrabsey? I do not know. But this I do know: As long as the hall and the Sanctum Sanctorum survive, then the future of the Faith in Wrabsey is secure.

In the name of Him who Dreams,

I am yr. affect. cousin,

Israel Martyr.

About "Rapture in Black"

Originally appearing in *Crypt of Cthulhu* #57, St. John's Eve 1988, "Rapture in Black" has been significantly revised and updated for its reincarnation here. Though written independently of Michael Shea's "Fat-Face", "Rapture in Black" spontaneously parallels it in many ways. This is altogether appropriate since the shoggoths appearing in Shea's story are natural allies of the deep ones who figure in Rainey's. One can only speculate, in light of these striking and eerie links, whether both tales do not share some subtle inspiration form a certain suboceanic Dreamer.

Rapture in Black

by Stephen Mark Rainey

The storekeeper saw her through the plate glass window, her black cloak billowing in the cold wind as she strode rapidly down the sidewalk. He saw her almost every evening about this time, on her way home from wherever she worked, he guessed. She was a rare face in a city of faceless millions: very attractive in a sullen, melancholy sort of way; reminded him a bit of the Gothic crowd that used to flow in and out of his shop to buy the latest Bauhaus, Sisters of Mercy, Xymox, and so forth. This one was different, though. Not as radical a dresser as the Goths, but still conspicuous in a crowd: tall and slim, with wild, coal-colored mane, pale complexion. She typically wore all black, tight-fitting apparel, lately with an overcoat or cape as the cold weather set in. She had to be pushing 30, separated or divorced—maybe a frustrated lesbian. Her thin, dark-painted lips never smiled, but her turquoise eyes still had a little gleam of humor in them. She'd been kicked, and kicked hard, but never beaten.

She occasionally came into Hot Wax and sorted through the CD's, sometimes the used records, always browsing, only occasionally buying. She liked '80's stuff, mostly obscure pop: Lena Lovitch, Bronski Beat, Psychedelic Furs, Bryan Ferry. Last thing she'd bought was the first album by The Pet Shop Boys.

The storekeeper took note of these things.

A greasy kid wearing leather came inside, admitting a burst of Lake Michigan wind, headed for the record bins at the back of the store. Hot Wax didn't take used records any more, so when the stock was picked bare, that would be it for old LP's. Would have to change the store name from Hot Wax, the storekeeper reckoned, as it didn't quite jive with the glossy sparkle of the CD's that filled all the racks.

The tall woman was gone from view, probably already at her front door. She lived two doors down, in the upstairs loft over one of the shops. Lived alone. Lincoln Park wasn't the worst neighborhood in Chicago, nor the best, but a single female living in this place certainly had more balls than he did.

* * *

Maria saw them on the street corner from her apartment window, as she expected, just as she had for the last five nights: two overcoated figures, faces hidden under wide-brimmed, gray fedoras. They stood side by side, occasionally leaning to one another as if in guarded conversation, never moving from their chosen positions. As usual, they remained there for about half an hour, then moved on, disappearing down Lincoln to address whatever business such men had to address.

The routine had begun last Sunday. Maria had noticed them only by chance and paid them no mind beyond a quick glance. Then she had seen them again on Monday night, at the same time—just about six in the evening, not long after she'd gotten home from work. On Tuesday, she intentionally had kept an eye out for them, and at the appointed hour they had appeared, completed their ritual of standing around for thirty minutes or so, then moved on. For the last two nights, curiosity aroused, Maria had gone to the window at six o'clock and waited for them to appear. They had. And tonight, Friday night, it seemed they would not deviate from this eccentric schedule.

Maria settled herself on the couch, her knees on the seat, her elbows propped on the back so she could watch out the living room window overlooking Lincoln Avenue. She had partially closed the miniblinds, allowing her to see out without being visible from the street. A goblet of blood-colored burgundy waited patiently on the window sill beside her, and, so it wouldn't get bored, she took a polite sip from it.

Life was good. No more working nights now that she'd finally gotten out of that damned production job at the *Tribune*. She'd acquired a spot at Comstock Associates writing advertising copy—strictly an 8-to-5 shift, little overtime, paid holidays and vacation. She had plenty of money, plenty of time, and, always, plenty of fermented grapes to keep her company while she watched old geezers who were probably gay go through some peculiar mating ritual. Life was sweet.

She was 29 years old, divorced.

The two men on the street huddled together to confer briefly, then returned to their vigilant stances. The cars and passersby carried on obliviously as always, unobstructed by the twin figures who might as well have been newly grown trees. Maria had the impression that those hidden faces occasionally rose to peer at her window, but she couldn't be sure, not from this distance.

She softly caressed the smooth, blood-filled crystal on her window sill. Her goblet was almost empty. When she had used him up, she would forget him and go on to another. She could be just as cold as he, using him with no remorse or regret. It was her way.

He's better than the last man I had, she thought, staring into the rich depths of the liquid. *I use him, he uses me—and if I'm gentle with him, he won't hurt me in the morning.*

There'd been, what, six or seven men since Jim had gone his own way?

Maria sighed, shifting on her knees, wondering what the gang from work was doing now. Often on Friday nights, they'd leave the studio together and empty some beer joints. Sometimes Maria left alone, other times with company she'd met over the course of the evening. She'd begun to think she should start charging for her time; the men were certainly eager enough and went back satisfied to their wives or parents or whomever. No one from the office crowd ever seemed to care what the hell she did on her own time. They'd decided not to go out tonight, so Maria was left to her own devices, something she'd decided had become rather dangerous. Wine and coke became close companions on solitary weekend nights.

She'd been lucky so far, no strange contagions resulting from these trysts that she'd repeatedly sworn to give up—only to find herself again and again accepting whatever invitation was offered. She'd tried it with a couple of women, just as a taste test. It had been okay. The men were physically more satisfying, but the girls had more passion. More honesty.

The men on the corner leaned to each other again, and this time Maria was certain she saw a gleam of light reflect off an eyeball aimed at her window. She drew back automatically, though she knew that with her lights off they could not possibly see in. They'd been down there for half their allotted time. Maybe, eventually—perhaps tonight—they would deviate from their established routine. Maybe? Variety is spice, and you know that's nice—

Music. I need music.

Maria had worn out all her records and CD's. REM was old. Gabriel was old. Springsteen was very old. The radio sucked.

Hot Wax.

I will go down to the record store and buy an album. The atmosphere in Hot Wax suited her. It was small, with good sound. Upstairs they had a leather and jewelry shop. *I will buy a CD, maybe an LP—or maybe a new jacket, or earrings, or a bracelet. I will pass by the men on the corner and see what they look like up close. Maybe I'll taunt them, just for fun.*

I love this idea.

She killed her drink and stood up, tossing her long hair behind her. Then into the bedroom to don her traveling clothes: black turtleneck bodysuit, black leggings, black suede boots—and, best of all, flowing black cape.

At one time she'd considered tattoos and piercing. Thank God she'd abandoned that notion. She could only imagine herself at 60 still wearing such adornments. One really would have to be mad.

Her raven hair hung in sleek, glossy waves, well past her slim shoulders. When the wind blew, as it always did in Chicago, whipping her hair like a fluttering black banner, she looked absolutely imposing. She knew this, and enjoyed it, but always bore in mind how transient the physical was. One day, all too soon, she would lose this, and the idea stung her. But for now, here, even on Lincoln Avenue, she would sometimes draw stares. And that was nice.

After she'd thrown her cape over her shoulders, she grabbed her pocketbook and glanced hurriedly in the mirror above her cluttered dresser. Very good. Violence Jack glowered approvingly from the Japanimé poster on the opposite wall. She was ready.

Down the creaky, spiral staircase to the front door. She loved the antique feel of the ancient building; the old-fashioned atmosphere complemented the Dante-like decor she'd provided her apartment. It tended to overwhelm the men she brought home, but that too was good. She was always the one to do the sending away.

When she pushed open the door to the street, a gust of wind slashed at her, lifting her cape regally behind her. Hot Wax lay to the left, the two men to the right. She headed for the gay pair, head bowed, hair billowing, eyes occasionally lifting to study her quarry. She beat a purposeful march toward them, an elegant, vampiric figure with a long stride, heels clicking soundly on the sidewalk. She sensed that two pairs of ghoulish eyes watched her from beneath those wide-brimmed hats. As she approached, she felt them tense up, like wild animals sensing a threat.

Excellent. I do believe they're afraid of me. How lovely.

She slowed her pace, kept her eyes aimed at the sidewalk until drawing up just in front of them, when she raised her head to regard them curiously. The hats were pulled low over their foreheads, overcoat collars turned up around their necks. Bright eyes glistened in the dark faces, met hers.

She was momentarily chilled. The faces, what she could see of them, looked wet and pallid. The staring eyes were round and bulged mysteriously. Fish-like. They both had short, stubby noses and thick, moist lips. *They must be brothers*, she thought. *How kinky.*

My God, they're ugly. No wonder they dress like that.

She passed them slowly, then circled around just behind them and started back in the opposite direction. As she turned, she remained close enough so that her wind-filled cape brushed one of them. To her surprise, she felt him stiffen and utter a low, snake-like hiss. *Jesus, they're animals*, she thought. Bizarre, sometimes, what came out of the closet.

She glanced back, smiled sweetly, and went on her way toward the record shop, aware of what a juvenile, foolish thing she'd just done. These days, you could get killed for—

Suddenly, behind her, she heard a thick voice say something like, "*Erlyuh neh thoolu fthagon.*" Foreigners; it figured. Not Russian, she knew that much, nor German—but some kind of coarse, guttural tongue, maybe Finnish or something. Almost as though a fish had acquired the power of articulate speech.

Go home. Who the hell needs your kind, anyway.

Well, their half hour was almost up. They'd disappear shortly, she supposed. *I'll do my business, pick up some fun new things, then go back to the impatiently waiting bottle of my Italian lover.*

She passed her own front door and continued on to Hot Wax. The sidewalks were beginning to teem with the Friday night socialites, for this section of Lincoln housed plentiful night spots, most of which she'd seen the inside of at least once. Just the fact they drew so many people her age helped assure her she was neither alone nor lonely in her solitary apartment. After all, whenever she felt like it, she could go out and meet people. And at least for one night, they'd accept her.

She turned into the small shop, from which blasting speakers spat Queensrÿche all over the sidewalk. Happily for her, only a smattering of patrons currently sorted through the CD racks; she hated it when too many bodies choked the aisles in the already cozy space. The drab-looking storekeeper gave her a quick, disinterested glance, which she met haughtily. What she needed was some mood music, something melancholy yet beautiful, like Albinoni's *Adagio for Strings*. However, this was the wrong shop for that kind of thing, so she would have to settle for some early OMD, or perhaps This Mortal Coil.

Ah, the romance of morbidity.

She made her way through one of the narrow aisles, flipped through a bin, and picked up *Dazzle Ships* by Orchestral Maneuvers in the Dark. '80's. Good. She still preferred the music of her youth, for she'd developed and refined her tastes in her early twenties, had never adapted to the resurgence of heavy metal, the obnoxious repetition of rap, or the pure banality of grunge.

Now to go upstairs, check out the jewelry section, maybe find some new earrings. Something silver. Something flashy without being gaudy.

As she started for the stairs at the rear of the shop, the bell above the front door jangled, and she saw a familiar, overcoated figure push his way inside, followed by another, identically clad creature. A stab of apprehension almost sent her running up the stairs, but she continued at a calm, leisurely pace, knowing that her face must have gone ghostly white. The half-hour had not passed; QED, the men must be coming after her. Usually when anyone trailed her, it was of her own design—whenever sex was the evening's goal. But these guys—no way. Obviously, sex was not on their minds.

Damn it! Why the hell had she felt so compelled even to attract these guys' attention? It was too dangerous to play around with strangers, and she knew that. *She knew that.* Too late now for regret. Surely, though, they could mean her no real harm, not here, where there were other people around. She had never even really considered that anything more deadly than the threat of AIDS might accompany these characters, the risk to her being nonexistent. Besides, she was far from a helpless female. She knew the pressure points, the lethal targets. Her lean, muscular arms and legs were fast and potentially dangerous. She had, out of necessity, decked a couple of overly ambitious gentlemen in her time. The gold and silver rings adorning her fingers could inscribe a nasty note in one's flesh, or even blind. If it came down to confrontation, she'd happily leave these fellows with some extremely unpleasant memories of her.

Not to mention she kept a canister of tear gas in her purse. Her fingers dipped inside, closed around the metal cylinder.

A bearded clerk sat behind the upstairs counter, gave her a disinterested glance. The air was warm and held a rich, musky, leather scent, which she savored. She went to one of the racks of hanging jackets and positioned herself just behind it, where she could see the stairs. From below came a heavy clumping, and a moment later the fist of the figures appeared, shuffling clumsily up the steps. The second followed at his heels, and Maria clenched the canister in her fist. All too plainly, they were coming after her. She took a deep breath to steady her nerves. *Easy ... easy ....*

The first man reached the top and turned questioningly to the clerk behind the glass-topped counter. To her surprise, the lanky, bearded man nodded toward her. The shiny eyes beneath the hat met hers—and she shuddered in revulsion, for something about them seemed not quite human. Forcing herself to remain calm, she placed the CD she was carrying on top of the clothes rack and turned to face her apparent aggressors, her left hand flattening into a rigid blade while the other drew the canister from her purse, keeping it out of sight behind her back.

Her voice clear and unwavering, she said to the first one, "Is there something I can help you with, sir?"

No response. The man behind the counter left his spot and headed toward a door at the rear of the room, through which he silently disappeared. It closed gently behind him. The lead creature took a shambling step toward her, heaving a deep breath that seemed to gurgle deep within his chest. Maria held her ground, preparing herself to counter with the gas.

A snake-like hiss issued from the lead man's throat, to be answered by a similar sound from his partner. A mottled hand rose and reached for her—

and she was stricken with horror, for the pallid appendage was webbed, like the fins on a fish.

What the hell?

The hellish hand shot like lightning for her throat, so fast she barely had time to react. Her left hand swiftly lashed out, parried the oncoming missile. Simultaneously, she thrust the gas canister into the brute's face and fired a burst straight into his eyes. Then she spun on one toe like a furious ballet dancer, swinging her left leg up into an unstoppable roundhouse kick. Her boot tip caught the overcoat just below the belt line, connecting with a gratifying, solid blow to the groin. To Maria's shock and dismay, the only response was a muted "hmph" and a momentary pause in the creature's advance.

The gas hadn't so much as fazed him.

With unexpected speed, the second figure moved to her right, flanking her, placing the rack of leather coats between them, hurrying around behind her to pinion her between them. Her only hope now would be to get past the one in front of her, blocking her passage to the stairway.

The kick—not to mention the gas—should have dropped the son of a bitch! Only slightly daunted, Maria raised her right hand to chin level, still clutching the canister, then punched with all her strength. Her first flew into the dark gap beneath the creature's sunken chin with enough power to shatter any normal man's Adam's apple. Again, the man-shaped thing took almost no notice. But the force of her strike dislodged his wide-brimmed hat, which popped up to reveal the features hiding beneath.

Maria froze in disgust. The football-shaped head protruding from the high-collared shoulders had no hair, either on top or on its loathsome face. No eyebrows, no eyelashes, no hint of a beard. The skin was shiny and flaccid, with a fishy, greenish tinge. The ichthyoid eyes gaped at her, lidless. Yellowish pupils glared at her with a disturbing lack of malice—of any feeling whatsoever. Ambivalent, dead-looking eyes. They had no place in the head of any earthly creature.

Reeling with shock, Maria could not avoid the webbed hands that closed around her shoulders from behind. She pulled away—so hard that she overbalanced and sprawled to the floor, knocking her head against the base of the metal clothes rack. Her breath hissed through her lips and she suddenly realized what it meant to see stars.

She was given no chance to recover. Powerful hands gripped her biceps, pulled her roughly upward until she rested on her knees. The figure from behind grasped her by the waist and lifted, its grip cold and clammy even through the fabric of her body suit. The cape was torn from her shoulders, and the two creatures dragged her toward the door at the back of the room, which swung open as if on cue. Beyond—somewhere far below, it seemed—something moved. Something large and heavy.

Maria did not have enough air in her lungs to scream. As she was pulled into the darkness, she felt the floor turn slick and wet. The bearded store clerk stood framed in the doorway, peering hesitantly past her, as if also afraid of what lay in wait for her.

Painfully, she twisted her head around, and in the dim light shining through the open door she saw a wide, curving staircase leading down into sightless depths. The bare stone glistened with a blackish-green coating of mucus, like the trail of a giant slug. Again she heard a sound from below: a thick, gurgling hiss, followed by a heavy rustling. And in the moment before the bearded man slammed the door shut with a low curse, she caught a glimpse of something moving up the stairs, something quite large that gleamed wetly, the surface of which writhed and pulsated wildly—something that had many arms waving like sea-stalks in the air.

Now she found the power to scream, but her voice only echoed in to the blackness below. She knew that no one in the shop could hear her—or would help her even if they could.

Something wet and snake-like curled around her ankle and wormed its way toward her thighs. A rough hissing sound burst from the unseen mass below, as if something with no vocal cords was attempting to form words.

Then she felt herself being dragged downward. Her head struck hard stone as she went over the edge of the first step.

Consciousness tried to exit, but somehow lingered, keeping her horribly aware of what was happening to her. She bumped down the next step, and then the next, as another slick, prehensile arm encircled her torso, to explore her body with a cold, questing tip. The scream that tried to escape was suddenly stifled as the obscene appendage lunged upward, flowing past her lips and into her throat, choking her—but stopping short of working into her windpipe. More of the cool, fleshy members rustled out of the darkness to caress her legs, her breasts, her buttocks. One of them managed to pop the snaps at the crotch of her bodysuit.

All the while, she was pulled down, down. The staircase seemed endless, yet Maria knew that somewhere, deep in unknowable vaults beneath the city, it *would* end.

* * *

The storekeeper sat nervously in his chair behind the counter, keeping an eye on the couple of patrons browsing the bins. A disturbing scuffle had broken out upstairs a few minutes earlier, but, thankfully, it had been quickly silenced. When all had been quiet for a full five minutes, he stood and went to the stairway to remove the rope and the sign that read UPSTAIRS CLOSED FOR CLEANING. He returned to his seat and took the money from a young man in leather with a nose ring buying a Frank Sinatra LP.

An odd one in an odd city.

He hated being a disciple. Yes, he did. The masters had lured many a young woman for their own purposes on many occasions, drawn her into a place where they had "influence." They never needed to stoop to breaking and entering, or any other form of abduction which might leave traceable evidence. Usually, these young ladies were not even missed for a significant length of time, and, when they were, foul play was seldom suspected. They were whores, or drug addicts, or just unfortunates who didn't have families nearby. Usually the police came to the conclusion that they'd gone off on some fling, or had skipped town in hopes of finding something better.

The storekeeper shifted apprehensively as the two overcoated figures shuffled down the stairs and silently left the shop, each casting a severe glance in his direction. One of them had something in his hand that he thrust inside his coat—the girl's pocketbook, the only remaining trace of her, which they would dispose of immediately. As they shambled away down the sidewalk, he gulped fearfully, but breathed a sigh of relief as they disappeared.

That poor girl. He'd found her attractive, would have liked to have gotten to know her. He could usually put them out of his mind, but this one was different. *Nothing so tragic as the death of a beautiful girl*—

If only she were just going to die. He knew from the whispered stories that she would be eaten alive by the denizen of the depths—but only after living through the tortures of Hell.

For he had caught a glimpse of what another disciple had brought through that door months after they'd taken their last victim—that small, shapeless mass that writhed and gurgled—a parody of a human child, its arms and legs nothing but waving ropes of gray flesh. Surely, that thing had not been the product of mating in the usual sense: no, more a parasite that gestated in the woman's body, inserted there by the true, asexual "parent." Unlike the natural creatures of the earth, where the dominant female often devoured her mate after their ritual—whatever the god of the darkness was, it feasted after its offspring was born.

To avoid being dragged into the depths himself, the storekeeper cooperated with the strange figures that he had never seen other than behind their coats and hats. He knew the moment he betrayed them, his life was forfeit. But for his willingness to serve, he was promised great rewards in the life after this one. He had to have faith. The thing in the darkness demanded it.

For he could never escape them. The staircase in his building leading to the underground lair was but one of many throughout the city. He knew of a similar staircase that hid in the rear of the bookstore across the street ... in the bar on the next block of Diversey ... in the cellar of the church over on Seminary. The network was vast ... efficient ... and flawless.

If the propagation continued, their numbers would keep increasing. And one day—God in Heaven forbid—they would come out.

He saw a lone figure crossing the street, coming toward his shop. Silently he begged her to turn away, keep going—

Do not come in here—

She walked past the shop without a glance toward him.

He saw the two overcoated figures suddenly appear again. They had found new prey. They would stalk her, study her, determine if she were a suitable host-mother—

The storekeeper turned away from the sight of his customers, bowed his head. And wept.

About "Live Bait"

Yes, it remains possible to fill an Innsmouth story with surprise and with reversals of perspective. "Live Bait" is sufficient evidence of that. In some ways the theme of the story might be said to lurk just below the surface of HPL's original: If the Innsmouth people were dangerous monsters, what are we to say of a government that would move in, destroy the town, and ship the inhabitants out to domestic concentration camps? The federal raid on Innsmouth is eerily reminiscent of the United States' treatment of the Japanese during World War II. The final submarine assault on Devil's Reef reminds one of the "final solution" of bombing Hiroshima and Nagasaki, while the internment camps in which Japanese-Americans were quarantined are dead ringers for those to which the Innsmouthers were shipped by the trainload. I hardly need point out that American wartime propaganda caricatured the Japanese as monkey-men, in much the same way Lovecraft's Innsmouth fish-faces are caricatures of the Polynesians with whom the Innsmouthers interbred.

"Live Bait" appeared first in *Cthulhu Codex* #9, November 1996.

Live Bait

by Stanley C. Sargent

Three employees of Alderman Distribution, Inc., had turned down the assignment, which involved spending at least two full days in Innsmouth, before Charles finally accepted it. Not having been raised in New England, Charles had known nothing of the frightening tales about the legendary town, but he had heard many rumors since accepting the assignment. The government had nearly obliterated the town of Innsmouth in the '20's, but he found that unremarkable in itself. Even the FBI's intense secrecy on the subject made sense, especially if Innsmouth had indeed harbored an extensive bootleg operation.

Arrangements had been made for Charles to stay with an elderly couple, Mr. and Mrs. Joshua Hunt. During that time he was to inspect the local fishing operation, answer any questions Mr. Hunt might have, and, if all went well, get the marketing agreement signed. After hearing the jokes about the toady "Innsmouth look", Charles had carefully scrutinized the snapshot of the Hunts he had been shown. Legend had it that the "look" became noticeable as one reached maturity. Both of the Hunts were well into their sixties, but they looked perfectly normal in the photo.

The company fully intended to complete its planned multimillion-dollar marketing supply network and could not allow unfounded rumors to hinder the successful execution of the operation. A widely read fictional tale, penned in 1931 by a fellow named H. P. Lovecraft, kept the Innsmouth legend alive, but several of the board members had heard other stories about Innsmouth. Subsequent delvings into FBI records via the Freedom of Information Act only raised more questions. The company might have to deal with journalistic headlines like "Monsters Produce Your Food" in the tabloids, but Charles was expected to return with first-hand knowledge disavowing the whispered tales of frog-beings.

Charles had read the story and been briefed about the ugly rumors. He was sure all the supernatural implications were simply bunk, yet it was part of his assignment to determine whether any of the mumbo jumbo would seriously interfere with Innsmouth's contract for delivery of regular fish allotments. Proctor and Gamble still hadn't quashed the fundamentalist rumor-mongering that saw in their moon and star logo the sign of the Antichrist. And such rumors could be expensive.

He left Arkham in the early morning, driving east at a leisurely pace through lush summer landscape. Beyond Newburyport, however, the general character of the landscape began to change, its verdancy yielding to monotonous tans and grays as sand and marsh overwhelmed the vitality of the terrain. The changes even began affecting his imagination; he found himself imposing unsavory images upon the passing scenery.

A tall variety of wild grass had grown abundantly here in spring, but only dry, yellow stalks remained, slowly bending in one direction, then the other, as if crushed by the passage of unseen things pursuing the taunting whispers of a vagrant wind. Here and there Charles noted the tumbled remains of weathered foundations that once had been houses. The piles of ancient stonework seemed to clutch desperately to sand and stunted bushes, as if trying to stay above the surface a little longer before being overwhelmed, to disappear forever from sight.

Five miles from town, a huge metallic object along the road caught his attention. He slowed the car as he approached the object, not only intending to get a better look, but also hoping the distraction might rid him of a growing despair created by mile upon mile of depressing scenery.

He stopped the car and stepped out, enjoying the opportunity to stretch his legs. Walking around the car, he peered into the deep roadside ditch. Lying at the bottom, on its side, was the wreck of a gray, old fashioned flat-top bus, its tires long ago rotted away and the windows nearly free of glass. It matched Lovecraft's description of the bus Joe Sargent had driven so long ago between Innsmouth, Arkham, and Newburyport. The wind had heavily battered the destination sign, now fallen from the driver's window. Once it had announced "Arkham-Innsmouth-Newb'port", but vandals had altered it to read nonsensically "Arm In mouth." The graffiti sprayed across the body of the bus itself, however, made Charles quickly return to the car and hit the gas. Above a number of juvenile renderings, someone had carefully written:

THE LORD HATH SPAT OUT ABOMINATION,
AND YET DOTH IT THRIVE IN INNSMOUTH!

Later, as he approached Innsmouth itself, he found himself wondering just how long ago those frightening words had been written and by whom. He refused to even consider why they had been written.

* * *

His first real view of fog-draped Innsmouth helped to ground him in reality again. The place had changed greatly during the sixty-five years since Lovecraft had described it. Even from a distance, he could see the sprawling urban areas had been nearly leveled, and in the fading twilight, he could see that the steeples of Innsmouth's unholy churches no longer pierced the horizon. One thing, however, adhered precisely to Lovecraft's description—the nauseating stench of rotten fish. It pervaded the air and even the tiny droplets of salt mist which left his face neither wet nor dry.

He drove through the dank, empty streets of Innsmouth, turning finally onto Federal Street. The Hunt residence was easily located after only two further turns. A few scrawny chickens ran loose on the few dusty acres centrally occupied by the stark features of an immense Georgian farmhouse. The structure desperately needed paint but appeared solid and in good repair. Parking the car near the gate of a stone fence, Charles followed a path through a small, rather sad vegetable garden to the entrance.

* * *

The warm, old-fashioned comfort of their parlor was unfortunately offset by the coldness of the Hunts themselves. They greeted him cordially, pretending not to notice as he studied their features, finding nothing unusual.

Mrs. Hunt proved to be a tall, well kept woman, her steel-gray hair tied back in a prudent bun. Though not unfriendly, her manner was withdrawn and discouraged conversation. Joshua Hunt bore himself commandingly, his intensely serious demeanor enhanced by a stark bone structure, small beady eyes, and rigidly unyielding mouth. His skin bore testimony to decades of exposure to the elements but belied any suggestion of taint.

Within the hour, Charles and Hunt were discussing business over a conservative meal, silently served by Mrs. Hunt. The men addressed each other by surname, Hunt rigidly avoiding any real congeniality. Apart from his neatly ironed overalls, Hunt's coldly dignified manner reminded his guest more of the owner of a multimillion-dollar conglomerate than of the representative of a few hundred fishermen.

Charles had expected the evening meal to consist mainly of fish, but Hunt informed him that very few of the locals ate fish. He explained, "When a man spends his life a-catchin', cleanin', and smellin' nuthin' but fish, he ain't much pleased ta sit daown for a meal o' the same." This surprised Charles, but it made sense.

The formal, icy atmosphere proscribed any reference to the town's nefarious reputation. Charles realized he would have to find the answers to those questions elsewhere.

The Hunts retired early, by their usual routine, and Charles was directed to a room located in the vacant upper story. He almost immediately fell
asleep, unable to resist the heavenly softness of the down comforter on the
four-poster bedstead.

* * *

In the morning Charles sat alone at the table as Mrs. Hunt served breakfast,
explaining that her husband had left at dawn with the other fishermen and
would return, at best, just before sunset. Meanwhile, it had been arranged
for Frank Quesenberry, a neighbor boy, to "escort" Charles "wher'ver business deems ness'ry." The woman's careful choice of words caused Charles to
despair of any unofficial sightseeing, yet he was relieved to learn he would
not be spending the day with Hunt.

A few minutes later an awkward, friendly 14-year-old knocked, came
in, and introduced himself. The handsome lad sported a mane of wavy black
hair under a cap bearing the initials of Arkham's Miskatonic University. In
T-shirt and jeans, Frank seemed a typical teenager to whom Charles, only
twenty-four, could easily relate.

Once outside, Charles decided to take the initiative to organize the day.
"Well, Frank, let's see now. I suppose the first thing we should do is—"

"I knaow what ye be wantin' to see, no daoubt," Frank interrupted. "Ye
wan' ta see the places that writer talked abaout in his tale." He smugly
added, "Tell me that ain't right, Mr. V."

The unexpected challenge took Charles by surprise.

"Well, yeah, if any of those places really exist. But how did you know I'd
read the story, and what makes you sure we're talking about the same one?"

"Juss 'cos we's isolate' don't mean we ain't smart," Frank insisted.
"There's only 'un story I e'er heard abaout 'cernin' this backwater ditch, an'
nub'dy comes here 'thaout readin' it fust."

Before Charles could respond, Frank interjected, "Nub'dy!"

Though speechless for a moment, Charles soon recovered. "So, do any
of those places still exist?"

"That feller knowed this taown a'right. Only problem's most o' the
places got blowed up or burnt daown back in '28 durin' the hoopla, so thar's
nuthin' left o' most 'ceptin' trash an' holes in the graound. Them G-men
e'en 'creted up any tunnels they faound that didn't fall in by the'selves."

Amazed at the boy's candor, Charles suggested a visit to the remains of
the churches of the Esoteric Order of Dagon.

"Fust thing the G-men did was burn them demon chu'ches," Frank
answered without hesitation. "That's haow they faound most o' the tunnels."

Charles was sure the punster in Lovecraft had been responsible for the town's hotel being dubbed the "Gilman" in the story, but at the mention of the name, Frank surprised him. "The Gilman Haouse? That's still standin', but thar ain't much ta see. Didn't git awl burnt up like most o' taown, but got 'ficiently scorched.

"They blowed hell aout o' the docks an' the wharf; slums on the water-front got burnt ta naught. None o' that's wu'th seein', but yer wish is my command, Mr. V.!"

Charles looked down to see Frank cock one eyebrow and, in his best imitation of Bela Lugosi, add, "At least fer naow!" The amateur imitation combined badly with Frank's rustic accent, striking Charles as funny. Frank took the laughter as a compliment.

Charles took the opportunity to inquire toward visiting notorious Devil Reef. Frank rolled his eyes, shook his head, then proceeded to scold the adult.

"Naow use yer head, Mr. V. The best fishin 'raound here's done just pas' the reef, an' wuth boats aout thar a'ready, they'd be hell to pay fer 'sturbin' things. 'Sides, I ain't up ta raowin' all the way aout thar an' back an', well, no 'fense, but ye ain't 'sactly up to it neither."

Staring directly at Charles, Frank continued, "They's nuthin' thar any-ways. Folks say they used to be some kind o' hell temple aout thar, built by them deep 'uns while the reef was 'neath the tide. The reef goes up an' down, with sometimes a whole week betwixt risin's, an' wun day it jest popped up with a temple sittin' thar! Nub'dy knaows 'sactly what 'come o' it, but they's nary a stone left naow. Nuthin' out there 'cept rocks, fish, an' slime—an' the smell, o' caorse. I'll take ye to the green where the chuches was, then I'll shaow ye whut's left o' Gilman House arter."

Charles nodded his agreement as they officially began the tour.

* * *

Frank readily agreed that the area of town north of the Manuxet River would make the perfect setting for a horror film. The destruction there had been tremendous, yet for sixty-odd years the rubble had remained relative-ly untouched. The story had described that area as being occupied by empty buildings with dark, boarded windows that stared at passersby, but Charles felt they now resembled the seared and blasted ruins of Hiroshima. Many structures had collapsed, at times colliding with those beside them, causing the devastation of entire blocks. Before Charles could ask if any bodies had been removed after the fire, Frank volunteered a gruesome anecdote about a horde of strangely deformed and inhuman skeletons some children had found just a few years ago in the crumpled debris of a warehouse.

Recently, Frank continued, much of the wreckage had become too dangerous for exploration, yet no one had taken the warning seriously until an eight-year-old had been crushed beneath a building as it folded in upon itself. In places, even narrow streets had to be avoided due to threats posed by precariously leaning edifices and disintegrating façades.

A little more than two hundred people had survived the disaster. Some had moved on, but those who stayed had claimed the abandoned homes of wealthier districts as their own. Given that second chance, they had vowed the deep ones would never infiltrate the town again.

By late afternoon, Charles had seen enough for one day. The tour had been disappointing, but he still asked Frank to show him around the next day for a few hours. He readily agreed, and Charles thanked the "young man." Pleased at the appellation, Frank strutted off toward home.

Charles had much to consider. Part of his task was to separate fact from rumor, history from superstition, and this was proving far from simple. On the one hand, the locals plainly resented the slanders Lovecraft's fiction had bequeathed them, almost as if it had been his story which had led the federal government all but to obliterate the town. Yet on the other hand, they seemed naturally to acknowledge the almost reportorial accuracy of the tale! And this acknowledgment expanded, in Frank's case, even to the existence of the inhuman deep ones! Charles had expected, indeed, still expected to confirm some reasonable explanation for the town's destruction. So far, none was forthcoming. Could it be that the nightmarish rumors had come to be believed even among the people of Innsmouth?

* * *

The second evening meal with the Hunts did not go as well as the first. Charles waited until the meal was nearly over before attempting to engage the old man in conversation, offhandedly mentioning some of the places he and Frank had included in their tour. He realized his mistake as Hunt's face abruptly flushed crimson with anger.

"Thar ain't no need fer yer diggin' inta the past, Varley. Trauble's ne'er fergot sa long as ut's fodder for needless conversati'n', an' the past's got nuthin' to do with our 'greement with yer comp'ny. Tell Frank he's to shaow ye to the fish pack'ry daown in the 'dustr'al part o' taown tamorrow; then ye kin peruse the boats at day's end. Anythin' else's just a-nosin', an' we dun't hold ta nosin' here."

Mrs. Hunt had left the table, remaining in the kitchen until table-clearing time.

"Naow I ain't a-orderin', mind ye, but I'd r'mind ye o' a sayin' we got 'raound here—'Ever' fox smells his aown hole.' I s'ggest ye ponder its meanin'."

Stunned at Hunt's reaction, Charles tried to think of a tactful response, but Hunt stood up, tossing his napkin onto his empty plate. The anger left his voice as he added, "That's all I got ta say, so I'll be a-biddin' ye g'night."

Charles went up to his room shortly thereafter, making note of things he needed to ask Frank.

* * *

His sleep was troubled by nightmares. He dreamed of being awakened by eerie chanting, then running to a window overlooking the ocean. Moonbeams skipped across the surface of lapping tides, but, as clouds blocked the moonlight, he observed a multitude of strangely colored beams, moving like fireflies beneath the breakwater near Devil Reef. It had seemed real, but it could only have been a dream, as Devil Reef was not visible from his window.

* * *

The next morning Charles told Frank how he had upset "old man Hunt" the previous night.

"Ye shudda 'spected that, knowin' he ain't as easygoin' as me. Dun't ye get it, Mr. V.? Folks 'raound h'yar hate the deep 'uns with a passion, an' they sure's hell dun't want no r'mindin' of 'em. 'Twus 'cos o' them demons that the taown got awl messed up, an' 'ssumin' they's dead an' gone now, thar ain't no point in yer raisin' ghosts."

Again Frank spoke of the deep ones as if he himself believed in them. Could he possibly mean only that the Innsmouth folk hated the *rumors* of the deep ones for all the mischief they had caused? Then something else occurred to him; he asked what Hunt had meant about the fox.

Frank burst into hysterical laughter. "That's a good 'un!" Then, trying to compose himself, Frank responded, "I'm sorry, that's jus' his way—hittin' folks with some sayin' or other. He tells me I talk 'nuff to make a fartin' dog shit hisself! Yers is an ol' 'un I musta heard a hundert times. I a'ways figered it fer havin' a differnt meanin' 'pendin' on the sitch-ation.

"The fox is a cur'yus an' distrustin' critter. When he comes back home arter bein' aout huntin', he sniffs 'raound his burrow afore goin' in, case some other critter craw'ed in thar since he's been gone.

"I'd say Hunt was a-warnin' that if'n yer too cur'yus an' 'spicious 'baout everythin', it's more'n likely, like a fox sniffin' his aown arse 'ole, yet cud end up in *serious deep shit!*" The boy broke into fits of uncontrolled laughter.

Charles knew the boy was enjoying not only his joke but also the opportunity to freely curse before an adult.

* * *

It took them over an hour to tour the Water Street packing plant. A metals refinery originally, the plant appeared to be well organized, efficient, and clean, but Charles' calculations of the volume of fish being processed fell far short of those proffered by the foreman. He said nothing but felt something was being kept from him. The quantities of fish added up to less than half the volume Innsmouth claimed it regularly processed. If the quotas were being filled, Charles would like to know how.

Frank was to leave at noon to help out at home. The boy had been whittling a small block of wood all morning, so, before he left, Charles asked him about the queer figure he had produced.

"Is that your interpretation of a deep one?"

"That's right," the boy responded, extending the completed figure for Charles' inspection.

"I take 'em in ta Arkham an' sell 'em. Taourists buy 'em as cur'yos'ties."

Charles took the piece from the boy, noting the excellent craftsmanship reflected in the depiction of a misshapen frog creature crouched in a semi-erect stance as if about to lunge or hop. It was well executed, but something about the piece did not seem right. He handed it back to the boy, commenting, "Pretty gruesome, but he seems almost more terrified than terrifying."

Frank retrieved the figure scrutinizing its features. He didn't respond to Charles' comment, however, until he was leaving, his back to Charles. Almost as an afterthought, he then replied, "I see jus' whut ye mean. Funny haow that is."

Charles wished he could have seen the expression on the boy's face at that exact moment.

* * *

On his own now, Charles headed directly for the only place Frank had refused to take him—the old Marsh mansion just off Lafayette Street. His excellent memory and sense of direction made it easy for him to navigate through the streets northward toward the river.

The story proved accurate once again as he passed the ruins of Zadok Allen's old fire station on Pine Street, long ago reduced to a mere pile of scattered bricks. He repressed the desire to explore, knowing he must hurry if he were to complete his investigations before he was due to inspect the boats of the incoming fishermen.

A short distance up Washington Street, he came upon the ruins of its bridge. The barn-like covered bridge had fallen into the gorge of the Manuxet years ago, but he easily forded the shallow stream the river had become. Once across the river, he need only follow Washington Street to his destination. Surely he could recognize the Marsh mansion, based on the story's short description combined with scattered bits of information he had pried out of Frank.

The boy had been extremely reluctant to discuss anything connected with the Marsh family, especially the members who had vanished shortly before the FBI raid. The Marsh mansion clearly represented the ultimate terror to the population of Innsmouth, for in the sixty-seven years since its abandonment, none had dared cross its threshold. Instinctively, Charles felt that the key to Innsmouth's mystery lay somewhere in that house. For over sixty years Innsmouth had remained stranded somewhere between reality and fantasy, but Charles refused to leave it there.

He wound his way through the dilapidated industrial and commercial areas, then through the burned out remains of slums that had reportedly been infested with deep ones. Fifteen minutes later, he stood before the largest private home in Innsmouth, its third-story and attic windows retaining only tattered remnants of the shutters that had once protected its secrets.

Extensive and probably once-beautiful parterres led the visitor, via twisting paths that slyly traced esoteric symbols, to the entrance of the house. The front door was unlocked, but, as he entered the foyer, Charles was struck by an unbearable stench far worse than that of any fish. Burying his face in his clothing, he inhaled deeply before approaching the intricately cobwebbed staircase directly before him. As he reached for the banister, he was overcome by the suffocating odor; he gagged before surrendering to a reversal of his digestive functions.

As the room slowed its spinning around him, he willed himself to composure. More determined than ever to continue, he brushed innumerable spidery strands aside as he propelled himself upward toward the revelation he was sure awaited his discovery.

Charles continued beyond the second- and third-floor landings to the attic level, irresistibly drawn to a pair of ornate doors at the end of the shadow-slashed hallway. Dust enveloped everything, and as he passed the tiny particles leapt into the air before being pulled back by gravity to obliterate his footprints.

He finally halted, facing two eight-foot filigreed doors. Without hesitating, he enclosed their solid gold knobs in his hands and, bracing himself, turned them both as he simultaneously thrust the doors inwardly. What he beheld vanquished forever his doubts concerning Innsmouth's abominable history.

* * *

He stood just inside some kind of deranged temple, staring at the bloated, mutilated visage of one with whom he had become well acquainted, having repeatedly shared the other's adventures. As the fellow had not committed his name to the written page, Charles found himself without a means of addressing Lovecraft's narrator.

Minutes later, his physical and mental numbness began to subside. In an effort to retain his sanity, he focused upon his surroundings and, with utmost reluctance, the hideous altar stone that supported the remains of the narrator.

He stared at murals adorning the walls with cosmic contradiction. Breath-taking colors delineated both human and ichthyic figures as they intermingled, subtly twisting and entwining, as they were transformed into hideous, otherworldly atrocities.

The altar itself had been carved from a single basalt boulder in the semblance of a crouching, mutated frog or fish. The tip of each digit of its paws boasted a metallic overlay in simulation of the taloned being that had acted as the model for the sculpture. The most salient feature of the ebony sculpture was its mocking, defiant expression, stemming from the coldness of the blind, unblinking eyes which presided over a lolling, foot-long tongue depending from a factitious maw.

Charles turned from the sight, concealing his face in his arms. He fought his weakness, forcing himself again to confront his surroundings. It was then that he noticed a word written in crimson letters across the wall behind the altar. "TRAITOR" was delineated in letters over two feet in height, but in order for him to read the smaller writing beneath, he had to maneuver around and behind the filthy altar, carefully avoiding contact. Then, standing just inches from the inscription, he read:

> Though he be one of us, in this way we repaid him who betrayed us—he who caused our land to be burned and our seas to explode. By his changing form and need for those of his kind, the traitor returned; thus were we granted the opportunity for revenge. The punishment is meet in the slowness of its taking, that the traitor, though forever branded, may join us as we raise our voices in the praise of Lord Dagon, in Y'ha-nthlei beneath the sea. Iä R'lyeh! Cthulhu fhtagn! Iä! Iä!

Charles knew that if he were to comprehend any of the madness around him, he would need to examine, even touch, the abomination on the altar. Studying it, he was reminded of toads which, after being crushed beneath the unrelenting wheel of a car, shrivel in the sun's heat as they transform into parchment-dry imitations of their former selves. The entity's prominent features were certainly those of a frog or toad, yet its overall bearing recalled

that of a man. The couchant body concealed its feet and hands, unnatural-
ly tucked beneath the torso. The body was mottled blue and gray, though
the underside or stomach area paled to ivory. The eyes and mouth were
closed, their details oddly blurred.

Charles cried aloud, "What in the hell did they do to you?" in the unan-
swering silence.

Finally he forced himself to reach out, his fingertips lightly grazing the
surface of the creature. Tiny particles pulled free as he retracted his hand,
creating minute holes or tears in the overall structure. He jumped back
quickly, shocked at the disintegration he saw beginning in the thing. The
gossamer figure erupted in the draft resulting from his sudden movement,
shattering silently into fragments which were further reduced to fumes that
quickly dispersed. Only when nothing at all remained of the figure did
Charles begin to understand the terrible nature of the deep ones' punishment.

The narrator had returned to Innsmouth in 1930, two years after alert-
ing the FBI to the anomalies present among Innsmouth's population, naive-
ly expecting to be welcomed by his fellow deep ones; instead, they had
flayed him alive, exacting their revenge by inflicting unimaginable pain
upon him. They had rightfully blamed him for the devastating attack which
eradicated their population. By flaying the traitor, they had "cleansed" him,
much as a fisherman cleans a catch by scraping the scales from its body.
They had performed their ungodly surgery with such exactitude that the
flesh had been incredibly maintained as one seamless pelt, carefully removed
by immersion of the flesh as it was being stripped from the living victim.

Then they had set the skin upon the altar, shaping the dermal envelope
to appear solid, that it might serve both as a warning and as ghostly
guardian of the mansion's secret.

Charles had by now half-consciously formed the hypothesis that the
deep ones did exist after all, but as a dangerous human cult among the
heretical Dagon churches. Its members presumably profited from allegorical doctrines concerning some superhuman immortality they had attained
through cultic initiation. Perhaps the psychotic narrator had mistaken these
claims for literal truth. Yet he had been right about one thing: Monsters
they were in actuality. They must have been to punish him in this fashion.

Despite the unspeakable torture the narrator had endured, Charles
realized with a start that, according to Lovecraft's story, the victim would
have survived due to its newfound organic immortality! Survived to accompany his torturers as they returned to Y'ha-nthlei, deep below Devil Reef,
that they might spend eternity blasphemously glorifying that aqueous
blight they called Dagon.

In this case, Charles fantasized, he would have merely destroyed a
phantasm, the long discarded slough of a creature absolved of its sin. In any

case, his action had earned him the right to any secret the immaterial sentinel had protected.

He was assaulted again by the sudden, overwhelming intensity of the room's revolting atmosphere combined with its ubiquitous stench. Together these strained to force Charles from the temple. Yet as he staggered toward the exit, he noticed some clothing piled against the wall opposite the altar. Subsequent investigation confirmed his initial speculation—the old-fashioned suit was a garment the narrator had discarded long ago. Searching through the pockets, Charles found a sheet of yellowed stationery, a letter addressed to Howard Phillips Lovecraft:

My Dear Mr. Lovecraft:

You will be pleased to learn that I stand upon the verge of attaining my goal. The cousin I rescued from a mental institution in Canton, Ohio, is quite advanced in his physical transformation and has already visited legendary Y'ha-nthlei beneath the waters of Devil Reef. The blasts of depth charges two years ago caused extensive damage, leading to much of the population's emigration to similar strongholds in this and other oceans—but the place is extant! At present, I excitedly await the return of my cousin with those who shall welcome me among them.

It is essential that you receive this information, as it must be added to the text of the story you are writing at my behest. The piece will truly be your own, though based upon events I have related to you. As I explained when we met, I deem it vital that all be told to others who are ignorant of their inhuman heritage. I remind you also, if I may, that it is imperative my identity be kept secret, that the publication of my tale may cause no member of my family any suffering or embarrassment.

You may be interested to learn that Capt. Marsh's former inner sanctum not only provides me with shelter at present, but has also proven most intriguing in its mystery. Yesterday I discovered by accident that this room accesses a hidden stairway leading to an underground construction. By applying downward pressure to the tongue of this room's beast-shaped altar, one may gain access to a tunnel which burrows to the harbor shore nearest the watery entrance to Y'ha-nthlei. The altar revolves upon an astounding series of levers and pulleys to reveal the stairs below.

Now, sir, before I bid you farewell, I wish to inform you of certain arrangements I have made with my solicitor. I have been, as you know, dubbed "missing" by the authorities. As I have no intention of ever returning or having any need for property, I

have directed my attorneys to deliver the full proceeds of the sale
of my substantial estate to you alone when, at the lapse of 7
years, I shall be declared "legally dead." Please accept the proceeds as a token of my appreciation for all the aid you have so
kindly given me. My attorney will contact you in early
September, 1937, concerning this distribution of the proceeds of
my estate.

Now I must close as I hear the approach of those I have so long
awaited and yearned to join.

The letter supplied what the story had lacked: It was signed ROBERT
OLMSTEAD. Olmstead's delusion, then, had been complete, his last words
filled with a terrible irony he would not live long enough to appreciate.

Without further pause, Charles let the long-unsent missive slip to the
floor as he ran to the hideous altar and pressed down the graven monster's
tongue. A grinding and whirring ensued as the altar slid aside, exposing a
stairwell which he quickly descended despite the worsening miasma. Upon
reaching the bottom, he flung himself into the shaft of the ensuing tunnel,
greatly relieved that the batteries of his pocket flashlight were fresh.

* * *

He hurried through the long-unused passage, hoping to reach the harbor
before the fishermen returned for the day, oblivious to the otherworldly
design of the intricately carved bas-relief that stretched the entire length of
the tunnel. After nearly an hour the tunnel widened, and he found himself
confronting a portal cut from native stone to represent the head of a colossal fish, its gaping mouth providing egress via a continuing passage. As he
paused to study the sculpture, he spied a seam in the adjacent wall, tracing
the outline of a door.

The sculpted door, he felt sure, would lead to the harbor, so he pressed
instead against the other door, which opened into a dark storeroom. Still
aware of the passing time, he carefully maneuvered through that room to
another door, a normal one.

Refusing to consider what might lie on the other side of the door, he
opened it cautiously and peered out. Seeing no one in the well lit area
beyond, he stepped through and was immediately confronted with a huge,
glass-walled tank of water. Looking further, he saw he was within the concrete walls of a warehouse containing ten or more of the gigantic tanks. His
legs were shaking now as he realized that the tanks were much too large for
any logical function in the processing of fish—unless he was in the old
Marsh refinery, now run by deep ones!

Putting his face to the glass of the nearest tank, he gazed into the murkiness of its dirty water. Seconds later he screamed as a pair of inhuman eyes looked back at him through the clouded translucence. Jumping back, he ran to the nearest open door and threw himself through its welcome opening. In those few steps, he traveled all the way from terror into absolute madness.

* * * * *

He stood, slack-jawed, on the threshold of an abattoir of the damned; there was no other way he could describe it.

There were approximately fifty web-pawed deep ones to his immediate right in a cage, huddling protectively round what Charles assumed to be a priest of Dagon, crowned with a ceremonial tiara of gold. Most of the beings were naked, though a few wore tattered remnants of clothing as if attempting to conceal the slimy wet nature of their squamous skin. Their panic-stricken expressions bore striking resemblance to that which Frank had reproduced from these living models. They were, of course, no mere cultists, but rather living specimens of the terrible fish-frog men described so luridly by Lovecraft. Charles had at last discovered precisely what was fact and what was fiction in the town of Innsmouth.

A wave of their doleful wailing washed over him as the prisoners gibbered and flopped behind the bars. Charles was sure, however, that he could detect perfectly enunciated English phrases mixed in with scattered bursts of otherwise alien, guttural speech.

Far worse was the sight opposite the cage. Six creatures, in various stages of butchery, yet definitely very much alive, were suspended from the ceiling, hung upon great hooks that had been torn through their spinal ridges. The six breathing slabs of meat bleated and tittered pathetically as their life blood splashed down into run-off troughs cut into the concrete slaughterhouse floor. Their uncanny pleas reminded the listener of their forsaken humanity.

Charles noticed the caged creatures suddenly stiffen, pulling back to bark and snarl gutturally at him. He stepped back in fear, just as a powerful hand slapped down on his shoulder.

"Naow yer in the shit, Mr. Fox."

Pulling away, Charles quickly turned to confront the speaker, Joshua Hunt, and the leering men behind him.

"What the hell is going on here?" Charles demanded. "What is this insanity?"

A smile spread across Hunt's face. "Ye wanted to see aour works, Varley, an' naow ye seen 'em all. This is where we keep aour supp'mental stock o' fish meat, in case we need to fill aour quota."

Hunt stood with one foot in a bloody trough, pointing. "Ye got yer older deep 'uns o'er here; some says the big shot is o'er a thousand years old. But ol' meat's tough, so we only use the face ten'acles—they say yer can't tell 'em from squid ten'acles. E'er eat cal'meri, city feller?"

Pointing next to the half-butchered deep ones, Hunt bragged, "But the young 'un's meat is ideal fer mixing' in with minced fish, fer breaded patties an' fish sticks like ye city folk loves sa much. Nice thing is they dun't die, so's ye can chop big fillets off'n 'em, then throw 'em back inter the ocean so's they'll grow more."

Hunt's smug look enraged Charles. "This is inhumane, to say the very least!"

Hunt laughed scornfully, his braying echoed by the other fishermen.

"*In-hu-mane*, he says! Yer dun't know the ha'f o' what them damn thengs done to this taown, an' give 'em ha'f o' chance, they'd do lots wuss. E'er hear tell o' a *sea shoggoth*? If'n yud e'er seed 'un, yud feel same as us. Well, these critters was a-plannin' on havin' a few shoggoths drop by to visit us Innsmouth folks afore we faought back." Seething with fury Hunt spit on the floor at Charles's feet. "The deep 'uns ain't nuthin' but filth, goddamn—!"

Charles screamed his interruption, "Yet you're willing to feed that goddamn filth to thousands of unsuspecting people! It could poison them or cause genetic mutations that won't show up for generations. You can't possibly know what the effects might be in time!"

"Yer think we care abaout ye aoutsiders?" screamed Hunt. "J. Edgar Hoover did his best to keep 'em aout o' Innsmouth, but his hands was tied. Arter it was all over, nub'dy'd let us normal folks leave; they cut off the power an' aour fresh water. It weren't spring yet, an' lots o' good folk died o' the cold—some jus' starved to death. The folks in Arkham an' e'erwhere else, they hoped we'd all die so they cud furget 'baout Innsmouth.

"Hoover, though, he was a good 'un. Mebbe he liked dressin' up like a girl an' wuss, but he had a worser problem than keepin' his druthers a secret! E'er notice his kinder toady shape, an' how his eyes got kinder poppin' and a-bulgin' as he aged? Yessir, he were part deep 'un, an' none o' yer folk e'er did figure that aout! He wanted us su'vivers o' the raid kep' quiet an' was willin' to let ever one of us die ta 'complish it.

"We're gonna rebuild Innsmouth with the profits from this new fishin' deal, an' to hell with all ye aoutsiders! No matter what happens, we'll be awlright—'cos we don't eat fish!"

Two men came from behind Hunt, each grabbing one of Charles' arms.

"Shud we put 'em in with the deep 'uns, Joshua?" asked one of the men.

The old man flushed in fury as his voice boomed with rage. "Are ye aout o' yer goddamn mind? Think, man!"

The man lowered his head, shamed by the reproof. Hunt strode over and lifted Charles' face by the chin.

"Gent'emen, this is a human bein'," he said calmly, his volume rising as he continued. "We can't be puttin' human bein's in amongst demons! They'd tar him 'part like a ragg'dy doll!"

Those words should have reassured Charles, but he did not trust Hunt. The man had been thoroughly poisoned with unreasoning hatred, a hatred that made him as alien and dangerous as the deep ones.

Feigning pity, Hunt smiled at Charles, then spoke in gentler tones. "I cud'n bear the thought o' them faoul things a-rendin' this man." His smile became a sneer. "'Sides, wha' ud aour big city cus'mers think if they was to find *hambu'ger* mixed in with ther fish? Why, it ud be the end o' all we been a-workin' fur!"

Charles choked back a scream. There was no mistaking the evil in Hunt's voice now; Charles knew he was going to die.

"Put him in one o' the storerooms raound back while I think haow to handle this," Hunt instructed the men holding Charles. "He might be th' start o' a whole new in'stry fur us."

Hunt did not even glance in Charles' direction as the hysterically terrified man was led away. Rather, he nodded to young Frank, who stepped forth from among the fishermen.

The boy hurried over, listened to Joshua's instructions carefully, then chuckled dryly.

"Ask yer dad to drive ye to Arkham, son," Hunt said to the boy. "I need ye ta find aout the curr'nt askin' price fur graound chuck."

Frank hesitated. "Sure, Uncle Josh," he replied, "but don't ye 'spect they'll be a-sendin' more folks to find aout what became o' Mr. V.?"

Hunt smiled, put his arm around the boy, and whispered, "I sure hope so."

About "Devil Reef"

This ingenious tale has points of contact with Lovecraft's fiction, but not quite the ones you might expect, and the result is authentic, yet offbeat. Lovecraft's own fiction is informed by Lord Dunsany's at a deep level, and those sometimes apparently recessive genes manifest themselves here. "Devil Reef" owes as much to "The Terrible Old Man" as it does to "The Shadow over Innsmouth." It works because of the semiotic equivalence between Kingsport and Innsmouth, both port towns opening onto the Oceans of the Unknown. Glasby's tale falls neatly within a well defined subgenre to which Henry Kuttner's "The Hunt" and Stephen King's "Popsy" belong. These stories are one niche over from tales like "The Terrible Old Man", in which a mundane crook overreaches himself with hood-hubris by picking the wrong victim. The idea there is not much beyond that of a story of a petty crook messing with the big boys. No, the kinds I am thinking of here play off the very different dichotomy Richard L. Tierney delineates between the philosophical-esthetic chill of supernatural horror and the very different blunt-ended terror of a mundane threat: getting ambushed by rap artists in a dark alley, let's say. These stories, like Glasby's, are implicitly tales of divine justice. In them, the supernatural horrors which slap down the mundane bad guys take the role of the God who is otherwise absent in the universe of the horror story.

This story appears here in print for the first time.

Devil Reef

by John Glasby

Gino Corsi saw the black reef for the first time through the grime-smeared window of the bus he had boarded almost an hour earlier in Arkham. Even though the tide was coming in, the long jagged line of grim rocks stood out clearly against the rolling white breakers of the Atlantic, yet for him it held a lure that went much deeper than the old tales of mysterious lights seen there at dead of night when there was no moon and the fishermen's stories of fine sailing ships that had been wrecked on those dangerous rocks.

It had been in Boston that he had first encountered whispered rumours concerning legend-shrouded Innsmouth, tales which had whetted his desire to visit this hoary old fishing port on the coast where the Manuxet enters the Atlantic off Kingsport Head.

Few people, he had been informed, ever cared to visit this ancient, decaying place, not merely because of its desolated isolation and inaccessibility, but because of the nature of the folk who lived there. Backwards and decadent, they kept to themselves, never mixing with their neighbours along the coast. There had also been unsubstantiated rumours of peculiar vanishments among outsiders who had gone there for one reason or another, together with murmured accounts of pagan rites, devil worship, and black magic.

While such information as this may have excited the curiosity of an antiquarian or student of ancient American history, Corsi was neither of these. His interest in Innsmouth was more basic and materialistic than this.

What prompted him to obtain more cognizance of the town and its inhabitants was the vague report he had received from one of his acquaintances that there had been, and almost certainly still was, a prolific trade in gold ingots and various articles of gold jewellery emanating from Innsmouth. One or two items were on display in certain museums in

Massachusetts, although it had to be said that in spite of their almost price-less value, all possessed intricate designs which were peculiar in the extreme.

So far, no one had positively identified their origin, although all author-ities agreed that the general designs were either batrachian or piscatorial in nature, vaguely resembling Polynesian art. Certain tales maintained that this precious commodity came from pirate hoards buried on Devil Reef, lying about a mile offshore from Innsmouth, and it had occurred to Corsi that if there were any truth in these evasive rumours, much of this wealth might still be there, waiting to be claimed by anyone sufficiently deter-mined to get his hands on it.

It had been in Arkham, however, that he had learned more concerning Innsmouth. While Arkham with its old gambrel-roofed houses and narrow, twisting lanes and cobbled alleys was full of dark, elder mysteries of its own, the people in certain quarters were a polyglot mixture of East European extraction who had little love for their neighbours along the coast and who, in the right circumstances, could be persuaded to gossip about Innsmouth. Much of what they said was clearly intended as a warning, intimating that Innsmouth was not a wholesome place to visit and certainly not one in which to stay the night.

It was from an old man of Polish origin that Corsi learned several inter-esting facts, after loosening the octogenarian's tongue by plying him with a liberal amount of strong liquor.

More than a century earlier, the oldster averred, Innsmouth had been a prosperous town with no hint of the nightmare that was to come and, undoubtedly, much of its wealth at that time was derived from privateering rather than the fishing industry.

Then the bad times had come, not only to Innsmouth but to the whole of Massachusetts, although even then that period marked the begin-ning of the shipping trade which was to take Innsmouth sailors to many strange and exotic ports in the East Indies and among the islands of the Southern Seas.

Whether it was as a result of these sea voyages that so much gold was brought back to Innsmouth, or there really were pirate treasures hidden on Devil Reef, the octogenarian would not speculate, but it was undeniable that several of the families there, particularly the Marshes, Gilmans, Eliots, and Waites, attained great wealth and influence at this time. Yet something else had come with this prosperity, something dark and evil which had appeared so insidiously that few could put a date to when exactly it had all started. Certainly it was at that period that strange things began to happen in Innsmouth.

The fishing trade, which had declined almost to the vanishing point, suddenly boomed around Innsmouth and the noticeable avoidance of the adjoining communities gradually assumed the form of a one-way traffic between Innsmouth and the surrounding area. While the Innsmouth folk continued to pay frequent visits to neighbouring towns for certain essential supplies, visitors to the town were actively discouraged until, following the closure of the railway branch line from Rowley, the only remaining link was the dilapidated road which meandered over the marshes and stretches of windblown sand, crossing numerous tottering wooden bridges over the narrow tributaries of the Manuxet.

Tales began to spread abroad of devil worship based upon some weird pagan religion brought back by Obed Marsh and Hiram Tilnsley from the Polynesian islands of the Pacific and of human sacrifices carried out on Devil Reef at certain times of the year. While the aged anecdotist himself did not subscribe to such fancies, he averred that it was true the normal Christian sects in Innsmouth faced rapidly dwindling congregations and eventually left the town altogether, their churches either falling into ruin and decay or taken over by some new cult whose high priests were chosen from among the most prominent Innsmouth families.

From what the old man had personally seen, all of the Innsmouth people had a funny look which distinguished them from all others along the coast. Some of the more superstitious Arkham folk maintained that this was due to interbreeding with slaves brought back by the old sailing captains from the South Seas. Whatever the truth might be concerning Innsmouth, the old man had wheezed warningly, many people from outside had gone there, including a number of government officials, and they had never come back. No hint of their whereabouts was ever uncovered.

All of this might have deterred a lesser man, but Gino Corsi was not a man to be put off by such idle gossip, especially where a fortune in gold was concerned. However, in the event that there might be trouble, he had taken the precaution of packing his bag with two heavy-calibre automatics fitted with silencers and several packs of ammunition. These, he felt sure, would afford him any protection he might need and could also persuade any of the inhabitants to divulge any information needed to lead him to this horde of gold.

As the wheezing bus rattled along the uneven, potholed highway leading into Innsmouth past Kingsport Head, Corsi cast an appraising glance over the town, now clearly visible in the wide valley. It was far larger in extent than he had supposed, stretching from the warehouses near the waterfront back towards the hilly country where the Manuxet tumbled over falls on the western edge of town. Yet from what he could make out, much of the place seemed devoid of life, as if entire sections had been abandoned and given over to rot and decay. Over everything lay an air of oppressive depopulation.

Most of the older buildings were in various stages of ruin with windows broken or boarded up, roofs sagging dangerously where the Atlantic gales had ripped them wide open. Even the streets appeared deserted as the bus made its way through the outskirts between rows of once-stately Georgian houses. While the mere sight of the place would have been enough to put off any normal traveller, this apparent emptiness and dearth of life was ideally suited to Corsi's purpose.

The fewer people there were around, the easier it would be to discover all he wanted to know and, if necessary, get a boat out to Devil Reef, search for the gold, and then make off with it before its loss was discovered. If these folk were as isolated and backwards as he had been led to believe, he did not anticipate too much trouble in that respect. Naturally, he would have to be discreet in his questioning and, as a last resort, he would have no hesitation in using the weapons he had brought with him to extract the information he wanted.

The bus finally pulled up in a wide square and Corsi got out, clutching his bag tightly. The driver, a repellent-looking individual with curious, wide-staring eyes, did not give him a second glance and remained seated behind the wheel, his thick, stubby fingers clenched tightly around it.

The instant he alighted, Corsi was assailed by the overpowering fishy stench, a fetor so mephitic that it almost suffocated him. It seemed to come from the direction of the large building he had noticed on the journey into town, a relatively robustly constructed structure near the wharves. Clearly, the fishing industry was still thriving along this part of the coast. It was only with a tremendous effort of will that he was able to keep his heaving stomach under control.

In Arkham he had been told that there was still a hotel of sorts in Innsmouth and, glancing around him at the decaying buildings which fringed the square, he spotted the three-storey building which had obviously seen better days. There was a square wooden sign outside which proclaimed it to be the Gilman place and, going inside, he approached the desk, placing his bag carefully on the floor.

There was no one in sight in the dusty lobby and no sound at all. His first impression was not very reassuring. Since few visitors ever came to Innsmouth, he considered it possible that even this hotel was deserted, left to dust and rats, and he did not relish the idea of spending the night elsewhere in this spectral town.

On one side of the scratched wooden desk he noticed a small brass bell and after banging it several times with the flat of his hand he was rewarded by the sound of shuffling footsteps coming from somewhere inside, and a moment later a curiously stooped figure emerged from the rear.

Corsi's first perception was one of degeneracy and malformation and a feeling that the man suffered from some obscure congenital disease which had transformed him into this pathetic caricature of a human being. There was also a queer *floppiness* about his slow movements as if his limbs were boneless, and the wide, staring eyes were virtually lidless and set too far apart, giving him an oddly piscatorial look.

"I shall want a room with meals," Corsi said harshly, keeping his emotions under tight control. For the first time since leaving Boston, he felt an odd shiver of apprehension. It was a sensation he was not familiar with and he forced it down quickly.

"You want to stay here, stranger?" There was an unmistakable hint of surprise in the hoarse, croaking voice. "But nobody stays in Innsmouth, leastways not overnight."

"I have business here," Corsi retorted belligerently. "I may be staying for some time."

Gilman, for such Corsi assumed him to be, hesitated momentarily, then turned without a further word and unhooked a key from the small rack on the wall. He slid it towards Corsi across the desk.

"Where is the room?" Corsi asked.

"Third room on the left at the top of the stairs. Yuh'll eat at seven."

Taking the key, Corsi picked up his bag without further comment and climbed the creaking stairs, knowing instinctively that Gilman was watching him closely.

He had expected the stairs to lead only to the third floor but then noticed there were two further flights going up. Evidently there were other floors at the rear of the building which he had not noticed from the square. He guessed they might have been hidden by the prominent cupolas at the front. The stairs ended on the fifth floor, just under the roof, and inserting the key in the third door along the short corridor, he pushed it open to find a small room with thick curtains drawn across the window, letting in none of the daylight.

Thick dust stung the back of his throat as he tugged them aside. Outside was a weed-infested courtyard, roughly flagged, and beyond it a veritable sea of roofs above which reared three tall spires which had evidently been churches in bygone days. All three were in various stages of disrepair.

Checking his watch, he saw that there still remained three hours before seven, giving him ample time in which to explore part of the town. First, however, he needed some idea of the general layout of the place. Unzipping his bag, he took out a pair of powerful binoculars and returned to the window, adjusting the focus until everything sprang into startling clarity. The view from his room lay towards the landward side of Innsmouth, showing

the narrow, winding streets and alleys of what had once been the main res-
idential quarter, filled with fine Georgian houses and green spaces.

Now lying like a smothering blanket over everything was this strange
dearth of life and activity. Only in one place did there appear to be anything
going on: a large building perhaps three quarters of a mile away having a
large wooden board above the partially concealed entrance. Several of the
letters were almost completely obliterated, but he could make out enough
to tell him that this was the Marsh Refining Company. So that was where
much of the gold was refined into ingots. This indisputable fact, that work
was still going on there, raised his hopes to fever pitch, so much so that the
binoculars trembled slightly in his hands as he fought to hold them still.

Turning slightly, he surveyed the entire visible panorama until the massive bulk of Kingsport Head came into view with the river flowing swiftly
beside it. For a second a shiver of nameless dread passed through him, for
there was a house perched right on the very edge of that sheer drop into the
ocean. It was not, however, the fact that a house had been built which
caused him to quake inwardly. It was really quite a simple fact, but one
which went beyond all reason.

There were wide windows and a door on that side of the building which
faced the sea, yet no hint of solid ground outside! The door opened onto thin
air with nothing but a drop of perhaps three hundred feet below it!

What insane perversity had caused anyone to build such a place, he
could not imagine. Unless the house had been used for contraband during
the old smuggling days and any unwanted guests, forced to flee in that
direction, would step to their deaths on the needle-pointed rocks far below.

He replaced the binoculars in his bag and, after thrusting one of the
heavy automatics into his shoulder holster, went downstairs. There was no
sign of the deformed proprietor and, pocketing the key, he went out into the
square. By now it was later afternoon and the lowering sun threw grotesque,
warped shadows across the streets which radiated from the square.

This time there were a few folk about and he could not help noticing
their shambling walk and the strange cast of their features as they eyed him
sullenly and with an open animosity. Clearly these people were highly suspicious of strangers and if the talk of pagan rites and a plentiful supply of
gold were true, they had good cause. As far as the idea of blasphemous rituals being carried out, Corsi didn't give a damn about that. As far as he was
concerned, they could worship whatever heathen gods they liked. The gold
was another matter and the sooner he obtained some definite information as
to its whereabouts, the sooner he would get out of this decadent place.

Making his way along a broad thoroughfare whose faded sign proclaimed it to be Fish Street, with the muted thunder of the waterfalls on the
Manuxet in his ears, he paused abruptly at a junction with a dingy lane that

clearly led off in the direction of the waterfront, for through a wide gap where one of the more ancient buildings had been demolished at some time in the past, he made out the distant breakwater and beyond it, lying in a black bar across the horizon, the serrated outline of Devil Reef.

A few moments earlier, he had spotted a dark shape entering the alley, and from the brief glimpse it had appeared to possess a more normal shape and gait than the other inhabitants he had seen. A quick look along Fish Street told him there was no one in sight apart from a couple of figures in the distance, their back to him. Slipping into the shadowed alley, he hurried after the man, catching up with him a few minutes later.

The youth, for such it turned out to be, jerked visibly as Corsi grabbed him roughly by the arm and thrust him into a weed-choked opening between two crumbling buildings. Deliberately, Corsi allowed his jacket to fall open, revealing the automatic in its holster, watching the expression of petrified fear on the youth's face.

"Just answer a few questions and nothing will happen to you," he said harshly.

"What is it you want to know?"

Corsi felt a grim satisfaction as he noticed the way the other kept his gaze fixed on the gun. Frightened men usually told the truth.

"You don't look like the rest of the Innsmouth folk I've seen, so I reckon you don't come from here. What's your name and what do you do here?"

"Henry—Henry Forbes. I work as a fish packer down at the wharf. Look, mister, I don't know much about Innsmouth. I live in Newburyport and only come into town four days a week. I—"

"All right. All right," Corsi interrupted sharply. Imperceptibly, he increased the pressure on the youth's arm, gripping him tightly. "I understand from certain friends of mine in Boston that there's a fortune in gold here in Innsmouth. Do you know anything about it?"

He saw Forbes hesitate and it seemed that the fear mirrored in his eyes suddenly went beyond that of the gun in Corsi's holster. For several seconds the youth's mouth worked but no words came out beyond a disjointed mumble in which Corsi could distinguish nothing. Then, gradually, Forbes took a firmer hold of himself and his muttering assumed articulation.

"Everybody here pays in gold, mister. They say it was all brung to Innsmouth by old Captain Marsh more'n a hundred years ago. There's precious stones, too, but what I've seen, they ain't like ordinary diamonds and rubies. They're a funny color and shape and have a queer look to 'em. The Innsmouth women wear 'em when they attend the services in the Temple o' Dagon yonder."

Forbes pointed a trembling hand in the general direction of the town center. "Say, you ain't thinkin' of stealing some of it, are you?"

Corsi gave a faint smile, feeling inwardly satisfied by the youth's responses. "That's the general idea," he said grimly. "Seems to me they've got too much of it stashed away in this town. I guess they won't miss a little of it."

Forbes shook his head agitatedly. "Don't try anythin' like that, mister. You'll never do it. They won't let you out of the town alive. Maybe that gun will stop some of 'em. But there are *others* they keep shut away most o' the time and only let 'em out at night. A bullet won't stop *Them.*"

"I'll take my chances on that. Just tell me where this gold is kept. Is it out yonder on Devil Reef?"

"Look, mister, I only know what little I overhear at work an' what I've sometimes seen o' nights. Believe me, you'll go the same way as all the others who came uninvited to Innsmouth."

Corsi shifted his right hand a little closer to the gun butt at his shoulder, felt the youth stiffen abruptly under his grasp. Maybe it would have been better to have got hold of one of the true Innsmouth stock for questioning, he thought.

"All right. I'll tell you everythin' I know." Forbes was stammering wildly now, the words tumbling over each other as he forced them out. "They reckon that Captain Marsh and some o' the other captains brung a whole heap o' gold trinkets and jewelry from someplace in the South Seas. Maybe a lot of it is still kept somewhere on Devil Reef because I often see folk goin' out there after dark. Some of 'em row out in boats but most swim out yonder. There's supposed to be rocks there that have funny carvings on 'em and deep caves that go right down under the sea. Plenty o' places where they could hide all this gold an' bring it back to Innsmouth whenever they need it."

Corsi gave a satisfied nod. He felt certain the youth was telling the truth and what he said sounded logical. Even though there were undoubtedly plenty of places in the town where such a fabulous horde could be concealed against the unwanted attentions of Revenue officers and Customs officials, that dangerous reef offshore would make a far better hiding place.

He slowly released his grip on the youth and stepped back. "Just one more thing," he said inflexibly. "You say most of the folk come out after dark, so there'll be more on the streets then." Already Corsi's thoughts were moving in the direction of stealing a small boat from along the waterfront and rowing out to the reef once night had fallen, but if what the youth had said was true, it would present certain problems in getting there from the Gilman place.

"They hold their services after dark," Forbes said tautly. "And it sure ain't healthy for any outsider to be abroad in town after nightfall."

Corsi mulled that over in his mind. Perhaps the problems of getting to the waterfront might not be as insurmountable as he had thought. Once most of the folk were inside their pagan temples the streets should be relatively deserted. All he had to do was keep his eyes and ears open and seize the opportunity. If his venture should prove successful and the sea conditions were favourable there might be no need to take the grave risk of returning to Innsmouth. Instead he might be able to take the boat further along the coast until he reached a suitable landing place and then head back for Arkham with his haul.

"All right," he snapped. "You can go. But keep our little conversation to yourself. It won't be too difficult for me to find you if I should get the idea that you've talked."

He watched the youth hurry off, then turned and made his way slowly back to the hotel. By now, the sun had set and it was growing dark. The only source of illumination inside the hotel lobby was a single bulb set close to the ceiling above the desk. Checking his watch, he saw that it wanted half an hour to seven.

Fumbling his way up the stairs, he remained in his room until it was time for the appointed meal. The small dining room contained only three tables, each spread with a dingy cloth. Since there appeared to be no other guests, he chose the table in the corner where he could watch the door with his back to the wall.

The meal, which consisted mainly of fish, was served up by a woman in her late fifties, whose repellent features were even more pronounced than those of the proprietor. The long, sloping forehead and almost complete absence of a chin made Corsi shudder and the fact that she did not speak a single word repulsed him even further. As he ate he studied her closely, unable to make up his mind whether this curious affliction which seemed to have overtaken so many of the residents of this town was due to some odd disease which had struck Innsmouth at some time in the past, or was a result of some rare form of interbreeding possibly, as some had suggested, with people brought back from distant ports during the frequent sailing expeditions of a century or so earlier.

Inwardly, he was glad when the meal was over and he could return to his room under the roof. Locking the door securely, he crossed to the window, seated himself in the rickety old chair, and looked out into the night. From his vantage point, so high up, he could view a large area of the town. Apart from the various warehouses, decrepit factory buildings, and ancient spired churches, his room occupied one of the highest points in Innsmouth.

He would have preferred a room situated at the front of the hotel from whence he could have kept a close watch on the region towards the waterfront, but he did not dare risk moving from where he was for the time being.

For almost an hour he sat there, straining to pick out the faintest sounds and slightest movements which would indicate that the local inhabitants were abroad. Occasionally, he thought he detected odd, furtive noises beneath him inside the hotel, but he put these down to the proprietor and the woman he assumed to be Gilman's wife going about their nightly chores. Outside, everything was still and silent, a deathlike hush which began to eat at his nerves.

After a while, however, he became aware of other nocturnal sounds which he found difficult to identify. There was a vague, overall impression of stealthy movement down below, clearly emanating from the dingy side streets around the back of the square, but this was interspersed at irregular intervals by curious croakings and bass ululations which were so totally alien to human speech that he doubted they could have been uttered by normal human beings.

In spite of the reassuring weight of the automatic under his left arm, Corsi could not repress a shudder as those bestial sounds grew louder, and for one frantic instant, he imagined they were converging on the hotel. Had he been seen, in spite of his precautions, talking with that youth? Instinctively, he removed the weapon from its holster and checked that it was loaded before pushing it back.

As the minutes ticked away, he realized that he was in no immediate danger, for the sounds swelled to a crescendo and then diminished as whoever uttered them moved on towards the town center and away from the hotel. He waited impatiently for a quarter of an hour after they had faded into silence before making a move.

Picking up the bag, he tiptoed to the door, turned the key silently in the lock, and let himself out into the short corridor. There was now no sound inside the building and the creaking of the stairs sounded ominously loud in his ears as he descended to the bottom floor. There was no sign of the proprietor or the woman in the lobby, and he guessed they had gone to join the others in their worship of their heathen god.

Trying the street door, he found it to be locked, but Corsi had been prepared for this eventuality. Taking out the automatic, he smashed the lock with a single shot, the weapon making scarcely a sound. A quick glance around the square told him it was empty and, keeping a tight grip on the automatic, he made his way as quietly as possible to the opposite side, keeping in the shadows.

Now his actions would have to be governed entirely by instinct and what he had managed to see from the bus. The fishy stench still pervaded the air, thick and repugnant in his nostrils, as he darted into a narrow street which, judging by the faint sound of breakers on the shingle, led in the direction of the sea.

He was almost halfway along the street when a fresh sound reached him, a sound which sent a finger of ice brushing along his spine and urged him on at a more rapid pace. To call it a devilish chant would be to disregard its abnormal abomination and shuddersome overtones. It was a bane of nature which should have had no place in normal human experience. It was truly the most shocking sound Corsi had ever heard in his entire life. For an instant he was oblivious to his surroundings as his mind tried to conceive of the creatures gathered inside that Temple of Dagon, shrieking and yelping their horrific invocations to such an outrageous deity.

Then he pulled himself together, forced himself to concentrate upon his objective, one which, if successful, would make him rich for the rest of his life. He reached the end of the street and had just turned into an evil-smelling alley when the sound of guttural voices almost immediately ahead brought him to an abrupt halt. Pressing himself into a shadowed doorway whose door had long since fallen from rusted hinges and been removed, he waited breathlessly, his finger tight on the trigger of the automatic.

Seven hideously misshapen figures suddenly emerged in single file from a low arched opening some twenty yards away, and he almost gasped aloud as they hopped and slithered across the rough cobbles. The sight of their faces would have caused a more sensitive man to faint on the spot. Corsi did not faint, although he was shaking uncontrollably by the time the group had vanished around a nearby corner. He had the unshakable impression that, just before they had disappeared, the last creature in the line had turned and stared directly at the place where he was concealed.

Drenched in perspiration, he forced himself to move on. What those *things* were he could never tell, for some of the abnormalities of shape and proportion were indescribable. For the first time, it was borne upon him that many of the old tales and rumours circulating about Innsmouth were nothing short of the literal truth. Only the overriding thought of all that gold ready for the taking steadied his shaken nerves sufficiently to keep him moving in the direction of the waterfront, which he reached some fifteen minutes later.

Here the wharves and warehouses were in an even more decrepit state than those closer to the middle of town. Great piles of fallen masonry lay where they had collapsed over the years. In places, the sea had torn huge chunks from the breakwater. Only the boats drawn up alongside the decaying jetty seemed in good condition, in stark contrast to everything around them.

Fortunately for his sanity, there were no other fresh sounds in the vicinity, although he could still pick out the undulating wail of that unearthly chant in the distance. He consoled himself with the knowledge that as long as it continued, he might be reasonably safe from discovery. Cautiously, he made his way down to the water's edge, casting a quick, appraising glance along the row of boats before finally choosing one which looked small enough to be handled by one man.

Thrusting the automatic back into its holster, he stowed his bag in the stern, cast off the rope, and clambered on board, pushing the boat out with one of the oars. Slipping the oars into the rowlocks, he commenced to pull strongly away from the abandoned waterfront, uncomfortably aware that soon he would be in full view of anyone in the maze of narrow alleys which edged down in that direction. He had known all along, however, that this was a chance he would have to take; there was always the possibility that, even if he were seen, any watcher might believe him to be merely one of the inhabitants rowing out to the reef, since this appeared to be a common occurrence among these curious folk.

Although the tide was now on the turn, beginning to sweep in once more, Corsi made steady progress, occasionally glancing over his shoulder in the direction of the long stretch of midnight blackness that lay about a mile out. Each time it looked dark and featureless but then, when he reckoned he was about halfway to his destination, he saw something which brought the perspiration boiling out afresh on his aching limbs.

Towards the northern tip of the reef a light had sprung into existence, a pulsing glow which waxed and waned in an oddly hypnotic manner, pulsating fitfully to some alien rhythm.

So there was someone out there on the reef, evidently signalling in some manner to a recipient in Innsmouth. Somehow, although he knew there was frequent traffic between the town and Devil Reef, he had hoped that everyone would be at that hellish ceremony. But now that those on the reef had given away their presence and position, he knew where the greatest danger lay. It raised the very definite possibility that his approach would be noticed and—

A sudden splash in the water drew his attention away from the reef and for the first time he noticed the strange phosphorescence of the sea: a pale greenish luminosity etched with widening ripples that spread out from some point astern of the boat as if something big had broken the surface and, almost immediately thereafter, vanished.

Peering into the surrounding darkness, he had the impression there were shapes swimming all around him, just beneath the swelling waves: dimly seen outlines that glided easily through the water, seemingly keeping pace with him as he pulled hard on the oars, heading the boat towards the southernmost tip of the reef, well away from that oddly gleaming light.

Even the thought that these were nothing more than dolphins brought little comfort. Too many strange things were happening around this myth-haunted town for his liking, and the sooner he got his hands on some of this gold and made his getaway to a point further up the coast, the better.

By the time he grounded the boat on a narrow, sloping shelf of black rock, his nerves were stretched almost to the breaking point. Here the fishy smell was even more pronounced than in the town, an overwhelming fetor that was almost tangible. Only by a sheer effort of will and the thought of what might lie hidden on this reef, possibly just within his grasp, kept him from jumping back into the boat and rowing as quickly as he could away from this accursed black reef.

He judged the source of the weird glow to lie some three quarters of a mile to the north of his position and, taking up his bag, he carefully made his way up the treacherously sloping rocks, keeping his head down, not knowing how many Innsmouth folk might be on the reef.

In his ears was the booming roar of the Atlantic breakers smashing against the seaward side of the reef, which he judged to be some forty yards wide at this point. Very soon, in spite of the hazardous nature of the rocks, he reached the highest point of the reef, drenched in the ice-cold spray from the fearsome waves. From his vantage point, he could just make out the odd glow he had noticed earlier and now saw that it emanated from a tall, stone monolith that jutted some twenty feet into the night sky.

Who—or what—had erected that ghoulish menhir, he had no idea, nor what strange natural, or unnatural, mechanism was causing it to glow in such a manner. Now that he was so close to it, he could just discern curious designs etched deeply into its rough surface, but from the impressions he received he had no wish to take out the binoculars and examine them more closely.

Then all thought of that fled his mind as two singular facts caught his attention. The first was the more alarming of the two for there, close to the spot where the opalescent column reared up from the bare rock, a multitude of ghastly shapes were emerging from the pounding surf, slithering up onto the sea-running rocks. Dear God, what were those monstrous forms? The piscatorial odor was now infinitely stronger and more pungent. Shaking uncontrollably, Corsi watched, unable to move, as creatures more fish than men formed a blasphemous ring around the gleaming stone.

Surely these were not to be counted among the inhabitants of Innsmouth? Or were they those things the youth had warned him of, kept out of sight behind shuttered windows, allowed to swim out to this accursed reef to do homage to some pagan god? His mind instantly rejected the latter possibility. No matter how far along the line of inbreeding or unknown disease they had progressed over the decades, normal men and women could never have sunk to this bestial appearance. Had they uttered any sound in parody of human speech, Gino Corsi would undoubtedly have gone insane at that terrible moment.

The second thing he saw in almost the same instant was a dark, irregular shadow on the rocks facing the seaward side of the reef. That it was not simply some rock formation delineated by the faint starshine, he recognized at once. Rather it was an opening of some kind, although whether manmade or natural he could not be certain.

Very slowly, he lowered himself down the smooth side until he was level with the black shadow, calming himself enough to work his way across until he stood before it, feet perched on a low, outjutting ledge. Spray stung his eyes so that for several seconds he was unable to make out any details. Then, wiping the salt water from his smarting eyes, he saw that this was no cavern formed by nature. Fully ten feet wide and almost twice that in height, it was roughly heptagonal in shape, flanked by double columns of smoothly chiselled rock bearing ideoglyphs which represented monstrous beings that could surely have no place in the normal evolution of life on Earth. Judging by the erosion which had clearly taken place, however, he doubted if these columns had been fashioned less than two thousand years earlier.

For a moment, the memory of what he had witnessed on the other side of the reef kept him from moving deeper into that yawning chasm, which seemed to lead down into malodorous gulfs of midnight blackness. Then the thought of all that gold asserted itself and he went forwards, feeling his way along the salt-encrusted walls, aware that there were steps of some kind beneath his questing foot. Yet even in that pitch blackness, he could tell that these steps had never been designed for human feet, for they appeared to be inordinately narrow and pitched at a peculiar angle.

As he progressed downwards, the dull booming of the sea roared even more loudly in his ears and there were shocking antiphonal echoes welling up from the hidden depths in front of him. How far those steps descended into the solid rock he could not tell, for after reaching fifty he ceased his mental counting, as there suddenly came the realization that the darkness before him was no longer absolute. A hideous greenish glow appeared, waxing brighter as he forced himself downwards.

Now in the spectral gleam he was able to see that the walls of the shaft were not as featureless as he had supposed, for in places the whitish coating deposited by centuries of saline saturation had chipped away. When he saw the grotesque carvings and glyphs graven into the rock, he withdrew his trailing hand, shuddering inwardly.

With the insistent knowledge of those creatures present on the other side of the reef and the possibility of imminent discovery uppermost in his mind, he descended the remaining steps as hurriedly as he could. At any moment, that silent horde might come streaming down here and even the weapons he possessed might not be sufficient to stop all of them. The sooner he found what he was looking for and made his escape from the reef, the better.

Suddenly, the walls ahead of him fell away, revealing a huge open space and Corsi saw that he had come upon a truly stupendous sight, one which momentarily took his breath away. Never had he anticipated anything like this.

Stout stone columns supported the roof which loomed more than thirty feet above his head, all lit by the eerie virescent luminosity. Corsi saw all of this in a single glance, but any initial queasiness he felt evaporated instantly as he saw a circle of smaller pillars in the center of the vast open space with a large graven altar in the middle and behind it. Glittering and sparkling in the radiance lay pile upon pile of unearthly trinkets: tiaras, bracelets, and ornaments all fashioned predominantly from gold, many set with lustrous, scintillant jewels. Never in his wildest dreams had Corsi imagined such a treasure trove. And to think it had lain here all these years, virtually unsuspected by anyone outside Innsmouth.

Running forwards, he bent to examine it, letting the various pieces sift through his trembling fingers. His first surmise, that this was a pirate horde taken from the galleons of Spain, was instantly dismissed. Never had he seen gold bearing this uncanny lustre, and even with his past experience, it was impossible to identify the precious stones which seemed to him to have no earthly origin.

From what strange, out-of-the-way corner of the world Captain Marsh and his contemporaries had brought all of this, he did not like to think. For some queer reason, he had the feeling that these precious artifacts hid a disturbing, sinister past, rather like the recently discovered treasures found in the tomb of Tutankhamun about which he had read with avid interest in the newspapers. Apart from the obvious strangeness of the gold of which they were primarily composed, the workmanship held a subtle *alien* quality which sent a little nervous shiver along his spine.

Then his natural avarice took over, exerting a tight control on his emotions. Plunging his hands deeply into the nearest pile, he began stuffing the objects into his bag and then into his pockets, inwardly visualizing what the jewel fences of his acquaintance in Boston or New York would say when they saw his haul.

Even though he might get only a fraction of their true worth, it would certainly be enough to set him up for life in the style he wished. Furthermore, there would be no awkward questions asked as to their origins, since it was doubtful if anyone outside of Innsmouth knew of their existence.

He straightened up and it was then he became aware of a faint sound superimposed upon the dull, booming reverberation of the sea: a curious flapping sound which abruptly conjured up the most frightening fancies in his mind. Turning swiftly, he saw them coming down the steps, hopping grotesquely from one to the next: a veritable horde of misshapen forms, and the fact that some of them were not even remotely human was the most nerve-shattering fact of all.

Reflex action instinctively took over from the initial paralyzing horror. Without hesitation, he raised the heavy automatic and squeezed the trigger several times, hoping that if he succeeded in killing several of them, the rest might scatter and provide him with the chance of breaking through their ranks and up those hideous steps to the outside, where he might be able to outdistance them to the waiting boat.

He saw the heavy-calibre slugs strike home in the scaly, greenish flesh yet, incredibly, they kept coming forwards as if the bullets had no effect on them whatsoever. For a wild, mind-numbing instant, he continued to fire at them, until the dull click of the hammer told him the gun was empty.

Desperately, he tugged at the second weapon in the leather holster but before he could drag it free, they were on him. Slippery bodies exuding that hateful fishy odor surrounded him, cutting off all hope of escape. From behind him, there came the sound of stone grating on stone as a second group threw their combined weight against the massive altar, thrusting it aside on some concealed central pivot.

Struggling futilely, Corsi was borne backwards towards the salt-encrusted walls of a wide shaft that sank vertically into the rock. For a heart-stopping moment he teetered on the brink of the shaft and then he was falling—

Shrieking madly, he struck something gelatinous and yielding which broke his fall. His thin scream was cut off sharply as the breath was knocked from his lungs by the impact. Whatever it was, it had cushioned his fall and apart from being severely shaken, he guessed no bones were broken. For a while he lay where he had fallen, sucking air into his heaving chest. Then, with an effort, he struggled to his knees on the uneven surface, twisting his head around to take stock of his surroundings.

The shaft had precipitated him into a vast cavern, even larger than the one above, and the floor into which he had fallen appeared to be completely covered by this phosphorescent mass which he guessed to be some previously unknown species of seaweed, for there were a number of massive rope-like strands clinging around the distant walls of the mammoth chamber.

Rising to his feet with difficulty, swaying slightly as he tried to maintain his balance on the slippery surface, he allowed his gaze to wander around the curved walls, searching for some possible egress which might lead him back to the surface. He could see nothing, although it was possible that some concealed tunnel might exist behind one of those ropy ramifications along the walls if he could only pry it loose.

A swift, appraising glance told him that the tunnel mouth just above his head was far too high to be reached. Even if it were possible to climb it, it would only take him back into that fearsome chamber inside the surface of the reef.

No, a thorough search around the walls seemed to afford him his only chance of getting out of this pit. Unsteadily, he began to move forwards over the irregular surface, then stopped in sudden horror and bewilderment. Some distance away, between him and the far wall, the rubbery substance moved. A large area slid aside to reveal an immense, oval opening, yards across.

It was then, in that moment of supreme terror, that Gino Corsi screamed and screamed and screamed as the full horror of what he was seeing struck home.

The opening was a single red eye that glared at him with a malevolence which transcended anything he had ever known! And when those rope-like strands around the walls began to move ....

About "The Transition of Zadok Allen"

Though the biblical ring of the closing section of "The Shadow over Innsmouth" has been remarked often enough, it has generally escaped notice that the biblical and Dunsanian flavor of that section might serve to link the tale with Lovecraft's canon of Dunsanian stylistic pastiches. When we recall that one of these, "Celephaïs", transpires in a harbor town called Innsmouth, well, who can fail to see a connection just waiting to be made?

And hasn't it occurred to you to wonder what finally happened to Zadok Allen, blabber-mouthed booze-bibbler? This wasn't the first time he'd blabbed, after all, and his "halfway-covenant" Dagonism had saved him from being simply rubbed out before. In light of the final disclosure that the people of Innsmouth were not hostile even to interloper Olmstead, why should we continue to suppose that they posed old Zadok any threat either? So what happened?

"The Transition of Zadok Allen", which first appeared in *Cthulhu Cultus* #1 (1995), is a speculative attempt to sew up these holes in the Lovecraftian fishnet.

The Transition of Zadok Allen

by Lewis Theobald III

Some time in the autumn of 1930 an Ipswich fisherman was hauling in his nets and noticed amid his flopping prisoners a metal cylinder which gleamed in the harsh sea sunlight. Leaving the fish to his sons who worked with him, he busied himself with the peculiar object. At first he thought it a stray length of pipe, but as he turned it over in his hands he found it was a sealed tube of exquisite workmanship, pale gold in color and carefully etched with the designs of fabulously fishy beasts and mermen. It was only a little corroded by the sea.

That night by lamplight, when he had a few moments to examine the strange artifact more intently, he found he could unscrew one end of the tube. Inside was an inscribed roll of an unusual parchment. My father (for I was one of his sons with him in the boat) soon decided to donate the metal case to the Newburyport Historical Society once he learned they already possessed a related piece, a golden crown of some type. I asked him why he did not attempt to sell the thing, but he seemed to feel it had wrongly come into his hands, and that he should be better off the sooner he divested himself of it. The written text, however, he kept for some reason. This I learned only years later when on his deathbed he bequeathed the scroll to me. I am fairly sure he had never even read it himself. But he could have. For it was in the familiar characters of our English alphabet.

Though written in English, the text was no less a mystery. I am transcribing it herewith in the hopes that someone with more information than I may yet read the brief account with more understanding.

The Testimony of Robert Olmstead

I imagined I had seen my last of the town drunk Zadok Allen following the abrupt conclusion of my interview with him on the rotting

wharves of decadent Innsmouth in connection with certain events
which have earned me a certain fame in some quarters and equal notoriety in others. I had found the old toper a ready source of information, especially once his tongue had been loosened by the ministrations
of Bacchus. In such a state of inebriated eloquence he was quite the
raconteur. At the time it did not even occur to me to take seriously his
fabulous tales of Innsmouth's remarkable past, and yet now I am in a
position to know that his yarns were scarcely half the truth, as distant
from the wonders they shadowed as the child's picture of his parents'
world is from the reality.

Such were the limits of my own self-blinded earth-gazing when I
believed I had seen, or all but seen, the death of Zadok Allen, snatched
away by his enemies for saying too much once too often. Following the
trajectory of his panic-bulged eyes, I looked away for an instant, turning back but a moment later to find him having disappeared with a
lightning speed impossible for however spry a nonagenarian.

It was only several months later, following certain monumental
discoveries relative to my own life and lineage, that I found myself
able to inquire further into the matter of my boozy companion's disappearance. I will now relate the true issue of those events, though in
the nature of the case I cannot make the reader to understand certain
references, and these may be more crucial to the meaning of the tale
than I realize, myself taking many things for granted that once
seemed utterly alien. So let our watchword in what follows be that
phrase from the scripture, "He that hath ear to hear, let him hear."

As old Zadok asked me once with a shaking voice, "Ever hear tell
of a shoggoth?" That fateful day I believe he found himself borne away
in an instant in the embrace of one of these creatures, great amoebic
clouds of living stuff, like unto the cloud-chariots of Jehovah and
Hadad in the myths of old. Yet it was not his fate to perish either in
the salty water or in the devouring acids of the thing's innards. Rather,
like Jonah, he rode safe in the belly of a living vehicle, softly ferried
within a bubble of wholesome air. Even now I cannot guess at his feelings during this unearthly voyage.

And when he found himself confronted by one of those entities he
had for so long feared and loathed, the deep ones? One feels certain
that the direct presence of this being must have both horrified Zadok
and calmed him. At once he felt the inevitability of the doom whose
descent he had feared for decades, and yet also the relaxing sense of
anticlimax that the reality can never be as dreadful as the expectation
of the unknown. He must have questioned, as I had earlier, whether

his own experience were real or the product of radical delirium tremens. But then the fish-frog spoke to him.

"Friend Zadok, rememberest thou not thy old comrade? Dost there yet remain no trace of thy childhood mate Hiram Gilman? Thou, too, art much changed with the passage of years. My pappy and thine were sailors together in the merchant fleet. Nay, 'tis not vengeance we would have with thee, but other business entire. I am sent to welcome thee."

First sure that it was some trap, Zadok at length was persuaded to understand the benign intentions of his captors. Surrounded by the comforting hues of the deep, Zadok sat and listened, and many matters were made plain to him. Had he never questioned how he had lived to so ripe an age, nigh unto the span of the biblical patriarchs? And why had he not long ago thought to flee a place he so feared as he did Innsmouth? Did he not recall what had been promised him as a lad when he had submitted to the Second Oath of Dagon? That rite had bound him to his town and his people. He had that day learned to shout the cry of the bacchantes of Dagon: *Iä! Cthulhu fhtagn!*, which no infidel may chant. And his sacramental joining with Father Dagon and Mother Hydra had been enough to secure for him a taste of eternal life. Only so had he been able to last out the decades on the streets of Innsmouth, albeit in an increasingly frail human form. The Third Oath would have caused the eventual change, and Zadok might have joined his fellows in blessed immortality beneath the seas.

Even now it was not too late. He might still find beneath the waves the peace that had eluded him for many decades. He would require no more the false surcease of the surface dweller's alcoholic poisons.

Finally he and his companion (whose outlines no longer seemed so repellent and frightening to him) reached the crystalline portals of Y'ha-nthlei, whose roofless palaces and coral palisades seemed to him little less than the Celestial City in some allegorical tale he had read almost a century before. He was the Pilgrim, and he had at last reached a culmination of a long and meandering progress. The salt of his tears mixed with the briny water about him as the great Being which bore him alighted before the mansion that should henceforth be his own. He realized with a start that the supply of air had long since run out, but that he breathed, like a frog, with no difficulty at all.

From that glad day Zadok dwelt amid the splendor of a thousand dreaming sea-bottom peaks, each taller than any Everest upon the forgotten surface. He wandered, when the mood struck him, through the garlanded streets of submerged Atlantises whose ghostly bells swayed with the drifting currents. He called the fishes by name and patted their narrow heads, danced with the squids and rejoiced to plumb the depths of unguessed chasms where deeper worlds of Elder aeons still lay spread. Girded and crowned like Neptune or Nodens, he bore his trident and shepherded the peaceful flocks of dolphin and nereid. The ears of the Trilobite Kings were attentive to his counsel, and the phosphorescent eels eschewed not his company. Only the rotting hulls of sunken ships reminded him of the world he had departed and which he increasingly suspected of being a childhood dream.

Zadok Allen reigns there still, as he will world without end, notwithstanding that below the cliffs of Innsmouth the tides of the channel pitch and toss the broken-spindled body of an old man who had often used to stumble along the lanes of the half-deserted fishing village.

About the Poems

Many of Lovecraft's *Fungi from Yuggoth* sonnets employ themes developed elsewhere in Lovecraft's stories. A couple of the *Fungi* mention Innsmouth, but these do not include the major motifs of "The Shadow over Innsmouth." These bits of eldritch verse fill that gap. You might ask, why bother? What can they amount to but summaries of the original story? If that's what you think, you have a lot to learn about poetry.

Cleanth Brooks did his best to prosecute what he called "the heresy of paraphrase." His claim was that one can never effectively paraphrase a poem for the simple reason that a poem is not, like prose, merely a vehicle for communicating an idea or some information. No, poetic language does something altogether different. As Gerard Genette says, the thing about poetic language is its "intransitiveness." It is a picture plane in itself, not a transparent window to enable you to see something else. Poetic language actually tries to do what Zen says all language does: It creates its own reality rather than conveying some other. Thus there is nothing to paraphrase, as if the form were negotiable and therefore negligible. In poetry, the relevant content is the content of the form (Seymour Chatman).

A neglected implication of the heresy of paraphrase is that it is only heretical in one direction. Because of the nature of poetry, it cannot be paraphrased without being destroyed (witness the degeneration of the sublime King James Version into the pathetic Living Bible). If one maintains the content while sacrificing the form, one has lost the content of the form, and that is everything. One has lost one's soul in gaining the world. But it also works the other way. That is, one may paraphrase prose into poetry readily enough, provided one has the necessary muse. Since it is nigh-incidental anyway, one may carry over the narrative content (in this case, the Innsmouth story), but the change in form (from prose to verse) creates a new content of the form, and something new, an Innsmouth poem, is born (or should we say "spawned?"), something quite beyond the original story. The content is the evocative magic built into the diction. "Salt-scented prophecy"—ah!

Virginia Anderson's "Shadow over Innsmouth" appeared first in *The Acolyte* vol. 1, #2, Winter 1942. R. Flavie Carson's "Innsmouth—Dread City by the Sea" first appeared in the *Nekromantikon* vol. 1, #2, Summer 1950. Ann K. Schwader's "After Innsmouth" was first published in *Noctulpa* #4, Spring 1990.

Three Poems

Shadow Over Innsmouth

by Virginia Anderson
(Dedicated to H. P. Lovecraft by Nanek)

We have forgotten some of mankind's ways:
The art of dying, or say ... Meroy's gift.
So when age grows upon us and our days
By span of man are numbered, the seas rift
And take us in. Then in the rites of old
We pledge allegiance where the strange pale gold
Of obscene Gods dispense eternal life
Wherein to glory, savour and renew. ...
Free from the world's alarms and strife
In ocean palaces of colalous hue,
Shedding the shape of man and doubling back
In form at least on evolution's track.

Innsmouth—Dread City by the Sea

by R. Flavie Carson

There was a city in a by-gone age
Built sturdily on sea-lashed, rocky shores,
A city deeply steeped in ancient lores,
Where dwelt the crone, the wizard, and the sage.

The city prospered for a time, until
The fishermen caught more than simple fish,
And wives were wont to brew a stranger dish
Than browned corn cake and mellow, bubbling ale.

The change came slowly, and there's none to tell
The date it started or the reason why,
And strange it was to see that city lie
Defenseless 'neath some curious, unknown spell.

But recently there has been brought to light
A tattered remnant of a diary page
A word of reference to that distant age,
Written by one who yet knew wrong from right—

("The blight is strange to see, and terror bleats
Forth from the heart of every citizen,
As ghost-like creatures, pale and wan and thin,
Slip through the darkly crooked, narrow streets.")

'Tis said that Innsmouth still exists today,
And though its name is changed to modern guise,
The night time passer-by still feels the eyes
Of ghostly creatures, flailing hands of clay.

And ever and anon, as night draws near,
The home-bound shudder from an ancient fear.

After Innsmouth

by Ann K. Schwader

I. Flight

Fear-driven as a beast, I fled that place
Where moonlight summons horrors from the sea;
Time-twisted hybrids of some ancient race
Whose every line suggests what Should Not Be.
Through underbrush and clumps of thorn I crept
To bring at last to Arkham my mad tale
Of elder rites thought dead which only slept ...
Grim government men listened, growing pale.

The night they dropped torpedoes off the Reef,
I woke still screaming. Fire engulfed my dreams;
Yet deeper waters drowned their futile schemes
& stirred in me recallings past belief.
Though Innsmouth's dying now, it leaves behind
Long shadow-marks of doubt across my mind.

II. Discovery

My mother's brother traced our Arkham line,
& killed himself soon after. Now, two years
Since Innsmouth's hell-soul spread its shade on mine,
I know the secret wellspring of his fears.
Our great-grandmother ... *what* was she, & how
Did Obed Marsh's madness taint our stock?
The truth of it arrives in nightmares now;
My thoughts turn darker daily with the shock.

Last night again I swam to Her below:
Twice-great-grandmother, daughter of the sea
& star-spawned Others alien to me. ...
My waking self distrusts such scenes, although
His visage in the mirror makes it plain
What sent the bullet through my uncle's brain.

III. Decision

Too often now, this inland wind brings
Salt-scented prophecy from Innsmouth's shore;
The whispered conversation of such things
As cannot die; or did, yet live once more.
I must not live at all: a pistol waits
Beneath my hand to end this sea-spawned voice
Which tempts me from my death with grander fates.
I strain—but cannot make my uncle's choice.

Iä! Y'ha-nthlei! City of our blood
Where ancient kinfolk call for my return
To long-drowned altars where strange votives burn
For Him who dreaming waits beneath the flood. ...
My journey to your depths begins tonight
To serve immortal till the stars turn right.

THE BOOK OF DZYAN

Mme. Blavatsky's famous transcribed messages from beyond, the mysterious *Book of Dzyan*, the heart of the sacred books of Kie-te, are said to have been known only to Tibetan mystics. Quotations from *Dzyan* form the core of her closely-argued *The Secret Doctrine*, the most influential single book of occult knowledge to emerge from the nineteenth century. The text of this book reproduces nearly all of *Book of Dzyan* that Blavatsky transcribed. It also includes long excerpts from her Secret Doctrine as well as from the Society of Psychical Research's 1885 report concerning phenomena witnessed by members of the Theosophical Society. There are notes and additional shorter materials. Editor Tim Maroney's biographical essay starts off the book, a fascinating portrait of an amazing woman.

5 3/8" x 8 3/8", 272 pages, $15.95. Stock #6027; ISBN 1-56882-198-0.

THE COMPLETE PEGANA

Lord Dunsany's fantasy writing had a profound impact on the Dreamlands stories of H. P. Lovecraft. This original collection is composed of newly edited versions of Lord Dunsany's first two books, *The Gods of Pegana* (1905) and *Time and the Gods* (1906). Three additional stories round out the book, the first time that all the Pegana stories have appeared within one book. Edited and introduced by S. T. Joshi.

5 3/8" x 8 3/8", 242 pages, $14.95. Stock #6016; ISBN 1-56882-190-5.

THE DISCIPLES OF CTHULHU
Second Revised Edition

The disciples of Cthulhu are a varied lot. In Mythos stories they are obsessive, loners, dangerous, seeking not to convert others so much as to use them. But writers of the stories are also Cthulhu's disciples, and they are the proselytizers, bringing new members into the fold. Published in 1976, the first edition of *The Disciples of Cthulhu* was the first professional, all-original Cthulhu Mythos anthology. One of the stories, "The Tugging" by Ramsey Campbell, was nominated for a Science Fiction Writers of America Nebula Award, perhaps the only Cthulhu Mythos story that has received such recognition. This second edition of Disciples presents nine stories of Mythos horror, seven from the original edition and two new stories. Selected by Edward P. Berglund.

5 3/8" x 8 3/8", 272 pages, $15.95. Stock #6011; ISBN 1-56882-202-2.

THE DUNWICH CYCLE

In the Dunwiches of the world the old ways linger. Safely distant from bustling cities, ignorant of science, ignored by civilization, dull enough never to excite others, poor enough never to provoke envy, these are safe harbors for superstition and seemingly meaningless custom. Sometimes they shelter truths that have seeped invisibly across the centuries. The people are unlearned but not unknowing of things once great and horrible, of times when the rivers ran red and dark shudderings ruled the air. Here are nine stories set where horror begins, with a general introduction and individual story prefaces by Robert M. Price.

5 3/8" x 8 3/8", 288 pages, $16.95. Stock #6010; ISBN 1-56882-196-4.

THE HASTUR CYCLE
Second Revised Edition

The stories in this book represent the evolving trajectory of such notions as Hastur, the King in Yellow, Carcosa, the Yellow Sign, Yuggoth, and the Lake of Hali. A succession of writers from Ambrose Bierce to Ramsey Campbell and Karl Edward Wagner have explored and embellished these concepts so that the sum of the tales has become an evocative tapestry of hypnotic dread and terror, a mythology distinct from yet overlapping the Cthulhu Mythos. Here for the first time is a comprehensive collection of all the relevant tales. Selected and introduced by Robert M. Price.

5 3/8" x 8 3/8", 320 pages, $17.95. Stock #6020; ISBN 1-56882-192-1.

THE INNSMOUTH CYCLE

The decadent, smugly rotting, secret-filled town of Innsmouth is a supreme creation of Howard Philips Lovecraft. It so finely mixes the carnal and the metaphysical that writers continue to take inspiration from it. This new collection contains thirteen tales and three poems tracing the evolution of Innsmouth, from early tales by Dunsany, Chambers, and Cobb, through Lovecraft's "The Shadow Over Innsmouth" to modern tales by Rainey, Glasby, and others.

5 3/8" x 8 3/8", 240 pages, $14.95. Stock # 6017; ISBN 1-56882-199-9.

THE ITHAQUA CYCLE

The elusive, supernatural Ithaqua roams the North Woods and the wastes beyond, as invisible as the wind. Hunters and travelers fear the cold and isolation of the North; they fear the advent of the mysterious, malignant Wind-Walker even more. This collection includes the progenitor tale "The Wendigo" by Algernon Blackwood, three stories by August Derleth, and ten more from a spectrum of contemporary authors including Brian Lumley, Stephen Mark Rainey, and Pierre Comtois.

5 3/8" x 8 3/8", 260 pages, $15.95. Stock #6021; ISBN 1-56882-191-3.

MADE IN GOATSWOOD

Ramsey Campbell is acknowledged by many to be the greatest living writer of the horror tale in the English language. He is known to Mythos fans for the ancient and fearful portion of England's Severn Valley he evoked in narratives such as "The Moon

Lens". This book contains eighteen all-new stories set in that part of the Valley, including a new story by Campbell himself, his first Severn Valley tale in decades. This volume was published in conjunction with a 1995 trip by Campbell to the United States. Stories selected by Scott David Aniolowski.

5 3/8" x 8 3/8", 288 pages, $16.95. Stock #6009; ISBN 1-56882-197-2.

THE NYARLATHOTEP CYCLE

The mighty Messenger of the Outer Gods, Nyarlathotep has also been known to deliver tidings from the Great Old Ones. He is the only Outer God who chooses to personify his presence on our planet. A god of a thousand forms, he comes to Earth to mock, to wreak havoc, and to spur on humanity's self-destructive urges. This volume of stories and poems illustrates the ubiquitous presence of Nyarlathotep and shows him in several different guises. Among them, his presence as Nephren-Ka, the dread Black Pharaoh of dynastic Egypt, dominates. The thirteen stories include a Lin Carter novella. Selected and introduced by Robert M. Price.

5 3/8" x 8 3/8", 256 pages, $14.95. Stock #6019; ISBN 1-56882-200-6.

SINGERS OF STRANGE SONGS

Most readers acknowledge Brian Lumley as the superstar of British horror writers. With the great popularity of his *Necroscope* series, he is one of the best known horror authors in the world. Devoted fans know that his roots are deep in the Cthulhu Mythos, with which most of his early work deals. This volume contains eleven new tales in that vein, as well as three reprints of excellent but little-known work by Lumley. This book was published in conjunction with Lumley's 1997 trip to the United States.

5 3/8" x 8 3/8", 256 pages, $12.95. Stock #6014; ISBN 1-56882-104-2.

SONG OF CTHULHU

Lovecraft's most famous portraitist was Richard Upton Pickman, whose ironic canvases of ghouls and humanity's relation to ghouls have become famous, even though they existed only in Lovecraft's keen imagination. Among HPL's writers, Randolph Carter and the tragically destined Edward Pickman Derby stand out. And of course there is Erich Zann, the inhumanly-great violist, whose powers are detailed in "The Music of Erich Zann," included in this volume.

In HPL, the artist is the detached observer of society, a cultural reporter of the sort whose function has since become familiar. But Lovecraft also saw a deeper role, one such as played by Henry Wilcox the sculptor in "The Call of Cthulhu": "Wilcox's imagination had been keenly affected. [He had] an unprecedented dream of great cyclopean cities of titan blocks and sky-flung monoliths, all dripping with green ooze and sinister with latent horror. . . . [and] a voice that was not a voice; a chaotic sensation which only fancy could transmute into sound, but which he attempted to render by the almost unpronounceable jumble of letters, *Cthulhu fhtagn*."

Here are nineteen Mythos tales, melodies of prophecy and deceit. *Cthulhu fhtagn*!

5 3/8" x 8 3/8", 222 pages, $13.95. Stock #6032; ISBN 1-56882-117-4.

TALES OUT OF INNSMOUTH

Innsmouth is a half-deserted, seedy little town on the North Shore of Massachusetts. It is rarely included on any map of the state. Folks in neighboring towns shun those who come from Innsmouth, and murmur about what goes on there. They try not to mention the place in public, for Innsmouth has ways of quelling gossip, and of taking revenge on troublemakers. Here are ten new tales and three reprints concerning the town, the hybrids who live there, the strange city rumored to exist nearby under the sea, and those who nightly lurch and shamble down the fog-bound streets of Innsmouth.

5 3/8" x 8 3/8", 294 pages, $16.95. Stock #6024; ISBN 1-56882-201-4.

THE XOTHIC LEGEND CYCLE

The late Lin Carter was a prolific writer and anthologist of horror and fantasy with over eighty titles to his credit. His tales of Mythos horror are loving tributes to H. P. Lovecraft's "revision" tales and to August Derleth's stories of Hastur and the *R'lyeh Text*. This is the first collection of Carter's Mythos tales; it includes his intended novel, *The Terror Out of Time*. Most of the stories in this collection have been unavailable for some time. Selected and introduced by Robert M. Price.

5 3/8" x 8 3/8", 288 pages, $16.95. Stock #6013; ISBN 1-56882-195-6.

All titles are available from bookstores and game stores. You can also order directly from **www.Chaosium.com**, your source for Cthulhiana and more. To order by credit card via the net, visit our web site, 24 hours a day. To order via phone, call 1-510-583-1000, 9 A.M. to 4 P.M. Pacific time.

Printed in the United Kingdom
by Lightning Source UK Ltd.
116780UKS00001B/18